"Don't go yet," he whispered. When he stroked the sensitive area along her jawline, she moaned aloud.

He touched his lips to her ear. He wasn't exactly kissing her, but he left no doubt in her mind that he was going to do.

Cydney flinched away from him. "Don't touch me," she managed.

"What do you expect me to do, Cydney?"

"I . . . I just don't want anyone to think that I kept my job because I slept with the boss."

He touched her cheek again. "When all of this mess gets sorted out, I'm going to get to know you better. I want to know you in every possible sense of the word."

Cydney shook her head ruefully, "I don't think so, Mr. Burke-Carter."

"Why not?"

"Because I don't know you from Adam."

He leaned close and whispered in her ear, "Take a lesson from the biblical Adam, Ms. Kelley."

"And what lesson is that?"

"One of the first acts sanctioned between a man and a woman was for Adam to know his wife."

FIRM
COMMITMENTS

Geri Guillaume

Pinnacle Books
Kensington Publishing Corp.
http://www.arabesquebooks.com

PINNACLE BOOKS are published by

Kensington Publishing Corp.
850 Third Avenue
New York, NY 10022

Pinnacle, the P logo and Arabesque, the Arabesque logo are Reg. U.S. Pat. & TM Off.

First Printing: October, 1998
10 9 8 7 6 5 4 3 2 1

Printed in the United States of America

I

"Yo, Mom! Are you sick or something? You goin' in to work today, or what?"

Thirteen-year-old Cameron Kelley leaned over his mother as she lay curled up in bed with a pillow clutched over her head.

"Five more minutes," Cydney Kelley mumbled, jamming the pillow over her ears.

"Mom, I just need to know one more thing. One more thing, Mom, and I promise I'll let you go back to sleep," Cameron insisted, grasping her by the shoulder and shaking her. He stood with a wrinkled shirt in one hand and an iron in the other.

"What is it?!" Cydney groaned, peeking at him with one eye.

"Where's the spray starch?"

"It's in the hall closet, right next to the spot where you found the iron." Cydney yawned, brushing his hand away.

Cameron started to walk away, then turned around again. "Okay, just one more thing, Mom. Will you iron my shirt for me? It don't look right when I do it."

"It *doesn't* look right," Cydney corrected automatically.

"That's why I need you to iron for me," he complained.

"Cam, please! Just give me five more minutes. I'll be up in just a little while."

Muttering to himself, Cameron closed the door to her room. *Slam!*

She watched it close behind him with one bleary eye. How did she manage to get any sleep at all—between the slamming doors, Cameron's constant questions, and the radio blaring from his room? She could hear him adjust the station to tune in to his favorite morning radio show.

"Turn that radio down!" Cydney shouted. She punched her pillow back into a comfy position, rolled over, and tried to ignore the not-so-subtle beeping of the alarm clock as it warned her that the snooze period was up.

"It's five minutes, Mom. Time to get up. Come on, Mom. Iron my shirt for me!" Cameron shouted as he headed back to her room.

Cydney groaned. *Why even try to get back to sleep?*

As Cameron pushed the door to her bedroom open, Cydney could hear the chatter of a popular radio personality. She groaned again. Nobody should be that cheerful in the morning.

The radio disc jockey was going on about a local publicity event—promising to give tickets away to any listener who could answer questions about the morning show.

"Since it's seven o'clock in the AM, we'll take caller number seven. Caller number seven, if you can give me the last seven songs we just played, and sing a few lines from each song, we'll give you tickets to next weekend's skate party sponsored by KSLM—the station with the *slammin'est* hits in the city. The lines are really lighting up. Folks must really want those tickets. Remember, caller seven is the lucky caller."

"Don't give those tickets away! Those babies are mine!" Cameron tossed the shirt and iron on Cydney's bed. "Yeah, buddy! Come to me skate tickets." He dove across the bed to reach for the telephone on Cydney's night stand.

"Boy, if you don't get off of my bed . . ." she said, her tone threatening bodily harm to her son. Cameron punched a button preprogrammed with the number of the radio station. The first time, the line was busy. In frustration, he punched the number again and again. He couldn't get through.

"Come on, come on!" Cameron urged. He could hear the DJ laughing as he offered condolences to callers four, five, and six.

"I know those songs. I know 'em. Let me through!" he begged into the phone. When he finally got a ring instead of a busy signal, Cameron let out a whoop that made Cydney jam another pillow over her ears.

"KSLM. Who's on the line?" the DJ asked.

Cameron almost dropped the phone is surprise. "Hey! What caller am I? This is Cameron Kelley"

"Hey! What caller do you want to be, Cameron Kelley?" the DJ teased him.

"Yo, man, I want to win those tickets. I wanna' be caller number seven."

"You're caller number seven, man. If you want those tickets for the skating party, all you gotta' do is give us the tunes."

"All right!" Cameron shouted. "I got the tickets?"

"Give us the tunes," the DJ repeated.

Cydney sat up, and tried to blink the sleep fog from her brain. Her son's voice seemed to be all around her. Cameron was in stereo surround sound! How could that be? He was standing there, right in her room. But he sounded funny. His voice was filled with static—just like the way Cameron's music sounded when it was blaring from his room. He was naming songs, and singing lyrics that she thought no thirteen-year-old should know.

"Oh, no! What time is it? I'm late!" Cydney shouted, jumping out of bed. She was startled to hear her own voice coming from the radio, too. Cameron clamped his hand over the phone, rolled his eyes at her, and hissed, "Mom, please!" He then turned back to the phone, and continued to list the songs.

"We have a winner! Cameron Kelley, we'll see you in two weeks at Jo-Jo's Skate House. Tell our listeners who plays the hottest hits in the city."

"KSLM!" Cameron shouted enthusiastically.

"Now stay on the line, Cameron, so I can tell you how to get your tickets . . ."

When the music started again, Cydney said, "Get off of that phone, Cam, we've got to go. I'm late."

Cameron nodded to show that he'd heard her, but he pointed to the phone to indicate that he was still on hold.

"If you miss your bus, I am *not* driving you to school. And I'm not giving you a note to excuse you for being late, either," Cydney warned.

Cameron opened his mouth to argue, but Cydney had already turned her back to dash into the bathroom. When she came out, she had a toothbrush frothy with toothpaste clenched between her teeth.

"I want you to come right home after school today. I'd better not hear you've been hanging out on the basketball court, either. There's leftover roast and potatoes in the freezer, so fix yourself dinner. Leave the chips and soda alone. I might be late coming home from work today. Do your homework before you turn on the television, Cam. When I checked your work last night, over half of your math problems were wrong. They were careless, little mistakes. I know you can do better."

"Yes, ma'am," Cameron said. Though most of her conversation was garbled as she brushed her teeth, he got the gist of what she was trying to say. He'd had plenty of practice trying to decipher her speech through her toothbrush. It seemed as though they were always running late. He had two choices. He could *not* understand her, and wind up getting into trouble for not following her directions. Or he could become an expert interpreter for his mother's many languages.

There was toothbrush talk—which listed his orders for the day. *Come straight home from school, Cameron. Do your homework, Cameron. Don't try to cook, or you'll set the house on fire like the last time, Cameron.*

And then there was the mad dash dialogue—which threatened him with the various ways she would make his life miserable if he didn't stop poking around. *Move your buns, Cameron, or I'll roast them for dinner. Get the lead out of your butt,*

Cameron, before I put my foot to it. Miss your bus, and you'll walk to school, Cameron.

After the instructions and the threats, was kiss-and-drop conversation. No matter how late she was running, or how exasperated Cameron made her with his school-delaying tactics, Cydney never failed to tell him how much she loved him— even as she was speeding away to work. She didn't always come right out and say it. He sometimes had to hunt for her meaning between final instructions. *When you get home, Cameron, keep the door locked. Don't leave the house unless you tell me where you're going. If you have to answer the phone, don't let anyone know you're home alone. I'll be home as soon as I can.*

This morning, Cameron listened with only half an ear to her daily routine. He was too distracted, too excited. He'd just won twenty tickets to the hottest skating party in the city. What did he care if he made it to school on time or not? Then again, he couldn't wait to get there to see how many of his friends had heard him on the radio. He jumped up. He had to get there! He had to get there so he could ask his best friends who else he should invite to the party.

"Get up, Cameron! Your bus!" Both of them turned to the window as the familiar grind of the huge, diesel engine roared up the block. The school bus paused a moment at the end of the drive, honked twice to see if Cameron was coming, then continued up the block.

He turned an apologetic expression to Cydney.

"Sorry, Mom."

"Sorry is as sorry does," she replied caustically.

"Can I get a ride to school today?"

Cydney glared at him with her hands on her hips. "I've got a good mind to let you stay at home."

When his face lit up, she said, "Don't look so happy. Then I'd call the truant officer and report you myself."

"Aw, Mom. That's really cold." He turned a wide grin on her, and said, "Did I tell you how much I like your new hairstyle. Aunt Courtney did a *slammin'* job."

Cydney automatically reached up, and fingered one of the

hundreds of teeny-weeny braids that fell past her shoulders in serpentine fashion. It had taken her sister two days to braid her thick, dark hair. She'd spent the entire weekend washing, conditioning, tinting, trimming, braiding, and sitting under the hair dryer with what seemed like a million curlers.

"You really like it?" Cydney responded tentatively to her son's obvious attempt at flattery. This new style was a radical departure for her usual, demure, single braid. It had taken her sister twice as long to convince her to try something new as it did to actually complete the style.

Cameron grinned even wider, thinking that even with a weak compliment like that, he could get his mother to agree to almost anything. "Wait until everybody at school sees you when you drop me off. Man, I'm gonna' have to hurt somebody for trying to put the moves on my mama."

"Go on, boy!" Cydney laughed. "I don't know who you're trying to fool."

"I mean it, Mom. You look great. They're not going to know you at work."

Cydney leaped back into action. "Speaking of which, I'll be heading out the door in ten minutes. If you're not ready, I'll be leaving you and your sweet talk right here."

Cameron brushed a lukewarm iron over his shirt. By the time Cydney had showered, dressed, and made a slice of toast, Cameron was still hunting for his other shoe.

"Mom, have you seen my red high-tops?"

"I don't wear your shoes, Cameron. How should I know where they are?" Cydney said testily. "I don't care if you have to go barefoot. Let's move it."

She grabbed her briefcase. "Now, where are my keys?"

"I don't know, Mom. I don't drive your car," Cameron said in passing. Cydney tapped him lightly on the back of the head with a rolled newspaper. "Don't get smart with me, Cam."

He said something under his breath. It was loud enough for Cydney to realize that he'd smarted off to her again, but low enough that she could still ignore it. She gulped down a glass of juice, then hurried to the door.

"Let's go, Cam. Hurry up!"

"I don't know why you're sweatin' this time clock thing, Mama. You know Mr. Mike doesn't care what time you get in as long as you put in the hours. And if the owner of the company doesn't care, why should you?"

"I know Mike is a little more laid-back than most entrepreneurs."

"What's an en ... tre ... pre ... ?" Cameron stumbled over the word.

"Look it up," was Cydney's automatic reply. "And I want to see it in a sentence when I come home."

Cameron groaned. Sometimes, he wished he never asked his mom questions. She always turned them into an opportunity for more homework for him.

"He knows I put in long hours," Cydney continued. "But he's not the only person I have to deal with. When I'm late, I'm the bottleneck. I push everyone else's work back. I don't want to deal with that on a Monday morning. So let's get moving!"

"Found my shoe. Now have you seen my gym shorts?"

"You have until the count of five to get your narrow behind in that car," she warned. "Starting now! One!"

Cameron came hopping toward her—his foot stuck in his tennis shoe as he laced it up.

"Two!" she continued.

He scooped up his backpack.

"Three!"

He stuck a piece of toast into his mouth.

"Four!"

After switching off the kitchen light, he hopped toward the door.

"Five!" Coincided with the slamming of the door.

Cydney brushed the crumbs from his face before kissing him on the cheek. "With seconds to spare." She closed the car door as he climbed inside, and gestured for him to buckle his seatbelt.

"Mom, are you going to pick up the tickets for me?"

"What tickets?" She'd completely forgotten about the event that had jolted her out of bed that morning.

"The KSLM tickets, Mama. Remember? I won twenty tickets to the KSLM skate party at Jo-Jo's the week after next. It wouldn't be out of your way. I mean, the radio station is right off the freeway."

"I can't get 'em this morning. But I promise I'll get them for you this evening—on one condition."

Cameron could almost feel another homework lecture coming on. "And what's that?"

"That you have your homework done, and done right, by the time I get home."

He knew it. He just knew she would tie it back to homework. "Bet!" Cameron said, vigorously bobbing his head.

"What does that mean? Does that mean yes?" Cydney wanted to know.

"Yeah, man. That means yes."

Cydney sighed. Every day was a new lesson in communicating with her son. From the first time he called her "mama" to the first time he called her "man" she had to constantly adjust to the fact that the life she created, and cherished, continued to distance himself from her. He set himself apart through his language, his style of dressing, his choice of music. (If you wanted to call that pounding, screeching, syncopated collaboration music.)

The harder she tried to understand him, and grow with him, the faster he managed to change one more facet of his personality.

Cydney smiled ruefully. She was only thirty years old—not so old that she didn't care to keep up with the latest fashion, language, and music trends. But she wasn't so young that she would feel comfortable trying to mimic them.

So, every so often, she did what she could to try to find some kind of middle ground—a change of a hairstyle, a piece of clothing to update her wardrobe, even adopting some of Cameron's idioms helped a little. Therefore, every time he said something she didn't quite understand, she asked him about it.

She pulled up to his school. "Remember, Cameron. Come right home."

"Remember the KSLM tickets," he countered.

"Homework," she volleyed.

"Tickets."

"Entrepreneur."

"Skate party."

"We'll see."

"Love you, Mom."

Cydney started to lean over to give him a goodbye kiss. She saw him stiffen, and look nervously out at the school yard where his friends might be watching. She shifted abruptly, and pretended she was reaching for something inside of the glove compartment instead. The look of relief that flooded Cameron's face amused and annoyed her at the same time.

He wanted to be a grown up so badly. She admired him for wanting to take on so much responsibility. But why couldn't he be her little Cam for just a while longer?

"Have a good day, son." She jerked her head in the direction of the school.

"Peace. And I'm outta' here," he said, forking his fingers into a V. Then he sauntered off to greet his friends.

Cydney's official hours were from nine to six. But by the time she'd parked, and waited for one her office building's terminally slow elevators, it was nine fifteen. There were two ways to enter her company's suite of offices. One way was past the receptionist. Cydney definitely didn't want to go that way. Maybe, if anyone hadn't needed her that morning, or if she hadn't received any phone calls, she could slip into her office, and no one would be the wiser.

"Oh, Ms. Kelley!" The receptionist happened to look up as Cydney stepped out of the elevator. She waved at her through the main glass door.

"So much for sneaking in the back way," Cydney grumbled. She plastered a wide, innocent smile on her face, and pushed through the door.

"Good morning, Joanie," Cydney said brightly.

"Uh-huh," Joan Kegler said in her "don't-give-me-that" voice. "You mean almost afternoon."

"Oh, really? What time is it?" Cydney asked, trying to sound surprised.

"Time for you to get your watch fixed, Ms. Kelley. You are fifteen minutes late for a very important staff meeting."

"Staff meeting? What staff meeting? Nobody said anything to me on Friday about a Monday morning staff meeting. Mike hates Monday morning meetings. You know he always says he's at his most creative on Fridays," Cydney rattled off a string of excuses.

Joan held up her hand. "If you were here at nine like you were supposed to be—"

The look Cydney gave her cut her off short. She was in no mood for a time clock lecture from Joan. Usually, she could take Joan's blatant jabs at her work hours. Joan only worked from seven in the morning until one in the afternoon. After that, another part-time receptionist occupied the front desk. Joan never saw the hours Cydney put in—long after the rest of the employees had gone home. Even her boss, Michael Megna, wasn't sure what time she usually left for the day. Mike hated to arrive early, and hated leaving late even worse. The fact that he had called a meeting so early made her nervous.

"They're in the front conference room," Joan said.

"Thanks, Joan."

"Don't mention it. By the way, Ms. Kelley, I love your hair."

"You do?" Cydney asked in surprise, again running her finger along a coiled braid. In five years, the woman had never complimented her.

"It suits you," Joan said.

As Cydney passed through the inner door and headed for the conference room, Joan muttered under her breath, "Suits you just fine, Ms. Kelley—dark and twisted."

II

Before turning the door handle, Cydney squared her shoulders and took a deep breath. While she collected herself, she took a minute to try to figure out what was going on inside. It was so quiet, she wondered if Joan had been mistaken. Maybe there was no meeting. Or even worse—maybe the meeting had already broken up. There was only one way to find out. She grasped the doorknob, and pushed the door open.

The entire staff sat or stood around the long, black lacquer conference table. Cydney looked toward the head of the table where her boss, and college friend, Michael Megna sat. She opened her mouth to apologize for being late, but Mike cut her off quickly with a negative shake of his head. He indicated that she should take a seat. Cydney glanced around the room again. Every available spot was taken. Where did he expect her to sit? The company wasn't that large—forty-three employees to be exact. Each and every one, except Joan, of course, had crammed into the room meant to hold only twenty comfortably.

"Here, Cyd. Take my spot." One of her coworkers who worked across the hall from her offered her his seat.

"Dion, what's going on?" Cydney whispered out of the corner of her mouth.

"Nobody knows. Mike wouldn't say a word until everyone was here."

"I'm the bottleneck again," Cydney groaned.

"Maybe not," Dion said. "Maybe he was waiting for *him*." He nodded toward the door.

Cydney had to crane her neck to see who and what Dion was talking about. If she thought the room had been quiet before she entered, it grew even more so when "The Suit" walked through the door.

It was obvious that he was an outsider. His clothes alone set him apart from the rest of the employees. Mike had always said that people did their best work when they were the most comfortable. If that meant that he had to allow people to come to work in jeans and a T-shirt, then he would allow it, as long as the outfit didn't push the bounds of good taste. There were very few abuses of Mike's lax dress code regulations because everyone generally agreed what those boundaries were.

If Cydney had to think of an exception to the come-as-you-want-to practice, it would have to be most of the members of the marketing department. To them, image was more important than comfort. They were the frontline to the outside world. If she'd heard the marketing director Vernon Castle say once, he'd said it *ad nauseam*—a company that looked successful generated success. Therefore, suits were the preferred method of dress for the marketers.

The Suit who walked into the conference room this morning must have written the book on dressing for success. With just a touch of snobbery and contempt, Cydney thought that she could feed herself and Cameron for six months on what that suit must have cost.

Cydney heard the woman on the other side of her give a low whistle of appreciation. "If that's who we've been waiting for, I'd say it was worth the wait," she said.

"I smell trouble," someone else whispered.

"Uh-oh." Cydney then heard someone else mutter.

"Uh-oh, is right," Dion agreed. "You know who that is, don't you, Cyd?"

She shook her head. "How do you figure that I'd know?" she whispered tightly.

"You're Mike's right hand. You mean to tell me you don't know anything about why *he's* here."

Cydney started to answer, but Mike stood up, and rapped his knuckles on the table. "I guess you're all wondering why I called this meeting," he began.

His voice cracked at the end of the sentence. He coughed a couple of times to clear his throat, took a sip of coffee, then began again. "First of all, I want to thank you guys for being so patient. You know, you all continue to surprise me . . . uh . . . and I want to say that it's been a pleasure working with you. All of you . . ."

His voice cracked again. Cydney thought that it sounded like more than a dry throat. He almost sounded *emotional.* Again, warning signals sounded in her head. Mike was a lot of things— a whiz kid, a wise guy, and sometimes even a womanizer— but he wasn't emotional. As he spoke to them, he sounded as if he was on the verge of crying. She could see it in his red-rimmed, swollen eyes and his quivering, lower lip.

Cydney looked around her. Everyone had the same confused and concerned expression on their faces. They all felt as she did, but no one wanted to speak up to say what was on their minds.

Well, if no one was going to speak up, she would have to. Maybe she wouldn't suffer any repercussions. She and Mike had a history. They had attended the same university, had even shared some classes. She had caught the bouquet at Mike's wedding. She was there for the birth of his first child, and she was there to comfort him when the child was prematurely called to heaven.

When Mike started his company, she was the first one he hired. She was the one he relied on to keep the company running smoothly. She had to say something, because it certainly looked like rough times ahead of them. "Mike, that almost sounds like a goodbye," Cydney spoke up.

"Does it? I didn't mean it to sound like that. Goodbyes are

so final. And this, if anything, isn't final. It's not the end of
the world . . . no, not by a long shot.''

"Mike, what are you talking about? What's going on?" Dion
demanded.

Mike opened his mouth to speak, then shut it again without
making a sound. He glanced over at "The Suit." Every pair
of eyes in the room followed Mike's gaze. For a moment, no
one said a word as "The Suit" seemed to take the time to meet
each and every gaze straight on.

"Maybe you ought to tell them, Mr. Burke-Carter."

Cydney's eyebrows shot up. Mike never said "mister" to
anyone. He didn't believe in titles. He always said that titles
were just ways to set people apart from each other.

"We're in trouble," Dion muttered to Cydney. She nodded
once, waiting for *Mr.* Suit to speak.

He moved to the head of the conference room, flipped off
the lights, and switched on an overhead projector. Then, he
placed a transparency on the projector that depicted the organi-
zational chart of the company.

Cydney studied it briefly. Before she could figure out a
few subtle changes in the chart, *Mr.* Suit announced in clear,
clipped words. "My name is Daryl Burke-Carter. As of eight-
thirty A.M. today, I'm the new owner of MegnaTronics, In-
corporated."

He paused dramatically, allowing the full impact of his
statement to sink in. The explosion of exclamation and deni-
als didn't seem to phase him, as he turned off the projector,
turned on the lights, then resumed his seat.

It was Cydney who found her voice to speak first. She
wasn't sure how she had accomplished that. A million questions ran through her mind. Was it true? Had Mike really
sold the company? Who was this Daryl Burke-Carter? Why
did Mike sell the company to him? Why hadn't Mike warned
them that this was coming? Why didn't he warn her? Why
couldn't she see this coming? Did they still have their jobs?
If not, would their last paychecks be delayed? What about

severance? Would they be granted that? If not, how was she
she going to meet this month's bills? Would she have to file
for unemployment?

The question that managed to work its way to the front of
all the others was, "What . . . what did you say?"

"I think I made myself clear enough, Ms.—?" Mr. Suit
raised his eyebrows in question to her.

"It's Kelley," Cydney supplied.

"First or last name," he asked, as he consulted a list of
names in a leather-bound binder.

"Last," she said coolly. What made him think that she could
allow him to casually use her first name after the bombshell
he just dropped on all of them?

"Cydney Kelley," he read aloud. "From the quality assurance department."

"Director," she elaborated. "I'm the director of the department."

"I'm going to try to make the transition as smooth as possible," he said, again making an effort to meet her gaze. "I
know you're all used to the way Mike runs his business. I'm
going to warn you now, we don't happen to share the same
philosophy. So, as time goes on, I'm going to fill you in on a
few quirks of mine, the first of which is that I make it a habit
never to repeat myself when I know my message has been
clearly received. Is *that* understood, Ms. Kelley?" He directed
his comment back to her.

Cydney felt her face burning with embarrassment. Just
because she was the first one to say something after that bombshell, did that mean he had to pick on her? What did he expect
her to say? Congratulations, and thanks for turning our world
upside down?!

The last time she felt this singled out was the seventh grade—
when her physical education teacher made her climb that *stupid*
rope for her strength and endurance examination. Cydney had
begged the instructor to let her try after the rest of the class
had been dismissed. She knew she'd never be able to make it,
not with so many people watching her. But her PE teacher

thought that she was either being shy or stubborn. One way or another, she felt it was her responsibility to break Cydney of either. So she stood there, trying every trick in the book to get Cydney up that rope. She cajoled; she teased; she scolded. None of the teacher's tactics seemed to work. Cydney stood there, with the rope clenched in her hands, and her shoes glued to the gym floor. When, out of exasperation, the teacher called her a name that no seventh-grader should have been called, Cydney burst into tears.

Up until that day, she had looked up to that teacher as a positive role model. She was a strong, African-American woman with, what seemed to Cydney, the best kind of job. She was a leader of young girls, a shaper of minds, attitudes, and bodies. But when she resorted to name calling, Cydney saw her idol topple. Her teacher was, in the end, just a woman who couldn't manage her own mouth—let alone a terrified teenager.

On that day, Cydney vowed that she would never put herself in a position where she could be ridiculed again. Instead of building up her courage, however, she built walls. She learned how to stay out of the spotlight. Once she'd made it to college, she always chose the larger classes, where she could remain anonymous. In her choice of careers, she always worked behind the scenes, choosing to let her work speak for itself.

The situation had to be pretty severe to make her speak out of turn. This seemed to be one of those times. And the rest of her coworkers seemed to understand that. If it were possible, the room grew even more silent as everyone waited for her response. Well, she thought, she could sit back and cry like she did back in gym class so long ago, or she could tell this gym teacher in a business suit exactly what he could do with this *verbal* rope he'd put out for her.

"Maybe I didn't make *myself* clear," Cydney said, with a noticeable edge in her voice. Out of the corner of her eyes, she saw Mike trying to signal her back to silence. He was shaking his head, and dragging his finger across his throat in a slashing motion.

"Yes, Ms. Kelley?" Daryl Burke-Carter rested his palms against the conference room table. "You were saying?"

"I . . . uh . . . I can only speak for myself," Cydney started. "But I have so many questions. I guess the first one that popped out seemed to be the most logical one to ask."

"Mr. Megna and I knew there would be plenty of questions—probably more than can be handled in a setting like this. And some of you may not feel comfortable expressing them in a group this size. So, Mike and I have developed a conference schedule." He went to his leather-bound folder again and withdrew a stack of papers. Then he divided each stack, and passed one half to his right, the other half to his left.

"We've tried to take into account those of you who telecommute, those of you who work flex time hours, and those of you who just can't seem to get here on time."

No one had to look in Cydney's direction to know he very well might be referring to her.

"If you have any trouble making the meeting time we have assigned to you, please let one of us know at the end of this meeting. We've got a few time slots open. So, in the time that we have left for this meeting, let's begin with some of the obvious questions. I'm sure you're all wondering if you still have jobs. The answer is yes . . . conditionally."

"Conditionally? What conditions?" Dion asked.

"I've thought long and hard about selling the company," Mike finally spoke again. "I tried every other option before making that decision—bank loans, venture capitalists, investors, performance-based salaries, even profit sharing. The truth is, I just couldn't stay afloat and keep you all. When Mr. Burke-Carter offered to buy me out, I accepted with the condition that he would have to keep eighty percent of the staff."

"And the other twenty percent?" someone else asked.

"Will have to go," Mr. Suit replied curtly.

"But only if we both agree." Mike softened the statement. "It has to be a mutual decision."

"Who decides who stays and who goes?" another employee asked.

"Whoever is the best butt-kisser," Dion muttered. When

Mike and Mr. Suit's eyes swiveled to that end of the table, Cydney was sure they'd heard him. And she was sure that, through guilt by association, she would be one of the first ones asked to leave because of Dion's comment.

"When will we know who will be cut?" Cydney asked.

"For the next couple of weeks, Mr. Burke-Carter and I will be reviewing our finances, our product line, and staff availability. We know this is a difficult time for all of you. I'm asking for your patience and your understanding. Things are going to be tense for a while. But let's try to concentrate. We still have a damn good product out there that needs our full attention."

We'll be on trial, Cydney thought. Each one of us will be expected to shine, if we want to keep our jobs. Maybe Dion was right. Maybe the best butt-kissers would win.

As she thought to herself, she kept her lips pressed tightly together. One careless, stray thought spoken aloud and she was as good as gone.

When Mr. Suit checked his watch, it seemed to be a signal to wrap up the meeting. He closed his folder with an audible snap. "Thank you all for meeting with us today," he said.

"As if we had a choice," Dion muttered.

"If I'm not mistaken, the first of the employee conferences starts in about ten minutes," he went on. "As I said, the time and place are listed on the schedules I've just passed out to you. In the meantime, if you have any questions, issues, or concerns that can't wait until your designated meeting time, please see my administrative assistant, and she'll schedule an interim meeting for you."

Cydney glanced meaningfully at Dion. Things were going to be different all right. Before, if anybody needed to talk, all they had to do was pop into Mike's office. No matter what he was doing, he always had time to talk to his employees. They were, as he often told them, the life blood of the company. Without them, there was no MegnaTronics.

Cydney rose slowly, gathering her purse and briefcase. "I need a cup of coffee and a good cry," she said, shaking her head.

"You'll have to hold off on that. I think Mike wants another meeting with you, Cyd," Dion indicated.

"Two meetings in one day? How am I going to get any work done?" she complained. She pointed to herself, and mouthed across the room, "You wanted to see me?"

Mike nodded gravely.

"Oh, Lord," she sighed. "Last one in, first one out."

"He won't dare fire you, Cyd. You're the best he's got."

"Yeah, but does The Suit know that?" she whispered over her shoulder.

Using a smile as a shield against her nervousness, she walked up to her boss . . . uh, former boss, she hastily corrected. "Hi, Mike," she said in a voice that sounded nothing like her own. So much for trying to sound cavalier and confident. Cydney thought she wound up sounding just plain chicken.

Mike gestured for her to sit down. He looked around, nodding to his employees as they filed past him out of the room. Some patted him on the back; others glared. Mike handled each response with the same enthusiastic response.

"What's up, Cydney?" he asked as most of the employees filed out of the room.

"Obviously not me . . . at least not on time," she said, trying to make a joke of her late entrance.

"Don't worry about that, kiddo. There's something else I wanted to talk to you about." He waited until there were only the two of them in the room before going on.

"Oh, now you want to talk. Why didn't you flap your gums before all of this came down on us?" she demanded.

"Don't be mad at me, Cyd. I couldn't say anything."

"Why, Mike? Why?! Couldn't you have at least—"

"No, Cyd, I couldn't," he cut her off. "Listen to me. I know you don't care much for office politics. You just wanted to be left alone to do your job. So, things I could have told you, I didn't, because I didn't want you to worry."

"Well, you certainly put my mind at rest today," she quipped.

"Cydney, when I first started to notice my business getting into trouble, I ignored it. You know why? Because we were still making money, hand over fist. That's why I could give out the bonuses and pay the raises all of you deserved. We kept getting contracts, so I didn't worry when some of the warning flags started.''

''What kind of warning flags?''

''I thought they were just administrative errors—bills that didn't get paid on time, notices that came in, clients who swore they'd paid on invoices but their checks we never received. All of it started to add up to something funny.''

''But you're not laughing,'' Cydney said softly.

''For a while, I was starting to get paranoid. I was starting to think that it was being done on purpose.''

''Like somebody was trying to sabotage you? Are you kidding?''

''I'm as serious as a heart attack. I started to smell takeover.''

''A hostile one. Right, Mike?'' Cydney insisted. She had to know if he didn't care anymore what happened to the company—or to them.

''You're damn right, it would be hostile. When I started MegnaTronics, I always swore they'd have to pry my business from my cold, stiff, six-feet-under fingers.''

''But you sold out to this Burke-Carter person. How do you know he wasn't the one trying to ruin you?''

''Because when I put the word out that I was looking to sell, I targeted him, not the other way around.''

''How did you hear about him?''

''Through some friends in the industry, I'd heard that he was looking for a company to develop. His usual line of work is consulting.''

''You mean telling people what to do. It isn't a stretch to see him in that position,'' Cydney said sarcastically.

''You sound like you don't like him.''

''I don't know anything about him,'' Cydney said quickly. ''How much do you know about him, Mike?''

''Enough to know that he's good at what he does. As soon as I filled him in on what was going on here, he was able to plug some of the leaks that were draining our resources. We were literally bleeding from a thousand cuts, Cyd. He got the business back on track. He's the reason why most of you will keep your jobs.''

"Did he ever find out who was doing this to you?"

"I think it's just a matter of time."

Cydney shook her head, "I don't know about him, Mike. It sounds a little strange to me. I mean, you know everything there is to know about your business. You make sure of that. How come he can just come in and be Mr. Fix-it in a flash and you couldn't?"

"He may not be Mr. Warm-and-Fuzzy, but he's sharp, Cydney. He knows his business. I trust him to put things back together again so that everyone will enjoy coming to work.''

"Did you have to sell to him, Mike? Did he make you do it?"

"No," Mike admitted. "I sold the business to him because I've done all that I can do here. I think another reason why somebody was able to do so much damage before I caught on was because I was getting lazy. I was getting lazy because I was getting bored. The thrill of building a business had gone. It was getting so that every day was getting to be a grind. That's when I knew it was time to get out. But just because I wanted to bail didn't mean I stopped caring for all of you. I'm sticking around long enough to make sure that all of my people get the best deal possible.''

"Thanks for hanging in there, Mike."

"No problem. I'd do anything for you guys."

"You know the feeling is mutual, don't you?"

"I was hoping that you'd say that."

"Why?"

"I have a favor to ask of you."

"What kind of a favor?" Cydney said suspiciously.

"You may not like it."

"Stop being so mysterious about it, and tell me."

"I want you to . . . uh . . . act as the official liaison between the employees and Mr. Burke-Carter.''

"Official liaison? I don't know if I like the sound of that, Mike. It sounds like you're asking me to be a corporate spy . . . a snitch.''

"That's not what I'm saying at all!" Mike sounded shocked. "You're the long-timer around here, Cyd. Everybody looks to you to set the example."

"Some example I set. I'm late for what could be my own funeral."

"Everybody in that meeting knew that you're the first one to stay extra hours whenever it's necessary. What I'm trying to say is that if you know of anyone who's having a really bad time with this change, let us know. Morale is going to dip pretty low. We want to do what we can before it hits rock bottom. One really bad attitude can poison the entire bunch, Cyd."

"Like Dion," she murmured.

"Like Dion," he agreed. "Don't think I don't know what he's probably saying about me right now."

"If I happen to overhear some of it, I'm not going to run back to tell you, Mike," Cydney said firmly.

"I wouldn't respect you so much if you did. All I'm asking you to do is help smooth out the transition. If someone has a complaint, and they want us to know, but they don't want to come to us, step in. If you want, you can even ask them if its okay before you come to us. That way, you won't feel like you're going behind anybody's back. People talk to you, Cyd. They share things with you. They might be a little reluctant to share them with me. And I know they won't go to Burke-Carter. Not yet . . . not until he's earned their trust."

"Do you think he can do that?"

"I wouldn't have brought him in if I didn't think he could run this company as well, or better, than I could."

"He seems so . . . so . . ." Cydney searched for a polite word for cold-hearted, son of a gun.

"I know." Mike grinned at her. "Maybe that's why I like him so much."

"You like him?" Cydney asked in surprise.

"It's kind of hard not to," Mike shrugged. "He's everything I'm not. We're complete opposites, but it works. I like to think

of him as a complement to my personality. He's yang to my yin. He's omega to my alpha. He's superego to my id . . ."
Mike would have gone on if Cydney hadn't held up her hand.

"All right, all right. I get the point," Cydney said dryly.

"So, will you do it? Will you help us make things run as smoothly as you can?"

"Well, I guess I don't have to like him to work with him."

"That's right, you don't."

She had only heard him speak for the first time today. Yet, there was no mistaking that voice. Inwardly, Cydney groaned. She should have remembered her promise to herself, and kept all negative comments about her new boss safely sealed behind her lips. She put her hand over her eyes and said to Mike, "Tell me I didn't just say that."

"Oh, you said it all right." Mike pointed his finger at her.

"Then tell me that *he* didn't hear that," she moaned.

"Oh, I heard it all right," The Suit said, moving around the conference table so that he was fully in her line of sight.

Slowly, Cydney climbed to her feet. Clearing her throat nervously, she began, "What I meant to say, Mr. Burke-Carter was that—"

"Ms. Kelley," he interrupted her. "I'm not here to win a popularity contest. I'm here to get this business back on its feet. If I have to endure a little behind-the-back griping, I'll do it. I've got thick skin. I think I can handle a little name calling."

"We weren't talking about you behind your back," Cydney denied. "Not the way that you think, anyway."

"I was just asking Cydney if she would be the unofficial spokesperson for the employees," Mike offered.

"I don't think we need one," Daryl said, dismissing the idea.

"I think you do," Cydney contradicted.

"And why is that, Ms. Kelley?"

"To be honest, I don't think anybody's going to talk to you—no matter how many of these scheduled conferences you've set up."

Mike cleared his throat as a signal for her to back down. Cydney ignored him. She'd already backed down once today. If she kept doing it, that Suit would start to think that she didn't have any backbone at all. "Don't get me wrong. Nobody's going to mutiny or not show up. They'll all come—promptly and attentively. But I doubt if you'll get any feedback. What everyone will do is sit there and listen to you tell them how it's going to be. No one will speak up because they'll be too afraid of losing their jobs."

"Even if we tell them that speaking their minds won't necessarily hurt them?"

"No one wants to take that chance, Mr. Burke-Carter," Cydney insisted.

"You should listen to her. She's right, you know," Mike said, nodding vigorously.

"So, what do you suggest that we do?" Daryl asked, adopting an open stance that was supposed to convey that he was willing to listen.

Cydney almost rolled her eyes. She'd been to those managerial, social skills seminars, too. At least, she'd practiced her skills enough so that it wasn't obvious that she was using the techniques she'd learned in those seminars.

"Go on and have your meetings. Just be prepared for what I told you is going to happen. There won't be much you can do over the next few weeks but show them what kind of a boss you're going to be."

"And those of you who don't leave, and who aren't asked to leave, will eventually adapt," Daryl finished for her.

"Listen to him, Cyd. He's making sense," Mike put in. Both Cydney and Daryl turned to stare at him. What was he—a one-man cheering section? "I'm just trying to keep the peace," Mike said, spreading his hands in a gesture of helplessness.

"I'm going back to work," Cydney said in a voice bordering on disgust. She headed for the conference door, but Mike called out to her.

"Hey, Cyd . . . Did you do something to your hair?"

She closed her eyes, shaking her head. That was enough!

No more spotlights for the day. She just wanted to fade back into her office, and not come out again until the proverbial five o'clock whistle blew. With a perfectly straight face, she turned to Mike and said, "Why no, Mike. What makes you ask?"

III

Nobody had to tell him that it was time to go. By four fifty-nine, MegnaTronics was a ghost town. Daryl walked the halls and noted all of the closed, dark offices. *So much for company loyalty*, he thought, with more than a small amount of sarcasm. He'd reviewed the project schedules of each department for the day and knew that most of the goals had not been met. But that was all right. This flight before finishing the job would soon change. He would see to that.

He tossed his portfolio into his briefcase, then closed it with a jaunty snap. And why shouldn't he gloat? He'd done what some of his colleagues said couldn't be done. He'd taken a business that was rotten through and through, almost on the verge of collapse, and had begun a drastic turnaround. It had taken almost a whole year of behind-the-scenes manipulation. He didn't want to tip his hand before he was ready to move on the company. There were too many others interested in what seemed to be the perfect business opportunity.

Daryl allowed himself the luxury of another self-satisfied grin. How long had he endured the not-so-good-natured ribbing from his colleagues when those who knew what he was trying to do threatened to snatch MegnaTronics right out from under him. When he thought about all of those others he'd beat out to get MegnaTronics, he had to congratulate himself. Those colleagues of his weren't slouches. He was up against some pretty stiff competition. Once they set their minds to taking over a company, you could usually count on their succeeding. This time, though, he wouldn't be outdone. He had nearly drained most of his personal resources. But he was determined to make them all jealous of his success this time.

He'd called in favors from his allies, bullied some, and bribed others (in a very loose sense of the word). Within a year, he'd plugged almost every leak in the MegnaTronics cash flow. As a result of all that hard work, he had finally won the right to announce himself as the man behind the helm of the company. And, as soon as he found a name that suited him, the name of the company would reflect the man who'd done so much to bring about the changes.

He was about to walk out the door when the phone rang. He snatched it from the cradle.

"Burke-Carter speaking," he said tersely.

"Hey, Mr. Big Time Business Tycoon. Did you forget we had a court reserved?"

Daryl groaned and sat down again. How could he have forgotten about the Monday night pick-up games he and his brother regularly participated in at the local YMCA? For a year, Daryl had looked forward to those Monday night games of basketball. Those games were the perfect stress relievers. There, at the Y, he could run, shout, and shower out his frustrations. He could then face the week, and the business world, with all of the sharp, competitive edge the game of basketball demanded.

"I'm sorry, Whalen. I got tied up at the office." Daryl leaned back in his chair, admiring his new office. He was proud of the plush leather furniture, the wide mahogany desk, the business awards that he'd won. They were stacked neatly in a corner, waiting for him to hang them up to show them off.

"So, how was the first day? Did you fire everybody yet?" his brother wanted to know.

"Who said I was going to fire anybody?" Daryl asked defensively.

"Hey, don't bite my head off. It was just a joke! Sounds like I hit a nerve."

"Talk like that is bad for business. Employees don't like it when you start messing with their money."

"Yeah, but won't the rest of your saplings be glad when you cut out the dead wood to make room for some real growth."

"Shana's had you working in that garden of hers again, hasn't she?" Daryl laughed. Whalen always picked up the terminology from his wife's latest project. Last week, it was astrology. Then, his brother's language had been peppered with talk of "moons in houses" and zodiac signs rising in and out of something or other.

"Don't laugh. By next fall, we'll be eating fresh fruits and vegetables picked from our own backyard. Speaking of backs—" Whalen began.

"Yeah?" Daryl sat up, suddenly made suspicious by his brother's too casual tone.

"Watch yours, big brother."

"What do you mean?"

"I've been hearing some things through the grapevine."

"What kind of things?" Daryl asked, his face hardening.

"Now, don't start getting that vein in your forehead. I can almost hear it throbbing over the phone."

"What kind of talk, Whalen?" Daryl repeated.

Whalen sighed. "It's just rumors . . ."

"Whalen!"

"All right, all right. I heard through some friends of mine, who know some people, who work with some other people who are in a position to know that . . ."

"Know what? Get to the point!"

"They're saying a lot of things."

"I want specifics," Daryl demanded.

"You've got them coming at you from two sides, big brother."

"Who, what, why, when, and where, Whalen? I can't get more specific than that."

"Everybody's not congratulating you on your new plaything.

Some of the big boys want your toys, brother. You know who I'm talking about, don't you?''

"Keller," Daryl breathed into the phone. One of his colleagues that he'd outbid for MegnaTronics didn't take the news too lightly. Dalton Keller didn't like losing —especially to Daryl, a man that he considered to be an upstart in the business. Keller, who was making deals long before Daryl could reach up to a desk to grab a phone, couldn't stand the idea that he could be usurped as Wall Street's whiz kid.

"I don't give a damn what Keller thinks," Daryl bluffed. "He's a sore loser."

"A nasty, sore loser. I wouldn't be surprised if you heard his name more than once while you're busy playing big business tycoon."

"I'm not playing this time, Whalen. I mean to stick with MegnaTronics and make it work."

"I know that. And I'm glad you've taken this venture more seriously than the others. The last time you cut out too fast. You left too many people thinking that you were just in it for a fast buck."

"And when it failed . . ." Daryl's voice trailed off. "Well, that wasn't my fault. I wasn't taking the blame for that one."

"Which made more people mad at you."

"I can't help that." Daryl was defensive. "But I can help MegnaTronics. Call it absolution if you want to, but I mean to clear my reputation."

"At all costs? You gotta' be careful how people are looking at you, Darry," Whalen warned. "You have to watch what people are saying about you."

"And what are they saying now?"

"They're saying that maybe you didn't play fair when you took over MegnaTronics, Darry. They're saying that maybe some of your tactics were a little too cutthroat, and there was a little too much under-the-table dealing going on."

"That's a damn lie!" Daryl said hotly. He leaped from his seat and paced his office. "Who's been saying it, Whalen? Tell me who. You know how hard I worked to get this company."

"I know that, and you know that, and anybody who really

knows you knows that." Whalen deliberately made his response nonsensical to lighten his brother's mood.

"Do you want to run that by me again?" Daryl asked, laughing softly.

"Sorry, I don't have the breath,"

"Who did you hear this from? I gotta' know, Whalen. I gotta' stop that kind of talk before it hurts any chance I have of rebuilding this company's reputation."

"Look, Darry, I'll tell you what I know as soon as I have something more concrete for you. In the meantime, watch your back."

"I will."

"And do yourself a favor."

"What's that?"

"Get yourself an ally."

"A what?"

"An ally, big brother. A friend in the company. You need someone who knows the score, and who'll keep you informed. You need someone who'll be loyal to the company and to you."

"Mike and I—" Daryl began.

"Uh-uh," Whalen cut him off. "He doesn't count."

"Why not?"

"Do I have to explain everything to you? You're the one with the MBA, remember? Mike is no good to you now because he's on his way out! He'll watch out for his employees as much as he can, but he's looking to get out of there. He's mostly watching out for himself. If his business goes down, it'll be unfortunate for him, but doubly so for you because you're the one who's sunk everything you've got into making it work. He's already made his money. He can just take it and run. If he doesn't take half the company with him when he goes, you need to find someone who'll make you as successful as they did him."

"One of my employees bluntly pointed out to me today that I might not be able to win the trust of anyone in this company," Daryl said.

"That sounds like the person you need by your side, big brother. Who was he?"

"What makes you think it was a 'he'?"

"I figured it had to be a he because no woman would talk to you that way."

"Figure again," Daryl said dryly.

"You mean you don't have all the women eating out of your hand?"

"Not even close," Daryl said, with a short laugh. If Cydney Kelley's reaction to him was an indicator of his ability to charm the ladies, then he might as well give up this line of business and join a monastery.

"What's the matter? Losing your touch?" Whalen goaded.

"What do you think I'm running here? A candy store? It's not as if I can go out and sample the merchandise any time I feel like it. I'm the CEO, for crying out loud. That means boss."

"Geez, Darry, it's not as if CEO means celibate employer's office," Whalen said derisively. "Because you're the boss, you can get any woman you want—that is if there are any worth having. Do you have any good-lookers in that brain trust company of yours?"

"I'll bet Shana loves to hear talk like that coming from you . . ." Daryl said, hinting that he was going tell Whalen's wife of his chauvinistic comments.

"You tell her I said that, and I'll deny every word of it."

Daryl glanced outside of his window, suddenly distracted by the parking lot lights flickering outside of his window. "Look, Whalen, it's late. I'm not going to make our game tonight."

"Well, I guess I'll just have to whip your tail some other time."

"You can beat me any time you want . . . in your dreams." Daryl laughed.

"Next Monday then?"

"Sure. Sure. I'll see you then."

"And Darry?"

"Yeah?"

"Congratulations, big brother. I'm proud of you."

"Thanks." Daryl started to hang up, then snatched the phone back to his ear. "Whalen? Whalen, are you still there?"

"Yeah, what is it?"

"I almost forgot. I'm holding a reception in a couple of weeks. I'm inviting the press and some of the investors to look at the new and improved company. Can you and Shana make it?"

"Nothing could keep me from it."

"It's a date, then. I'll call you back later with details and directions," Daryl said and hung up the phone. He took one last look at his office. *His* office! Then, like the rest of his employees, headed for home. How he liked the sound of that— his employees! Without realizing it, as he strode out to the parking lot to his dedicated parking space, he whistled tunelessly through his teeth.

Gritting her teeth as tightly as she gripped the steering wheel, Cydney fought her way through the evening traffic. She wanted to go home, too. But she couldn't. There was something she had to do first. She had to get to the KSLM radio station before the administration office closed. If the progress she was making was any indication of how the rest of the evening would go, she was in for a lot of trouble. She had to ask three different people for directions to KSLM. Each person she asked gave her similar directions, but none seemed right on target.

She was so disgusted, that she was *this* close to saying forget it (or something a little more colorful) and going on without stopping. But there would be no peace in her house, Cydney knew, until her son had those tickets in the palms of his outstretched hands. So, even though she missed the turnoff and could have easily kept going home, she swung around to get back onto the expressway. The traffic going in that direction was much heavier. What should have taken her fifteen minutes instead took her forty-five.

By the time she found the station, she was tired, hungry, and grouchy—a dangerous combination for the station, which catered to a more enthusiastic crowd.

"Just give me the tickets!" Cydney practically shouted to the secretary who tried to get Cydney to take T-shirts, bumper stickers, placards, and buttons printed with the radio station logo. "I don't want this stuff!" Cydney said, ignoring the items offered by the secretary. "What am I going to do with all of this?"

"You'll need them for the party," she insisted. "Think of them as party favors."

"I'd rather not think about them at all," Cydney said testily.

"You have to take them."

"Fine . . . fine . . . just box them up, and give me the tickets!" Cydney said, literally holding her temper, and her sanity, in check by sheer willpower.

"And if anybody asks you where you got these, tell them KSLM—the radio station with the *slammin'est* hits in the city!"

"Do they pay you to be that perky, or are you for real?" Cydney wanted to know.

The woman just smiled, and added an extra bumper sticker to the box.

"Yo, Mom! Where did you get all of this stuff?" Cameron asked, as he started to rummage through the box that Cydney let fall to the floor.

"You're kidding, right?" she asked. As if he couldn't read the fluorescent orange, green, and black logos. She shrugged out of her jacket, kicked off her shoes, and headed for the kitchen.

"You went by the station? You got the tickets?"

"I promised that I would, didn't I?"

"Yeah . . . but . . . I mean, I figured you might forget, or get tired, or something . . ."

You don't know how close you are to being right, she thought. She bit her lip to keep from admitting it. He had sounded so dejected when he thought she might forget. Seeing his face light up made all of her suffering worth it.

"I didn't forget. I didn't forget about the tickets, and I didn't forget about the homework, either. Let's have it."

Cameron groaned, but pulled out his backpack where he'd stuffed his work. Cydney scanned a three-page science essay he'd written. After circling a few misspelled words, she nodded her approval, then asked to see his math homework.

He handed it to her, smug in the knowledge that he'd gone over each problem three times to make sure he'd done them right. There was no way he was going to jeopardize his skating party over a careless error—not after he'd practically told the entire school about his big win this morning.

"Anything else?" Cydney prompted.

"Social studies." He handed her the final assignment. Cydney read over his work. After finding no errors, she said, "Okay, give me what you've got for entrepreneur."

When Cameron grimaced, Cydney laughed and said, "I bet you thought I forgot about that, huh?"

"No way, Mom. You never forget when you give me extra homework."

"You'd better believe it. Now give me that sentence."

Cameron recited from memory the sentence he'd scrawled on a crumpled sheet of notebook paper. "When I grow up, I want to be an entrepreneur."

"Did you even look up the word? I know you can do better than that!" Cydney accused him of trying to get out of work.

"An entrepreneur is a big shot, right? Somebody who takes chances, runs things, and makes a lot of money?"

"Uh . . . something like that," Cydney agreed.

"Then that's what I want to be," Cameron said, with a definitive nod.

"You can't argue with reasoning like that. Good job," she praised him.

"So do I get the tickets? Can I go to the skate party?"

"Let's see how you do the rest of the week, and then we'll—"

"Aunt Courtney's coming," Cameron broke in suddenly, turning his head toward the window to watch for her.

"How do you know she's coming?" Cydney asked.

"She just made the turn onto our street," Cameron said, and shrugged as he stuffed his homework into his backpack again.

Cydney wondered how he could hear a car coming that was still halfway down the block, but he couldn't hear her when she called him from his room to take out the trash.

Cydney peeked out the window, too, and caught a glimpse of dark gray as her sister's car rolled by her window. The car horn beeped twice to let them know that she'd arrived.

"Go see if your aunt needs any help." Cydney pushed her son toward the door. Courtney rarely came to her house empty-handed. Courtney was a shop-o-holic. She justified her urge to spend by buying for everyone. "And, Cam, I know I don't have to tell you how happy it'll make your Aunt Courtney if you invite your cousins to the party."

Cameron did some mental calculations. Because he had to invite his cousins, that meant two less friends he could ask along. He quickly reviewed his list. He knew that half the school would be at the party, if only as spectators. But his friends and the list of "want-to-be" friends who would be guests of the radio station were growing by the minute. He didn't want to risk cutting out someone more popular, or prettier, just to invite his cousins.

Cameron was a heartbeat away from complaining, but when he saw the look on his mom's face, he quickly clamped his mouth shut. If he gave his mom any excuse, she would snatch those tickets out of his grasp so fast, it would leave a smoking hole in his hand where the tickets used to be.

"Yes'm," he said, with as much enthusiasm as he could muster at the idea of inviting his cousins—Oscar and Adrienne. They were younger than he was—much younger and spoiled rotten. What else could they be with a mom who didn't know how to say no once they'd gotten her inside of a store. Any store, it didn't matter. Cameron had seen his aunt make even the most enthusiastic sales assistant weep with fatigue.

Cydney opened the door, and waved to her sister.

"Hey, baby sister," Courtney called out, waving a brightly colored shopping bag at her. "What's up, Cameron?" She kissed Cameron soundly on the top of his head as he grabbed the shopping bags that she indicated.

Courtney hurried up the drive, wobbling slightly on brand

new, six-inch, stiletto heels that she was trying to break in. "Girl, wait until you see what I've got for you! I have found the bargain of the century."

"No more of that bargain body splash, Courtney," Cydney said, crossing her index fingers, and backing away as if to ward off the "evil" that her sister brought with her in that bag. "The last bargain you found broke me out in a rash so bad I had to sit in an oatmeal bath for three hours to stop the itching."

"Well, if you'd read the directions . . ." Courtney shifted the blame to her sister.

"Who knew that the stuff would react badly to its own, coordinated body powder," Cydney said sarcastically.

"If it makes you feel any better, I wrote a nasty letter to the manufacturer."

"And what did they say?"

"Nothing. But they did send me a gift certificate for their coordinated hand lotion."

"If you've been using it, don't touch me or anything in my house," Cydney warned. "With my luck, the first time I'd try to clean anything that you'd touched, my whole house would spontaneously combust."

"Speaking of hot stuff." Courtney turned her sister's irritation to her advantage. "Girlfriend, have I got something for you!"

"What is it?" Cydney asked suspiciously.

"Come on inside and I'll show you. You'd better send Cameron to his room. Some of the stuff I've got in these bags are rated PG-13 and above."

Cameron groaned and said, "Aw, man! Female stuff."

"Don't knock it, Cam. In a few more years, you'll be a lot more interested in female stuff—especially in a couple of weeks. Are you inviting any girls to that party of yours?"

"You know about that, Aunt Courtney?"

"I heard you on the radio this morning, Cameron. Congratulations."

Cydney prodded Cameron gently—or what she considered gently. He rubbed the back of his head and muttered, "Ouch!

Okay, Mom. I'm doing it. See? Can Oscar and Adrienne come to the party that Saturday, Aunt Courtney?''

''That's all they've been talking about today. Of course they can come. Thanks for inviting them.''

''Like I had a choice,'' he muttered, just low enough for them to ignore him.

''Upstairs to the bedroom.'' Courtney waved Cameron on. ''And after you take those up, there are four more bags in the trunk.''

Cameron dragged his feet. He knew if he didn't do something fast he'd be their ''go get it boy'' for the rest of the evening.

''Can I go to G-Man's house, Mom? I don't need to hang around here while you and Aunt Courtney talk, do I?''

''G-Man? Who's G-Man?''

''You know G-Man, Mom,'' Cameron said impatiently. ''It's Gerald Thomas.''

''Where do these kids get these names?'' Courtney shook her head.

''Can I go, Mom? If I'm outta' here, then you ladies can do your thing without worrying about what I might see or hear.''

''Our thing?'' Cydney said, putting her hands on her hips, raising her eyebrows at him.

''That girl talk thing.''

''It's a school night, Cam,'' Cydney objected.

''Let him go, Cyd.'' Courtney took up for him.

''For calling you a girl, you'd let him go to the moon for the evening,'' Cydney said sarcastically.

''You'd better believe it,'' Courtney replied with a grin.

''Be home before nine o'clock,'' Cydney relented. ''And leave Gerald's phone number so I can reach you if I have to.''

Cameron had a vision of his mom calling him all the way from G-Man's house just to run some sort of errand for her. ''Yes, ma'am,'' he said, biting his lip to keep any smart remarks sealed tightly behind his lips.

''And don't forget the other bags!'' Courtney called out as she grabbed Cydney by the arm and pulled her into the bedroom.

* * *

"So, what do you think?" Courtney pulled suit after suit from a bag, and laid them out on Cydney's bed for her approval. Cydney fingered the material enviously. Summer wool, linen, and rayon blends of the latest styles and colors decorated the bed like a rainbow.

"Well?" Courtney prompted.

"They're perfect," Cydney murmured. She looked at the price tag of just a jacket alone, then said, "And pricey! Good grief, Courtney, do you know how much this one piece alone costs?"

"I have a vague idea," Courtney said cynically. "I'm the one who shopped up one side and down the other of the mall looking for just the right pieces. And you know what?"

"What?"

"I've got a pair of shoes to match every outfit."

"You and your twelve-inch stilettos. You're going to kill yourself on those high heels one of these days, Courtney, or kill somebody else by stepping on them."

"For your information, Queen of the Flat Soles, I do not buy twelve-inch heels. Even if they made them, I don't think I'd buy them. This time, I've got three-inch heels."

Cydney's eyebrows raised. "Since when do you wear sensibly heeled pumps?"

"I don't," Courtney said. "I didn't buy them for me."

"Then who did . . ." Cydney began, then stopped when her sister started to laugh.

"When you were checking out the price tags, did you check out the sizes, too? You know I'm not a size eight, baby sister. I didn't buy all of this stuff for me. It's for you."

"For . . . for me?! Are you kidding me? Why, Courtney? What did I do to deserve all this royal treatment?"

"Don't you even remember what today is, Cydney?"

"I know it isn't my birthday."

"So, guess again," Courtney prompted.

Cydney closed her eyes. She'd been so unsettled today, so

on edge. Somewhere, in the deepest corners of her mind, she knew the reason. But she thought that if she kept pushing it back, she could continue to pretend that the feelings she had hidden didn't exist.

"You had to remind me," she whispered.

"I don't know if it's a good sign or not that you've forgotten, baby sister."

"It means that I'm on the road to recovery."

"Or that you're in major denial," Courtney scoffed.

"It hasn't been that bad for me. Now that I think about it, I should be celebrating. Three years to the day I became a free woman again."

"I know it's been hard for you, baby sister, raising that boy—as sweet as he is—all by yourself, without any help from that—"

Cydney raised her hand to stop her sister's litany. She'd heard it all before. "I've had about all the stress I can handle today, Courtney. Don't bring him up. Let's just let my divorce anniversary pass without a mention of *him.*"

"Fine. I don't care. Pretend like he doesn't exist. But I don't like the way you've been existing."

"What do you mean?"

"Cyd, you're a beautiful woman. But no one would ever know it by the way you hold yourself."

"I let you change my hair," Cydney said defensively.

"And it got you some looks, didn't it? It turned a few heads."

"Yeah," Cydney had to admit. "Yeah, it did."

"I practically had to knock you down and tie you up to get you to change. With a new hairdo, some new clothes, and a little makeup—"

"Courtney, I don't have time to fool with a lot of *froufrou*," Cydney said impatiently. "I barely make it to work on time as it is."

"You're always late, so what's a few minutes more?"

"Well, I can't afford to be late anymore," Cydney said sullenly. Somehow, she didn't think that Daryl Burke-Carter would accept primping as an excuse for being late every morning.

"Cyd, I can show you a technique called the three-minute face. All it does is polish your look. I promise, you won't look made-up. No heavy stuff or crazy colors. You'll still look like your wonderfully earthy self."

"Then why bother with that stuff at all if I'll still look the same?"

"It'll be you, only better. Wait until you see the difference. Then ask me that question again. Come on, try on some of these things."

Cydney picked up a vibrant, yellow, two piece jacket and skirt ensemble.

"I can't wear this! This skirt is *way* too short. My knees will show. You know how I am about my knees."

"Your knees are not fat," Courtney said with a sigh. "Come on, baby sister. Loosen up. Get with it. This is the nineties. I'm talking nineteen-nineties, not eighteen. You have got to get out of those dark, boring, almost down to the ankle hoop skirts."

"Come on, Courtney. I'm not that bad."

"Do you have anything that falls above your knee? Anything? I dare you to find one thing in that closet that isn't blue, brown, or gray."

"No."

"Why not?"

"Because I don't want to," Cydney said stubbornly.

"Because you can't," Courtney countered.

"All right, so I'm stuck in a fashion trend."

"You mean fashion rut. But never fear, baby sister is here. I'm going to bring you to the present, if I have to drag you kicking and screaming all the way."

"Courtney, I appreciate everything you're trying to do. But you're not going to solve all of my problems by slapping a new coat of paint on me."

"I know beauty is only skin deep. But how can you get someone willing to scratch beneath your surface if you're always trying to fade into the background."

"I'm not like you. I don't feel comfortable trying every new fashion that those magazines say I should."

"I know you think I'm a little shallow sometimes, and that I use money as a substitute. But at least I have a substitute. What have you got? Nothing."

"What are you trying to do? Depress me?"

"Of course not. I just wanted to let you know that you don't have to be this way, baby sister. Tell me something. When was the last time you went out on a date? And I'm not talking about a night out with the girls. I'm talking about a one-on-one, you and a man date."

Cydney clamped her lips together. She reached for another suit, and held it against her.

"What do you think of this one?" she said, trying to evade Courtney's question. Courtney snatched the suit from her hands, "Hey, you! I'm talking to you."

"I heard you," Cydney said sullenly.

"Oh, for crying out loud! You mean you haven't dated in three years, Cydney?"

"Where am I supposed to find the time between work and raising my son to meet someone? Tell me that, Courtney."

"You find yourself a baby-sitter and you make the time, girlfriend."

"I'm too old to be hanging out in clubs."

"There are plenty of other places to meet men."

"Like where?"

"Church is always a good place to start. Or the library, or shows. Put your mind to it, girl. I meet men while I'm out shopping all of the time."

"You don't work, Courtney, so you're always in the malls. That's why you're always meeting men. You can't do anything with them anyway. You're married."

"That doesn't stop me from talking to them. There's nothing wrong with talking. Talking to them is like window shopping at Cartier's. A nice thought, but not a chance in hell of ever doing anything about it."

"When I'm out shopping, any man who might be interested in me is instantly turned off when they see me with Cameron. He's no help, either, with all that strutting and glaring he's been doing lately."

"Okay, so how about this idea. The next time I go out, if I meet anybody I think is interesting, I'll get his name and number and bring it back to you," Courtney suggested.

"Oh, there's a confidence booster for you. I hope to never be so desperate that I have to latch onto my sister's castoffs!"

"Three years." Courtney shook her head as if Cydney had been handed the death sentence. "That means you haven't had . . . that is . . . been intimate with anyone since your divorce?"

"Jason was my first love and my last," Cydney said softly. "I wasn't going to subject Cameron to a parade of men through my house just to try to fill the emptiness when my husband left."

"But, don't you miss it?" Courtney lowered her voice. "The feel of a man's strong arms around you? The sound of his voice deep in passion when he whispers your name? That warm, glowing feeling when you wake up in the morning, and look over at *your* man . . ."

"Now, that's a stupid question."

"So, what do you do when you want to . . . uh . . ."

"Exercise is very therapeutic," Cydney said with a wry smile.

"If you can find the time to jog, you can find the time to date," Courtney said confidently.

"And you think a few pieces of cloth and some face paint will get all of that for me?" Cydney sounded derisive, but on the inside, she knew her sister was holding out the glimmer of a promise for her.

It would be nice to have someone else to talk to, someone to share her thoughts, hopes, and fears with. Or, just to sit and be comfortable with.

"You've got to start somewhere. I say, let's start with the things I know you can change. Start on the outside where everybody will notice first. Why not rack up a few confidence points with some compliments. When you look good, you feel good. When you feel good, you'll act like things are good. And when you act like things are good, good things will happen to you. It's not scientific, but I know it works. Will you trust me?"

Cydney spread her arms, and fell back on the bed. "Work your magic on me, big sister."

Courtney pulled out another bag, and another, and another.

"I just hope everyone won't think I'm doing this for the wrong reasons," Cydney said.

"What everyone?"

"Everyone at work. I hope they don't think I'm changing my image for the new boss."

"What new boss?"

"Didn't I tell you? I guess I haven't had the time in between you completely making me over. Mike sold the business, Courtney."

"No! You're kidding!"

"No, I'm not. MegnaTronics has a new owner. We met him today."

"Him?" Courtney said. "Hmm . . . this smells of possibilities."

"I think you've been sniffing that atomizer for too long," Cydney teased, putting aside the fragrance bottle her sister had pulled from a shopping bag.

"What's he like? How old is he? Is he married?"

"He's a jerk," Cydney said flatly.

"How do you know?"

"A woman just knows these things."

"I wouldn't be trusting that female intuition, if I were you. Yours is a little rusty."

"He just rubbed me the wrong way," Cydney argued.

"You haven't been touched by a man in three years," Courtney scoffed.

"Are you trying to help me or not?" Cydney complained.

"I'm trying to help you. Now give me the details about this new boss of yours."

"Get it out of your head, Courtney. He's off limits."

"Why? Because he's your boss?" she demanded.

"Among other things."

"What other things?"

"I told you!" Cydney said in exasperation. "I don't like him. I don't like his attitude."

"Why? What did he do to you?"

"First impressions mean a lot to me, Courtney. He made a very bad one. Without preparing us, he just waltzed into the conference room, wearing a thousand dollar suit, and told everybody he was the new owner."

"So, what was his first crime? That he bought the company or that he has good taste in clothes?"

Cydney ignored the comment. "And then he told us that some of us would be fired."

"If some of you are deadweight at the company, then maybe some of you need to go."

"That's heartless, Courtney!"

"That's business, Cydney," her sister retorted. "The sooner you realize that, the better. You ought to be glad that he had the good sense to know that sometimes you've got to cut some people loose so that the rest can stay afloat."

"And I'm supposed to sit around feeling grateful while he decides who's going to stay and who's going to go?" Cydney said caustically.

"A one thousand dollar suit, did you say?"

"Didn't you hear anything else I said to you? The man has no tact, no compassion. Do you really think I'd be interested in a man like that?"

"Do me a favor, will you, baby sister?"

"What's that?"

"Let me work my magic on you tonight. And after you come home from work tomorrow, call me."

"Why?"

"I want you to ask me that same question again."

"I'm not going after a man like that, Courtney," Cydney said firmly. "And I don't want a man like that coming after me."

"Come over here," Courtney called to her sister with a crooked finger.

"You've got that look in your eye again, Courtney, and it's scaring me. What are you going to do?"

Courtney smiled a wide, knowing smile. "I'm going to give

you a makeover that will have every man in that place coming after you.''

''Just practice a little restraint with that magic of yours,'' Cydney warned. ''I'm not going in to work like some sort of sleaze on the make.''

IV

"Glad you could *finally* make it in to work this morning, Ms. Kelley. Mike has been asking for you for twenty minutes now," Joan Kegler said as she handed Cydney several slips of pink paper with her morning messages.

There went starting work with a new image, Cydney thought, checking her watch. She blew out a sigh of resignation. She'd wanted to make it to work on time so badly today. After her talk with Courtney last night, her sister almost had her convinced that she could do it all. She could have it all! She could be mother, sister, career woman, and woman of the world.

"Three-minute face, my left eye," Cydney muttered.

Trying to reproduce the so-called effortless face that Courtney had showed her took fifteen minutes to get right. But, she had to admit, the effect was remarkable. The new colors that they'd experimented with last night really did add a certain polish to her look. Even the receptionist noticed.

"That's a new look for you, isn't it, Ms. Kelley?" Joan commented.

"I just thought I'd try something different for a change," Cydney said casually.

"Uh-huh." Joan's reply was caustic. "You wouldn't be flashing a little more leg to try to keep your job, would you?"

Cydney's head snapped up. She was afraid that someone would think that of her. It would have to be Joan to make the first comment. Is that really how the new boss would see her? How could he? He didn't know what kind of person she was. He wouldn't judge her like that. Would he? Suddenly, Cydney wished she'd never worn the wonderfully vibrant, two-piece that showed not only her knees, but a healthy portion of thigh, too.

"Did Mike say why he was looking for me?" Cydney continued, glad that she was able to sound unbothered by Joan's comment.

"He said something about needing the Janski file."

Cydney nodded. "I guess he didn't get my note telling him that I'd already archived it. I'll get it for him."

"And Dion has been looking for you, too."

"Dion? Did he say what he wanted?"

"Contrary to popular opinion, I am not everyone's keeper." Joan snorted. "His office is right across from yours. Why don't you just pop in on the way to yours, and see what he wants."

Cydney thought irritably that if she were so inclined to pop anywhere, it would be to "pop" Joan right in the mouth. Let's see how many sarcastic remarks she could get through a fat lip.

"You have a good day, Joanie," Cydney said pleasantly.

That would teach her to be so sarcastic. Kill her with kindness!

Cydney dug out the keys to her office. As she headed in that direction, another employee waved to her through the window of his office.

"Good morning, Cydney!"

Cydney looked up, startled. It was Vernon Castle from marketing. What did he want with her? And why was he sounding so pleasant. He hardly ever had a good word for her—especially since his idea of a quality product and hers were as different as night and day. She didn't want to think how many times she had almost strangled him and members of his marketing team for promising a potential client an impossible product with an even more impossible deadline.

"Good morning, Mr. Castle," she said, letting him know by her tone that she wasn't in a mood to be trifled with today. "What can I do for you?"

"Actually, I was coming down to ask what I can do for you."

"Excuse me?" Now she was really confused! Had someone had another meeting without telling her it was scheduled. It sounded like he knew something she didn't.

Now there's a switch, she thought snidely.

"Here, let me help you," Vernon said, taking the keys from her hand and opening the office door. Cydney barely resisted the urge to shudder. She imagined a trail of slime left on the doorknob when he pushed the door open for her. As he shut the door, Cydney set her briefcase on the desk, and turned to face him. "All right. All gloves are off. What do you want, Vernon?"

Vernon shrugged. "I just came down to ask you to lunch."

"Why? What do you want?"

"Can't a man ask a beautiful woman to lunch without wanting something?"

"You are treading on very dangerous ground, Vernon Castle," Cydney said tightly. "I don't have time for your games."

"Can't you work me into your schedule?"

"Last chance. Tell me what you want or get out."

"I want to talk to you."

"About?"

"Oh . . . stuff like the direction for the company, our product line. Stuff like that."

"We meet once a month to discuss those issues. Why do you want to meet now?"

Vernon smiled. "Would you believe I'm an early bird?"

No, but I will believe you're a worm. Cydney's smile told him exactly what she was thinking.

"All right, all pleasantries aside. I'm just trying to rebuild a few bridges that I might have burned," Vernon said.

"Go on," Cydney prompted.

"Mike is on his way out. He made that quite clear. And some of us may be going, too. Not of our own volition. Mr. Burke-Carter made that clear. He's going to run his business his way. But he still needs help. He's going to need someone like me . . . and you, too, of course, to help him transition. If we present a united front, we may both be able to keep our jobs."

Vernon began to pace. "I know we haven't always seen eye to eye, Cydney . . . er . . . Ms. Kelley, but we can change that. We can be a formidable team if we stick together. With Mike gone, you're next in line to . . ."

"To what?" Cydney asked, her voice and eyes hardening.

"To be second in command. You know the business. You're Mike's right arm. But listen, we shouldn't be talking about this here. Why don't we talk about this over lunch?"

"That won't be necessary," Cydney said softly. "I get the gist of what you want."

"So, do you want to meet with me?"

"No," Cydney said bluntly.

"Don't make the mistake I've made, Ms. Kelley. Don't burn your bridges."

"I'll cross that bridge when I get to it," Cydney said. She reached for the door and held it open for him. "Have a nice day," she repeated, with the same venomous intention she'd had for Joan. No sooner had Vernon left, than Dion poked his head in the door. "Hey, Cyd."

"Oh, hi, Dion."

"You're late."

"So what else is new?"

"I don't know, you tell me."

"What do you mean?"

"Marketing doesn't usually grace us with their presence without a hidden agenda. What did creepy Castle want?"

"To schmooze me," Cydney said in disgust. "Can you imagine that? He's trying to get on my good side."

"Did he say why?"

"He said he wanted to unburn some bridges with me so that he can get next to Burke-Carter."

"Humph . . ." Dion said, deep in his chest. "With a suit like you're wearing today, Cydney, I don't see how creepy Castle could resist thinking he could get next to you. What's up with this new color? Are you sure you aren't planning to do a little schmoozing on your own?"

"Now don't you start on me, too, Dion."

"Somebody else has been on your case?"

"Who hasn't been? First my sister, then Joan, now you. I don't have time for this. Speaking of Joan, she said you were looking for me earlier."

"Yeah, I almost forgot. I wanted to know which booth you want for the charity bazaar."

"Booth? Bazaar? What bazaar?" Cydney said distractedly, as she started to pull several files from her briefcase.

"Come on, Cydney, snap out of it. You've been on the volunteer list for a month now. The bazaar is this weekend. We've finally decided which booths we're going to man. I'm giving you first pick of the one you want."

"I'm not doing a dunking booth, Dion. Swimmer's ear can be very painful."

"Okay, no dunking booth."

"And I don't want a kissing booth either."

"Shame," Dion teased her. "We could probably make a fortune off of creepy Castle alone."

"Another comment like that, Dion, and you can kiss my—"

"Ah-ah-ah," Dion chastised her, wagging his finger. "Remember, this charity is for the children."

"So, what's left?"

"There's the cake walk."

"Too tempting. I'd eat half the merchandise."

"And the softball throw."

"Can't do that. I threw out my elbow playing tennis with my sister."

"You don't play tennis!" Dion scoffed.

"That's why I threw out my elbow," Cydney said testily.

"You're running out of options."

"Then what's left?"

"We have two booths left, Cydney. We're sponsoring the children's face paints and one of the ticket booths."

"I'll take face paints," Cydney said. "They're using stencils, aren't they?"

"I think so."

"Then I can handle that."

"Should I put you down for the morning, afternoon, or evening shift."

"Knowing my track record for getting in on time in the morning, you'd better put me down for afternoon."

"All right, then. I'll see you Saturday at eleven thirty. The directions to the place are posted on the bulletin board in the break room."

"I'll be there with bells on."

"You don't have to. We've already got somebody from marketing to play the clown." Dion grinned at her. "I'm outta' here. Get back to work."

Cydney pantomimed cracking a whip, then buried her head in her work.

If it weren't for the rampant gossip about who would be fired first, the parade of strangers (though the official word was potential clients) through the office, and the total disruption of the familiar routine, Cydney thought irritably that she would never guess that the company was being run by a total stranger.

Even after almost an entire week, she knew almost nothing about the man who now made the majority of the decisions affecting their careers. Though several people had had their conferences with him, no one, so far, had come to her with any grievances. That meant either that they had confidence in Daryl Burke-Carter's ability to lead them, or they were too frightened to say otherwise.

Since no one had come to her to talk, she simply buried herself in her work, and counted down the days before it was her turn to meet with him. By Friday, she had almost convinced herself that things were back to normal. She woke up, late as usual. She spurred her son on with the same loving threats, and tried as always to slip past Joan.

"Hold on a minute, Ms. Kelley!" Joan waved at her through the glass door. "Where do you think you're going?"

"To my office," Cydney said, through a forced smile. "The same place I've been going for five years now."

"You know your meeting with the DBC is in ten minutes."

"The DBC?" Cydney shook her head uncomprehendingly. She didn't recognize the name of that company. She started to reach for her day planner to make certain that she hadn't scheduled two meetings for the same time.

"The Daryl Burke-Carter," Joan said, in slow, distinct tones as if she was talking to a small child. "Remember him? Your boss's boss. I thought that's why you came in all dressed up on a dress-down Friday," Joan said, indicating the brightly colored, two-piece ensemble that Cydney had chosen for today.

"That isn't the reason why I came dressed today," Cydney said, with thinly veiled annoyance. "I happen to have clients coming in today." Cydney glanced at Joan's scheduling book meaningfully as if to say, if she paid more attention to her job, instead of to what Cydney was wearing, she wouldn't ask such stupid questions. "I didn't forget about my meeting with Mr. Burke-Carter."

Behind her back, Cydney crossed her fingers. As a matter of fact, she had almost forgotten about him. She was so busy trying to pull together an inspiring presentation for clients she had arranged to meet today, that she didn't even consider this employee relations ploy Mike and Burke-Carter concocted.

"Well, you could have fooled me," Joan said.

"That shouldn't be too hard," Cydney muttered under her breath as she read through her morning messages.

"And while you're down at that end of the hall, stop in to see Mike. He needs another set of documents out of the Janski file."

Cydney groaned. Sometimes she wondered if Mike was part goat. The more information she fed to him, the more voracious he became. What did he do with all the data she researched for him?

If she hurried, she could dig out the Janski file for Mike and still make her conference with Burke-Carter. She thrust open the door to her office, dropped her briefcase to the floor, then pushed it with her foot. As it slid across the floor, it snagged her stockings, and pulled a filament of nylon from the door to the desk.

Seeing the run in her new stockings brought a word to her lips that would have grounded Cameron for the rest of his life if she ever heard him use it. Cydney then shrugged her shoulders fatalistically. There was nothing she could do about it now. Even if she was as organized and as well-prepared as to have a bottle of clear fingernail polish close at hand, the run was too long, and too wide to try to camouflage. She checked the clock in her office. There was no more time. Mike would just have to wait for the information from that file. If she wanted to salvage her second impression with Burke-Carter, she'd have to get to his office, and get there fast.

She checked her schedule once more to make certain of the arrival time of her clients. She had two hours. If she kept the meeting short, she could get that file to Mike, and still make it to the airport in time to pick them up. And maybe, if fate was with her, she'd still have a few minutes to spare to dash into a store to replace her torn hosiery.

After trying unsuccessfully to maneuver the run in her stocking so that it wasn't so visible, she took a deep breath, and forced herself to walk with confidence. The first thing she noticed when she approached Burke-Carter's office was that the door was closed. She shook her head, silently lamenting the passing of what she considered a golden age at MegnaTronics.

Mike almost never closed his office door. In fact, he was seldom in his office at all. He was constantly moving from department to department to see where he was needed most. And when you did find him behind the desk, he left his door open to encourage anyone to come to him whenever they needed to. That let everyone know that he considered any matter brought to him important. If it was worth your time to seek him out, then it was worth his time to help you work it out— one of the mottos Cydney thought she would miss after Mike was gone. Another change that Cydney didn't think she could get used to was the presence of the new boss' personal assistant stationed outside his door.

"Stationed is right," Cydney muttered to herself. The elderly woman, with iron-gray hair and matching suit, sat at her desk—pounding away at a computer keyboard with military-like precision. When the intercom buzzed for attention, she didn't miss a keystroke. She kept typing with her right hand, and picked up the telephone receiver with her left. Cydney thought, with an impish grin, that underneath the desk, she was probably filing with her left foot and taking dictation with her right.

As she approached the desk, the receptionist cocked an eye at Cydney.

"You're late," she said, moving the mouthpiece away from her frowning lips.

"It couldn't be helped, Ms . . . ." Cydney trailed off, looking around for a desk plate with her name.

"Pinzer," the woman said. "Dorothy Pinzer." For a moment, Cydney was certain the woman said Pinscher, as in Doberman. She bit the inside of her cheek to keep herself from laughing.

"Pleasure to meet you, Ms. Pinzer," Cydney responded, very carefully. She held out her hand. "Welcome to MegnaTronics."

"Mr. Burke-Carter had to take a phone call. But he'll be with you in a minute."

"I could always come back," Cydney said, turning to leave.

"Sit down in that chair and wait," the woman said sharply. Cydney resisted the urge to salute, and do an about-face. She settled uneasily in the chair Dorothy Pinzer indicated, and pulled at her stockings to try to make the run less visible. When her fingernail caught, and turned the run into a hole, Cydney groaned softly, and slapped her hand against her forehead. The noise drew Dorothy's attention. She looked up at Cydney, frowning at the interruption.

"Sorry," Cydney whispered, then gestured helplessly at her ruined hosiery. "I just . . . that is, I snagged my . . . oh, never mind! Sorry I bothered you." She put her fingers to her lips to indicate that she would be quiet.

Dorothy sniffed, then went back to her typing. Out of the corner of her eye, however, she continued to watch Cydney squirm—as if she was trying to find a position that wouldn't draw attention to her legs. Dorothy almost snorted with laughter. Even with a gaping hole, and the streak that ran from thigh to ankle, the woman still had a pair of legs that Dorothy knew would get no complaints, at least not from the male employees of MegnaTronics. That included, she thought with a sly smile, their new boss. She knew his tastes, having been his personal assistant for almost ten years now.

She glanced at Cydney again. Poor thing. She was probably as nervous as a cat in a room full of rocking chairs. Here she was, about to try to convince a perfect stranger that he should value her enough to keep her on for her competence and value to the company. Yet, all she could think about was her physical appearance.

Dorothy couldn't figure out why this Ms. Kelley was so worried. If Daryl Burke-Carter was the kind of man who judged worth by looks alone, then Cydney Kelley would be able to retire from MegnaTronics with a big, fat retirement bonus. But he wasn't that kind of man. It would take time, but sooner or later, they would come to recognize that they would never have a better boss. Dorothy smiled. By the time Ms. Kelley came out of that office, she would see it, too. But first, she had to get over her nervous jitters.

"Here," Dorothy opened her desk drawer, and held a small vial of clear liquid out to Cydney.

"What?" Cydney looked up, obviously distracted.

"Will this help, Ms. Kelley?" Dorothy toggled a bottle of clear fingernail polish at her.

Cydney's smile in return was genuine. "Thanks, but I think these stockings are beyond repair."

Dorothy checked the light on her telephone. It indicated that the boss was still on the phone. "If you make it really quick, you might be able to make it to the ladies' room and take them off before your meeting."

Cydney's eyebrows raised. That's all she needed was for everyone to think she was doing a strip tease for the boss.

"Well, if that skinny blonde on that nighttime soap opera can go hoseless, I think you can pull it off, too. No pun intended." Dorothy said, with a face as severe as a drill sergeant.

"I'll be right back," Cydney said. "Can you stall him for me?"

"Make it quick. Mr. Burke-Carter is a very busy man." Dorothy was all business again as she turned back to the computer. Before Cydney left, she tossed her another small vial of scented lotion.

"You might need this," Dorothy offered. Cydney looked at it dubiously. Since the incident with her sister, she was very reluctant to try anyone else's offered beauty products.

"Thanks, Ms. Pinzer," Cydney said, and ducked out of a side door into the ladies' room. She didn't even bother moving to a stall. She kicked off her shoes, slid her hose off, and stuffed them into the trash bin. She then squeezed a tiny pearl of the softly scented lotion into the palm of her hand. She sniffed cautiously. *Ummm!* This was much better than the bargain lotion that her sister had suggested. It felt silky to her fingertips. And when she smoothed the creamy liquid over her legs, she made a mental note to ask Ms. Pinzer where she bought it.

She knew that it was foolish to think so, but the combination of the new attitude her sister had insisted she adopt, the new suit, makeup, and the soft scent warmed by her hands made her feel invincible. Let Daryl Burke-Carter glare and growl all he wanted. Nothing could touch her. She felt so *empowered!*

Courtney was right! The first step toward feeling like you could conquer the world was telling yourself you could! She was good at what she did. MegnaTronics needed her as much as it needed that Daryl Burke-Carter—if it did need him. Obviously Mike Megna thought the company did; otherwise he would never have sold it. But she had to believe that the same held true for her. If Mike didn't need her, he wouldn't have hired her. He wouldn't have promoted her, and trusted her with so much responsibility. She had to believe that the new boss wouldn't dare consider firing her. She would march right in there and tell him exactly how good she was. And if that wasn't good enough for him, well he . . .

"He's off the phone!" she heard someone whisper urgently through the door. Cydney spun around just in time to see a flash of iron-gray hair disappear into the hall.

"On my way!" Cydney said, but Dorothy was already gone.

She was at her desk attacking a stack of invoices by the time Cydney made it back.

"Go on in." Dorothy jerked her head in the direction of the door without a break in her typing.

"How does it look?" Cydney asked, trying to nod surreptitiously at her legs.

"Fine. Just fine," Dorothy said distractedly, picking up a document from her printer. "Oh, and if he asks you about the delay, tell him you were waiting for *him* to get off the phone," she offered.

Cydney started to accept the advice, then froze before going in. Wait just a clock ticking minute! Her time was just as valuable as his. What did it say about how she valued her time, and her work ethic, if she could just hang around until he found the time to see her? She wouldn't say it.

Cydney tapped lightly on the door.

"Enter."

When she pushed the door open, she went from being irritated to incensed. He was on the phone again! He sat at his desk, in that cushy, oversized, executive's leather chair, with his back turned to her. He didn't even have the good grace to turn around and acknowledge her! She had a good mind to turn around and walk right out of there. He was the one who scheduled these conferences.

She caught a glimpse of a crisp, white sleeve as he rested his elbow against the arm of the chair. Without turning around, he whipped his arm out to impatiently wave her inside, then reached out to stab at the redial button on the telephone. After a moment, he punched the intercom.

"Dorothy . . ."

"Yes, Mr. Burke-Carter?" came the prompt reply. Cydney could hear the clicking of her fingers on the keyboard.

"Buzz me if I get a call from Benjamin Johnston."

"Yes, sir."

"And see if you can set up a meeting for all of the department heads for the middle of next week."

"Morning or afternoon?" Dorothy asked.

"Afternoon."

"Anything else, sir?"

"Would you order up lunch for me from that deli in the food court? They make a mean chicken salad sandwich."

"Chicken salad sandwich," Dorothy echoed. "Wheat, white, or rye?"

"Wheat. And could you . . ."

"Excuse me!" Cydney cleared her throat a little louder and a little more belligerently than she had intended. Enough was enough!

The chair made barely a sound as Daryl whisked around, preparing to give one of his employees another lesson in one of his many pet peeves. Running a close second behind repeating himself was being interrupted. He hated being interrupted. Patience played such a crucial part in the success of his business ventures. To win MegnaTronics he'd had to wait until every piece was in place before announcing his move.

His philosophy was that people who rushed couldn't be counted on to be careful in their work. He wasn't going to have that—not from his employees. The sooner everyone knew the rules, the smoother the company would run.

On the other end of the intercom, Dorothy cringed. Bad move, Ms. Kelley, she thought. The woman goes in late to a meeting, and she has the nerve to interrupt the boss?

Whatever reprimand was on the tip of his tongue to give to Cydney was lost as he opened and shut his mouth in mid-thought. He swallowed once—made even more difficult because his mouth had suddenly gone dry. He sat there, immobile, and regarded her from behind trendy, tortoiseshell-rim glasses that Cydney always thought of as the trademark for "buppies"—black urban professionals.

"Mr. Burke-Carter? Anything else?" The tinny sound of Dorothy's voice over the intercom broke into this thoughts. He was thankful for *that* interruption. He needed something to bring his mind back to what he was supposed to be doing.

''Never mind, Dorothy. And hold all calls, please.'' He set the phone carefully back into the cradle. Moving slowly, deliberately, to cover the fact that he'd been noticeably distracted, he checked his meeting schedule to make certain that he had the right person. There, in his appointment scheduler, in his own precise handwriting he'd penciled in: *Friday. 9:30. Cydney Kelley.* But the woman who stood before him now bore only a slight resemblance to the quality assurance director he'd met at the beginning of the week.

Come on, Daryl. Don't be dense, he berated himself. To think that this could be a different woman didn't speak too well of his powers of observation. Of course it was the same woman. It had to be. But why hadn't he noticed then what he was noticing now?

Why hadn't he noticed that crown of thick, glossy hair. Today she wore it in a French twist wound around her head. Several wispy, coiled braids framed her face. She hadn't worn it like that on Monday, had she? Yeah, she did. Even Mike had commented on it. He supposed that he was too busy being the big boss to notice.

And why hadn't he noticed her dark, almond-shaped eyes, fringed with lashes so deep and sweeping that he wondered if she had trouble seeing through them? Had she been wearing glasses then? Is that why he hadn't noticed her eyes? She might as well have been wearing a football helmet for all the attention he had given to her. He had made a concerted effort to look everyone in the eye on Monday. But, he'd missed these.

He must have been the one with the blinders on. Otherwise, he would have noticed lips so full and inviting that he couldn't get the image of sweet, luscious berries out of his mind.

This was the same woman. It had to be. She had the same voice, soft but deep, almost husky. It was the kind of voice that could hold his rapt attention—whether she was confronting him in the company conference room, or making, slow, sweet love to him in his bedroom.

Daryl blinked once. Now there was a thought that came out

of left field! Since when did he think about sleeping with his employees? He never had before. He had always kept business and pleasure separate. Echoes of the conversation with his brother came back to him. What was it Whalen had said? *He was the boss. He could have whichever woman he wanted.* A pang of conscience stabbed through him. Was he actually considering pursuing this woman? What was it about this one employee that had him blurring the line between his personal life and his professional life? It was Cydney Kelley herself. It had to be her. Or maybe not.

He indulged in a fantasy that the woman he'd confronted on Monday had somehow been replaced by a clone. Not an exact replica, but a definite improvement. Not too tall, not too short. But not average, either. His eyes flicked to her bare legs. Nice, he found himself thinking. *Very nice.* When she had stood up to him after everyone had left the meeting, he wondered why he hadn't noticed her long, lean legs.

Cydney shifted uneasily, following the direction of his gaze. Her sudden movement broke his concentration. Daryl's head snapped up. He was annoyed at himself. He didn't know whether he was irritated because he didn't see all of this in her before, or because he was seeing it now. If he had been blind to her, it must have been for a reason. Why couldn't he have remained blind? The last thing he needed was for his hormones to start making his decisions for him. If she was competent, then he would keep her. That's the only criteria he would base his employee selections on. He would remain cool, logical, and dispassionate.

The longer he remained silent, the more nervous Cydney became. When she saw him looking at her legs, and frowning in what she thought was disapproval, she almost wished that she hadn't taken Dorothy's advice. She'd rather stand there in the hosiery, gaping hole and all, than have her new boss find reason to fault her for her appearance. She didn't think she could take that kind of rejection. Not after all the soul-searching (and color matching) she and Courtney had gone through to find something that made her feel both comfortable and confident.

"I'm here for your scheduled conference," she broke the

uncomfortable silence. He didn't say a word, so Cydney started to back away. "But if you're busy, I can come back later."

Daryl stood, and by moving, broke the spell he'd put himself under. He indicated a chair directly across from his desk. "Have a seat, Ms. Kelley."

She slid carefully into the chair, making sure that the short hemline didn't creep any farther.

"I'm sorry to have kept you waiting," he said smoothly.

Cydney regarded him with a hint of suspicion. Was he making fun of her, or did he really mean it?

"Can I get you anything? Coffee? Or a soda?" he offered.

She raised her eyebrows in surprise. Civility? From Mr. Gruff-and-Granite? She wasn't sure what she expected when she walked in there, but she certainly didn't expect that from him. Was this how he charmed the other employees? Was this how he had won them over to his side so that they didn't see the need to come to her? *Kill them with kindness,* she thought again.

"No," she said in response to his offer. Then as an afterthought, "No, thank you."

If he could be civil, then she could make an effort, too. She willed herself to appear relaxed and confident. As she sat back in the chair, she crossed her legs, and laced her fingers over her knees. "I don't want to take up any more of your time than I have to, Mr. Burke-Carter."

Daryl almost frowned. What she really meant to say was *let's get this over with.* He didn't blame her if she was a little impatient. If it was any consolation to her, he was just as eager as she was to get this conference over with. He didn't like the way she made him feel right now. She unsettled him, made him lose his composure. Yet, at the same time, he also wanted to drag it on as long as he could. He wanted to notice more of what he hadn't noticed before.

Daryl moved to a side table to refresh his own coffee. "You let me worry about my time, Ms. Kelley."

But it's not just your time! I've got work to do, too, she was on the verge of saying. She opened her mouth, then shut it quickly. She was glad that his back was turned to her. She didn't want him to know just how close she came to sticking her foot in her mouth.

"I don't know if you're aware of it or not, but I have representatives from a software development company we've been wooing flying in in a couple of hours," she told him.

"Greg McAdams and Angela Dupont," Daryl said with a nod. "We've already been in touch."

"Then you know how important it is that I make a good impression. As much as I value this opportunity to chat . . ." Cydney almost gagged on her own words. "I don't want to be late."

"I'm glad you find this opportunity so worthwhile," Daryl said with a hint of sarcasm. "Don't worry. You won't be kept long."

Cydney wondered if she should read more into that statement. She wouldn't be kept long? Did that mean she would be let go?

While he busied himself with making coffee, Cydney took the opportunity to study him as critically as he'd studied her. Without realizing it, she made a face at his back. What was he doing talking to the potential clients that she'd developed? She'd been on the phone, back and forth, for weeks trying to convince McAdams and Dupont that their company and MegnaTronics would benefit from an alliance. It wasn't fair!

Come on, Cydney. Don't be childish! she chastised herself. Burke-Carter was the CEO. He had every right to be involved with any clients. It was in the best interest of MegnaTronics if he knew every aspect of the company's potential clients. After all, that's what made Mike so successful as a boss. Then again, Mike would involve her in any conversation that affected how she did her job.

She folded her arms across her chest and silently fumed. By going behind her back in talking to McAdams and Dupont, he had undermined her ability to appear in control of the situation. What did they talk about? She should have been a part of that dialogue. She didn't like the idea of meeting with them without every piece of knowledge at her full disposal. What if she slipped up and went against something they had already agreed to? She would look foolish, maybe even incompetent! No, she didn't like Burke-Carter's business ethics at all.

Yet, as she watched him pour strong, aromatic coffee into his mug, and raise the mug for an experimental sip, her frown was quickly replaced by an expression of something close to panic. She found herself focusing on the lean lines of his clean-shaven jaw. As she watched the motion of his lips when they closed over the edge of the coffee mug, she wondered how pliant his kiss would be. So far, she had only seen one expression from him—stern. But could that stiff-upper-lip expression soften if the right woman roused him to desire?

Uh-oh, she thought. *I'm in trouble.*

Bubbling just beneath the surface of what she thought was blatant hostility, another unexpected emotion began to push its way forward.

If you could call it an emotion, she mentally amended. What she was starting to feel was a pure and natural hormonal response to this man. At first, she tried to dismiss it as butter-flies—just nerves at the thought of meeting the boss one-on-one for the first time. It was more than that. It had to be something more.

Cydney thought she heard Courtney's voice echoing in her head.

Don't you miss it, Cyd? Don't you miss a man's touch? Not just a man, Cydney quickly denied. She missed her former husband. She missed Jason! Maybe that's why the image of Burke-Carter and his coffee unsettled her so much. Jason loved coffee. Every morning, before he headed off to work, his good-bye kiss always tasted of it. But he always put more cream and sugar than coffee into his cup. The memory of his kiss would linger sweetly in her mouth and in her mind.

Cydney clenched her jaw. It was just a cup of coffee! Was she losing her composure over a cup of coffee? She knew that caffeine had strange effects on people, but this was ridiculous! How could this man remind her of Jason? He didn't sound like Jason. He certainly didn't dress like him. Jason wouldn't be caught dead in a suit. He would be a T-shirt and jeans guy until the day he died. So what was it that had her angry and attracted to this man at the same time? What was it that caused the fluttering in her stomach to spread to all points beyond. It made her fingers tingle, her heart race, and her breath catch. And those were just the sensations that she was aware of. How could she know that it made her dark eyes more sultry, her lips increasingly inviting?

Cydney didn't know, but Daryl certainly did. He made himself stand at the coffee table a little longer than he had to in order to redirect his thoughts. Maybe a jolt of good, old-fashioned java would keep his thoughts from straying.

"So," he said, drawing out the word. "How are things going for you, Ms. Kelley?"

Cydney felt panic rise in her again. She didn't have time for small talk!

"Busy," she said honestly. "Very busy."

"You know, everybody says that around here."

"Maybe because it's true."

"Maybe not," he countered tightly. "According to my reports, productivity hasn't changed, but the quality of the product has dropped. So, if you all are busy, you're busy doing a whole lot of nothing."

Since when! Cydney thought defensively. She had worked too long and too hard for him to make a blanket statement like that. If productivity had slacked off, it could only be since he arrived. Who could work with pressure like the threat of layoffs looming over their heads?

Daryl glanced sharply at her and startled Cydney by saying, "Not just since I came onboard, Ms. Kelley."

She blinked. Had she spoken out loud? Or had he read her mind? By her expression, Daryl knew that he'd come pretty close to responding to whatever was going on in her head.

"Do you know why I've arranged these conferences?" he asked.

"To separate the wheat from the chaff?" Then she mentally kicked herself. *One of these days, Cydney, your mouth is going to get you into a world of trouble.*

"Is that the reputation I have around here? Hatchet man?" He sounded irritated—almost wounded. She watched him through hooded eyes stride back to his chair. She might not like his business tactics, but if there was one other thing she could say that she liked about the man, it was the way he filled his business suit. It was well made and tailored to fit his obviously athletic lifestyle. He'd hung the suit jacket across the back of his chair. That gave her the chance to note how the crisp, white, Oxford shirt accented his broad shoulders. He also followed the fashion trend of wearing suspenders that coordinated with a tie.

She tried to keep her eyes trained at his chest level. She didn't want her glances to betray her thoughts. What would he think if he caught her following the direction of his suspenders all the way to the waistband of his slacks? When he grasped the razor sharp creases of his slacks to adjust them before sitting down, Cydney couldn't help but wonder if his thighs were as rock hard as slightly rippling muscles in his legs seemed to indicate.

"I . . . I wouldn't know," she managed to say, raising her eyes to meet his gaze.

If he noticed her preoccupation, he didn't give her any indication.

"And why not? Aren't you MegnaTronics' team leader? Aren't you Mike's appointed true confessor?"

His mocking tone jolted her as sharply as the coffee had for him.

"Mike only approached me about the idea Monday. Since then, no one has come to me to talk."

"I would think that your phone would be ringing off the wall, Ms. Kelley."

"Well, it hasn't."

"And what do you plan to do about that?" He tapped his pencil against the palm of his hand. Cydney's gaze fixed on that pencil as if mesmerized. Okay, she told herself, so she wasn't staring at the pencil, but at the large hand that cradled it. She thought every detail about his hand would burn into her brain—from the smooth, underside of his wrist that was barely hidden by an expensive, leather banded watch, to his long, tapered fingers (wedding ring conspicuously absent). They were hands that had seen hard work. She could tell by vestiges of calluses in the palm of his hand. She wondered how his hands would feel, roaming over her, with his curious mixture of manicured care and calluses.

Stop it, Cydney! Get your mind out of the gutter! This is your boss—the man who replaced your friend!

Cydney ground her teeth, making her next question sound like a challenge. "What do you expect me to do?"

"All I expect from you is for you to do the best that you can. That's all I can ask from any of my employees."

"They're not your employees," Cydney said matter-of-factly. There was no malice in her tone, but the look on his face had her wishing again for some sort of clamp for her mouth. What on earth possessed her to say something like that! Was she trying to get herself fired? She tried to soften her statement. "At least, not yet, they aren't. They're very loyal to Mike."

"I told you that the transition will be difficult," he began.

"Don't sugarcoat it, Mr. Burke-Carter. Difficult won't be the half of it."

"You could help ease the transition."

"By being team leader, yes I know," she said a little impatiently. "What good can I do if no one will come to me to talk?"

"If you like, your first task as team leader for this company, is to go back and tell the employees that there won't be an eleventh hour reprieve. Mike Megna, for whatever reasons, gave you all up to me."

"You may have bought the company, Mr. Burke-Carter, but all that means is that you've got the controlling stock, the buildings, the equipment, and all the trials, tribulations, and triumphs that come with a business like this."

"I'd say that makes you all mine," Daryl said, too callously for Cydney's liking.

"You can't buy people," she insisted. "Not their loyalty, and not their respect."

He fell silent for a moment. He told himself that it was to digest the information she'd given him. Maybe that was part of the reason. The other part of him admitted that he wanted to sit and look at her for as long as he could reasonably justify. Leaning back in the chair and rocking slightly, he cradled his cheek and chin between his thumb and index finger.

"You told me that you didn't have to like me to work for me. Were you speaking for yourself, or do the others feel that way, too?"

"Why don't you ask them?"

"How do I know they'll be as open with me as you're being? What they say to my face may be completely different from what they say when I'm not around."

Cydney felt herself tensing. What did he expect her to do? Be a snitch? She'd already told Mike that she wasn't cut out for being a corporate spy. How could she make that clear to Burke-Carter, too?

"What ever happened to all of that thick skin you were bragging about, Mr. Burke-Carter?" The words popped out of her mouth before she considered how they would be perceived. Her question caught him so off guard that his only response was to laugh at her, and at himself for turning this conference into an accusation against her loyalty to the company. "I guess I did say that, didn't I?" he said.

"I may not have a photographic memory, but I think I am capable of remembering when I'm being chastised by the boss."

"I wasn't chastising you," Daryl denied.

"Oh, you don't call that chastising? What would you call it, Mr. Burke-Carter." Though she tried to keep her tone from sounding confrontational, she couldn't help sounding just a little stung. After all, he had embarrassed her. It had set her teeth on edge, and made her spine bristle.

"I suppose I would call it the way I meant for you to take it, Ms. Kelley—as a challenge."

"Why would you do that? Why would you come in and intentionally tick off your staff?"

Daryl squirmed slightly under her gaze. This was the first meeting that he'd had where someone had turned the focus on him. Cydney had been right when she said that the employees would be reluctant to tell him how they really felt about the change in command. He had held several meetings during the week. Each employee had responded to him literally like a robot.

He had asked open-ended questions to get them talking about themselves and their expectations for the company. What he wound up with was minutes full of dead silence after they responded yes or no to his questions. Some didn't bother to respond at all.

"This company was in trouble," he began.

"How much trouble?"

"You didn't know? I thought you and Mike were close."

"I thought so, too," Cydney replied.

"When I started my research to try to find a way out of your troubles, the one thing I noticed about the company was that it had a hell of a lot of potential. For one reason or another, that potential wasn't being tapped. I thought it needed a jump-start."

"And you thought a cattle prod would do it?"

Daryl laughed. "I guess I came on a little strong because I wasn't sure what I'd be up against when I came onboard here."

"Honey, not vinegar," she replied with a small smile.

"That might work if MegnaTronics employees were flies," he responded to her abridged homily. "What I need are worker bees. And since you seem to know the inner workings of the hive . . ." Daryl paused. Since when did he talk in metaphors? He was starting to sound as bad as his brother Whalen.

Then Daryl referred to the open portfolio which summarized Cydney's work history. As he ran down the list of all of the projects she had managed and was currently managing, his estimation of her abilities rose another notch. His brother's words kept coming back to him. Whalen had said to find someone who was loyal to the company. He'd said to find himself an ally. Could he convince Cydney Kelley to be as loyal to him as she was to Mike?

If he was going to sway her opinion of him, he would first have to stop antagonizing her. He had no doubt in his mind that that's exactly what he was doing. He just couldn't figure out why he was going out of his way to set her on edge. Maybe it was in retaliation for what she was doing to him.

"Can I count on you to keep me on my toes, Ms. Kelley?"

"Excuse me?" Now it was her turn to be caught off guard. What did he need a watch dog for? His little piece of information about talking with McAdams and Dupont let her know that he kept every aspect of the company under tight control.

Daryl tried a different approach. "I was just going over your work profile. You and Mike have worked very closely on the majority of this company's projects."

Cydney didn't respond. She wasn't quite sure how to. What point was he trying to make? When he looked at her expectantly, she shrugged slightly. "Mike and I have similar views on what makes for a successful product. We're a good team. If one of us slips up, the other is always there to take up the slack."

"Can I count on you to remind me when I'm slipping up, Ms. Kelley?" Daryl asked softly.

"Do you slip up, Mr. Burke-Carter?" she asked, raising an eyebrow at him.

"Occasionally," he admitted with slight shrug.

"That's good to know."

"Why?" Did she want to see him fail? Didn't she know that if he failed, the company failed, too? That meant everyone was out of a job.

"If I'm going to take on the extra work of being your watch dog," she said slowly, "I have to know my efforts will be needed as much as they're appreciated."

"You can count on both," he assured her.

"Then I'll do the best that I can to dog you every step of the way," she replied.

Daryl looked askance at her. She'd responded to his request with a little too much enthusiasm. He wondered if he should be reading more into her response than what was on the surface. Did she mean that she would stick with him through thick and thin? Or did she mean "dog" in the sense of treat him badly?

"I'm not sure if I know what I'm getting myself into, Ms. Kelley," he admitted as he held his hand out to her.

"You should have thought of that before you bought the

company," she said in the same sweet tone that she used to shrivel Joan Kegler and Vernon Castle.

Daryl laughed out loud again. Now, he knew exactly what she meant. One look into her expressive face, and he knew.

Cydney took his hand, and gave a firm, single shake. She couldn't help it, she found herself smiling in response. Maybe because she liked the sound of his laughter—deep and rumbling, like the warning of an oncoming storm.

As he stood there, clasping her hand, Daryl couldn't help thinking that he liked the way she smiled. It warmed him like sun rays. Thunder and sun—a rare combination. As opposite as two opposites can be, yet brought together by a higher power.

That's what drew him to her! It was a higher power. It had to be. What else would explain this overwhelming attraction he had for this woman? It was more than attraction. It was a connection. It had been there from the moment he first saw her. Only then, he had been too preoccupied with making a strong, first impression with his employees to notice it. Now that they were together, one-on-one, without distractions, he felt a pull toward her stronger than the forces that kept the planets aligned. And when he looked into her eyes, he knew she felt it, too.

Their mutual laughter died away.

Cydney drew her hand back, stood quickly, and maneuvered to put more distance between Daryl and herself. She placed her hands on the back of the chair and squeezed, as if she could erase the feel of him.

"Well . . . uh, I guess I'd better get back to work. The plane with McAdams and Dupont should be landing soon."

"You'll keep me informed with what's going on?"

"With your sources, I'm sure you'll know what's going on before I do."

"From what I've read about you, Ms. Kelley, you're more than competent," he said, referring to her personnel file.

Cydney's hopes soared. Did that mean she wasn't being considered for termination? Another part of her, a secret part that she didn't want to admit, wanted him to say that he admired her for who she was, not what she did. Maybe Courtney had been right. Maybe because he was her boss, she didn't have to rule him out.

"Keep up the good work, Ms. Kelley. Goodbye." He turned abruptly to his phone, picked up the receiver, and began to relay another message to Dorothy Pinzer.

Then again, maybe not. Cydney sighed.

V

"Not in a zillion years!" was Cameron's response to Cydney when she asked him early Saturday morning if he wanted to go with her to the charity bazaar.

"It'll be fun," Cydney cajoled.

"In whose universe?" He snorted. "No way, man. I'm not wasting my Saturday on some whacked out, lame games."

"It's for the children," Cydney insisted.

"I'm not a child."

"No, but you could help me with the others."

"Do I have to go?" Cameron complained.

"I'm not forcing you to go, Cam," Cydney began in a voice that let him know she was about to twist his arm in a way that only mothers could.

"Are you going to tell me that I can't go to the skate party if I don't go with you this Saturday?"

"I wouldn't do that to you."

"Then I'm not going."

"All right then, while you're here at home, I want you to do some things for me."

Cameron sat up in bed, his face panic-stricken. His mother always had a list of "some things" a mile long that she kept in reserve. Cleaning the entire house from top to bottom was just one of the tiny tasks on the list. If he didn't go with her, she was liable to have him mowing every lawn on their block, or collecting everybody's recyclables—and sorting them, and cleaning them, and delivering them to the recycling center.

"What time do we have to be there?" He sighed in resignation.

She kissed him on the top of the head. "Eleven thirty. Call a couple of your friends. Maybe they'd like to come."

"Please, Mom! Don't make me drag them with us. I want them to stay my friends."

"I promise, if you don't wind up having a good time, that you can pick what you want to do the next weekend after the skate party, and I won't give you any argument about it."

"Even if I decide that I want to go out drinkin' and gamblin' and doin' the nasty with a few college girls I know?" Cameron teased.

"Now, I don't have to worry about that because I know you would never, ever choose to do anything like that. Not even when you're grown and living on your own. Would you, Cameron?" she said, grabbing his ear and twisting just a little.

"Ow! Ow! No, of course not! It was just a joke!"

"See what a good sense of humor I have?" she said pleasantly. "Now call your friends, and tell them to be here by eleven o'clock sharp. Make sure you tell their parents where we'll be and what time we'll be home."

"And what time is that?"

"We should be back here around six."

"Great. I can hardly wait."

She kissed him on the top of his head and said, "I'm going to grab a quick shower and then I'll be downstairs."

Cameron did manage to get two of his friends to accompany them to the bazaar; but only after he promised them that they could each invite two friends to his skating party next Saturday.

"For that many people, you'd better make my mom believe that you really want to be here," he warned.

Cydney parked, then turned around to face the three boys in the back seat of the car. "I know I don't have to tell you how to behave."

"No, ma'am," Cameron said quickly. When his friends, G-Man and Hoops, didn't respond, he dug his elbows into their ribs.

"No, ma'am," they echoed.

Digging into her purse, Cydney gave them each five dollars. "Make it last, boys," she said. "That's all there is."

"We'll try not to bankrupt the bazaar with all of the prizes we'll win," Cameron said, rolling his eyes. For a moment, Cydney wondered where he got his sarcastic tongue. She didn't wonder for too long. When she realized that she was on the verge of a caustic reply herself, she knew exactly where Cameron had learned his behavior.

"Meet me back here at six o'clock. Got it?" she directed.

"Should we do that watch thing?" Hoops wanted to know.

"What watch thing?" Cydney asked, the beginnings of a smile tugging at her lips.

"You know, that thing they say on TV all the time. What is it, Little C?" Hoops directed at Cameron. "Sympathize our watches?"

Cameron flashed a worried look at his mom. If he didn't get this right, his mom would give them all a homework assignment before they got out of that car.

"Synchronize, man!" Cameron said, almost in desperation. "He means synchronize, Mom."

"Yeah, synchronize," G-Man took his cue from Cameron. He'd been on the receiving end of an extra homework assignment a time or two himself.

Cydney swelled with pride. "No, we don't need to synchronize our watches. Just be here as close to six as you can."

"Yes, ma'am," they said in unison, then scrambled to get out of the car. Cydney could hear her son warning them to be careful what they said around her. When she caught the word homework in his strident tone, she burst out laughing.

"What's so funny?" Dion surprised her by appearing suddenly at the driver's side window.

"Good grief, Dion!" Cydney jumped and clutched her heart. "What are you trying to do, scare ten years off my life? Don't sneak up on me like that."

"I wasn't sneaking. You just weren't paying attention. That's a first for you, isn't it, Cyd?"

"Never mind about that, just tell me where I'm supposed to go."

"Your booth is just off the main strip. Come on, let's get you down there. Pin this on." He handed her a bright yellow badge in the shape of a smiley face. Her name in bright orange letters was stenciled across it. Dion was wearing a similar badge.

All of the volunteers are wearing them," he explained. "As the kids come in, we tell them if they need help, to look for the big yellow smile."

"How's it going so far?" Cydney wanted to know.

"Not too bad. It was a little slow at first, but things are starting to pick up. I guess word of mouth is getting us more people."

"Is Mike here yet?"

"I haven't seen him."

"But you are expecting him?" Cydney pressed.

"Yeah, sure. Why are you looking for Mike? Don't tell me you're planning to work today."

"I didn't get a chance to debrief him on the meeting I had with McAdams and Dupont yesterday."

"How did it go?"

"Promising. We may be able to come up with some joint venture projects."

"That is good news. But maybe Mike isn't the one you should be debriefing, Cyd." Dion nodded at a figure standing at one of the booths.

"I don't believe it. Burke-Carter is here?"

"You could have knocked me over with a feather."

"Who's the sweet young thing with him?" Cydney asked, indicating Burke-Carter's lithe companion. She assumed they were together because they wore similar outfits.

"How should I know?" Dion shrugged.

"You mean he didn't introduce her when you went up to him?"

"I didn't go up to him. Why would I do that?"

"To thank him for showing up at the bazaar, Dion!"

"Are you crazy? He might think I was sucking up to him."

"Or he might think you were genuinely grateful for his participation," Cydney countered.

"Are you grateful for his participation?"

The way he said it made Cydney feel as if she had done something wrong.

"This is your project, Dion. You organized this charity event. As hard as it is to get people to give up their Saturdays, you'd think that you'd be out, bending over backward, trying to thank anyone over four feet tall who showed up."

Dion pursed his lips. "Yeah, I guess you're right. Come on. Let's go." He started for Burke-Carter.

"What do you mean us?" Cydney pulled back against the hand that had grasped her elbow. "You're the one who has to play host."

"You have to pass by him to get to your booth. You may as well go with me to suck up . . . I mean, say hello."

"I don't see why I have to go," she complained.

"You're a supervisor, Cydney. You're a leader. You're supposed to be setting an example."

"Shut up and start smiling," Cydney said through clenched teeth. "Maybe by the time we get to them, you might look like you mean it."

"Don't look now, but I think you're about to be hit up for more money." Daryl's companion nodded over her shoulder .

"What are you talking about?"

"Two volunteers with bright yellow badges and the phoniest smiles you've ever seen are coming this way. Don't turn around! If you move, they'll pounce on you."

Daryl grimaced. "Come on. If we walk away now, we can pretend that we didn't see them."

"You're losing him," Cydney prompted Dion as Daryl and

his friend started to meld into the crowd. She quickened her pace.

"Mr. Burke-Carter!" Dion called out heartily, waving his hand. "Hey! Mr. Burke-Carter!"

"We're caught," Daryl said, stopping in his tracks. Dion had yelled loud enough for the entire city to hear. If he kept walking now, he'd have to pretend that he was deaf for the rest of his life.

"Remember," his companion said, in a low whisper, "show no fear, but don't look them in the eye either. Once they make eye contact, they'll be able to convince you to do anything— including handing over your wallet."

"You've got an evil tongue, Shana. Did you know that? This is supposed to be for charity."

"Oh yeah? Well, there's being charitable, and then there's being a chump. Whalen sent me to make sure you know the difference."

"You tell my brother that I don't need a watch dog."

"We'll see," Shana said cryptically, eyeing the duo as they approached.

Daryl turned slowly. When he caught sight of Cydney leading Dion along, he took an involuntary step forward and waved them over to him as enthusiastically as Dion had called out to him. Shana was completely forgotten in his haste to get to Cydney.

Shana Burke-Carter, Daryl's sister-in-law, glanced up at him and saw his eager expression. *Chump,* she thought in disgust. Despite her warning, she knew he was about to give away every last dime!

If it had just been the man hounding Daryl for money, she probably could have minimized the damage to his wallet. But there would be no escaping the woman that accompanied him. She walked toward them with a determination that seemed to cut through the crowd and drive straight for them. Shana looked up at Daryl again. All thoughts of trying to avoid them had flown completely out of his head. If anything, he looked impatient for them to get there. Shana looked closer. No, not them, she mentally corrected. Her! He was waiting for her. Shana wasn't even sure if Daryl knew there *was* a male counterpart to the duo that approached them. And then it struck her—an idea that seemed so ludicrous at first, that she rejected it. But as the duo continued to approach them, and Daryl continued to have that "deer in a headlights" look, she thought maybe the idea wasn't so silly after all.

She didn't have to worry about Daryl giving all of his money away. In fact, that was the least of her worries. It was his heart she should be concerned about. If he hadn't completely fallen for that woman, Shana thought, he was fast on his way.

Shana studied Cydney with a practiced eye. Slightly out of fashion with the clothes, but still acceptable in the circles of those who made it a point to always be in style. She wore a short-sleeved white cotton blouse with tiny, delicate pink and blue flowers all over it. Cute. The little kids would be attracted to the friendly pattern. But why was she wearing the long denim walking shorts?

She doesn't like her legs, Shana thought in surprise. *That's why she's hiding them in weather as hot as this is.*

But at least she knows enough to wear sensible shoes. Shana noted that Cydney had worn a pair of tennis shoes known as cross-trainers, and two pairs of socks—one pink pair and one blue pair to match her shirt. That meant she knew enough about these bazaars to protect her feet against all of the walking she would have to do to drum up donations. She'd pulled her thick, dark hair high off in a pony tail tied with a bright pink ribbon.

"Hi," Cydney said, a little breathlessly, as she walked up to him. "I didn't expect to see you here, Mr. Burke-Carter."

"I didn't expect to be here, Ms. Kelley,"

"Then how did you wind up coming?"

"Mike called me this morning and asked if I would."

"We appreciate the patronage," Cydney said.

"Anything for the kids."

"Yeah, thanks for coming out, Mr. Burke-Carter," Dion broke in forcefully. He felt that if he didn't say anything, Cydney and Burke-Carter would ignore him completely. He *was* the organizer of the bazaar, and, as Cydney had said, if he didn't make an effort to appear grateful, he might not be able to rely on any more patronage for more of the scheduled charity events.

Dion held out his hand. Daryl accepted it, but his mind drew a blank. What was this man's name?!

"Er . . . your welcome . . ."

"Mr. Dixon was about show me to my booth," Cydney said smoothly. "Dion organized the entire event, you know."

The look Daryl turned on her was comically grateful. He supposed he should count that as one of her efforts to keep him from slipping up.

"You've done a good job organizing the bazaar, Mr. Dixon."

"The kids seem to enjoy it."

When Shana coughed delicately behind them and laid her hand on Daryl's elbow, Cydney spoke up quickly. "We don't want to take up too much more of your time. We just wanted to say thanks for coming out." Then she grasped Dion's arm and started to backpedal.

"Yeah, enjoy the bazaar!" Dion said, almost tripping as a result of Cydney's overenthusiastic guidance. She looked behind her once, gave a half-wave, then increased her pace.

As they moved away, Shana gave a low whistle. "Whew! Who were those masked volunteers! And they didn't even hit you up for money. It must be a sinister new ploy to lull you into a false sense of security."

"I think my quality assurance director has a little more tact than that," Daryl said.

"Your director? The woman?"

"Uh-huh," Daryl said distractedly, trying to figure out which booth Cydney and Dion were heading for. He should have asked. Maybe he could arrange a casual stroll by. After all, it was a charity event for the children. Watching Cydney walk away from him in those cute shorts had him feeling very charitable.

Shana tried a little investigative work to see if her theory about Daryl was correct. "They make a cute couple," she said casually.

Daryl swung, pinning Shana with a sharp stare. "They're not dating."

"No?" Shana said innocently. "How do you know?"

"I can't say for certain," he hedged.

"I just thought that since they came up to you together, and they had their hands all over each other that . . ." She let her voice trail off. She had no choice but to cut the conversation short. Daryl had already started after them, leaving her in the middle of the road.

"Somebody should come by to relieve you around two o'clock," Dion was telling Cydney as he shut the gate to the booth behind him. "If you need me, I'll be at the front, pressing flesh and acting grateful."

But Cydney wasn't listening. She was still kicking herself for what she thought was her stupid, schoolgirl behavior around Burke-Carter. When she'd gone up to him, she'd meant to sound suave and sophisticated. In her mind, all she managed was gushing. She couldn't help herself. He was so much more approachable outside of the office.

In those dark, severe suits he wore everyday, he was like an untouchable, but the clothes he wore today said anything but hands off. If anything, Cydney thought wickedly, the light, summer material said to her *feel free to run your hands all over me, Ms. Kelley.*

She sighed heavily. Maybe not. His companion was wearing similar colors. Couples who were really into each other were the ones who intentionally dressed alike. She could almost see it. Before the bazaar was over, they would be wearing matching T-shirts that said "Daryl loves what's-her-name and What's-her-name loves Daryl."

Cydney paused. What was her name? Then she slapped her forehead. Could she have been anymore rude? She'd barely looked at that other woman. If that didn't say crush on your boss, what did? Dion must have thought she was a complete idiot. She was the one who acted like she didn't even want to go near Burke-Carter. Yet, when she saw the man face to face, she didn't give Dion a chance to get a word in edgewise. If

Dion didn't think she was crazy, she knew Burke-Carter must have thought she was.

"So, is this where you'll be?"

Cydney jumped, nearly spilling the face paints and stencils on the ground.

"Uh . . . yes . . . I'm face painter for the next few hours . . . Mr. Burke-Carter," she added.

Daryl swung the gate open, and pulled a stool next to her.

"Do you need some help?"

Again, Cydney nearly dropped the paints. Was she going deaf, or did he just volunteer to spend the next few hours with her? Daryl Burke-Carter? Mr. You-Don't-Have-to-Like-Me-to-Work-With-Me?

"Sure." She shrugged nonchalantly, though her insides were slowly turning to mush.

Please, she silently prayed, *please don't let me say or do anything that might give away that this man is playing serious havoc with my hormones.*

"You're the booth boss. What do you want me to do first?" Daryl asked her.

"Would you clean these brushes for me?"

"No problem." As he reached for them, for the briefest moment, his fingers closed over hers. Cydney swallowed convulsively. She thought she'd held the brushes out far enough. She left him plenty of room on the brushes so that she could avoid touching him. The fact that he'd missed meant one of two things to her. Either the man had the worst hand-to-eye coordination she'd ever seen, or he'd touched her on purpose. Slowly, as if she was afraid to know the answer, she searched his face.

"Water soluble?" he asked her.

"What?" Cydney blinked and shook her head.

"Is the paint water soluble?"

"I believe so. It has to be non-toxic for the kids."

He nodded, and took the brushes from her without any indication that he knew of the tiny tumult that raged inside of her. Cydney fought to get a grip on her feelings. If he was going to be with her, in that tiny booth, she couldn't fly to pieces every time they bumped into each other.

Fortunately, there was a steady stream of children through the booth. Cydney barely had time to think about her situation as she laughed and teased the children as she painted. Once or twice, she looked over her shoulder, and found Daryl painting faces, also. She didn't know whether he felt her watching him or if it was a coincidence, but he looked back at her. This time, it wasn't difficult to read his expression. He was enjoying himself. He smiled at her, so Cydney smiled back.

"Having fun?" she had to ask.

"Better than a staff meeting," he said, before turning back to his work.

"Ain't it the truth!" Cydney laughed.

After almost two hours of steady painting, the stream of children had slowed to a trickle. Cydney checked her watch, then gasped out loud. She would have never dreamed that he would have hung around that long.

"It's almost two o'clock," she told him.

Daryl twisted his hand to glance at his watch, too.

"A quarter 'til," he corrected.

When he made no effort to leave, Cydney said hesitantly. "Won't your friend miss you?"

"She knows where to find me," Daryl said casually. He wondered if she was fishing for information. He noticed at their meeting earlier that Cydney had glanced at Shana, but didn't bother to introduce herself.

"What about Dion Dixon?"

"What about him?" Now it was Cydney's turn to wonder why Daryl was interested.

"I thought he'd be around, ready to take you to lunch or something."

"He's probably sneaked off to be with his girlfriend,"

"Then you and he aren't dating?"

"Me and Dion?" Cydney said with an incredulous laugh. "Whatever gave you that idea?"

Daryl shrugged, and busied himself with cleaning brushes. "Just a feeling," he said.

"I think your feelings need adjusting," Cydney said. Then she looked up. "Oh, I'm sorry. I shouldn't have said that."

"Don't be afraid to say what you think."

"Thanks for all of the help, Mr. Burke-Carter. But you really don't have to hang around here. If you want to go off and find your friend . . ."

Daryl handed the brushes back to Cydney. This time, he made it obvious—as she took them, he closed his hand over hers.

"She's probably sneaked off to call her husband," he teased her.

"Her husband?" Cydney wasn't sure how to respond to that. Was Burke-Carter the kind of man to mess around with a married woman? Just because he was supposed to be a straight-shooter in business didn't mean that philosophy spilled over into his personal life.

"My brother," he elaborated.

"Oh . . ." she said vaguely. Now she was even more confused. Was he playing around with his brother's wife? That would be even worse.

"I asked Whalen to post the location and time of the bazaar at the YMCA where he sometimes works out. He might be able to get some more warm bodies here for it. Then, he'll meet us here."

"Oh!" she said again, this time her face brightening.

He squeezed her hand gently, then stepped closer to her.

"You sound relieved," he commented. "Why is that?"

"Almost as relieved as you sounded when I told you Dion and I weren't dating, Mr. Burke-Carter," she returned. "Can you tell me why that is?"

"Maybe I should show you." Daryl zeroed in on her mouth. Up until now, he thought he'd done a pretty good job of keeping his feelings under control. Time after time, he found himself thinking about how he could maneuver her to kiss her. She had two habits that were literally driving him crazy within the confines of the tiny booth. She had the most enticing habit of pursing her lips and whistling as she painted. She also had a voracious sweet tooth.

He'd stopped counting the number of times she popped across the causeway to grab a sweet treat. As she painted, she munched on funnel cakes liberally sprinkled with powdered sugar. She would lick the sugar from her fingers before washing her hands at each painting request. Each time he caught her doing it, he had to focus his mind elsewhere. That's what made him take up the paintbrush. He had to keep his hands moving. He had to keep his eyes trained elsewhere. If he watched her blow an affectionate kiss to one more child, he thought he would have to close the booth down, and kiss her until he'd gotten the urge out of his system.

Now that the crowds had thinned, and he didn't have an excuse not to look at her, he was starting to forget the reasons why he shouldn't stay in that booth with her. The tiny voice inside of him—the one that had always guided him away from the women that he worked with—was slowly being drowned out by another. The other voice was louder, rebellious. It was the one that always guided him when he was ready to take a chance. It was the voice that got his adrenaline pumping. *Go on. Go for it. She wants you to,* the voice told him over and over again until he was almost ready to believe it. Despite the urging, there was just enough of caution in his weakening, warring other half, to keep him a respectable distance away from Cydney.

"Hey, girl. Where's Kate?"

The question, gruff and demanding, was followed by insistent pounding. Cydney and Daryl both took a discrete step away from each other, and turned to the front of the booth. A man Cydney didn't recognize leaned over the edge of the booth and peered under the counter.

"Who's Kate?" Cydney asked, shaking her head

"The woman who's supposed to be painting the brats!"

Cydney stiffened. She didn't like that man's tone. Worse than his tone, she didn't like his looks. She couldn't smell alcohol on his breath, but he definitely wasn't behaving normally. His eyes were red-rimmed, and he smelled of pungent smoke. She knew that smell. As much as she hated to admit it, several of the parties she attended back in college had closed off rooms where the smell of that smoke occasionally wafted out.

"There's no one named Kate here," she said calmly.

"Damn it! I want Kate! Get her out here now!"

She felt Daryl grasp her hand and try to pull her behind him.

"I think she has the next shift," Daryl said. He didn't know Kate from ketchup, but he wasn't going to antagonize this man. It was obvious to him that the man was as high as Georgia pine.

"She told me she'd be here. Kate! Kate! Get your narrow ass out here, girl!" the man shouted. Leaning farther into the booth, knocking paints and stencils everywhere.

"Cydney . . ." Daryl said softly, pushing her toward the rear of the booth. He didn't have to finish his sentence. He wanted out her of there.

"I'll get security," she said so low that only Daryl could hear her.

"Where in the hell do you think you're going!" the man growled. Cydney stopped in her tracks. Her heart pounded faster now, this time in fear. She opened her mouth, but her mind drew a blank.

"To get Kate," Daryl said quickly, then waved her on. She wanted to argue. She didn't want to leave him there. She didn't know what the man was capable of doing. "Go on, Cydney."

She nodded, then opened the door to the rear of the booth. As she opened the door, a young woman stood outside with hand raised as if she was about to knock.

"Hi!" she said in a voice so perky, Cydney knew she had no idea what was going on the other side of the booth. Cydney thought she hardly knew herself what was going on. "I'm Katie. I'm your relief. You can take a break now."

At the sound of the young woman's voice, the man looked up as the woman cried out, "Pauly!"

"Bitch!" the man bellowed. "Where's my money?! You owe me for that last dime bag. I want my money, and I want it now!"

He extended himself into the booth as if trying to grab her. But Cydney caught a flash of silver out of the corner of her eye that let her knew that he wasn't reaching for her empty-handed.

The next few seconds happened so fast for Cydney, that it would take her a couple of days to figure out exactly what transpired. She didn't have time to think—just react. She pushed Kate out of the door to the ground. She wasn't acting heroically, she was actually falling from a shove that Daryl had given her to get her out of the way. She landed on her backside in the sawdust covered ground. Though dust had flown up around her, and stung her eyes, she saw Daryl grab the man's wrist and bring it swiftly and forcefully over his knee.

The man gave a low grunt of pain as Daryl pushed him to the other side of the booth. He didn't have time to get up. The commotion attracted the attention of a couple of security guards. Then Daryl scooped up the gun with a paper sack and passed it to a security guard. Behind her, the woman named Kate sobbed, then scrambled up and ran. She hadn't gotten very far before security stopped her, too.

"Are you all right?" Daryl grasped Cydney by both of her hands and hauled her to her feet. He could feel her trembling through her hands. Cydney nodded in response, too shaken to say anything.

"Are you sure? I didn't mean to push you so hard. I just didn't want to take a chance that you'd get in the way."

Cydney smiled, touched that someone else was worrying about her welfare for a change. She held her hand out, then in a trembling voice. "See? Steady as a rock. How about you?"

"No harm, no foul."

"Was . . . was that a gun? Was he going to shoot her?" The full impact of what almost happened hit her suddenly, and forcefully.

"Nobody was hurt," Daryl insisted. He grasped her shoulders and squeezed. He was just moments away from drawing her close. Yet, something in her expression kept him from doing so.

She nodded again, then said, "Excuse me."

He released her. Cydney took a few steps away from him. And leaning against the booth for support, proceeded to bring up everything she'd eaten that morning. She looked back at the booth, shuddered, then added last night's dinner to the ground for good measure.

"Sorry I'm late," Daryl said as he slid into his seat at the family dinner table. He glanced around the faces at the table. They were all irritated at him. His father was drumming his fingers on the arm of the chair. His stepmother was indicating to the cook which platters she wanted sent back for rewarming. Since the Burke-Carters only had a couple of days out of the week where they could all be together, the family rule was that no one would be allowed to eat until everyone was present to say grace. He'd kept them waiting for a full twenty minutes. "I had to make a very important phone call," Daryl insisted.

"That call wouldn't be to someone in your new company, would it?" Shana asked with faked polite interest. "Like to your quality assurance director?"

"No," Daryl said emphatically, and gave her look that said *drop it.*

"How is she doing, by the way?"

"I don't know," Daryl said tightly. "I haven't spoken to her since this afternoon."

"Why not?" Shana pressed.

"I thought I made it clear that we wouldn't discuss business at the table," Daryl's stepmother broke in.

"This isn't business," Shana said innocently. "It's pleasure."

"It's business," Daryl said abruptly. "But none of yours. So let it go."

Shana started to reply, but broke off when Daryl's father, Harlan, broke in with, "Let's bow our heads."

Daryl immediately obeyed, but during the saying of grace, he sneaked a peek at Shana. She was looking at him, too, and laughing softly. She wasn't going to let it go so quickly. She thought she had something on him, and she was going to use it for all it was worth.

"I'm sorry you didn't get a chance to make it to the bazaar, Whalen," Shana said. "I had a really good time."

"You need to give me more advance notice when your company is sponsoring one of those things, Darry," Whalen said. "I might be able to get more folks involved for you. Pass the rolls . . ."

"I just found out about it myself," Daryl said. "It was very spur of the moment."

"Maybe next time you'll have a better time, Daryl," Shana said. "Spending all of your time at one booth must have been so boring!"

"I was just fine," Daryl said. "So . . . Tricia, they tell me you have a new exhibit opening up soon?" He quickly turned the topic of conversation to his stepmother. She usually couldn't talk enough about her art. If he was lucky, by the time she finished talking about herself, dinner would be over, including dessert, and they could all escape from the table.

Shana waited for a lull in the conversation before she turned the topic back to Daryl again.

"Then again, I guess when that man showed up with that gun . . ."

"What man? What gun? You didn't say anything about a gun!" Whalen glanced from Shana to Daryl. "What happened out there?"

"Nothing happened," Daryl insisted. "It was just some guy . . ."

"Some guy wasted out of his mind," Shana interrupted.

"Who was looking for some girl," Daryl continued.

"Some girl who owed him drug money," Shana put in.

"Who came to our booth," Daryl finished.

"Our?" Tricia was interested now. "Who was 'we'?"

"He can't tell you. That would be discussing business at the table," Shana said. "Or is it pleasure?"

"So, what happened?" Daryl's father pressed.

"Nothing really. I happened to be standing at one of the booths my quality assurance director was manning," Daryl said, and shrugged.

"Man, nothing," Shana said in derision. "She was all

woman . . . with legs clear up to her neck. And you didn't just happen to be standing there. Tell it like it is. You left me all alone to fight off those donation hounds and stayed with her for two hours."

Whalen looked over at Daryl and raised his eyebrows. Daryl said sullenly, "One hour and forty-five minutes."

"I want to know about the gun," Whalen insisted.

"And the drugs," Tricia put in.

"And the legs," Harlan ended.

"It all happened too fast. One minute we were there painting kids' faces . . ."

"You were painting kids' faces?" Tricia laughed. "Looking to branch off into my line of work, Daryl? Do you want me to make some calls to set up a showing for some of your work, too?"

He ignored her. "And the next minute, I was knocking some junkie on the ground. That's all there was to it."

"Sounds like something to me," Harlan said quietly.

"What do you want to bet that she thought it was something," Shana said, looking around the table for confirmation.

"I wasn't going to stand there and let him threaten my employee, or hurt somebody else."

"Especially an employee that looks like her."

"Will you leave Cydney out of this?" Daryl demanded.

"Cydney?" Everyone around the table echoed.

"It was business," Daryl declared, though he had the distinct impression that nobody believed him. "Just business . . ."

"Speaking of which," Whalen said quietly, "I need to talk to you after dinner."

Daryl looked up, partially concerned, but Whalen shook his head and mouthed, "Not now."

The dinner was excellently prepared as usual, but Daryl could hardly finish the appetizer, let alone the main course. He had almost managed to put the incident this afternoon behind him. Shana's meddling had stirred it all up again, especially his growing feelings for Cydney. And when Whalen had mentioned that he needed to talk privately, something told him that despite his lack of appetite, he would need some stomach-calming antacid before the evening was over.

Daryl skipped dessert and expected Whalen to do the same.

"Are you kidding. I've got a game in one week. I need all the carbs I can get," Whalen complained, reaching for a thick wedge of caramel-topped cheesecake.

"Bring it with you," Daryl said sharply. He indicated that he would be in his home office.

Whalen trailed behind his bother, cheesecake in one hand and a cup of coffee in the other. He shoved the door closed behind him as Daryl whirled on him.

"All right, what's up? What have you got?"

"A name," Whalen said, knowing perfectly what Daryl wanted to know.

"Spill it," Daryl said curtly. "And I'm not talking about the coffee on my rug, either."

"Do you know a D.J. Colton?" Whalen said, smiling a little at his brother's trademark fastidiousness.

"No. Should I?"

"I heard from one of my frat brothers who trades in stock and bonds that this Colton is an SEC investigator."

"And?"

"You're under a microscope, Darry."

"Why me?"

"You're moving too high, too fast. Getting MegnaTronics is just the final flag that got their attention."

"Everything I did to get that company I did on the up and up," Daryl said, his voice threatening.

"You're preaching to the choir, Darry. I know you. I know how hard you worked. But some people just don't like success stories. Especially not from people like us. We're not supposed to be successful. Don't you know that?"

"That's a crock of—" Daryl began.

"I'm only calling the play like I see it, big brother."

Daryl sighed. "This frat brother of yours, what else does he say?"

"For the next six months at least, every move you make is

going to be looked at up one side and down the other. As far as MegnaTronics is concerned, you'd better walk on water.''

''I haven't done anything wrong,'' Daryl insisted.

''Darry, that may mean something you may not want to hear.''

''And that is?''

''This woman in your company ...'' When Whalen saw Daryl start to bristle, he held up his hands.

''Shana is blowing this whole thing out of proportion.''

''Look, I'm the one who encouraged to you to get friendly with the employees,'' Whalen grinned. ''And there's nothing wrong with having a gorgeous friend. Hell, Shana used to be my best friend before I married her. And if, by some miracle, you decide to settle on one friend, just make sure that it's after this mess with the SEC dies down. The last thing you want is for someone you care about to get mixed up with some mess that wasn't worth it. Just play it cool for a while. Take some time off and think about it. Plan your strategy.''

''All right,'' Daryl said. ''Thanks for the advice, Whalen. And the info.''

''No problem, big brother. I just hope everything works out.''

Once she got to work on Monday, Cydney enjoyed about thirty seconds of fame. When she got to her office, there was a crowd of about ten employees standing outside of her office. As she walked up to them, they greeted her with applause and cheers.

''What's all this?'' she asked, smiling a little self-consciously.

''Like you don't know,'' Mike said, patting her on the back.

''It was on the news,'' someone called out.

''And in the paper.''

''That's all everyone is talking about—how you and Burke-Carter took down that drug dealer.''

''I don't know why everyone was so quick to put my name in it,'' Cydney said. ''All I did was duck.''

"Well, we had to congratulate somebody. Burke-Carter has been out of pocket all morning," Dion said.

"He's probably doing what we should be doing. Get back to work!" Cydney said, cracking an imaginary whip. She accepted a few more words of praise, endured a little more good-natured teasing about her being a vigilante, then retreated into her office.

Dion, however, was right behind her. He didn't say anything, he just took a seat in the rear of the office and watched her settle into her morning routine. After ten minutes of his silent companionship, Cydney swung around in the chair to regard him.

"Something I can do for you, Dion?"

"I'm just making sure you're okay."

"I'm fine."

"I feel really bad about what happened to you, Cyd."

"Don't worry about it. Nothing happened. Everything turned out just fine."

"If Burke-Carter hadn't been there . . ."

"But he was."

Dion paused, "What was he doing there, Cyd?"

"Helping out, I suppose."

"Why?"

"How should I know? Maybe he was feeling philanthropic."

"Or maybe he was just trying to feel you up."

"Dion, what are you talking about?" Cydney said, bristling a little at his accusation.

"You think I didn't notice the way he was looking at you when we went up to him Saturday? God, Cydney, his eyes were all over you."

"He had a woman with him, Dion."

"So, why did he need you?"

"Thanks a lot!" she protested.

"That's not what I meant to say."

"I know what you meant to say," she said, her tone softening.

"Maybe I'm speaking out of turn by saying this . . . but I just want you to be careful. I don't get a good feeling from this guy."

"Mike seems to think he's good people."

"Mike would take in anybody to save his precious company."

"And you're not glad of that?"

"Of course, I am. I like getting a steady paycheck as much as the next man . . ."

"Person," Cydney corrected.

"Whatever. Just be careful. I keep getting these vibes from that man."

Cydney took a deep breath. She'd been getting vibes, too, though she knew that they weren't the same as Dion's.

"Well, I've said my say. I'll get out of your hair now."

He opened the door, then stepped aside as Mike rushed in.

"Why don't I just get a revolving door," Cydney complained.

"Because then you couldn't have the pleasure of telling me not to let it hit me on the way out." Mike grinned at her.

"What do you need, Mike?"

"We've got another problem."

"What is it?" she asked, turning around.

"I just found out from . . ." Mike stopped in mid-sentence, staring curiously at her. "You did do something to your hair," he said, wagging his finger at her.

"How did you ever get to be the president of a company with your powers of observation?" she teased. "It's been over a week, Mike."

"I guess the same way I lost it," Mike retorted.

"Tell me about this problem." She brought him back to reason he'd come to her office.

"Oh, yeah. The problem. We just got a call from Shirley out on the west coast."

"Shirley Claiborne. She's the technical support administrator, isn't she? What's the problem?"

"She says the diagnostic software we sent her is acting strangely."

"Strange? Strange in what way?"

"It's flagging several files as possibly corrupted."

"Maybe they have an unstable system."

"No way. I went over their system with a fine-tooth comb myself last month. When we delivered the final software and the source code, I made sure that everything was working."

"And now it isn't?"

"Nope."

"Sounds like a virus to me," Cydney said, tapping her index finger against her nose in thought. "Could we have sent them infected disks?"

"I don't think so. We scan everything before we send it out. We scan the disks before and after we load the software."

"Then it has to be something on their end. We're not liable for that. They chose not to purchase our additional maintenance option package. It's out of our hands. We're not legally bound to help them."

"That's what Shirley said. But she was begging us to take a look. She's almost certain that some of the files that the software has flagged have been deleted. If her system crashes, it could mean her job."

"It might be good for business if we take a look at their system," Cydney agreed. "I'll need a team."

"Name it, you got it."

She glanced at Dion who was still standing in the door. "Dion, you know how to build a quick, down, and dirty test case that could reproduce their problem. You want in on this project?"

"Count me in, Cyd."

"Who else?" Mike prompted.

"Give me Marty. He's the summer intern, but I think he's most up to speed with the coding that went into the diagnostic software."

"Is that it?"

"And Keshia," Cydney ticked off on a third finger. "She knows the software from a user perspective. And Truang Le. He's been brushing up on the latest viruses. If it is a virus Shirley's got, he'll know what kind, and how to get rid of it."

"All right. I'll have them in the conference room in fifteen minutes for you."

"I'll grab Shirley's file, and meet you there."

"I'll have Joanie order us in some lunch," Mike offered.

"Crank up the coffee pot, Joanie. It looks like we're going to be here for a while," Mike called over the intercom. "Joan?" He called again when he didn't get an answer.

Cydney checked her watch. It was almost 11:30 P.M.

"Joan left a long time ago. And so did the afternoon receptionist," she told him.

"We should have bugged out of here when they did," Dion muttered under his breath. "You don't see the new bossman hanging around to fix a problem that we aren't going to be paid overtime for. He hasn't been available to us all day."

Mike glanced at Cydney. Now would be the perfect time for her to practice a little team leader damage control. Cydney nodded at the nonverbal message. She stood up, stretched, and said, "Hey gang, how about a little break."

"Oooh, yes," Keshia said, rubbing tired muscles in her neck.

"Time for a trip to the little boy's room," Truang Le said.

"Anybody hungry? I could make a snack machine run," Cydney suggested. "Who's got change?" She started digging through her pocket for loose coins.

"Forget the sodas and chips." Marty looked up, sniffing the air. "Do you smell that? It smells like—"

"I smell shrimp fried rice!" Keshia said excitedly.

"You people have been staring at a computer screen for too long. Those cathode rays have fried your brains. That's probably what you're smelling. Fried shrimp brains," Cydney said, shaking her head in mock dejection.

"I know Chinese food when I smell it," Keshia insisted. "At lunch time, I practically live in a little dive of a place call Mr. Woo's Wonderful Wok."

Smiling in friendly condescension, Cydney said over her shoulder as she started out the door. "I'm going to get myself some coffee and a danish. The rest of you can munch on imaginary wonton if you want to."

"Nothing imaginary about it."

She had to stop abruptly to keep from plowing into Daryl as he sidestepped her to place several large bags on the conference room table.

"Mr. Woo's!" Keshia said, reaching for a bag. "Oh, just smelling the bag alone will put five pounds on me."

"I could take it back, if you want," Daryl said, making a mock swipe at her bag.

"Meaning no disrespect, Mr. Burke-Carter, but touch this bag and you draw back a nub," Keshia warned.

"I wasn't sure what everyone liked, so I got a little bit of everything on Mr. Woo's takeout menu," Daryl said as everyone gathered around the table, and started to inventory the bags.

"We've got shrimp fried rice over here," Marty called out.

"And steamed sprouts here." Truang Le held up another bag.

"Baby back ribs and egg rolls."

"Sweet bread."

"Steamed rice."

"Egg drop soup."

"Broccoli and chicken."

The list went on and on.

"Still want that coffee and danish, Cyd?" Keshia teased her.

"You are so cruel. Now shut up, and pass me another five-pound-adding egg roll."

"Hey, thanks for the spread, Mr. BC," Marty's appreciation was barely recognizable as he filled his mouth with crunchy, fried wonton.

"Thank you all for sticking it out." Daryl was genuinely grateful that they had been working so hard for so long. *His employees!* He was so proud.

"For all the good it's doing us," Dion said. "We've tried everything and we still keep getting the same result."

"Mike told me that maybe they have a computer virus?"

"It's a virus all right, and a nasty one. It selects certain program executables at random and treats them as corrupted files. You know, like those temporary files that you get whenever you have to reboot your system. Those files are never any good. They just clutter up space, so as a rule, we delete them.

When our diagnostics software goes in to find any corrupted files, it flags them and deletes them. The problem is, it's also deleting the executables. That means they can't run their software." Dion slapped at his computer monitor in frustration.

"But the little bugger is tricky to find," Marty said.

"If we don't have the virus, and can't duplicate the problem here, how do you expect to fix it?" Daryl asked.

"We've logged onto their system. We thought maybe we could manipulate their units by remote to find the problem. But their database has radically changed since last week."

"Why is that a problem?" Daryl wanted to know.

"They're supposed to keep two databases," Cydney explained. "One database is the test database. We're supposed to have an exact copy of that one. When we make a change, they make one, and vice versa. That's the only way we can keep track of which updates, if any, are the cause of the problem."

"They've put a bunch of files in directories that shouldn't be there. So, we don't know which files are copacetic and which ones are totally bogus. Come here and see what happens whenever we think we've got a hold of it . . ." Marty crooked his finger at Daryl.

Daryl rose and stood beside Dion and Marty.

"Take a look at this, Cyd," Dion waved her over. "This is what happens when I shut their unit down."

"Wait, Dion. Before you shut it down, change the autoexec file. I want to see each command in the start-up sequence."

She watched as he gave a series of commands to begin the shut down. He started the system again and said, "Now look what happens when the system is booted up again."

"Watch the start up sequence," Marty said, pointing to a series of seemingly meaningless statements that scrolled up as the computer started again.

"That went by too fast. How can anybody see what's going on with all of that scrolling by so fast?" Daryl asked.

"Put a few pause commands in the autoexec batch file, Dion," Cydney directed. "Then start it up again."

Dion followed her direction. This time, the monitor froze every fourth line of text that scrolled up the screen.

Cydney peered closely at the monitor. "Who put our diagnostics command line in their start-up sequence?" She wanted to know. "See that? Our software application is set up to run when they start their system. Did you do that, Dion?"

"Nope. Other than what you told me to change, I haven't touched their start-up commands. As far as I know, our software application shouldn't be starting unless the user types in the command to start it."

"Check the diagnostics files. How many have been flagged as corrupted?" Cydney asked.

"Thirteen," Marty said promptly. "That includes two hidden, system files."

"Start the system again," Daryl directed.

"But don't bother shutting everything down. Just do a hard reboot, then count the files again," Cydney added.

Daryl glanced at her, though she didn't seem to notice. Her gaze was trained on the computer screen where Dion and Marty worked. Her expression indicated that she was deep in thought.

Dion typed the request again. This time, when the diagnostic software started again, it came back with sixteen corrupted files.

"That sneaky, little bugger!" Marty exclaimed. "It's hiding in the boot up sequence. No matter how many scans we did, unless we could scan during start-up, we would have never found it."

"There are a few software packages out there that can root out those kinds of viruses," Truang Le informed them. "I subscribe to an electronic bulletin board that offers services like that. I can connect from my office and see if anyone has come across a virus like this and a fix. If there isn't heavy network traffic, I should have an answer for you in an hour."

"Hold up there, Truang Le. What if you do find something? Do we have authorization to use it out there? We're not under contract, which means we may not be paid. But will we be liable if we crash their system? I don't know about you, but I don't carry around a multi-million dollar insurance policy in my back pocket," Dion complained.

Truang Le looked to Cydney and Mike for direction. She turned to Daryl.

"We think we've found the problem. We didn't cause it, but if we try to fix it and make things worse, what then?"

"Maybe we could just tell them what the problem is and recommend a course of action," Mike suggested. "That's the best way I know to cover our butts."

Daryl looked at the tired, expectant faces around them. "If you do find a fix, Truang Le, we have to test it; I mean, really beat it up before we send it on. And we can't do that there. That means, we'd have to have a perfect test case set up over here—a controlled test case that won't affect the rest of their system in case it doesn't work right. Mike and Ms. Kelley here have assured me that you people are the best at what you do. If you think there's a chance that we can't get it to work, then I say scrap it. Tell them what we've found, and let's close up shop. But if you want to keep the reputation of miracle workers that MegnaTronics have formed, then go for it. Whatever happens, whatever you decide, I'll back you one hundred percent. I'm going to get on the phone and talk to someone who'll authorize the funds to compensate you for all the work that you've done so far. Contract or no contract, the caliber of work that you've done here tonight is worth more than a dinner. Don't you think? Let me know what you decide to do."

After he left the conference room, the room remained silent. After a few seconds of contemplation, Mike said, "Well, what are you slackers and hackers waiting for? Let's purge that virus!"

"I guess that means we're going for it," Cydney said.

"Go let the boss man know, then, team leader," Dion said, jerking his head in the direction of the door.

As Cydney passed by her, Keshia patted Cydney on the back.

"Go get'em, tiger."

"Good job spotting that boot virus," Marty called out to her.

* * *

The door to Daryl's office was closed when Cydney approached it. She checked the phone on Dorothy's desk, and found one light blinking. He must be on the phone. Oh, well. Scratch that idea. She turned around, thinking that she could always talk to him later. Much later. In fact, the later, the better. If she never had to talk to him again, it would be so much the better for her taunt nerves.

"You don't have to leave," Daryl opened the door, and saw Cydney make a fast retreat. "I'm on hold while they get the company president connected to a conference call."

"The president?" Cydney said. "At this time of night? I'm impressed."

"Don't be. We go back a long way. You needed something from me, Ms. Kelley?" he asked, indicating the reason for her being there.

Yes, oh yes! I need you to stop being my boss, and start being my own, personal love toy! she thought with delicious wickedness.

"I just wanted to let you know that we decided to keep going. We feel pretty confident that we can fix their system. We're going to give it our best shot, anyway."

He nodded.

"Is that what you were hoping for?" she asked.

Daryl smiled broadly. "More than I hoped for."

"I think feeding us had a lot to do with it," Cydney teased. "If you hadn't brought us food, you would have seen a stampede out of there."

"Now, you don't really mean that, do you?"

"No, of course not. You've . . . you've got a good group of employees," she said. With the speech, and maybe the food, too, he'd gone a long way toward winning the respect of the employees.

"Does that mean I've earned them?"

"You're on your way," she agreed. "Keep showing that you trust us."

Daryl turned his head as he heard a voice from his speaker phone, "Hey, Burke-Carter, pick up. Is anybody there?"

Daryl suddenly grasped Cydney's hand. "I want you to sit in on this conference call with me."

"But, I don't . . ." she started to protest.

"You do now," he responded. He indicated a chair for her, the settled into his own.

"Did I disturb your beauty rest, Elise?" he directed at the voice at the other end of the line.

"You need it more than I do, Darry," came the playful retort. The woman on the other end suddenly became all business. "So, what's up, Burke-Carter? They tell me you found a nasty old virus on some of my units."

"That's right. I have my quality assurance director, Cydney Kelley, sitting in on the call, Elise. She's the one who discovered how it works."

"I appreciate the effort, Cydney."

"You're welcome. But I don't want to celebrate too soon. The true test will be if we can find an application that will purge it, and rebuild your fragmented database. We may not be able to get your original files back, but we think we can restore full functionality to your system."

"You think, but you're not sure?"

"There's no way of telling the full extent of the damage to your database. We don't know when the virus was introduced. We don't know how long it has been there just waiting for a trigger like our diagnostics program to activate it. You do keep backup copies of your database, don't you?"

"Of course we do. But what good would it be to restore our original files if the virus is just going to destroy them again? Burke-Carter, what are you and your team of whiz kids going to do about it?"

"What do you expect us to do?" Daryl asked, glancing at Cydney.

"Fix it, of course. It doesn't take a genius to figure that one out."

"And it doesn't take an accountant to know that time and effort like this is expensive," Cydney retorted. She looked up in alarm, clamping her hand over her mouth. *Turbo tongue strikes again,* she thought.

Daryl shook his head, but he was grinning. "She's right, you know, Elise. You conveniently neglected to sign on the dotted line that pays us for additional work after we handed over the software and the source code."

"That almost sounds like an extortion ploy. How do I know that you didn't plant the virus to squeeze some more money out of us?"

"You know me better than that, Elise. I don't operate that way. Check your logs. Before Mike Megna left you last month, your system was in perfect working order. You signed the authorization to go from test units to live production yourself. Would you have signed if you thought the software was defective?"

"You know that I wouldn't. So, what are you trying to tell me, that you won't fix the system unless we fork over some more cash? I think you've done your homework, Daryl. You know things are a little tight for us right now."

"Maybe we can work something else out."

"What do you suggest?"

"That you don't say evil things about us to others in the industry if we don't fix your problem."

"Is that all? There's got to be more. What's the catch?" Elise prompted.

Daryl nodded at Cydney.

"And if we do fix it, that you give us the names of twenty potential contacts that you've personally spoken to and made glowing recommendations for us."

"Only twenty?"

"We're not greedy," Daryl continued.

"You've got a deal. So, when do we know the results?"

"We've got a team committed to working on your problem until it's solved," Cydney guaranteed.

"I'll call you again in the morning to give you a progress report," Daryl promised.

"Talk to you then."

"Later, Elise," he said, breaking the connection.

Cydney jumped up, pleased with the result of the conference call. "Yes!" she said, clasping her hands together. "If everything goes as planned, we could keep MegnaTronics rolling in contracts.''

"You think they can repair the damage to the system?"

"Now that we know what we're looking for, I'm sure that we can fix it," she said.

"How sure?" Daryl insisted.

"Pretty sure," she said nodding.

"Pretty," he echoed softly, referring more to how she looked to him at that moment than to how she felt about the success of their latest project. "I think so, too. In fact, I know so."

He moved from his chair, to perch on the corner of his desk. He wanted to be closer to her—to know that he could reach out and touch her if he wanted to. How he wanted to! Shana's teasing on Saturday had forced him to admit that that's exactly what he wanted to do. It was all he could think about the entire weekend. As he sat in Sunday morning church service, not even the threat of God's wrath could stop him from thinking about how close he'd come to kissing her on Saturday.

He'd spent the entire day out of the office today to keep himself a safe distance from her. With an occasional call in to Dorothy to check his messages, and a few connections from his modem and computer to the unit in his office, Daryl convinced himself that he could work just as effectively at home as he could at the office. He'd thought that maybe, if he didn't have the temptation of strolling past her office whenever he got the urge to see her, he could concentrate on work. He didn't return to the office until after nine, when he thought everyone would be gone.

When he'd come in and found them all still working, he felt an odd mixture of frustration and anticipation. He realized that he couldn't just avoid her. He had to find some way to work with her without wanting her. Somehow, he had to see her as just another employee.

But she was so close! Not just physically, but emotionally and mentally, too. He was certain that he could feel her heart and mind reaching out to him. He knew because his heart and mind were racing just as quickly to meet hers.

"I meant to call you this weekend," he began.

"Why?"

"To check up on you."

"Don't bother. As you can see, *I* made it into work." Her comment jabbed him. Did she know he'd been avoiding her? If so, did she know the reason why?

"You're right, I should have been here. But I'm here now."

Cydney grabbed the edge of the desk, and pulled herself to her feet.

"I'd better go," she whispered, almost in desperation. "They may need me."

They may need her? *He* needed her!

"Wait!" he called out to her. A thousand, wildly conflicting emotions communicated themselves in that one word.

Cydney froze, then shook her head. No, she had to go. She had to go now! It was late. She was tired. She was losing it— her composure, control, and her excuses not to act on the emotions flaring inside of her.

"Wait, Cydney," he repeated. He had called out to her, meaning to ask her not to go. Yet, part of him wondered if he was also asking himself to wait. Should he give himself more time before jumping headfirst into the pool of emotion that he saw reflected in her eyes?

Cydney closed her eyes, wanting his touch, and at the same time berating herself for needing him.

"Cydney," he said, taking her hand in his and drawing her closer so that her thighs rested against his. She went to him willingly, yet Daryl felt her tremble when he touched the back of his hand to her cheek.

"Don't go yet," he whispered, cupping her face with both hands. Then he smoothed her hair away from her face, and toyed with the dark, braided coils that had escaped her elaborate, French knot. When he stroked the sensitive area along her jawline, she moaned aloud.

He touched his lips to her ear. He wasn't exactly kissing her, but he left no doubt in her mind that he was going to do. The warmth of his words against her skin quickened her pulse.

"I wanted to be here," he told her.

"Then why weren't you? People were starting to wonder . . . to talk."

"What did they say?"

"Nothing that a thick-skinned entrepreneur like you couldn't shrug off," she said coyly.

"I'm not as bulletproof as you think, Cydney. Some things do get to me."

"Like . . . like what?" she stammered.

"Like this," he said, pressing his lips to the warm section of skin below her chin.

Cydney flinched away from him. "Don't touch me," she managed, in a slightly stronger voice.

When he leaned forward again to test her resolve, Cydney physically forced him away from her.

"I said, don't!"

"What do you expect me to do, Cydney?" How could she stand there, looking like she looked, feeling as he knew they both felt, and not expect him to want her? But he already knew the answer to that. Even though he was the one who held her immobile so that she could not leave, she was the one who demonstrated so far the real strength. She pulled away from him when he didn't have the strength to do it himself.

He allowed his hands to drop to his sides, muttering a terse expletive.

"I . . . I just don't want anyone to think that I kept my job because I slept with the boss," she said.

"No one would think that about you, Cydney. I've only known you for little while, but I know you better than that."

"As shaky as things are around here, how can you say what people will believe and what they won't believe?"

"You know them better than I do."

"Then trust my judgment," she insisted.

As she started to leave, he touched her cheek again. "When all of this mess gets sorted out, Cydney, I promise you, I'm going to get to know you better. I want to know you in every possible sense of the word. I want to know you better than any man has ever known a woman."

Cydney shook her head ruefully, ''I don't think so, Mr. Burke-Carter.''

''Why not?'' He raised an eyebrow at her.

Then, with a ghost of her former, flippant tone, she said, ''Because I don't know you from Adam.''

He leaned close and whispered in her ear, ''Take a lesson from the biblical Adam, Ms. Kelley.''

''And what lesson is that?''

''One of the first acts sanctioned between a man and a woman was for Adam to know his wife.''

VI

Cydney hit the snooze bar on her alarm clock for the fourth time since it first went off. Yet, she felt no great hurry to leap out of bed. One of the last things Daryl told them all before they left for the night, was that they could take their time coming in.

She rolled over, and jammed the pillow over her head. It wasn't because she was trying to drown out the pounding music from Cameron's stereo. He'd left for school over half an hour ago. Instead, she was trying to drown out the pounding of her own head and heart at the mere thought of what almost happened last night in Daryl's office.

No! She sat up straight in bed. No more Daryl, she reminded herself. He was her boss. He was Mr. Burke-Carter. And if she wanted to keep any shred of her professionalism intact, she had to keep reminding herself not to think of him in such a familiar way.

"Oh, man!" she groaned in despair. How could she avoid thinking about him like that. He hadn't left her thoughts all night. It was a wonder she'd gotten any sleep at all. Every time she closed her eyes, his face was there. As she lay in her bed, any way she turned, she half expected to see him lying next to her. If she heard any little noise in the night, she half expected it to be him, coming to her. The way she had left him last night felt so open, so unresolved. It was like he was haunting her. Snatches of phrases, remembrances of glances, vestiges of his touch wove their way into her dreams so that what little sleep she'd managed, was fitful and disturbed.

"Forget it!" she threw back her covers. She wasn't going to go back to sleep. She might as well get up, and go to work. Yet, the thought of facing *him* in the light of day bothered her. Was she a good enough actress to pretend that nothing had happened between them? Should she even try? Maybe the best way to handle this was to confront him directly.

As she showered, dressed, and prepared a meager breakfast that she didn't have the heart (or the steady stomach) to eat, she rehearsed over and over in her mind what she would say. She would be polite, but firm. She would be sympathetic, but sincere. Somehow, without jeopardizing her job, she had to let him know that there could never, ever be anything between them.

If anything was going to come between them, Daryl thought, it would be her job. Cydney was good at what she did, and was proud of her accomplishments. She had a right to be. Looking over her personnel file, he saw situation after situation where she had pulled off what seemed a miracle. Even if she didn't know the answer to a problem herself, she knew how to get the most out of the people around her so that together, they came up with the solution.

That situation last night was the perfect example of her expertise. Once they'd finally delivered the solution, and everyone was trying to wrap up and go home, Cydney was the first one to remind their client how much praise the people at MegnaTronics deserved. Watching her, Daryl had the distinct impression that she was doing a little PR work. She was laying the groundwork in case some of the people in that room last night were selected as candidates for corporate downsizing.

He snorted at his euphemism. Corporate downsizing? That

sounded almost as bad as workforce reduction. He meant lay-offs. That's what it all boiled down to. Cydney had been watching out for them, trying to open another avenue for them in case things didn't work out at MegnaTronics. Yes, it was obvious to him that she loved her work. And, if she could help it, she wouldn't do anything to jeopardize her job. The reputation she had built here was practically beyond repute. In one, careless moment, he could have destroyed all that she'd worked for. Could he blame her for nearly pealing rubber out of the parking lot to get away from him?

Daryl checked his watch. It was almost eleven. He'd asked his administrative assistant Dorothy Pinzer to let him know when Cydney came in. So far, she hadn't. He wondered if Cydney was avoiding him. He hoped not. He needed to talk to her. Actually, he needed more than that. But that was the crux of the reason for the conversation. He wanted to apologize to her for letting his hormones get the upper hand. He would assure her that it wouldn't happen again. He was an adult, for Pete's sake—a professional.

What could he have been thinking? He was her boss! By acting like a raging, hormonal teenager, he put them both in an awkward position. Cydney had only barely scratched the surface when she reminded him how their behavior might be viewed by the other employees. If there was even the slightest hint that she kept her job by something other than the merit of her work, the other employees, no matter how friendly they might have been, could make her life miserable.

He'd seen it happen too many times before. In companies that he managed, he always made it a point to know exactly which employees were dating. Some people thought he was being nosy and out of line for inquiring about them. But he had his reasons for wanting to know. Office romances among peers were hard enough. But between supervisor and subordinate? That was just asking for trouble. When those relationships went sour, and all the ones that he had seen did, that left the door wide open for disputes that should have remained private, reduction in the quality of work, and the always dreaded threats of harassment suits. More good workers were lost that way than he cared to admit.

Heaven forbid he should ever find reason to have to dismiss Cydney. There was barely a chance of that happening with her work history. But, by failing to keep his mouth shut and his hands to himself, he left MegnaTronics wide open to the possibility of that kind of trouble. No, he sighed, he would have to nip this in the bud—and fast. He admired Cydney, and to be honest with himself, he desired her, but nothing was worth losing the business he had worked so hard to save. Coworkers, yes. Friends, maybe. But lovers? Never. Impossible. When she came in to see him, he would just have remember that. He nodded once in satisfaction. Platonic. Perfunctory. Professional—where she was concerned, that was his new motto.

''Mr. Burke-Carter?''

His intercom buzzed, interrupting his thoughts. Before he could reach over to answer Dorothy, his office door flung open, and Cydney strode through the door. Without a word, she closed the door behind her. She must have bypassed her office, and come straight to see him. Her car keys jingled in one hand as she walked, and her briefcase was clutched tightly in the other hand. She strode up to his desk, and set the briefcase on the floor with a thud.

Uh-oh! Daryl thought. If he thought that she was going to excuse his behavior last night with a mealy-mouthed apology, he was sadly mistaken. He was going to have to do some fast talking to keep the storm clouds threatening in her eyes from completely overwhelming him. He pushed back in his chair, subconsciously putting a little more distance between them. She looked as though she could leap across his desk and strangle him with her bare hands.

Cydney folded her arms across her chest. *Look at him!* she silently raged. How dare he sit there, looking fresh as the morning dew—calm, cool, and collected when she'd had barely two hours sleep. If he thought she was going to let him get away with putting her emotions in turmoil, then pulling back as if nothing had happened, he had another thought coming. He couldn't just dismiss her feelings like that! She wouldn't let him. She was willing to take ownership of her behavior of last night. He had to be held responsible for his.

"You!" she drew out on a ragged breath. "Because of you, I'm a total wreck this morning! I barely got a lick of sleep. I've got bags under my eyes the size of shopping carts. My stomach is all in knots. I couldn't hold down my breakfast, and my head hurts so bad, I wish it would just explode and put me out of my misery."

Daryl privately thought that he couldn't imagine her looking more desirable. He didn't dare tell her that now.

"How about a cup of coffee," he suggested softly. It seemed the most noninflammatory thing he could think of.

She nodded once and watched him as he poured her a cup. When he gestured toward cream and sugar, she shook her head. She didn't want it diluted. She wanted it strong, as strong as battery acid. She wanted it to tear through her insides to help her keep her raw edge. She needed to feel anything but that overwhelming attraction she had for him.

"I'm sorry you had such a rough night, Cydney," he said. He smiled wryly, and said, "If it makes you feel any better, you weren't suffering alone."

She looked up at him. "I have a hard time believing that," she admitted.

"Now, why is that so hard to believe? Is that a general statement about men and their ability to express their feelings, or is that directed specifically at me?" He perched on the corner of his desk and regarded her in that curious mixture of amusement and annoyance.

Cydney shrugged. "You don't strike me as the type to have any weaknesses," she admitted. "And even if you did, I can't imagine anyone in your line of work admitting that you did."

"In my line of work," he echoed.

She nodded. "To get as far as you have, I know you've had to make some tough decisions. The stress has to get to you sometimes. But to be successful, I know you have to keep it in. I know you can't let your competition know where your weak spots are. Under that kind of pressure, you're bound to crack. We were both under a lot of pressure last night, maybe that's why we . . ." she stopped abruptly. "Wait a minute!"

"What is it? What's wrong?"

"I didn't come here this morning to make allowances for what happened between us last night. I came here to tell you . . . no, to warn you that it had better not happen again. I can't go through another night like I had last night."

"And you think I could? Cydney—" He backed himself up physically and emotionally. "Ms. Kelley," he amended. "I've been doing some soul-searching, too."

"The least you could do is have the decency to look like you've suffered." She gestured at his expensively tailored suit. "Not a crease out of place, not a rumple, not a crumple. Forgive me if I have a hard time believing you."

He tapped on his chest, indicating his heart. "It's all crumpled in here."

"Now you're making fun of me!" she said tightly. "This isn't funny! My professional reputation is at risk here!"

"I know . . . I know . . . and I am sorry. That's why I wanted to see you this morning. I wanted to apologize, and to try to set the record straight."

"Go on," she indicated, with a tight nod.

"I'd like to say what happened last night was a fluke, a one in million occurrence."

"Then why don't you? Do you make a habit of seducing your employees, Mr. Burke-Carter?"

Cydney's words stung him, as she had intended them to. The thought that he may have taken her work lightly hurt her.

"Do you?" he countered.

"Me?!" Cydney was genuinely shocked that he would suggest that she had chased after him. She shook her head, too flabbergasted to get out a decent retort.

"Oh, don't look up at me like that," he said. "Don't act like it's not in you."

Cydney stood up quickly. This conversation wasn't going at all like she had imagined that it would go. All the way in to work, she'd imagined him practically groveling for her to forgive him. She had even extended the fantasy to him telling her how valuable she was to the company, and how he could never dream of firing her.

"Mr. Burke-Carter, I need this job. Otherwise, I'd have to kill you for saying something like that to me."

"But you feel justified saying the same thing to me?"

Cydney bit her lip. Okay, maybe she was out of line. But under the circumstances, she felt like she had to use every weapon in her arsenal to gain back the self-respect she thought she had lost by practically falling into his arms. She clenched her hands into fists so tight, she felt her nails bite into her flesh.

"You think I went after you?" she asked incredulously. She closed her eyes. Could Joan Kegler have been right? Could she have gone through her rapid transformation to attract attention to herself? She certainly didn't protest too loudly, or too strenuously, when Daryl had turned his eyes on her. Suddenly, she felt sick to her stomach. If that's what he thought of her, there was no way he could ever evaluate her on the merit of her work. And she would never know if any of her future successes were based on her efforts, or through subtle manipulation by him.

Shaking her head, she said in a low voice, "No . . . I don't need it that badly."

He took a step toward her, but she backed away. "I'll save you the trouble, Mr. Burke-Carter, of wondering just how far I'd go to keep this job."

"What are you talking about?"

"Effective immediately, I quit."

"What did you say?" Now he was the one without a clever retort.

"I make it a habit never to repeat myself when I know my message is heard loud and clear!" She echoed the words he'd used at their first meeting back to him. Then Cydney headed for the door.

"Cydney, whoa! Slow down! Let's sit down and talk about this."

He went after her. He had to. This wasn't an act she was putting on. This wasn't a ploy to gain his sympathy. She wasn't bluffing. She was going to walk out of that door and never come back. She grasped the door as he clutched her wrist.

"Wait, Cydney, please. Let's not let our emotions get the better of us again."

"Don't you see? It won't work," she said. "We crossed the line. We can't go back. One of us has got to go. And everybody knows that as far as the money is concerned, I'm a hell of a lot more expendable than you are."

"This company needs you."

"And what about what I need? I need to feel . . ."

"Feel what?"

"Respected," she said stoutly. "Self-respected," she added. "I can't do that when every time I look at you, I feel . . ."

"What do you feel?" he pressed. He raised her hand to his lips, but she snatched it away.

"Something I shouldn't—not with my boss anyway."

"And you think quitting will solve our problem?"

"Life should be so easy," she said in derision. "No, that won't solve our problem."

"Then, don't go," he insisted. "Don't go without giving this some more thought."

"That's all I did last night was think. I couldn't get it out of my mind. I kept playing in my mind over and over what happened in here last night. And for the life of me, I can't explain what got into me. I just know that if being around you is going to make me lose my . . ." She started to say mind, then quickly corrected herself. "My sense of what's right and wrong, then I know I don't have a future with this company anymore. Can't you see that?"

"What I can't see is myself letting you out of that door," he retorted.

"Don't worry. I won't try to sabotage the company," she said snidely.

"That's not what I'm talking about, and you know it."

"No, Mr. Burke-Carter, I don't know it. I don't know anything more. I just know that I've to get out of here. Now!"

She grasped the door, and backed out. Ignoring the strange

look from Dorothy Pinzer as she turned around and fled toward her office.

Daryl went back to his own office. Back to neutral corners, he thought in disgust as he threw himself in his chair. He felt like he had just gone ten rounds with a heavyweight boxing champ. As he sat, mentally licking his wounds, he wondered how things had gotten so crazy. He certainly hadn't expect this when he came in this morning. He wasn't sure how he imagined it, but it certainly didn't end up with one of his best employees walking out of the door.

Daryl stared down at her personnel folder. As extensive as the information was about her work record, the folder said absolutely nothing about how to get her back if she ever decided she wanted to leave the company. That information was more of a personal nature. What he needed was personal advice about how to get to Cydney Kelley.

He turned to his phone, placed the receiver to his ear, and stabbed at the button labeled MM.

"Mike, here," Cydney's former boss picked up his extension.

"Mike, it's Daryl. When you've got a moment, can you come down here. I need your advice."

"Yeah, give a minute to wrap up here, and I'll be right down."

"Thanks."

"What's up?" Mike wanted to know, as soon as he poked his head into the door.

"Come on in, and shut the door. I don't want this leaking all over the company just yet."

"Something wrong? Did some of the investors back out?"

"Not investors. Employees. One to be exact."

"Dion? I kind of figured he would be the first to bow out."

"No, not Dion."

"Then who?"

"Cydney Kelley."

"What?!" Mike exploded. "Have you completely lost your

mind? Why did you fire the best thing that ever happened to this company?''

"I didn't fire her. She quit.''

"When?''

"Fifteen minutes ago.''

"Why?''

"What is this? Twenty questions? What difference does it make? All I need to know is how to get her back.''

"It all depends on what made her leave in the first place. Was it money?''

"No, it wasn't money,'' Daryl said tightly.

"Are you going to make me pry it out of you? I need the facts, Daryl, if I'm going to help you.''

Daryl rested his elbows on his desk, and steepled his fingers. "It goes no farther than this room,'' he said quietly.

"You ought to know by now that I can keep my mouth shut when I have to. What happened between you two, Daryl?''

When Daryl shifted uncomfortably and looked away, Mike caught a glimmer of what was causing the problem. "Tell me that you didn't . . . that you and she didn't . . .''

"No, we didn't,'' Daryl finished for him.

Mike then started to laugh. "But you want to, you dog, don't you?''

"Look, are you going to help me get her back, or aren't you?'' Daryl asked testily.

"Man, you move fast. It hasn't been a full two weeks yet. But I can't say I blame you. She's a very attractive woman. And smart. And single. What more can you ask for?''

"I can ask her to forgive and forget what a damn fool I've been so far. I can ask her not to give up a career I know she's worked hard for, one that she loves.''

"So, when did all of this come down? During your conference? Last night while we were busy chasing down bugs?''

"Something like that.''

"Just how far did you go?'' Mike asked, an envious gleam in his eyes.

"Will you give it a rest!''

"Not going to kiss and tell, are you?''

"Mike," Daryl said, his tone clearly threatening.

"Okay, I'll be serious. There's nothing funny about losing your right arm. That's what she was to me, you know. My right arm, and my third eye, and all of those wonderfully, catchy phrases you use to let everybody know how important she is."

"So, what do I do?"

"If I were you, I'd let her go for now. Give her a chance to cool off. I know Cydney. I know she won't say anything to anybody. Not yet. She keeps private conversations private. You can trust her to do that."

"And?"

"Then tonight, I'd make a beeline for her house, and give the best damned groveling act you've ever put on in your life."

"I don't grovel," Daryl said stiffly.

"If you want her back you'd better bend those knees, Mr. CEO."

Daryl leaned back in his chair, blowing out a sigh of frustration.

Mike regarded Daryl curiously. "From all of the stuff I've read about you in those publicity rags, I didn't think you'd fall for a woman like Cydney."

"Who's said anything about falling for her?" Daryl asked defensively.

"So, you're telling me it was just a lust thing?"

"I'm telling you that I don't know what it was. Whatever it was, it doesn't belong here. She knew that. That's why she's cutting MegnaTronics loose."

"If I were you," Mike began again, "I'd rethink what happened between you."

"I told you, it's best if we forget and move on."

Mike shook his head. "You're the boss. That means you're supposed to know best. But if it wasn't love, or at least something close to it, why such a drastic reaction from the both of you. I mean, if it was just hormones, there are ways to cure that. Not meaning to be crude, my man, but if it's just sex you were both after, you find somebody else, she finds somebody else, and you both let nature take its course. Come back to work the next morning, and everything is back to normal. Have you ever thought about that?''

"No," Daryl admitted. "I didn't look at it like that. That kind of stuff doesn't happen for real, does it, Mike?''

"You mean love at first sight?" Mike teased.

"Yeah.''

"I don't know. You tell me. What does it look like from where you're standing?''

"One big mess," Daryl sighed.

"So, what are you going to tell her when you go to see her tonight.''

"I honestly don't know." Daryl looked up at Mike. "Mike, you know her better than I do. And she trusts you. Why don't you . . .''

"Nope." Mike shook his head quickly. "She's your employee now. If you want her back, you've got to deal with it.''

"It gives me the sweats just thinking about it.''

"What do you mean? You're the man! You can handle anything. And your reputation with women alone should give you all the ammunition you need to get her back.''

"Forget all of that stuff you read, Mike. You can't believe any of that. All of that was just PR hype.''

"So, all of that stuff about you and a different woman every week—''

"If you read between the lines, you'll know that most of those women were my relatives.''

"Now that's kinky.''

"Will you get your mind out of the gutter. Most of those events you read about were charity functions. My family is big on donations, Mike. Somebody had to be there to represent us.''

"If I had to tell you anything about Cydney, it's this—Just treat her how you want to be treated.''

Daryl shot Mike a dirty look, which Mike didn't miss.

"Oh, but that's part of the problem, isn't it?''

"Of course that's part of the problem. I treated her like I

wanted her to treat me, instead of remembering that boundaries should have been set by employer and employee.''

"So, what are you going to do if she decides not to come back?''

"Find another right arm," Daryl said simply.

Mike shrugged fatalistically. "I guess you don't have a choice. The show has got to go on. But I have a harder question for you.''

"What's that?''

"What are you going to do if she decides to come back?''

VII

Cydney stood at the stove stirring a steaming pot of noodles, her back to her son. She had been going over and over in her mind how to tell him about her leaving her job. She glanced over her shoulder, Cameron stood in the doorway, munching on a piece of uncooked pasta.

"Come here, Cam. I could use a hug."

"Sure, Mom."

She squeezed him tight—so tightly, she heard his ribs squeak. "My baby . . ." she murmured.

"What's the matter, Mom?"

"I've got something to tell you, Cam. You may not like what you hear."

"You're gonna' tell me I can't go to the skate party! Aw, man!" Cameron jerked away from her.

"Skating party? You're worried about a skating party when I just—" she cut off abruptly, choking back tears she'd promised herself she wouldn't shed. She'd promised herself that she would be strong and optimistic. Some pillar of strength she turned out to be. She needed *him* to be strong now. Everything was falling down around her, and he was worried about a skating party.

"Cameron, listen to me very carefully," Cydney said gravely. "Things are going to be very tight around here for a while."

"So, what else is new?" Cameron retorted, then regretted that he had. The look she gave him told him that she wasn't going to tolerate any more foolishness from him. Whatever happened to her today was serious—really serious.

"Cameron, I . . . uh . . . I'm not working at MegnaTronics anymore."

"You were laid off?"

"No," Cydney said, her eyes hardening to agates.

"Were you fired?"

"No."

"Then what happened?"

"I quit."

"You quit! Why'd you do that?"

"It's kind of hard to explain?"

"What's so hard to explain? You said, see you later, alligator, and now we don't have any money or any way to get some! That's not hard."

"Cameron, try to understand. I had to go. I didn't have a choice."

"What do you mean you had to go? What do you mean you didn't have a choice? Has somebody been bothering you up at the job, Mom? This isn't one of those sexual harassment things, is it? Because, if it is, you know you can do something about that, don't you."

Cydney almost smiled. "What do you know about sexual harassment?"

"I know nobody had better be putting the moves on my mom, I know that much! You let me catch somebody putting their hands on you! It'll be the last breath they ever draw!"

"Cameron!" Cydney said, her tone clearly shocked and disapproving. "You know I don't approve of fighting." But a secret part of her rejoiced in his need to protect her. This was a side to him she had never seen. Though she had told him over and over never to start fights, she didn't want him to grow up being anyone's punching bag either. He swelled up to his full height—all five feet and ninety-five pounds of him.

"And what would you do if I told you someone was interested in me?" she asked cautiously.

"Hurt him," he said, without blinking an eye. At that moment, Cydney almost despaired of ever finding someone whom she and her son could share their lives with.

But then, Cameron started to laugh.

"I'm serious!" Cydney said, putting her hands on her hips.

"What would I do?" Cameron repeated. "I could get one of those lawyers that you see on TV all of the time."

"You watch too much TV," she scoffed.

"Well?"

"Well what?"

"Do you want me to call one of those sexual harassment lawyers or not?"

"Oh, good heavens, no!" Cydney said. "It ... it wasn't anything like that at all." She mentally asked for forgiveness for that tiny misrepresentation of the truth. It wasn't such a stretch. What happened between her and Daryl wasn't harassment. He didn't threaten her, or belittle her. It made her uncomfortable not because she didn't appreciate the attention, but because she felt it was out of place. To be more honest, it was out of time. It was just too soon.

"So, you walked out for nothing?" Cameron prompted.

"I had my reasons."

"Is there any chance of you asking for your job back?" Cameron asked glumly.

"I don't think so."

"So what are we going to do?" He looked up at her with eyes so serious that Cydney actually considered calling Daryl back, and begging for her job.

"We aren't going to do anything. Not yet, anyway. We especially aren't going to worry. We're okay for a while."

"Will we ... will we have to go on public assistance?" Cameron said the words as if the very thought was enough to bring him to the brink of ruin.

"I don't know," Cydney said truthfully. "Maybe we will.

Maybe we won't. Whatever the case is, I don't want you to worry about it, okay? It's not the time for that yet. What I want you to do is finish your homework.''

"Done that," he said distractedly. Cydney could almost guess what was in his mind. At his school, she knew how the kids of families on government assistance programs were treated. They were teased unmercifully and ostracized. At this tender stage of his self-esteem, to become one of them would seem like the end of his world. Any popularity he thought he would have gained as a result of the skating party, would come to a screeching halt.

If that happened, she could almost see him want to change to a school where they either didn't know of his family situation, or didn't care. Maybe he would be too embarrassed to go to school. Maybe he'd be a dropout, and end up without an education. He'd be trapped in a low-skilled, low-paying job. He'd be so depressed, maybe he'd turn to drugs to bring himself out of it. Or maybe he'd start experimenting with sex! He might even get a girl pregnant. He had a friend at school that he denied (maybe a little too much) that he liked. What was her name? Would it be her?

Cydney could see it so clearly. Cameron junior, in diapers, sitting on her knee, and begging "Granny" for a cookie. She'd be a grandma! At thirty! Cameron, no! Not her son! She wouldn't let it happen. Surprising him with her fierceness, Cydney wrapped her arms around her son again in a tight hug.

"Mom! You're choking me!" Cameron gasped.

"Sorry," she murmured. "I'm sorry. I just didn't want you to worry. Everything's going to be all right. I'm not going to let Cameron junior down."

Cameron pulled away, his face puzzled. "Mom, what are you talking about?"

"Nothing. Never mind. I'm tired. I think I'm going to take a long, hot bath to relax. I'm expecting Aunt Courtney to swing by, so if she does, don't say anything just yet about what happened on the job today, okay? I want to break the news to her myself."

"No problem."

"I've got spaghetti warming on the stove. Stir it every ten minutes or so. I don't want it to stick to the bottom and burn."

"Yes'm."

"And do me a favor. Mix up some iced tea, will you, Cam?"

"Do you want me to bring some up to you?"

"Would you please. That would be so nice." She kissed him again on the forehead, and headed for her bathroom.

Cydney tossed a handful of scented bath crystals into the tub, added several capfuls of bubble bath, and filled the tub with water as hot as she could stand without scalding herself. The tub was partially full by the time Cameron brought her a tall glass of freshly made iced tea. He also brought her a stack of her favorite magazines, and one of his portable radios.

"Hold on a minute," she said, putting her hands on her hips and regarding him suspiciously. "Who are you, and what have you done with my son?"

"Aw, man! That's really cold. I thought you could use a little taking care of. You had a rough day today."

"You can say that again," Cydney responded. She turned away before Cameron could see angry tears well up in her eyes again. "Thanks, Cam. I needed it," she said, her voice husky.

"And don't worry about cleaning up after dinner. I'll do that."

"If I'd known I'd get this much cooperation, I would have quit my job a long time ago," she teased.

"Don't even joke like that, Mom," Cameron said as he closed the door behind him.

Cydney toyed with the radio until she found the station she knew would be playing old-fashioned, down-home blues. She wanted to listen to someone else be depressed for a while. She knew that if she could get one good cry out of her system, she would feel better. Of course, crying never solved anything. But after a long crying jag, she could square her shoulders, lift up her chin, and see her way through her problems without those pesky tears getting in the way.

After some tentative testing with her toes, a little splashing to stir the bubbles up, she sank into the tub with the words of a familiar tune on her lips.

The music from the living room stereo drowned out the noise coming from the television, which competed with the sound of pounding as Cameron beat on the countertops with wooden spoons to the rhythm of a song he was hearing in his head.

Maybe that's why he didn't hear Cydney shouting from the bathroom for him to get the door when she heard someone leaning on the doorbell.

Grumbling, she climbed out of the tub, wrapped a huge towel around her, and sloshed to the top of the stairs.

"Cameron! Get the door!" she yelled, just as he called up to her, "I got it, Mom!"

She spun around, muttering something about getting that boy's ears checked.

Cameron went to the door, calling out, "I'm coming, Aunt Courtney!" He flung the door open, expecting his aunt to thrust more shopping bags into his arms. Instead, he found himself eye to chest with a double-breasted, charcoal-colored suit.

"You're not Aunt Courtney," he said, before he could recover from his mistake.

"No, I'm not."

Cameron's eyes narrowed. "Who are you? Are you selling something? If you are, you can just turn around and get back into your . . ." Cameron looked around the man's shoulder to take note of his car. "Jag! Man, you drive a jag?!"

"Yes, I do. Now will you answer a question for me."

"What do you want?"

"Is this the Kelley residence?"

"Yeah."

"I'm looking for Cydney Kelley. Is she home?"

"Maybe." Cameron's impressed preoccupation with the car quickly wore off. Who was this man? And why was he looking for his mom. This had better not be the man who tried to put the moves on her. "What do you want with her?"

Daryl considered answering. This was a child; and he didn't

make it a habit of discussing his business with children. Then
again, he'd already alienated one Kelley today. He could see
the strong resemblance in the boy who stood blocking his way.
He and Cydney had the same huge, dark eyes, the same high
cheekbones. And they certainly had the same guarded nature.
Was this her son?

"I'm here to see Ms. Kelley about a job," he said truthfully.

"Oh, well, you're too late, Mister. Mom doesn't work for
MegnaTronics anymore."

"I know," Daryl said softly. Something in his tone, or maybe
in his expression, suddenly made the boy go from mildly suspicious to openly hostile.

"Hey! Are you that guy that bought MegnaTronics?"

"I am," Daryl said calmly, in the face of the rising storm
in the boys eyes.

"You're the man who made my mom quit!" Cameron took
what he thought was a menacing step toward Daryl. Though
he was underweight, and undersized, Cameron thought he could
still do a little damage to this man if he could just get in one
good punch. "You made my mom cry. Did you know that,
mister? Huh? Did you know that?" His voice was low and
tight, not unlike Cydney's when she announced her decision
to leave.

Cameron moved as if to close the door. Daryl's hand shot
out, and held it open. In that obvious show of strength, both
knew who was the victor.

"Look, son, is your mother home or not?"

"Don't call me son."

"I'm not going to ask you again."

"She's here," Cameron said sullenly.

"Can I speak with her *please?* It's very important."

Cameron eyed Daryl once more, then stepped back. He turned
and yelled, "Mom, you'd better get down here. Now!"

Cydney sat up quickly from lounging in her bath. Something
in Cameron's voice worried her.

Maybe he's burning the house down, she thought. Or worse.
Maybe her sister Courtney had bought something so hideous

that even Cameron was afraid to open the packages. She wrapped the towel around her again and dashed for the stairs.

"Cameron, I told you to keep an eye on that pot on the stove!"

She was half way down the stairs, tucking the end of the towel under her arm. Water dripped from her hair where a few braids had worked their way from her loose knot. As she skipped down the stairs, she left a trail of bubbles behind her.

Uh-oh, Daryl thought, *here we go again.*

The words that he'd prepared leaked out of his brain like quicksilver. He wasn't prepared for this sight of her. Not like this. Why wasn't he? He'd rehearsed for almost a full hour of what he would say to her once he saw again.

By the time he'd pulled into her drive, he was proud of himself. He had it all worked out. He was going to tell her what an asset she was to the company. He was going to remind her of all of the clients that relied on her for such efficient, effective service. He had intended to draw on her relationship with the other employees, and how they looked to her for guidance. Now his carefully prepared speech seemed lame and unconvincing. All he could think of was how desirable she looked—bubbles and all.

"Uh, Mom . . ." Cameron began, then spoke louder to speak over the stereo that was still blaring. "Mom, you have company."

She hadn't noticed him yet. Daryl thanked the skies for the brief respite he'd been allowed to compose himself. As quickly as shutting off a switch, he shuttered his expression. By the time she noticed him, he thought, he would be the model of professionalism.

Cydney's head snapped up. Cameron wouldn't announce her sister that way. When she saw Daryl, she literally squawked in surprise, and skidded to a halt.

She grasped her towel to keep it from falling to her feet, then grasped the banister to keep her feet from sliding out from under her. Daryl saw several emotions flash across her face. She registered shock first, then embarrassment.

"What are you doing here!" she cried out, partially out of anger, and partially to make herself heard over the stereo.

"He said he came to talk to you about your job, Mom," Cameron spoke up.

"Cameron, what I did tell you about getting in the middle of adults' conversation," Cydney said sharply. "And turn that thing down!"

"Yes'm," he muttered, as he started for the stereo.

Cydney took a deep breath to regain her composure. She'd directed her hostility at her son when he really didn't deserve it.

"Do me a favor, son, and check on dinner for me," she changed her tone so that it was more conciliatory.

He nodded. Before he walked toward the kitchen, he detoured past the stereo. As he adjusted the volume, he gave Daryl a long, hard stare.

"Move it, Cameron," Cydney said. The look wasn't lost on her. She couldn't help wondering if Cameron had made the connection between her episode at work and their visitor tonight. Was he now planning a slow, painful punishment for her ex-boss?

She waited until her son had disappeared into the kitchen before speaking.

"Is it true?" Cydney asked Daryl then. "You came to talk to me about work?"

"That was my intention, yes."

"So what do you want to talk about?" she demanded.

"I can't talk to you like this, Cydney," Daryl said, looking away from her. "It's a little distracting." He gave a brief smile and said, "It was bad enough watching you in that yellow suit of yours."

Cydney almost smiled. Was he admitting to another weakness? *Now you know how I feel every time I look at you,* she thought. "Give me a minute. I'll go up and change." She started up the stairs, then as another thought occurred to her, she turned around and called out, "Cameron, could you come out here, please?"

Cameron poked his head out of the kitchen door. Cydney

could tell by the red stains around his mouth, that he'd decided to start dinner without her.

"Cameron, this is my boss, Mr. Burke-Carter. Daryl, this is my son," she made introductions. Daryl held out his hand, not sure if the boy would take it or not. Cameron glanced up at his mom. She was smiling. At least, she didn't have that pinched look on her face. Maybe that meant everything was going to be all right. Cameron took the offered hand, but he still sized up the potential threat to his mom. Daryl tried not to smile when Cameron squeezed his hand harder than necessary for the supposedly cordial introductions.

"Mr. Burke-Carter and I have something to discuss," Cydney said. "Would you mind eating dinner in your room?"

"Mom, you said I couldn't eat in my room anymore after finding that week-old hamburger," Cameron began.

Cydney gave an embarrassed, apologetic glance to Daryl. "I'll make an exception this time. But if I find any more food under your pillow—"

"You won't," he promised.

"And no TV," she warned. "Read a book, or something."

"Yes, ma'am," he said enthusiastically, not bothering to ask whether or not comic books counted.

Cydney tucked her towel tighter around her, and skipped up the stairs. As much as he wanted to, Daryl made a conscious effort not to watch her as she left. The towel she wore around her was thick, but short. He could easily imagine what would be revealed as she climbed the stairs. He felt her son watching him like a hawk. So, he strayed over to the mantel to study the collection of pictures.

"Are you one of *the* Burke-Carters," Cameron asked, moving to stand beside him.

"If you're asking what I think you're asking, the answer is yes."

"Your dad Harlan Burke-Carter is a doctor. He's got a whole medical complex named after him. And your brother Whalen is a basketball player. He could have gone pro right out of high school. Your mom, I think her name is Sadie . . ."

"Sada," Daryl corrected.

"Yeah, that's right. She's an artist. Once, on a field trip to the art museum, I saw some stuff she did at an exhibit. Man, that stuff was totally dope."

"That means good?"

"You sound like my mom!" Cameron laughed. "What is it with your generation?"

"I think every generation has asked that question of the previous one."

"Anyway, I don't know what that other lady does, the one your dad married after he and your real mom broke up."

"She's an artist, too—or wants to be one. How come you know so much about my family?" Daryl was curious.

"You're in the papers all the time."

"You read the newspaper?"

"In social studies," Cameron nodded. "We have to study up on current events."

"If there's one thing my family is, they're always involved with some current event or other."

"I know. Your family makes big bank. That means rich," Cameron translated.

"We do all right."

"Yeah, right." Cameron took Daryl off guard with his next question. "How come you fired my mom, Mr. Burke-Carter? What did she do to you that made you not like her?"

Daryl shifted his gaze back to the pictures on the mantel. Wasn't the kid supposed to be eating in his room? Daryl continued to stare at the pictures, hoping Cameron would get the hint that he didn't want to discuss the issue with him. But Cameron wasn't going away—not until he had some answers.

"I didn't fire her. She quit."

"Yeah, that's what she said. I just wanted to make sure that she was giving me the straight 4-1-1."

"You think your mom would have a reason to lie?"

"Man, don't be dense. Of course, not. But she would try to spare me. She doesn't want me to get all upset. I know she loves that job. She's worked so hard, so why would she quit? I thought it was one of those sexual harassment things. If it was, I told her I'd beat the guy up first, and then I'd call a lawyer. You know, those ones on TV.''

Daryl wondered just how much Cydney told her son.

''And what did she say?''

''She told me it wasn't like that, and that I watch too much TV.''

''Oh. Well, she's right about that. You can never read too much,'' Daryl said, looking up in the direction he thought Cameron's room would be.

''So you came here to ask her back?'' Cameron asked, ignoring the look.

''Something like that.''

''So you do like her?'' Cameron pressed.

''Don't you have some homework or something to do, Cameron?''

''Been there, done that. I just want to know. I mean, I saw you checking her out.''

Was this a test, Daryl wondered. Was Cameron waiting for him to say the wrong thing so he can ''beat him up, then call a lawyer''? What if he answered no? Would that give Cameron an excuse to act out the aggression he'd seen in the boy's eyes when he first answered the door? Daryl could almost hear him demand—How come you don't like my mom? You don't think she's good enough for you Burke-Carters? Once Cameron figured out who he was, was he trying to set him up with her? Was his question meant as subtle permission?

Or what if he answered yes? Would Cameron then become the overprotective man of the house and defend his mother?

''Your mother,'' Daryl began, ''is one of the smartest, most competent women I've ever met.'' There, that sounded safe enough.

''My dad didn't think so,'' Cameron picked up a picture off of the mantel. It showed a younger Cameron, a smiling Cydney, and what Daryl assumed was the father as they stood in front of the entrance to a theme park. One of those ridiculously cartoonish, costumed characters was in the background, waving a flag and gesturing at the sign announcing the park's grand opening.

"I was just a kid when he left, but I remember," Cameron said solemnly. "He used to call her names . . . He made her cry, too. Maybe that's why she quit him, too. They got a divorce."

"Cameron Jason Kelley! That is quite enough!"

VIII

Cydney stood at the bottom of the stairs with her arms folded across her chest. Her breathing was so ragged, Daryl could see her nostrils flare. Her arms barely restrained the rise and fall of her chest. It seemed to Daryl that if she could char them both where they stood with the fire blazing in her eyes and the heat of embarrassment burning in her cheeks, she would. She jerked her head in the direction of the stairs. "Go to your room right now, young man."

"But I haven't finished fixing my food yet," Cameron objected.

"Maybe you'll remember that the next time you use your mouth for saying things you shouldn't instead of eating."

"Yes, ma'am."

"And while you're up there, I want you to look up the word discretion in the dictionary. When I finish with Mr. Burke-Carter, I want to see it in a sentence."

"Aw, man!" Cameron groaned, but he trudged up the stairs. A moment later, they heard strains of music coming from his room.

Daryl waited until he was out of earshot before saying, "He

didn't mean anything by it, Cydney. He was just making conversation.''

She shook her head. ''He was just making me seem like some pitiful, rejected hag is what he was doing.''

''I didn't get that at all from him.''

''Okay, maybe I did overreact just a little. Maybe. I don't want you to think that I set him on you to get your sympathy.''

''Why would I think that?''

''So I can get my job back.''

''I came to you. Remember?''

''Why did you come?'' she asked.

''I had to come and try to get you back. Mike threatened my life,'' he teased her.

''Good!'' She made him feel better by laughing at his attempt at levity. Cydney gestured for him to take seat. Daryl chose to sit on a comfortable looking couch, while Cydney perched in an armchair across from him. She curled her lean, supple legs under her. Now that Cameron was out of the room, Daryl didn't try to hide his interest her. His eyes swept over her—full of heat and deliberate intentions. There went his plans for keeping his mind on business! If she had come down wearing a business suit, it would have been better for his concentration.

Instead she wore a simple, white cotton blouse with tiny little buttons shaped like raspberries down the front and a pair of faded, denim jeans that molded to her perfectly. When she tucked her feet under her, Daryl saw that she wasn't wearing any shoes. He almost smiled. The woman could even make bare feet look sexy! The thing that really got to him was that he didn't think she was doing it on purpose. That is, he didn't think that she went out of her way to drive him crazy. She was too comfortable in her outfit. It was obviously one that she wore— and wore often. It was just his luck that he was already primed to want her. She could have come down those stairs in combat fatigues and army boots. It wouldn't have mattered.

''So tell me again how much you want me back,'' she said, propping her chin on her fist and smiling at him.

''I checked on your project load, Cydney. You personally manage, or at least consult on, twenty of MegnaTronics contracts. Currently sixty of our contracts are still active. That means you manage one third of our business. I would be an idiot to let you go."

"And your mama didn't raise any fools," she teased him in return.

"You'd better believe it."

"Oh, I love it!" Her laughter rang out. "With admissions like that, how could I refuse to come back? That tells me that you know where your bread is buttered and who butters it."

"So you will come back?" he asked, raising his eyebrows in surprise. "That was easy enough. Mike said I had to get down on my knees and beg you to come back."

"Maybe I should be a hard nose and make you go through with it. It would be interesting to see to what lengths the CEO of a soon-to-be *Fortune* 500 company would go to keep a valued employee."

Daryl's pulse quickened. She could reduce him to begging all right, but not to take her back to work. If she didn't stop looking at him with those big, brown eyes, he would beg to take her upstairs. His eyes kept straying to the row of buttons of her blouse.

"I can't force you to come back, but I wish you'd reconsider. Everybody knows you love your work. It shows in the quality and in your commitment to it," he forced himself to repeat the phrases he'd concocted to get her to stay with MegnaTronics. If he could convince her that he was only interested in her for her business acumen, then he maybe he could convince himself, too.

"So, do you want me back bad enough to give a raise?" Cydney leaned forward to ask. Daryl caught a whiff of something scented and flowery. It was probably due to the bubbles of her bath. The thought of her, glistening, wet, and naked was his undoing.

"Yes, Cydney," he said, his voice hoarse. "I want you bad enough."

Cydney blinked, caught off guard by his tone. "We are still talking about my job, aren't we?"

Daryl shook his head. "No," he said bluntly.

"Then we're back to square one," she said, resolutely. "I'm sorry your drive out here was such a waste of your time."

"You let me worry about my time," he said automatically.

"I can't go back to the office if every time you walk around the corner, I get mush-brained," Cydney declared. She wanted to say hot and bothered, but decided to keep the conversation neutral in case Cameron happened to hear any of it.

Daryl leaned forward, resting his elbows on his thighs, his hands clasped tightly to prevent himself from reaching out to touch her. "Look, Cydney, something is obviously going on between us. I've felt it and you've felt it, so we can't deny it. Maybe it's all smoke and no flame. Or maybe it's something that will burn long after the name MegnaTronics is forgotten. Whatever the case, you can't throw away a career because of it. We've got to go on in spite of it."

"How do I know?" she asked softly. "How do I know which will it be? Fizzle or flame?"

"Kiss me," he said, as casually as if he'd asked to shake her hand.

"What did you say?" she gasped.

"You have a hearing problem, Cydney?" he teased. "Why am I always repeating myself around you when I don't have to. I said kiss me."

"Why would I want to do that?"

"You mean no one ever explained the birds and the bees to you?"

"I'm not kidding," she warned.

"Neither am I. We're both curious. As long as the tension is there, and we deny it, we'll never have any peace."

Cydney shook her head in silent denial. She didn't want to admit it. She'd done almost everything in her power to deny that he affected her so deeply. Yet, imagining how his lips would feel against hers was literally driving her crazy.

"Curiosity killed the cat," she tried to laugh.

"I've got nine lives," he responded.

"Oh, what the heck. Let's just do this, get it over with, and get on with our lives." With what she thought was a casual shrug, and a glance over her shoulder to see if Cameron was anywhere near, she moved next to him on the couch.

"I feel like a teenager, necking on my parents' couch," she said, and laughed a little shakily to cover her nervousness.

"That's you as a teenager up there in that picture?" Daryl asked, indicating one of the pictures.

This time her laughter was genuine. "Oh, good grief! You've been looking at those?"

"It gave me something else to think about while you were getting out of that towel," he said, and raised his eyebrows at her à la Groucho Marx.

"I was fifteen," she said. "And that was my junior prom. I was a nervous wreck then, and I'm a nervous wreck now."

"What made you so nervous back then?"

"Because that's where I got my first real kiss," she admitted. A look came over her that was bittersweet. Daryl glanced over his shoulder at the picture again. He didn't know how he didn't notice it before, but Cydney's date in the picture was the same man Cameron had indicated was his father. For the briefest second, Daryl experienced an irrational surge of jealousy. Though it was impossible, he wished that he had been the one to taste of Cydney's sweet kiss for the first time. He resolved to make up for lost time and make this experience with her now worthy of remembrance.

He touched his index finger to the uppermost button of her blouse. "I don't know why you're so nervous, Cydney. You've filled out considerably since then."

Cydney started to pull away.

"Oh, no you don't." He drew her back again.

"I didn't count on being made fun of."

"I'm not laughing at you, Cydney Kelley," he said huskily. He brushed his lips against her ear. "It looks good on you."

She closed her eyes, and shivered unconsciously. It wasn't so much what he said, but how he said it that made her tremble. He made her feel like the most desirable woman in the world.

As if a light switch had suddenly been flipped in her mind, Cydney now knew what it was about Daryl that reminded her so much of her former husband. It was the way he made her feel!

With just a look, Jason Kelley used to make her feel like every woman in the world. She was strong, yet sensual, delicate, and demanding. Daryl was looking at her that way now.

"You're not so bad yourself, Mr. Daryl Burke-Carter," she said, smoothing her hands under his jacket and over his shirt.

It was the first time she'd ever referred to him by his first name aloud. He liked the sound of it. He liked the look of it on her lips. He liked it a lot. It set his pulse to racing. She could tell by the beating of his heart. And when she touched her lips to the underside of his jaw, she felt his warm skin pulse against her lips. She inhaled, taking in the scent of his aftershave. She also moved her face slightly from side to side, feeling the beginning of his five o'clock shadow.

Courtney had been so right! She had missed this. Face to face, chest to chest, heart to heart—how could she have deluded herself into thinking that she could fill this void? How she ached to be filled now! It hit her like a wave, drowning out the last reserve of resistance she had against him. She clutched his shirt with both hands in something close to desperation. He covered her mouth swiftly with his own, swallowing her moan of surrender. He plundered her lips, drawing them into his mouth as eagerly as he would if the ripe, sweet berries depicted by the buttons on her blouse were real.

As greedily as he took from her, Cydney was eager to give. When he pressed her back against the cushions of the couch, she drew him down to her. He settled over her, moving his hips in a timeless rhythm that she'd thought she would never experience again. For three long years she had denied that she needed this contact. How could she? How could she have thought she could live without this delicious sensation of heat, and motion, and the promise of ultimate release.

"Cydney!" Daryl groaned, when she reached for him. She ran her hand along the length of him, pausing at the clasp to his slacks. Daryl grasped her wrist, squeezing gently to communicate both his need and his caution. "Your son," he said, his voice ragged.

"Cameron!" Her eyes flew open, looking around for him. She could still hear the music blaring from his room. "What am I doing? Have I lost my mind!" she said aloud more to herself than to Daryl.

What if her son had come down and found her behaving like some sort of sex-starved maniac? All of those talks of abstinence she had drilled into his head would seem worthless. What would he think of his mother then? \

That I'm still a woman, a tiny voice reminded her. She would always be his mother, but did that mean she had to give up feeling like a woman? More specifically, a woman in need of tenderness? Of companionship? Of love?

Cydney stood up quickly, and moved to the far side of the room. She found herself at the pictures on the mantel. Her eyes fell on the picture of herself the last time she had felt so loved. *The very last time* . . . Jason had chosen one of the happiest days in her memory to announce the fact that he didn't want her anymore. The trip to the theme park was supposed to be the start of a turnaround in their relationship. They'd had some rough times the previous months. But what couple didn't have its troubled times? Cydney agreed to the family outing, fully intending to put her whole heart into a reconciliation.

Yet, after almost a month of counseling and attempts at reconciliation, Jason decided that he simply didn't want to try anymore. One moment, they were at the park, laughing, loving, being a family, the next moment—nothing. When they pulled into the drive, he let her and Cameron out of the car, then started to back away. He'd come by for his things later, he'd said. And just like that, he was gone.

For a moment, Cydney's vision blared. She blinked, and found her face scorched with streaming tears. With trembling fingers, she reached up to swipe the tears away. She couldn't believe that it could still hurt so badly. Not after all of this time. She thought she had gotten over the worst of it. After all, she had her career. She had her sister. She had her son. She had her involvement in the church. With all of that, her life had seemed to be full. So why was she feeling so empty and aching?

Daryl could see her shoulders shaking. Was she crying? Had he made her cry again? Part of him wanted to go to her. He wanted to take her in his arms and hold her until everything that had ever given her pain had faded way. He didn't want to face the possibility that maybe he was responsible for it.

The other part of him told him to leave. He should get out of there before she was forced to turn around and confront him. He certainly didn't want that. On his way over here tonight, he had told himself that he would avoid a confrontation at all costs. He didn't like the way he'd felt after the last one; and he certainly didn't like the thought of how he had made her feel. Maybe it was best if he just left. *That's it, Daryl,* he told himself, *just turn around, and walk out that door.* If she came in to work tomorrow, then he would have accomplished what he set out to do. And if she didn't . . . well, he had given it his best shot. She was a grown woman—capable of making her own decisions. What was he going to do? Throw her over his shoulder and drag her back to MegnaTronics caveman style? No. That wasn't his style. So what was the alternative? Wait around here all night while she made up her mind? That wasn't his style, either. That is, it didn't used to be.

He stood there, feeling foolish and angry over his own indecision. What was the matter with him? Why was he just standing here like an idiot?! He should say something. Do something! But what could he do? What could he say to bring down that damned, impenetrable wall she had erected around herself again?

"Your spaghetti's burning."

Cydney turned to face him. Her expression was puzzled. "What did you say?" she could barely speak through the lump in her throat.

"Didn't you leave dinner on the stove? I think it's burning," Daryl elaborated.

"Oh!" She blinked as if to clear her brain, then moved quickly toward the kitchen. "That boy! He must have turned up the heat."

"Or somebody did," Daryl muttered under his breath.

It was quite possible that after that kiss, they'd sent the

mercury in the thermometer rising several notches. He followed behind her, holding open the kitchen door as she pushed through. Grabbing a pot holder in one hand, and filling a cup of water with the other, Cydney tried to salvage what was left of supper. As soon as she took the lid off, a plume of smoke rising from the pot of spaghetti wafted toward the smoke detector. Within seconds, the sound of the alarm competed with the music blaring from Cameron's room. While Cydney reached for the pot, Daryl reached for the kitchen window. He raised it as high as it would go, and drew back the curtains. To quiet the alarm, he grabbed a dishtowel, and waved it several times in front of the detector.

"That's just great!" Cydney said in disgust, dumping the entire, scorched mess into the disposal. She followed that with a box of baking soda. As the disposal ground away, she stood, with arms folded, glaring at the sink as if it were the cause of all of her problems. Daryl took a position on the far side of the kitchen. He also stood with his arms folded. But his attention was focused on her.

After she cut off the disposal, he cleared his throat to get her attention.

"*Ahem!*"

She glanced up at him, her eyes as hard and as cold as glaciers.

"Yes?" she said, in a voice so chilling, he almost forgot that it was the middle of the summer. He could have chosen that moment to walk out again. But something that Mike had said kept coming back to him. Something that couldn't easily be shrugged away was happening between them. They were reacting far too strongly to what should have amounted to inconsequential matters. That told him that their feelings for one another, whatever they were, ran strong, and they ran deep. Feelings like that didn't come along often. He wasn't going to walk out on them simply because he didn't know the right words to express them. Somehow, he would find the words. In the meantime, he hoped Cydney was a patient woman. He fully intended to hang in there with her until she told him she didn't want him around anymore.

"So which was it?" he asked.

"What was what?"

"Flame or fizzle?"

"Something tells me we're not talking about the spaghetti, are we?" She looked underneath her lashes at him.

He shook his head no. "I'm talking about our little experiment out there on the couch." He jerked his head in the direction of the living room. "I can tell you from where I'm standing, that my, er . . . flames are shooting about a thousand feet into the air. How about you, Cydney?"

Cydney leaned back, using the kitchen sink as her support.

"Me, too." She looked so forlorn when she admitted her feelings to him, that Daryl thought it was appropriate to keep his reaction to her admission low key.

"Are you gonna' stand there grinning like an idiot, or are you going to do something?" she demanded, putting her hands on her hips.

"What do you want me to do, Cydney?"

Cydney lowered her eyes. "You don't want me to answer that."

By the smoldering look that came to her eyes, Daryl had a pretty good idea of what she was thinking. It wasn't too hard to figure it out. After all, his thoughts were moving in the same direction, and had been for some time.

"Sure, I do," he said softly. "Just not now, and not here."

"Daryl, what are we going to do?" Cydney asked, almost in desperation.

"You could order in a pizza," he said, deliberately misunderstanding her.

"Will you be serious!"

"That's the first time anyone has ever accused me of not being serious," he said thoughtfully.

"I was just trying to think what we should do about Megna-Tronics."

"What about it?"

"It's obvious that you're not going to give up your position at the company. And you're not going to let me give up mine."

"And?" he prompted.

"Don't you see the potential for . . . for gossip, and innuendoes, and speculation? What do you think that's going to do to the work environment around there?"

Daryl closed the distance between them. Taking her face in his hands, he assured her, "If there's a problem, we'll handle it."

He sounded so confident of their ability to face the storm of controversy when everyone found out about them, that for a moment, Cydney was tempted to accept his simple assertion. She leaned her head against his shoulder and sighed. Then, as if a sudden thought occurred to her, she pulled away.

"What is it?" he asked. "You left another pot burning on the stove?"

"Very funny. I just thought that I'd better warn you, I don't always make it into work on time."

"No!" he said in mock surprise.

"And some days, I don't want to be there at all. And you'll know it, too."

"Maybe, on those days, I can do something to make the day seem a little more bearable," he suggested, running his thumb lightly over her lips. Cydney shivered unconsciously, and raised herself up on tiptoe for a kiss.

"Promise me that there'll be no special treatment for me. I don't want everybody mad at me for being the boss' pet."

"I promise that between the hours of nine and six, or whatever time you happen to make it in or whatever time you'll leave, there'll be no special treatment. There, does that make you feel better."

"It's still going to be hard," she said, biting her lower lip with worry.

"Hard's not the half of it," he retorted. "More like torture. Do you know how difficult it's going to be to concentrate, knowing that you're just down the hall and I can't kiss you, or touch you, or even look at you the wrong way?"

"I think I'll have an inkling," she said sardonically. "So, as long as we're off the clock, where do we go from here? And if you make any more cracks about finding something to eat, I'll . . ."

He touched his index finger to her lips. "I wasn't going to. But I was going to suggest that we make some plans to talk. I mean really talk. We need to give our heads time to find out what our hearts already know."

"Oh," Cydney breathed. "That's so beautiful. Did you make that up yourself?"

"No," he laughed at her. "I think I heard it in a song somewhere."

"I don't even know what kind of music you like," she said, shaking her head and wondering what she'd gotten herself into.

"I can tell you for a start that it isn't that," Daryl said, indicating the direction of Cameron's room. "Why don't you let me take you and Cameron out for dinner somewhere?"

"I can't. My sister is coming over tonight."

"Then how about tomorrow?"

"That's out, too. I have Wednesday night church service."

"Thursday's out for me. I have dinner with my family every Thursday and Sunday. Hey! Maybe you could . . ."

"Oh, no I couldn't!" she said, her eyes reflecting her panic. "I'm not ready for meeting family yet. How about Friday?"

"I can't have dinner with you Friday, either. I have a previous engagement."

"A date?" she suggested, trying not to sound jealous even though she felt it.

"With my cousin Amanda."

"Good old cousin Amanda," she murmured.

"Not too old, but plenty good. You'd like her."

"We're running out of days of the week, Daryl. This isn't going to be one of those 'have your secretary call my secretary' relationships, is it? Because if it is, we're in big trouble. I don't even have a secretary."

"No, it isn't going to be one of those relationships. I promise. How about Saturday?"

"I can't. Cameron won this party over the radio at a skating rink, and I . . ."

"I'm a very good skater," Daryl said enthusiastically.

"You? Really?"

"Now there's one more thing you know about me. What if I pick you and Cameron up and take you to the party?"

"I'd like that."

"What time should I come by?"

"The party officially starts at six-thirty. I . . . uh . . . may have to take off a little early from work Friday to get some errands done. Cam's going to have me tied up all day Saturday. I just know it," she said in chagrin.

Daryl shook his head in mock dejection. "Look at you. We're an item for all of twenty minutes, and already you're trying to take advantage of me."

"In the middle of my kitchen is not where I'll try to take advantage of you, Daryl Burke-Carter," she said, and smiled in a way that would have made him let her have the entire week off if she'd asked. Daryl leaned forward, and started to kiss her again.

"Hey, Mom!" Cameron shouted from the top of the stairs. "Something's burning!"

"That's a really smart kid you've got there, Cydney," Daryl murmured as he started to back away from her. "But his timing leaves something to be desired."

"You let me worry about the desire," Cydney said, closing the distance between them again. She pressed her lips to his, quickly and decisively before she lost her nerve and the moment. She could hear Cameron trudging down the stairs.

"See you tomorrow?" Daryl asked.

She nodded. "Tomorrow."

IX

Though they both had commitments that week, both Cydney and Daryl found themselves proposing, and then discarding, excuses for getting out of them. Faithfully, they followed through on each and every one of those previous commitments. People depended on them. And some of those plans had been made months in advance. As much as they looked forward to seeing each other, they couldn't allow their lives to be disrupted. Somehow, they just had to make do until they could find time to be with other.

With each, casual contact, however, they found it harder and harder to stay resolved to their previous promises. Whether they passed each other in the hall, or managed to sit in on a joint meeting, or even read the same memos, it both fueled and frustrated their need to see each other just one moment longer.

Cydney found herself mentally keeping track of all of the missed opportunities she had to see Daryl. Did he need some information about a client? She could have been the one to give that information to him. Was someone giving a presentation about a particular aspect of the company? She was a longtime member. She knew almost all there was. Why couldn't she be the one to give the presentation to him? Was a group getting together to grab a bite to eat? Why didn't someone invite Daryl along? She had to keep reminding herself that to them, he wasn't Daryl . . . He was Mr. Burke-Carter. As long as she was with them, she had to remember to call him that, too.

If it weren't for the telephone calls they shared in the late night hours, she thought she really would lose her mind. If she made it home before he did, she wasn't ashamed to leave a message on his answering machine. She laughed at herself, telling herself that she was addicted to the sound of his voice. The answering machine provided the quick fix she needed to get her through until he could return her call. And if she happened to be out late, she would sometimes go through three or four messages where he had called her several times, too impatient to wait for her return call.

What they talked about for several hours at a time, Cydney could barely remember the next day. It was the act of sharing that was so important to her. She would lie in her bed, listening to him tell her of his dreams for the future. Each time he would say, ''we're going to do this'' or ''we're going to do that,'' he wasn't just talking about the company. He was talking about her! As the days and nights passed, it became clearer and clearer to her that he was including her in all of his plans. Finally, too sleepy to hold up her end of the conversation, she would drift off to sleep until he laughingly called out to her.

During Thursday night's conversation, he brought her back to wakefulness by wickedly describing to her in detail how and where he intended to make love to her for the first time. Each scenario he described grew more creative and more risqué.

''I'm hanging up now, Daryl,'' Cydney said with her most prim inflection.

''Why? Are you coming over to see me?'' he said hopefully.

''No. I'm going to take a cold shower.''

''Those don't work,'' Daryl said in derision.

''How do you know?''

''What do you think I've been doing all week? I can't wait until Saturday gets here. I can't wait to hold you again, Cydney.''

"Me, too. I wish you were here."

"Hold onto that thought," he murmured. "See you tomorrow."

"Good night, Daryl," she said, then on a whim, blew a kiss into the phone.

"When you get off the phone, Cyd, can you help me pull together a Request for Information package for the clients coming in next week for that reception?" Mike stuck his head into Cydney's office and whispered loudly.

Cydney swiveled in her chair to look at him. "What happened to that sample RFI that I gave you for that conference you attended last week?"

"I gave it away to a potential client."

"You gave away your only sample?"

"It was the only potential client who showed any real interest in our products. Hopefully, the bodies we'll pull into the reception will warm to us."

"All right, I'll pull another one together for you. But do me a favor, Mike. Make some copies. Do you want to pull those letters from the Janski file? They speak pretty well about us and they've agreed to be references for us for anybody who calls."

"Sure . . . sure, that sounds good."

"Do you want to give me back the file?" Cydney held out her hand.

"What makes you think I have it?" Mike said sharply.

"Because I gave it to you, last week some time. Don't you remember?"

"I'm sure you never did," Mike said.

Cydney flipped in her day planner back to the day she thought she'd checked off that she completed that task.

"It's not in my stack of files. I thought for sure . . ." her voice trailed off.

"Well, you didn't," Mike sounded impatient.

Cydney closed her eyes, thinking hard. Ever since she and Daryl decided to try their relationship, she'd worked extra hard to make certain that her thoughts of him didn't distract her from her work. One of the first things she knew employees would say once they knew was that he let her slack off. If those accusations came about, she wanted them to be just that— accusations with no substance.

"Hello! Earth to Cydney!" Mike snapped his fingers at her.

Again Cydney turned a puzzled expression to Mike. He'd never used that tone with her before. She slanted her head and asked, "Are you all right, Mike?"

"Yeah, I'm fine. Why do you ask?"

"You sound a little out of sorts."

"I guess I've got fishing on the brain. That's what I'm going to be doing a lot when I leave here, you know."

"No, I didn't know. Well, you deserve the break."

"Yeah, the company's in pretty good hands between you and Daryl." Mike glanced slyly at her and said in the friendly, teasing manner she knew so well, "Speaking of hands . . ."

She raised her eyebrows at him. She didn't know how much he knew. But for the sake of discretion (she never did get that sentence from Cameron) she thought she'd better play it cool.

"Yes?"

"How would you like to be his right-hand woman?"

"What . . . what do you mean?" Cydney asked, and hoped the quaking she was doing on the inside wasn't coming through on the outside.

"I wanted to see how you felt about being made a VP."

"A vice president? Mike, are you serious?"

"Of course I'm serious. I should have done it a long time ago. While I've still got some say so around here, I want to give you a promotion."

She put her trembling hands to her mouth and stared wide eyed at him.

"I don't believe it!"

"Believe it, kiddo. I've got a draft recommendation sitting on my desk right now. Of course, it'll have to be approved by the boss and some controlling stock members, but I don't think there'll be a problem."

"Oh, thank you, Mike! Thank you!" Cydney leaped up and flung her arms around Mike's neck.

"Your welcome, kiddo. You deserve it. You hung in there with me through it all—through flush and lean." Mike patted her on the back in turn. Then, on impulse, kissed her briefly on the cheek.

"Cydney, I wanted to tell you . . ."

"Mike, you shouldn't . . ."

"Ms. Kelley, have you . . ."

Three voices spoke in unison. Mike had started to tell Cydney how much he admired her, while Cydney started to tease him about office rumors and how it would look if anyone walked in on them. Neither Mike nor Cydney would ever know what Daryl wanted—for his was the third voice.

He took one look at them embracing in the middle of her office, then closed the door with a definitive jerk toward him.

"Oh, great!" Cydney sighed, while Mike muttered something more colorful. "I'd better go after him." She started for the door.

"You'd better not," Mike said, grasping her wrist.

"I have to, Mike. You don't understand."

"Yes, I do. And I'm telling you, you'd better not go."

"Why not?"

"So far you two have been pretty good at playing it cool, Cyd. I don't think anybody suspects that he's hot for your body and you're hot for his. If it weren't for a conversation that Daryl and I had the day you quit, I don't think I'd be able to figure it out, either."

Cydney opened her mouth to deny his assertion, but she decided against it. Mike used to be her boss, and he was still her friend.

"I'm glad you didn't insult my meager intelligence by telling me that nothing's going on between you two. Give him a few minutes to digest what he saw. Let him sort out what he thought he saw from what was actually going on. I told him that I was recommending you for a promotion. And he knows how you'd likely react to that bit of info. He'll piece it all together, and then he'll come back here, feeling like a jackass."

"Are you sure?" Cydney asked dubiously.

"Positive. But if you go to him now, Cyd, while he's still worked up, he may not be able to separate the man from the boss. I wouldn't want him to say anything as your boss that he'd regret saying as your man."

Cydney blew out a long breath and said, "I've trusted you before, Mike. I'm not going to stop now."

"You'll see. Play your cards right, kiddo, and you may get more than a promotion out of this."

"Why don't I see about pulling together that RFI for you. If you need me, I'll be in the archive room looking for that file."

"I'll be sure to pass the word along to you-know-who when he comes back," Mike promised.

Daryl had just one word for Mike, and it sounded to him a lot like *castration*. What did Mike think he was doing, putting his hands on Cydney like that? And what was she doing letting him do that to her? Damn her! Did she have to have every man in that office panting after her—including himself?!

He slammed his door to his office behind him, and threw himself into his chair. The thought that another man might want her as much as he did made him furious. The idea that she would even allow another man to touch her made him secretly afraid.

He knew, and regretted, that he had little time to give their fledgling romance the attention it needed to flourish. At work, no matter how much he wanted otherwise, he had to be the boss. He had a company to run. That meant putting aside his personal feelings for the sake of every employee under his guidance. They depended on him to make the decisions that would keep the contracts, and subsequently the cash flow, coming in. He couldn't afford to let himself get distracted.

Back to work, Daryl. Back to work, he repeated as a mantra to keep his mind focused. He had to. If he let himself think about what was going on in that office between Mike and Cydney, he would have to commit murder. What galled him

WE HAVE 4 FREE BOOKS FOR YOU!

FREE BOOK CERTIFICATE

Yes! Please send me 4 *Arabesque* Contemporary Romances without cost or obligation, billing me just $1 to help cover postage and handling. I understand that each month, I will be able to preview 4 brand-new *Arabesque* Contemporary Romances FREE for 10 days. Then, if I decide to keep them, I will pay the money-saving preferred subscriber's price of just $16.00 for all 4...that's a savings of almost $4 off the publisher's price with a $1.50 charge for shipping and handling. I may return any shipment within 10 days and owe nothing, and I may cancel this subscription at any time. My 4 FREE books will be mine to keep in any case.

Name _____

Address _____ Apt. _____

City _____ State_____ Zip _____

Telephone ( ) _____

Signature _____ AP1098
(If under 18, parent or guardian must sign.)

Terms and prices subject to change. Orders subject to acceptance by Zebra Home Subscription Service, Inc. .
Zebra Home Subscription Service, Inc. reserves the right to reject or cancel any subscription.

was that she didn't even have the decency to look sorry that she'd been caught kissing Mike.

As much as it stung him, he replayed the image in his mind. Okay, maybe they weren't exactly kissing. But they were hugging! No, it wasn't quite a hug either. What was it then? She was standing there, with her arms leaning against his shoulders. Did that mean she'd just broken from an embrace with him? Or was she about to embrace him?

When they had both turned to him, they looked surprised— but not aroused. Did that mean that he'd gotten there before something happened between them? Or did it mean nothing was actually going on?

It doesn't matter. Mike shouldn't have been standing that close to her, Daryl complained. Never mind that they'd been friends and coworkers for as long as there had been a Megna-Tronics. Never mind that Mike would soon be leaving the company. As a parting token of friendship, Mike had even suggested to him to give Cydney a much-deserved promotion.

Suddenly Daryl groaned aloud, and slammed his head against his desk.

"Idiot!" Mike must have been telling her about the promotion! "Stupid! Stupid! Stupid!" he pounded his head against the desk. Then, realizing that giving himself a headache on top of a heartache probably wouldn't improve matters, he sat up and rubbed his forehead. For a brief second, he considered the idea of hitting his head even harder. Maybe, if Cydney saw that he was in pain, she would be willing to forget her own pain, the pain he must have caused with his silent accusation.

"Damage control time." He stood again and strode toward Cydney's office again. This time, he knocked before entering.

"Ten minutes, forty-five seconds," came the reply. Daryl opened the door cautiously and found Mike sitting in Cydney's chair, with his feet propped on her desk. He held a sports watch in his hand, adjusting the stop watch function. He looked up at Daryl. "That's how long it took you to figure it out."

Daryl closed the door behind him. "So where does that rate on the idiot meter, Mike?"

Mike sighed. "I'm afraid that's pretty high, my man. But cheer up."

"What have I got to be cheery about?"

"You rate pretty high on the she-gives-a-damn-how-you-feel meter. She wanted to come after you, but I stopped her."

"Why? When we could have straightened it all out so much faster than . . . what was that time again?"

"Ten minutes and forty-five seconds," Mike supplied promptly.

"It's hard enough having to put on this mask for the sake of the other employees," Daryl said, shaking his head. "I want to be as open as I can with her."

"You're too open, Daryl, my man."

"Does it show that bad?"

"Only to me. Like I told her, you two have got everybody else practically fooled."

"So, where is she?"

"In the archive room pulling together an RFI for me."

"I've got to talk to her."

"Do you think you can be a big boy now? No jealous hysterics?"

"I'll behave."

"Come on then, let's go."

"What do you mean us?" Daryl held out his hand to stop Mike. "Where do you think you're going? I don't need an audience, Mike."

"Exactly. Somebody's got to stand guard at the door."

"Thanks for volunteering, but I think I can handle this. What's it going to look like if you're hanging around the door? Don't you have something better to do?"

"And miss out on the office romance of the century? I don't think so."

"I don't want you there, Mike," Daryl insisted.

"Bummer. All right, I'll stay out of the way."

Cydney heard the door open, but she didn't move. She was sitting in the middle of the floor, with several open boxes around

her, trying to find the right combination of documentation that
would make for an impressive presentation.

The archive room was large and full of corridors created by
shelves of boxed information. She didn't think she would be
in anyone's way if she stayed where she was. So, she continued
to flip through files, and didn't bother with checking to see
who had come in.

"I know I gave him that file," she muttered to herself. "It's
not here. It was on my to-do list to give to him and I don't
have it. I must have given that file back to Mike."

"Cydney . . ." She heard a voice call out to her. It was
Daryl. She could hear his footsteps echo in the large room, but
she couldn't see him. Daryl corrected himself in case they
weren't alone. "Ms. Kelley?"

"Over here, Mr. Burke-Carter." She followed his example.
As his footsteps grew louder, she thought she could hear the
pounding of her heart growing louder, too, as she grew more
apprehensive waiting for him. She just knew that he was coming
after her to tell her that it was over—quicker than it had begun.
She just knew that he'd found her not to apologize, as Mike
said he would, but to dismiss her from his life, or worse—
from the company.

So many emotions ran through her so quickly, that she barely
had time to sort them out. She knew that she was angry—
angry because he had accused her without giving her the benefit
of the doubt, and without giving her the chance to explain.
Even if she had done something wrong, didn't she deserve the
chance to apologize? Were his feelings for her so shallow and
insecure that he couldn't stand the thought of another man
touching her—even in friendship?

As angry as she was, she was also oddly flattered. The same
jealousy that made him insecure also endeared him to her. The
type of selfishness that wanted her all to himself made her feel
valued. Near the end of her marriage with Jason, she had started
to feel as if he didn't care if she danced naked on the tabletops
in a room full of sex-starved maniacs. She didn't know which
felt worse—feeling overvalued or undervalued.

Running close behind her anger was fear. She was afraid

that she could never trust her instincts again. Her first instinct at first sight of *The Suit* told her he was trouble. Her instincts told her to stay away. More than that, her instincts told her to run away as fast as her dimpled knees could carry her.

Falling for him was such a bad idea. His being her employer was just one of the reasons why she'd told herself to stay away. The differences in their business philosophies alone put a gulf between them. He was the proverbial mover and shaker. He forced the business community to bend to his will and his wants. Cydney didn't believe in that heavy-handed approach. She believed that you could push people too far. Sooner or later, someone had to push back. When that happened, who would fall? Would MegnaTronics suffer under Daryl's firm-fisted approach?

She didn't even want to think about the differences in their personal lives. He moved and operated in a world that she knew only through television and glamour magazines. His family was always in the spotlight, while she had made an art form of fading into the background. If you could believe those magazines, Daryl had a different woman with him on every public occasion; while she had done her utmost to cut dating from her life.

The overwhelming affect he had on her senses was another reason she was so wary of him. When he was around, she couldn't think straight. Her heart raced so fast, she could barely breathe.

By the time Daryl caught up to her in the archive room, she was a bundle of taut nerves. It showed in her face. She stood, with a stack of folders clutched tightly against her chest and looked as if at any moment she would bolt out of there.

Daryl felt his chest tighten. As long as he had breath in his body, he hoped never again to be the reason for that look on her face. "Do you have a moment?" he said, as he approached her.

As if I'm going to tell the boss I'm too busy for him, she thought sarcastically.

"I wanted to talk to you," he began, then realized how lame that must have sounded to her.

"About?" she asked, in clipped tones.

"About what happened in your office." He glanced around him.

"There's nobody here," she assured him. "And about what happened in my office, it wasn't what you thought," she said, shaking her head.

"Yes, it was," he contradicted.

"No, it wasn't!" she countered. "If you would have just waited a moment, you would have seen that I was just thanking Mike for telling me about . . ."

"The promotion. I know."

"You know?"

He nodded once.

"If you knew, why did you let me think that you were upset with me?" She took a step toward him. Was he playing games with her? Was he purposefully trying to find all of the buttons to push that would make her react? A dirty name to call him was on the tip of her tongue.

Daryl read the look perfectly. "Go on and say it. I guess I deserve it."

"How do you know what I was going to say?"

"Because I've been calling myself the same thing, Cydney."

"I don't understand you, Daryl."

"It took me a while to figure out what was going on, but I finally did." Daryl smiled and said, "Ten minutes and forty-five seconds to be exact."

"You're losing me," Cydney said, shaking her head in confusion.

It was just a figure of speech for Cydney, but Daryl took it literally. "Never again, Cydney. I promise. I won't lose you again. Not like that. If it means I have to talk about what's bothering me all night long. I won't lose you again to a misunderstanding. I guess I got a little crazy . . . No, jealous. Don't take this the wrong way, Cydney, but for a minute, just a minute . . . when I saw you with Mike, I didn't trust you."

"Maybe it's too much to ask that you trust me so soon. There's still so much we don't know about each other. This is happening just too fast, Daryl. Maybe we should . . ."

He stopped her next words by placing his fingers lightly against her lips.

"Don't start thinking like that now, Cydney. I admit that I jumped to a wrong conclusion. I wasn't thinking straight. Believe me, it won't happen again. If you back away from me now, we may not ever be able to get back to where we want to be."

"And where is that?" she asked. "I need to know, Daryl. I need to know where I stand with you."

"I want to get to know you. I want to know everything about you. The sooner, the better," he insisted.

"No, I don't think that's a good idea. Maybe we should back off. You saw for yourself how quickly we can get the wrong impression. Shouldn't that tell you something?"

"What it tells me," he said, placing his hands on either side of her shoulders, "is that I want you. And I don't want anyone else to want you. If that's moving too fast for you, then we're just going to have to get you up to speed. Because I'm not slowing down, Cydney. I don't want to. I want you so badly that sometimes I can barely concentrate on work." He slid his hands along her arms, enjoying the sound of her rustling silk blouse against his fingertips. "Do you know how many times a day I've considered calling you down to my office, locking the door, and making love to you right there on my desk?"

"No," she said, choking back the sudden constriction of her throat. "Tell me."

"A hundred times a day! A hundred times a hundred times a day. When I saw Mike touching you when I knew I couldn't, I could have wrung his neck."

"Well, you're touching me now," she whispered.

"Touch me back, Cydney." Daryl didn't care if it sounded like pleading to her. He didn't want to leave any doubt in her mind how he felt about her. "Touch me like you did that night at your home."

"You mean like this?" she whispered, sliding her fingers along the front of him.

"Yes!" he hissed, moving closer to her. "I mean exactly like that."

"Kiss me, Daryl," she then urged him. "Kiss *me* like you did then." She'd barely gotten the words out of her mouth before Daryl was doing exactly as she'd asked. He placed his arm around her, and maneuvered her farther into the shadows.

When he leaned toward her, and covered her lips with his own, Cydney felt a jolt through her that sent her head reeling. He wasn't kissing her like he did that night. It wasn't even close! The kiss that night had been pleasant. It had given her an inkling of the passion they could share. But that kiss had also been controlled, almost orchestrated as if they were playing by some mutually agreed-upon rules. They were testing each other—getting used to the idea of touching and teasing and tasting.

This kiss was different. Fueled by almost an entire week of denial, Daryl's kiss was meant to strip away her defenses and draw every ounce of desire from her. For a brief moment, Cydney panicked. If she gave in to this kiss, it would leave her emotionally exposed. Whether tearing down the walls of reservation she built around herself, or worming through the tiniest chinks in her self-preservation armor, this kiss, if allowed to continue, would break through all of her defenses. Once inside her heart, he would know of her years of loneliness and denial. Yet, he would also know her capacity for love. He would never be satisfied with her attempts to distance herself from him. He would know that her sarcasm, and her indifference, was all an act.

Exposing her vulnerability to him was more frightening to her than the thought of his rejection. She had never really believed that he would want her anyway. When he'd left her standing in her office with Mike, despite her initial pain, she had secretly breathed a sigh of relief. He had let her off the hook. She didn't have to come up with any excuses why their relationship had failed. He had already done it for her.

But by kissing her like this, he was letting her know that he wasn't going to let her go so easily. This kiss was both passion and possession. He had once told her that he wanted to know her as no man has ever known a woman. If he achieved that, he would have such power over her. She couldn't allow that.

Not now. She wasn't ready for this unveiling. She needed time to decide if she wanted to expose herself to him. And if she decided that she didn't want him to know her, she needed time to build another defense.

As if he'd read her mind and felt her slipping away from him, Daryl gripped her tighter. He silently vowed to hold her until he'd smothered that glimmer of doubt, and resurrected the spark of desire. Grasping both of her wrists with one hand, he raised them over her head. With the other hand, he started to undo the buttons of her blouse. With each button, he punctuated his progress with a kiss.

Once her blouse fell open to him, he released her hands. If she was going to back away, she would do it now. If she rebuttoned her blouse and walked away, then he would have to admit defeat. But if she stayed, if she continued, then he would know. *He would know!*

She stepped away from him and saw disappointment cloud his eyes. But when she slid her blouse off her shoulders and let it fall to the floor, disappointment was quickly replaced by desire.

Daryl jerked his tie away from his neck as if it strangled him.

"You're not afraid someone's going to walk in on us?" Cydney asked.

He shook his head, and started to tear at the buttons on his shirt.

"Don't," she said, gently slapping his hands away. "One missing button you could probably explain away. But several of them?"

She took over. With each button she undid, she mimicked him, and kissed him over and over. The taste of him, and the feel of him against her lips spurred her on. If she had any misgivings at all about touching him, they faded now. His soft moans of pleasure empowered her, and gave her the permission she needed to continue. She drifted lower, planting kisses over his shoulders and chest. She lifted his undershirt from his waistband, and trailed soft moist kisses down the planes of his abdomen.

He grasped her by the shoulders and lifted her to face him. "Cydney, I'm running out of time," he said hoarsely.

"You mean you have to go back to work?" she asked, purposefully misunderstanding him. "Maybe you could ask the boss for a longer break."

"I'm at the breaking point now!" he ground out. He moved against her so there would be no mistaking his meaning.

Cydney began to writhe, matching his movements. She felt his hands on her thighs, lifting her skirt and lowering her hosiery. When he touched her between the juncture of her thighs, the rush of heat and warmth made her knees buckle. Weakly Cydney clung to him, asking shamelessly for release from the prison that had kept her alone and afraid.

"Daryl, please . . ." she begged. The strain of her emotions boiling so near the surface took a rational, self-controlled Cydney and turned her into a woman she barely recognized. "I need you!" she whispered raggedly, and moved against him with growing urgency.

Daryl hesitated. For a moment, the shining light of sanity pierced through the fog of wanton desire. Just as he had remembered about protecting Cydney from Cameron and the sight of their lovemaking, he remembered where they were now. At any moment, anyone from the company would walk in on them.

"Wait, Cydney. This isn't how I want to make love to you for the first time. Not here . . . not like this . . ."

Cydney tore herself away. "We can't go on like this, Daryl. This is making me crazy!"

"I know . . . I know . . . Me, too," he soothed.

"So what are you going to do about it?" she challenged.

"Ask me again on Saturday," he promised. "The skating party is still on, isn't it?"

"If it isn't, Cameron will never speak to me again."

He rebuttoned her shirt and adjusted his tie. When Cydney reached for his belt clasp, Daryl grasped her hands. "I don't think you'd better go there," he warned her.

"I'm only trying to help," she insisted, but flashed him a wicked smile.

"You're just making it worse! How am I going to get back to my office looking like this?"

"You could always tie your jacket around your waist," Cydney suggested.

"I think you're getting some kind of cruel pleasure seeing me this way, Cydney."

"It strokes a woman's ego knowing that the man she wants enjoys being stroked," she admitted.

"Then it's official?" he asked, suddenly serious.

"What's official?"

"Am I the man you want?"

"Yes, Daryl, you are the man I want."

"Not Dion."

"No."

"And not Mike?"

"Of course not—or any other man in this company that you can name."

"No more misunderstandings?" Daryl said, grasping her chin and lifting it to look into her eyes.

"None. Certainly, no misunderstandings on my part."

X

Cydney couldn't understand it! She'd just fit into those jeans last week. Now, as she stood in front of the mirror, struggling to fasten several silver buttons of the popular, button-fly jeans that Courtney had bought for her, she found herself wondering how she could put on the extra pounds so quickly. In a flash, it came back to her—last Saturday's funnel cakes! She knew she shouldn't have eaten that seventh one.

Finally, she gave up in disgust. She peeled off those jeans, and pulled on the *old reliables*. Cameron would just have to deal with the embarrassment of having a mother that preferred comfort to being cool.

"Yo, Mom! Ain't you ready yet?" Cameron called out to her.

"Aren't ready yet," Cydney corrected.

"Why not!" Cameron then demanded. "How come you're not ready? You're the one who told your boss to meet you here at five thirty. And you're not even ready."

"I'll be ready by the time he gets here!" Cydney shouted. The words were barely out of her mouth when the doorbell rang.

"No, you won't be," Cameron muttered as he trudged down

the stairs. "I know one thing. I know I'd better not be late to my own party."

"What did you say, boy?" Cydney called out. Though she could barely hear him, she knew him well enough to know that he would be in the mood to say something sarcastic.

"Nothing!" he called back to her. "I didn't say nothing."

"Anything," Cydney muttered under her breath.

Cameron flung the door open, then jerked his head in the direction of the stairs. "She's not ready yet, Mr. Burke-Carter."

"Somehow, I'm not surprised. That's all right. That'll give us a chance to talk. Can I come in?"

Cameron stepped aside, and motioned for Daryl to take a seat on the couch. "Talk about what?"

"I wanted to make sure you're all right with me taking you and your mom to this party."

"You mean if it's okay if you and my mom go out," Cameron amended as he perched on the arm of a chair.

"Something like that."

"Why are you asking me?"

"Because you're the man of the house."

"And you wanted to make sure you gave me my props . . . That means respect."

"I know what it means. That's exactly what I mean to do."

"What if I said no?" Cameron said belligerently. "What if I said I don't like it. Would you back off? Or would you sneak behind my back?"

"You know your mother better than anyone, Cameron. You tell me what she would do," Daryl said evenly.

"If I asked her to, she'd cut you loose like a bad habit, man. Just like that!" He snapped his finger dramatically.

"So, what's it going to be?"

"Yeah, I know my mom," Cameron said quietly. "I know she needs somebody. Maybe that somebody is you. Maybe it ain't . . . isn't," he corrected himself. "But I wouldn't be givin' my mom her props if I got in the way of her trying to figure it out for herself. I know she likes you . . ."

"How do you know that?"

Cameron grinned. "You want the straight 4-1-1?"

Daryl leaned forward and whispered, "Give it to me straight. How do you know she likes me?"

"The same way I know you like her. It's all in the eyes, man. When she's talking about work, she gets this funny look on her face. And I guess it's the way she's singing all of the time like she used to. And smiling . . . and puttin' on makeup trying to fix herself up . . . not that she really needs all of that stuff, you know."

"Thank you," Cydney said sarcastically from the stairs. Daryl looked up. She was wearing those jeans again! This time, instead of the little shirt with the raspberries, she wore a dark, knit shirt that clung to her, a denim vest, and black boots.

"Hey, Mom. Mr. Burke-Carter and I were just having a little talk. Man to man. You know, doing that male bonding thing."

"Is your butt bonded to the arm of that chair? Get off of my furniture like that, Cameron Jason Kelley!" Cydney tried to sound severe, but she found herself smiling anyway.

"Yes'm." Cameron hopped up immediately. "Can we go now? I want to get there before all the skates in my size are gone."

"Oh, that reminds me," Daryl said in a deceptively, casual voice.

"What?" Cydney and Cameron said in unison.

"In the trunk of my car, Cameron, there's a little something for you."

"A present?"

"You didn't have to do that, Daryl." Cydney shook her head.

"I know. I wanted to." Daryl tossed Cameron his keys. Cameron headed for the door, then stopped abruptly. "Mr. Burke-Carter?"

"Yeah?"

"About what we talked about . . ."

"What about it?"

"What if it had gone the other way? Would you . . . would you still have told me about the present?"

Daryl liked to have believed that he would. He'd avoided

telling Cameron about the gift because he didn't want to be accused of trying to buy the boy's acceptance.

"Yes." Daryl nodded. "By the way, if they don't fit, we can still swing by and exchange them."

Cameron tore out of the door. Cydney heard the keys jingle as he fit them into the lock of the trunk. Then he gave a whoop of surprise.

"What did you get him?" Cydney asked.

"Something I'd hoped he didn't already have. I should have asked you first, but I got into the store and I guess I got a little carried away."

Daryl broke off as Cameron *whooshed* into the house wearing a pair of brand new roller blades. He also wore a sleek, black helmet with matching knee and elbow pads.

"*Bitchin'!*" Cameron yelled, as he zoomed past them, into the kitchen, and through the dining room.

"What did you say?!" Cydney shouted as he glided past her again. She reached out, grasped his collar, and jerked him toward her. Cameron flailed wildly, trying to gain his balance.

"I mean . . . man, these are so cool, Mr. Burke-Carter. Thank you!"

"That's what I thought you said," Cydney said in satisfaction.

"How do they fit, Cameron?"

"Like I was born with them on."

"Take them off, now. It's time to go."

"Aw, man!" Cameron groaned. He coasted outside where he'd left his shoes. As Cydney pulled the door behind her to lock it, Daryl whispered seductively into her ear, "Don't worry, Cydney. I didn't forget about you. You'll get your present later."

Cydney swallowed convulsively. The sound of his voice, the nearness of him set her pulse racing. "Will I have to take mine off, too?" she replied, trying to sound unbothered by his blatant invitation.

"The quicker, the better," he insisted.

"But, Cameron . . ."

"Don't worry. Everything's going to work out. Trust me."

* * *

"Trust me," Daryl was saying, grasping Cydney by the hand.

"I'm not getting out there! Are you kidding! Those psychos on skates will run me down and flatten me into road kill." She hooked one arm around the safety railing while Daryl tugged on the other arm.

"I'm not going to let anything happen to you," Daryl insisted.

Cameron glided up to them, grinning, and breathing heavily from his exertion on the skating rink.

"I coulda' told you that you wouldn't get Mom out there, Mr. Burke-Carter. She doesn't know how to skate." He shouted to be heard over the music.

"I can skate," Cydney said belligerently. "I just don't want to."

"I think she's chicken!" Cameron goaded her by making clucking noises.

"Cut that out, Cameron!" she warned.

"Come on out on the floor and make me."

"Are you going to let him get away with that, Cydney?" Daryl urged her. "Come on out. I promise, I won't let you go. I won't let you fall."

She looked distrustfully at the mass of bodies weaving in and out of each other—chaotic, but strangely hypnotic as they all seemed to find the pulse of the music.

Carefully, Cydney stepped onto the polished, wooden floor. With one hand grasping the railing, and the other clenching Daryl's she pushed off with one foot, and then the other. Cameron glided backwards in front of her, still taunting her and daring her to catch him.

When one of his classmates whizzed past him, he spun around, calling out.

"Yo, G-Man! Hold up! I'm right behind you."

Daryl grasped Cydney around the waist, holding her tightly against his hip.

"Don't go too fast," she warned him.

"That's not my style." He grinned down her.

"No?" she asked, raising her eyebrows at him. "And just what is your style, Mr. Burke-Carter?" Cydney said primly.

"I take it slow," he whispered against her cheek. "To make it last."

He maneuvered behind her with his hands firmly grasping her hips. When she felt herself losing her balance, he righted her again, but not before he held her against him long enough to let her know how her touch was affecting him.

"I think I'd better warn you, Daryl," Cydney began.

"About what?"

"When we do get a chance to be alone, I don't think I'll be able to practice much restraint."

"And that's supposed to scare me?" he said with mock derision.

"You don't understand," Cydney said, shaking her head.

"What don't I understand?"

Cydney cleared her throat nervously. "I . . . I . . ."

"What is it, Cydney?" The look on her face did scare him. She'd had that same fight-or-flight expression when he had found her in the archive room back at MegnaTronics.

"It's just that . . . I haven't . . . that is, I haven't . . . you know . . . since . . . my divorce."

"You mean you haven't . . . since your divorce?"

She nodded tightly.

"Cydney, are you trying to tell me that you haven't been with anyone since your divorce?"

"That's exactly what I'm trying to say!" She breathed a sigh of relief. She couldn't find a delicate way of saying that her emotions were dangerously near the breaking point.

Daryl maneuvered closer to her, holding her against him as they glided around the rink. "Then I'd say you were overdue for a little T-L-C, Cydney Kelley."

"T-L-C?"

"That means tender loving care," he explained.

"You sound just like Cameron," Cydney laughed in response.

* * *

"Cameron, who's that out there with your mom?"

Courtney flagged down Cameron as he glided past her. She'd arrived late to the skating rink—after stopping to buy new outfits for Oscar and Adrienne. She didn't want publicity shots taken of her children in something they'd worn to the skating rink before.

"That's Mr. Burke-Carter," Cameron said. "Her new boss."

"She's skating with her boss?"

"Yeah."

"Excuse me?" Courtney turned the that's-not-how-you-respond to adults face on him.

"I mean, yes, ma'am. He picked us up. That's his jag out there."

"You know, I wondered whose car that was."

"He bought me these new skates. *Bitchin'*, huh?"

"Very nice," Courtney said distractedly, as she tried to keep an eye on the couple. It was obvious they hadn't noticed her, yet. They were too wrapped up in each other. They glided along, slowly and carefully, even though the music was hard pounding and skaters were whizzing past them.

"You know, Aunt Courtney, I think he has a thing for her," Cameron observed.

"So I noticed," Courtney said. She could see Cydney's beaming smile from half the rink away. Courtney then looked down at Cameron. "How do you feel about that, Cameron?"

Cameron shrugged. "He's okay. He made sure to give me my props. That means he gave me my respect."

"Thanks for the translation. You don't mind if your mom dates him?"

"He makes her happy, Aunt Courtney. I don't have a problem with that. Besides, his family is rich. He'll know how to treat her like she needs to be treated."

"So, Cameron," Courtney began. "What are you doing after the party?"

Cameron shrugged again. "I don't know. Going home, I guess."

"How would you like to spend the night at my house tonight. Oscar's got some new video games. He's been practicing."

"He couldn't beat me in a million years."

"Why don't you go tell him that. He's in the arcade room somewhere. So, it's okay with you? You're spending the night at my house?"

"You're just trying to fix it so that they can be alone tonight," Cameron accused her.

"Can't put one past you, can I, Cam? Do you have a problem with that?"

"No problem, as long as he uses protection."

"Cameron!" Courtney said, clearly shocked. "You're only thirteen! What do you know about things like that?"

"My mom always gives me the straight 4-1-1, Aunt Courtney. When I ask her questions, she answers."

"And you've asked her about sex?"

"I asked her about sex," he admitted. "And she explained to me about love."

It was true love. It had to be! Nothing short of that could have made Cydney get out on the skating rink and put her life at risk at every turn of the wheels under her feet. Despite Daryl's assurances, she continued to stare distrustfully as the skaters moved around them. When one skater threatened to shoot between them, Daryl quickly pulled her aside—spinning her around so that she was no longer in front of him, but behind him. She didn't have time to shout at the discourteous skater, before he'd maneuvered back to her position of security.

When she thought she'd fall back, she reached behind her, grasping his hands, his shirt—whatever she could hold onto to keep from embarrassing herself with an uncoordinated tumble to the slick floor. Cydney cried out, partly in fear, partly in laughter. She could only imagine how ridiculous she must look.

"Don't worry. I've got you," Daryl whispered confidently into her ear. "I'm not letting you go, Cydney. Not ever!" To emphasize his point, he pulled her closer against him, his chest against her back, so that she could feel his heart beating soundly.

It was the feel of him—warm, yet unyielding—behind her that did more to boost her confidence than all of his spoken assurances.

Words, Cydney thought with a touch of regret, could be deceptive. A master of words could make her believe anything. After all, the words she'd spoken as a marriage vow led her to believe that she and Jason would be together until death parted them. She didn't want to make that mistake again. She needed assurances of another kind. She'd heard it in Daryl's voice. She needed to see it in his eyes. She forced herself to turn around.

When he felt her twisting away from him, he slowed to the barest crawl. He didn't speak, but waited for her to say what was written on her face.

"Do you know what you're saying, Daryl? Do you really know what that means when you say that to me?"

"I hope it means as much to you as it means to me," he replied, and gently touched her face.

"I think we're going around in circles," Cydney said with a wry smile.

"We're in a skating rink. That's what we're supposed to do," he teased in return.

"I'm serious, Daryl!"

"So am I, Cydney! What else can I say to convince you that I enjoy being with you? I want to spend time with you, Cydney. I want to know everything about you. I care about you, and for you, and I want to be the man you care for, too. Is that simple enough? Do I have to repeat myself?"

"No, I think you're coming in loud and clear, boss man," she relented.

"Speaking of loud and clear . . ." Daryl said, looking over her head across the skating rink. "Who is that woman waving and pointing and trying to get your attention?"

Cydney craned her neck around to see. She started to laugh. "That's my sister Courtney. Push me over there, and I'll introduce you." She spun around so that Daryl's hands were in the small of her back. When she got close enough to the safety railing, Cydney grasped it with both hands and pulled herself, hand over hand, toward Courtney.

"I finally made it!" Courtney called out.

"You stopped and shopped before you came out here, didn't you?" Cydney accused, as she pulled alongside her sister.

"Not for me. It was for Oscar and Adrienne. They had to have new outfits for the party. So—are you having fun yet?" Courtney smiled, and glanced at Daryl.

"A blast!" Cydney responded immediately. She *was* having a good time. She suspected that much of her amusement had absolutely nothing to do with the crowd, the skates, and the music, and had everything to do with Daryl's company.

"Courtney, I'd like you to meet someone," Cydney said, then smiled a little shyly.

"Pleasure to meet you, Mr. Burke-Carter," Courtney said, quickly holding out her hand to greet him. She wanted to spare her sister the awkward moment of deciding whether to introduce Daryl as her boyfriend, boss, or any other term that would call attention to the newness in her life. "How in the world did you convince Cydney to get out there? A person could get killed trying to work their way into that crowd!"

"Are you kidding? Daryl's a wonderful skater. Once I saw he wouldn't let me fall, I just jumped right out there!"

"Yeah, right," Courtney said, giving Cydney that "tell me another story" look. "I'll bet he had to drag you, kicking and screaming, all the way."

Cydney glanced up at Daryl. "You're going to let her get away with that?"

"Hey, she's your sister. I don't get between family disagreements," Daryl said, holding up his hands and backing away.

"Oooh! I like this guy already. You'd better hang onto him, Cyd."

"With the way those skaters are zoomin' past, you think I'm going to let go?" Cydney said, deliberately misunderstanding her sister's true intention.

"Speaking of zoomin' skaters, I ran into Cam a little while ago."

"He's having the time of his life. I'm glad he won this

skating party." Cydney smiled tenderly, then looked around. "Where is that boy, anyway?"

"I think he's with Oscar in the arcade room. You know kids and video games. Once they start having fun, you won't be able to tear them away." Courtney said. "What time is this party supposed to break up?"

"Ten."

"Ten o'clock?!" Courtney snorted in derision. "Who's running this party—a bunch of old men and women? It seems a shame to cut the kids' fun so early. It is a weekend, you know."

"I know that," Cydney said defensively. "But I have to follow the sponsor's rules. And I'm not about to send a message to the other parents that it's okay to keep thirteen-year-olds out to all hours of the night."

"The other parents can do whatever they want to entertain their kids. I'm talking about Cam."

"What about Cameron?"

"He and Oscar sure do want to keep playing video games." Courtney sighed heavily and wistfully, making Cydney immediately suspicious.

"And just what do you want me do about that?"

"I know! You can let Cam spend the night at my house tonight!" Courtney said, brightening as if the idea suddenly came to her.

Cydney glanced sharply at her sister who was trying, and failing, to look completely innocent. Then she looked back at Daryl.

"Are you going to let her get away with that?" Cydney demanded again.

"Get away with what?" Daryl asked, with equally feigned innocence.

"You know what," she accused them both. "With this obvious attempt to set us up."

He held up his hands again and said, "I told you, this is between you and your sister."

"Then it's settled?" Courtney pressed.

"I'll have to check with Cameron first."

"I've already done that. It's all cool with him."

Cydney shook her head. ''If I thought that you—''

''That I what?'' Courtney interrupted. She leaned forward and whispered, ''That I care enough to want to see you with a man who obviously makes you happy?''

''Is it that obvious?'' Cydney sounded surprised.

''You're positively glowing,'' Courtney said promptly, then lowered her voice even further. ''But that's gonna' be nothing compared to the afterglow when you and the bossman . . .''

''Sh!!!'' Cydney waved her sister away from her.

''What are you shushing me for? You don't want him to know how much you want him?''

''I don't want the whole world to know.''

''You won't be able to stop the gossip once they see his car parked outside your house. There's something about a parked car, especially a strange one, that gets all the tongues wagging,'' Courtney warned her.

''Then we'll just have to park in the garage, instead of the driveway,'' Cydney said and grinned mischievously at her sister.

The drive back to Cydney's house was both the longest and the shortest drive she'd ever taken. It seemed long because the anticipation of what was to come literally stretched the moments to hours. The drive was also much too short. By the time Daryl pulled into her drive, she still hadn't made up her mind whether now was the perfect time to share all the intimate details of herself. The threat and the promise to reveal details that she had only imagined and that they had often joked of during their late night talks was staring her right in the face.

As Daryl turned off the ignition, she closed her eyes, waiting expectantly. When he didn't move, didn't say a word, she opened her left eye to peek at him. He was staring straight ahead with his hands still gripping the steering wheel.

The silence between them was so great—too great. She had to say something.

''Well, here we are,'' Cydney said with forced brightness,

then bit her lip. *Good grief, Cydney! Could you have said anything more lame?* she chastised herself.

"We made it safe and sound," he responded. Cydney thought she heard just a hint of a tremor in his voice, too. It was then that she realized that he was just as terrified as she was! Now that Courtney had given them the perfect opportunity to be alone, the pressure to perform must be enormous! *Among other things* . . . Cydney thought wickedly, then burst out laughing at the thought.

"All right, what's so funny?" he turned to face her, half smiling. "Are you going to let me in on the joke?"

"You're already in on it," she said, gasping and laughing and wiping tears from her eyes.

"What do you mean?"

"You are the joke . . . and so am I."

"I don't get it," he said, still puzzled.

"Will you look at us? Just look at us! For weeks now we've been bragging about what we'd do once we finally had a moment alone together, and now look at us! We're so scared, we can barely look at each other."

Daryl chuckled softly. "I guess you have to be careful what you ask for."

Cydney took a deep breath and squared her shoulders. "Why don't we just take this one step at a time. Do you want to come in for a cup of coffee?"

"I'd love to." Daryl slipped the car keys into his pocket, climbed out, then walked around to help Cydney from the car. He watched as she walked away from him, fishing around in her purse for her house keys. Seeing the seductive sway of her bottom as she walked, it didn't take long for his initial jitters to start to fade. He stood close to her as she fit the key into the lock. The faint traces of her perfume caught and held his attention. He reached out, and touched the back of his hand to her cheek. Her skin was warm and smooth. And when she smiled at him, he felt the last traces of his reluctance drain away. How he wanted her! And nothing was going to get in the way of having her.

During the week, he had to compete for Cydney's attention

with forty other needy adults. Tonight, for several hours, he'd
shared Cydney with what seemed like a hundred precocious
thirteen-year-olds. Now, he wanted her all to himself. He
wanted her to look at him and only him. When she spoke, he
wanted it to be to him, and about only them. And when he
touched her, he wanted their passion to consume each other.

He leaned forward and brushed his lips lightly against hers.
When she turned to him, and placed her arms around his neck
to draw him close, restraint quickly turned to sweet aggression.
He grasped her hips and jerked her toward him.

Cydney gave a little gasp of surprise. She didn't know why
his touch should startle her. Several times tonight, he'd performed the same action. With tender attention, he'd kept her
from falling at the skating rink by helping her keep her balance.
But this time, his attention was not to keep her aloft, but to
unsettle her. He wanted her to fall—to fall immediately into
his arms. He needed *her* now—Now!

"Open the door, Cydney," he said on a ragged, indrawn
breath, "or it'll be out here and right now."

Reaching behind her, Cydney fit the key into the lock, turned,
and kicked the door open with her foot. Grasping her derriere,
Daryl lifted her across the threshold and carried her into the
living room. He wanted to carry her upstairs, to the privacy
and security of her own bedroom, but he didn't think he could
make it that far without losing the last shred of restraint. It had
shattered the moment Cydney reached between them to caress
him—whispering with unabashed urgency, "Right here, Daryl!
Right now!"

She pulled him toward her, and whether by fate or design
(he wasn't sure which, and at the moment didn't care) they
toppled onto the comfy cushions of the couch. Cydney unfast-
ened his pants, while he struggled to pull her blouse over her
head. Her ample breasts spilled from the gossamer material
into his demanding hands. His lips closed around one nipple
as he suckled her—drawing from Cydney a deep-throated
moan. He moved to the other, giving the same solicitous attention.

"Daryl, please!" she cried out, moving under him so as to leave no doubt about what he must do to fulfill her yearning. She was certain that if he didn't come to her soon, she would burn like a cinder under the heat of his touch. Daryl kissed her deeply to soothe her, then took only a moment to reach into his back pocket for the small, foil wrapper.

"I want you, Cydney Kelley," Daryl whispered as he smoothed his hands against her back to draw her closer.

"Then you can have me, Daryl Burke-Carter," she gave permission. Her voice was husky with passion as she urged him. "Take me!"

At the blatant invitation, Daryl positioned himself over her, and thrust deeply. As he entered her, Cydney cried out, and clutched his shoulders. She squeezed her eyes shut tight; her breathing was rapid and shallow.

Daryl mentally cursed himself. Damn it! He should have been more careful! She'd told him that she hadn't made love since her divorce. He didn't stop to think that it would take time for her to get used to him. Like some sort of inexperienced, hormonal teenager, he had to come to her without finesse or regard for her feelings.

"Sweetheart, I'm so sorry! Did I hurt you?!" Daryl started to pull away, but Cydney grasped him in desperation.

"If you leave me now, Daryl Burke-Carter, so help me, I'll never talk to you again!" she threatened. "But like I said before . . . we take it one step at a time."

"Lead the way, sweetheart," Daryl urged her.

"Like this," she began. Placing her hands on either side of his hips, she pulled him toward her again. Slowly releasing her hands, she allowed him to pull away until he'd almost left her. She repeated the gestures until, with a barely perceptible nod, Daryl indicated that he understood. Moving with deliberate slowness, he reestablished a rhythm that allowed Cydney to relax. A soft sigh escaped her lips.

"Yes . . ." she praised him.

That single word did more to inflame him than all of the passionate phrases that he could call to mind. When she repeated her encouragement, he heard an edge in her voice. Somehow he knew that the strain was not from discomfort, but from building desire. She arched toward him again, taking him deeper inside of her with each thrust. It didn't take long before impatience began to manifest itself in her movements.

Her body thirsted for more. She had passed the plateau where she thought she should be cautious. Now, there was only need—pure and unadulterated. She gripped his shoulders, digging her nails into him so that he winced. But he understood. She was spiraling away from him, rising fast on emotions too strong to contain. With a touch, she meant to show him how he affected her.

She took his face between her trembling hands and brought him to her lips. Daryl was equally eager to kiss her. For days, he'd fantasized about the fullness of Cydney's lips and the pliant, dueling tongue darting and daring him to capture it.

She swallowed his moan of pleasure, and took equal pleasure in knowing that right now, he needed her, as much as she needed him. The need was so great. It was too overpowering. She couldn't hold on. She couldn't contain it. It was carrying her farther and faster than she wanted. She clutched his shoulders, whispering in dismay.

"Daryl, I can't hold on . . . I can't wait!"

"It's all right, sweetheart," he murmured. "Go on. Let go! This one's for you."

Cradling her hips, Daryl surged forward, withdrew, then came to her again. No restraint, no regret, but with complete commitment to giving her pleasure, Daryl met her again and again with the full force of his passion. Gasping and holding him as if he were her lifeline, Cydney threw back her head and surrendered to the wave that she had tried to stay ahead of. She felt herself lifted higher, and higher. And when she thought that she would rocket wildly into space, never to be seen or heard from again, she heard Daryl's tender encouragement in her ear, guiding her back.

She opened her eyes, staring at him in wonder and gratitude.

Cydney touched her hand to his cheek. "Thank you," she murmured. She felt a little silly for saying it. It seemed inadequate after the intensity of emotions she'd shared with him.

Daryl stared down her with an equally, foolish grin. "Any time."

Cydney started to chuckle. Laughter bubbled up inside her—explosive and uncontrollable,

"You want to tell me what's so funny?" he asked.

"You want to tell me why we couldn't even wait to take the rest of our clothes off?"

Daryl craned his neck to look around. They'd managed to get out of their shoes and shirts; but his pants were still around his knees while Cydney's jeans were hooked over her left foot.

"Man!" Daryl whistled in mock awe. "You know what this means, don't you?"

"What?"

"We'll have to make love again, and get it right this time."

"I thought it was pretty perfect the first time," Cydney said, raising an eyebrow at him.

"Flattery, Ms. Kelley? What are you trying to do? Swell the boss's head?" Daryl asked her.

"Something like that," Cydney said, with a wicked gleam, and reached between them to stroke him. Daryl responded just as she thought he would. He quivered and began to move his hips so that he slid through her questing fingers.

The mood shifted quickly from teasing to tension. Without breaking contact, Daryl raised to a sitting position and brought Cydney with him. She straddled him, her knees burrowing into the cushions of the couch. With the slightest movement of her hips, she brought from him responses more passionate, more powerful than she could hope for from a man who prided himself on his ability for self-control.

Cydney placed her hands on his shoulders, leaned forward, and brushed her breasts against his lips. When Daryl opened his mouth to take the offering, she leaned away from him, laughing slightly.

"Oh, it's going to be like that, is it?" he asked, with a hint of mock warning.

She planted a quick kiss on his lips.

"Just need to know my effort is appreciated," she teased him.

"Yes," he said, with the same fervor that she'd encouraged him.

"Yes?" she repeated, moving her hips rhythmically. She increased the tempo.

"Yes, Cydney, yes!" he echoed. Smoothing his hands along her back, he undulated in time to the rise and fall of Cydney's breast swaying before him.

Though she had intended to give him the intensity of pleasure he'd given her, Cydney felt the heat rising inside her again. Watching Daryl's face change as she moved over him, sent a shiver of excitement coursing up and down her spine. With a groan that poured deep from within him, his expression went from laughing to longing.

On any other man, that expression would anger her, maybe even repulse her. But on him, and with him, she felt an odd sense of womanly pride knowing that it was her touch that brought those feelings to him. She leaned toward him again, and this time, allowed him to capture a swollen nipple between his teeth and tongue. Cydney clasped her hands behind his head, drawing him closer into the warm folds of her flesh. His tongue, warm and rough, switched from one breast to the other. Faster and faster, he lathed her, making Cydney cry out—reveling in the sheer abandon of flesh against flesh.

She increased her tempo, rising and falling against him. Her breath came in short, staccato bursts, punctuated with softly uttered words that shamelessly proclaimed her pleasure. Words that Daryl knew she would never use in polite company poured freely from her lips. Instead of being bothered that she would know and use those words with him, Daryl found himself strangely more aroused. He felt himself harden inside of her and twitch uncontrollably. His own release was imminent. As much as he'd wanted to prolong the moment, she had pushed him to the edge. With his hands firmly encircling her waist, he rolled Cydney onto her back.

"My turn," Daryl declared, in a voice made hoarse by thinly restrained passion. He slid his hands to her hips to hold her immobile against him, then surged forward—deep and demanding.

Instead of resisting the obvious display of male desire and dominance, Cydney became more pliant, more receptive. How could she deny him fulfillment and satisfaction? It was his virility, his prowess, that drew her to him. He had shown he could be tender and considerate by giving her pleasure. This was the proverbial flip side of the coin. She had been the aggressor. Now she was going to prove that she could accept as graciously as she'd taken.

Daryl stiffened, then surged forward once more—signaling the culmination of his release. In an explosion of warmth against his cheek, Daryl sighed, and finally settled against her. He rested for only a heartbeat, before withdrawing.

Cydney stroked his hair, his shoulders, and his back to still the pounding of his heart. It thudded in his chest. When he tried to rise, to remove the bulk of his weight from her, Cydney moaned in dismay and drew him back to her.

"Don't move yet," she whispered. "Lie still for a moment."

"I'm not too heavy for you, am I?" he asked in concern.

"No," she shook her head, smiling at him. "Not at all."

"I will be in a minute," he promised. "I'll tell you what . . ." He rolled onto his side, cradling Cydney's head in the crook of his elbow. Then Daryl tossed his leg over hers, warming her. Now that they were still, the air against her exposed skin had raised goose pimples. He stroked her arms, her back, her thighs. Cydney sighed and snuggled against him.

"Now I know why you're so good in business," she said, with a sleepy yawn.

"And why is that?"

"Your willingness to compromise," she yawned deeply and closed her eyes.

"Having an understanding partner helps," he said.

"Ummm-hmmm," Cydney said driftingly.

"I want you to be mine, Cydney Kelley," Daryl went on in hushed tones. She nodded a couple of times, but he wasn't sure if she'd heard him correctly, or understood exactly what he was asking her. When he heard the deep, rhythmic breathing that told him that she'd fallen asleep, Daryl said with a wry smile, "I'll have my secretary get with yours on our pending merger, Ms. Kelley." Then, he kissed her on each eyelid.

Cydney's eyelids flew open. Her heart froze in terror. Something was wrong—really, really wrong! For one thing, she was lying on the wrong side of the bed. She never slept on the left side of the bed. Never! She squirmed just a little, testing the odd side of the bed. It didn't even feel right. Where was the little dip in the mattress that molded to her rear so perfectly?

The bed creaked softly, but not because she'd moved. God, someone was in her room! Not just in her room, but in her bed. Slowly she turned her head, then broke into a wide, foolish grin. How could she have forgotten? She was sure that if she told *him* that she'd forgotten, it would wound even his strong, male ego.

Lying beside her, Daryl stretched and flung one arm over his eyes. He'd pushed the comforter from around his chest until it draped loosely over his hips and legs. Then he took a deep breath, drawing attention to what Cydney thought must be the most magnificent male torso she'd ever seen. Carefully, she raised up on one elbow and stared down at him.

"Beautiful," she murmured, barely resisting the urge to reach out and touch him. Long, lean, and bronze—could he be real? Or was he a figment of her imagination? Maybe he was some Egyptian god who'd taken human form to seduce her. When the first rays of sunlight streamed into the room, would he disappear and leave her with only the memories. She shook her head fiercely. No, she wanted more from him than memories, so much more than that.

The thought of what he'd given her tonight aroused in her a sleeping giant. It was only a sample, a portion. Just think what they could share given more time and much-needed patience. As much as she'd enjoyed their lovemaking, she knew that they'd rushed. They'd hurried through like two children sneaking candy, afraid that an adult would come along and take it away.

The next time, she silent vowed, *and she would make certain that there would be a next time*, she would take it slow and easy. She would savor each touch, each caress. She would explore every facet of her rekindled passion.

Daryl drew another deep breath.

"That's right, bossman," she whispered. "Get all the sleep you can. You're gonna' need it."

She glanced over at the clock. It was four thirty; too late to think about sending him home before the neighbors saw that a strange car had been parked in her drive all night, and too early to think about waking him for breakfast. Careful not to wake him, Cydney slid from under the covers and headed for the kitchen. That's not to say that she couldn't enjoy a small cup of decaf coffee. It was so seldom when she woke up early enough to enjoy anything. Maybe a little cup, in peace and solitude, was the first step in her resolution to slow herself down.

She tiptoed out of the room, down the stairs, and through the living room. In the middle of the floor, her foot brushed against a piece of cloth. She bent down to pick it up, then held it affectionately against her cheek. It was Daryl's shirt. She looked around to make certain that he hadn't followed her down, then sniffed deeply of the cotton material. The scent of his cologne brought the memory of his touch sharply to her mind. Without wondering whether or not he'd mind, she slid the shirt on and buttoned a few of the buttons.

As the material brushed her bare skin, she imagined that it was his hands running along her skin. She shivered, and resolved herself to get the coffee started. If she didn't do something to keep her own hands busy, she would rush right back up those stairs, and throw herself on top of him—asleep or not.

The thought of being a ravisher made her laugh softly to herself. She could almost see it now. Like a swashbuckling hero from an old movie, in a fluffy shirt, skintight breeches, and high, leather boots she'd burst in on the sweet, demure captive, sweep him off his feet, and carry him away to a secret romantic hideaway where she would have her way with him.

Chuckling at the image, Cydney mixed cream and sugar into a large mug. Then, on second thought, she started to put together a small sandwich, too. A little bread, some cheese and lettuce, a piece of deli turkey and low-fat mayo. And maybe she could add some chips, and a piece of fruit. And goodness that last wedge of pie looked good! After all, she'd exerted herself quite a bit tonight—last night, she corrected herself. She began to hum a little tune.

That's how Daryl found her. With her back to him, she was slicing the sandwich, humming, and nodding her head and swaying those seductive hips in time to the music. It hadn't taken him long to realize that she was gone. What took him the longest was finding his pants. When he'd carried her up the stairs to put her in bed, it had been bare skin to bare skin. He didn't think she'd mind. She'd snuggled against him, murmuring softly in her sleep. Now, closer to the light of day, he wasn't sure how she'd react to him. Would she be embarrassed, bothered by their unrestricted lovemaking?

He thought the best way to approach her would be as close to normal as possible. He'd heard her in the kitchen moving around as he slid into his pants. Yet, he was having a harder time finding his shirt. He shrugged, "Forget it."

He could smell the coffee brewing and decided that his need for the coffee was greater than his flair for fashion. He pushed open the kitchen door and found Cydney, in that shirt, singing softly and swaying. At that moment, Daryl wished that he hadn't taken the time to put on his pants. They'd just get in the way again. He leaned against the door, with his arms folded against his chest, watching her.

She loaded all of her spoils onto a small tray, then spun around. On seeing him standing there, Cydney let fly a terse expletive as the tray nearly fell from her startled hands. The tray tilted, sloshing coffee against the sandwich and pie. Before she could right it again, Daryl crossed the room in a few quick strides, and plucked the tray from her hands. He shoved it onto the counter.

"I thought you might like . . ." Cydney began, gesturing weakly toward the soggy mess.

"I do," he muttered, dragging her to him in a kiss so fierce that she literally gasped for breath.

"I, uh . . . put on your shirt," she pulled her face away to begin.

He reached under the draping material to stroke her breasts. "I know. It looks good on you. Very sexy."

"You think so?"

"Yeah," he grinned down at her. "Yeah, I think so."

"That's too bad," Cydney said, heaving a mock sigh.

"Why?"

"Because if you minded, I'd have to take it off."

"It looks terrible on you!" Daryl quickly amended. "Call the fashion police! Surrender that garment!" He began to unfasten the buttons. When the two halves of the shirt fell open, revealing her to him again, Daryl lifted Cydney quickly onto the counter. She reached for the clasp of his pants. "These don't do a thing for you either," she said raggedly. "I think you should get out of them."

Daryl let his pants slide to the floor. He stepped out of them, and in doing so, moved toward Cydney. She clasped her ankles behind his back, moving against him.

Oh well, Cydney thought in resignation. *So much for patience!*

Daryl smoothed her hair away from her face and kissed her forehead, the tip of her nose, and both cheeks.

"This could become a habit," he said.

"One I don't mind if I never break," Cydney responded. She returned his kisses, matching him move for move.

"Hold that thought." Daryl stepped away from her, and scooped up his pants. He needed them after all. That is, he needed the condoms he'd tucked into the pocket.

"I'd rather be holding onto you," Cydney said. Then with an impish grin, took the packet away from him.

"That's what I like about you, Cydney Kelley. You're a take charge kind of woman."

She crooked her finger at him. "Come on over here, Daryl Burke-Carter, and I'll show you what other kind of woman I can be."

"You're the boss," he said amiably, and wrapped Cydney in his arms.

XI

Daryl called the early Monday morning managers' meeting, but his mind wasn't on what he was doing. More times than he cared to admit, he found himself referring to his notes to keep track of the key points that he wanted to make. He kept his nose almost buried in his portfolio. It was either look down at his notes, or look down the conference table where Cydney sat. He couldn't afford to do that. Each time he thought of glancing in her direction, memories of the past weekend came back to him with almost painful vividness.

Daryl knew it was going to be a difficult morning meeting the moment Cydney walked into the conference room—*surprisingly on time!* When she first walked in, he saw her not in the dark, conservative suit she wore. Instead, he saw her dressed only in his shirt, open to the waist. He saw her breasts, firm and full, peaking out at him from underneath the cotton material. He looked past the neatly coiled French twist, and saw her with her hair spread on the pillow as he leaned over her in love. Daryl's eyes met hers; the smile on her face told him that she knew exactly what he was thinking.

Daryl reached for his mug, gulped down his still steaming coffee, and hoped to high heaven that it was decaffeinated. The last thing he needed was for the caffeine to stimulate his already overactive imagination. He told himself that somehow he'd have to get through this meeting without looking at Cydney. And if that wasn't possible, he'd have to make damn sure that he didn't slip up, and call her by any of the endearments that he'd lavished on her this weekend.

"I'm sure everyone is aware of the open house this, uh . . . Friday," Daryl said, referring to his notes again. "The hours are from six thirty to nine. Attendance is mandatory, unless there are extenuating circumstances."

"Such as?" one of Daryl's managers asked.

"Abduction by aliens," another employee suggested.

"Not good enough. If they're advanced enough to lift you off the planet, then they're advanced enough to tell time. Have them get you back here by six o'clock sharp," Mike broke in. He then leaned and whispered to Daryl, "We're both still in agreement. I don't need to be there."

"You sure you don't want to reconsider. This was your baby, Mike."

"Like any parent, I've gotta' let go sometime. This is as good a time as any."

"If you're sure."

"I am."

"I'll have my assistant circulate a memo reminding everyone about the function," Daryl said, then snapped his portfolio shut.

"I'll make certain that all of my people are there on time, ready to meet and greet our potential customers with our usual professionalism and charm," Vernon Castle, director of marketing smiled down the table at Daryl. "The dress is black tie, right, Mr. Burke-Carter? Don't worry, my department will be ready by five o'clock."

"You keep a tux hanging in your office, Vernon?" Cydney teased.

"You'd be surprised what I keep hanging down there, Cyd," Vernon returned. His gaze swept over her, then indicated with a slight nod at his crotch to indicate where she should begin her search.

Daryl's back stiffened. The look, and how Vernon intended it, wasn't lost on him. He glanced at Cydney to see how she would respond. She wasn't looking at him. Instead, she pretended to yawn delicately behind her hand. One of the other managers snickered loudly, followed by another snort of laughter from another employee.

Daryl chose that moment to break in.

"No, Vernon, black tie is not mandatory. As much as I wish it were otherwise, I know every employee can't afford the luxury of buying or even renting a tux for just a few hours. Pass the word along to come in your Sunday best. And next year, after we've won all the contracts to keep us out of the red, the company will pay for all the formal wear for the employees for next year's event. Now, if there are no more issues, let's get the week started."

He tucked his portfolio under his arm and headed for the door. It took every ounce of his self-control to keep from "hanging-out" in the conference room for a chance to talk to Cydney. Though she gave no indication of needing to talk to him, or needing him for anything at all. He should have known that Cydney would be able to take care of herself. He was secretly glad that she hadn't looked to him for verbal and moral support after Vernon's comment. If, according to her wishes, they wanted to keep their relationship private, he couldn't afford to be perceived as leaning heavily on his employees whenever one of them did something he perceived would bother Cydney.

Yet, he couldn't let Vernon get away with making such blatant, sexual innuendoes—whether it was directed at Cydney or not. There was one thing he could do in defense of her and still not look like he was protecting her. He would recirculate the company's policy manual. And with it, he would strengthen the statement regarding the company's policy on sexual harassment. He didn't approve of it, and he wouldn't tolerate it.

He swung by his assistant's desk, picked up his messages, then retreated to his office. There were three calls from his brother Whalen and a message from someone he didn't recognize. A potential client, maybe? He stared at the tiny slips of pink paper for a moment, then tossed them on his desk. He didn't feel like returning any of the calls just yet. He didn't feel like doing anything except escaping from the office with Cydney by his side. Maybe they could sneak off somewhere, go to a park, a movie—anywhere as long as they were together.

He shook his head.

"Pathetic, Burke-Carter," he said to himself. The only thing on his mind was Cydney. She hadn't left his thoughts all weekend. He was thinking of her as he drove away from her house Sunday morning. He kept thinking about her through the Sunday morning church service, and during dinner with his family. He couldn't wait to call her on the phone that night. Three times he called, and three times he had to leave a message. Where was she! Didn't she know that he was literally aching to hear the sound of her voice again?

"Call me, no matter what time you get home, Cydney." The third message was almost a plea.

At twelve fifteen in the morning, the phone rang. Daryl caught it on the second ring.

"Cydney?" he said hopefully before saying hello.

"How'd you know it was me? Suppose I'd been some other woman. You'd be very embarrassed," Cydney said.

"No other woman would be ringing my phone this time of night."

"Good answer," Cydney said smugly. "Sorry to call so late."

"Don't be. I couldn't sleep until I'd heard from you."

Cydney's heart warmed. "We had a shut in at our church tonight."

"What's a shut in?"

"It's like a slumber party and a revival rolled into one," Cydney explained. "We don't sleep much. We sing a lot, and pray a lot, and renew our promise to attend church more regularly. Most of the members are still there. But since I wanted to be sure to be at work on time, I had to leave."

"Cydney," Daryl began tentatively.

"Umm-hmmm?"

He then smiled. He recognized that sleepy-sounding "umm-hmmm''. The thought that she was getting ready for bed without him made him jealous.

''After this weekend, how are we going to go back to work like nothing happened? Can you honestly pretend that it's business as usual?''

''I don't see where we have a choice, Daryl. We have to.''

''What if I said that I don't want to pretend?''

Cydney sat up in bed, wide awake now. Her heart pounded in something close to panic. ''Now, you knew this would come up when you convinced me to give this relationship a try.''

''I know,'' Daryl sighed. ''I know.''

''So, what are you trying to say.''

''I'm just saying that it's going to be hard to pretend that I'm not absolutely crazy about you.''

She smiled into the phone. Daryl could hear it in her voice when she said, ''If I come in late, take two-hour lunches, steal office supplies, and leave early every day, will that give you enough ammunition to treat me like the other employees.''

He laughed in turn, then stopped abruptly. ''Who takes two hour lunches?''

''I'm no snitch,'' Cydney said, lowering her tone in a conspiratory whisper. ''But if I were you, I'd check the expense reports coming out of marketing.''

''Will you be serious, Cydney? How long do you think we'll be able to hide what's happening between us?''

''For as long as it takes.''

''It takes to what?''

''I don't know!'' Cydney said in exasperation.

''Then why'd you say it?''

''Because I couldn't think of anything else to say.''

''You're probably tired. I'll let you go.''

''Don't let me go,'' Cydney said. ''Just let me get some sleep.''

''I want to be there with you, Cydney.''

''And I want you to be here,'' she responded, her voice husky.

''Then let me drive over there. Let me be with you tonight.''

''I . . . I can't.''

"Because of Cameron?"

"Yes. You understand, don't you, Daryl?"

"I understand, and then again I don't. Cameron's a smart young man, Cydney. He knows we were together last night. And he knows we were doing more than holding hands all night long."

"There's a difference between knowing and *knowing*," Cydney said. "I don't know how he'd react if he woke up and saw a strange man coming out of his mother's bedroom. Let him get used to the idea that his mom wants to date first, Daryl. And then maybe . . ."

"You're hiding me from your son. You're hiding me from your coworkers. Are you sure you aren't hiding me from yourself, too?"

"What is that supposed to mean?"

"Maybe you're not used to the idea that you want to date, Cydney."

Cydney fell silent, then asked softly, "Is this our first argument?"

"We're not arguing. We're disagreeing."

"That's what I used to tell Cameron right before my divorce."

Daryl heard the bitterness and remoteness in her voice. He had to do something to draw her back to him. "Then if we're arguing, when can we kiss and make up?"

"If you don't like pretending that we aren't seeing each other," Cydney began, "why don't you pretend that you're holding me tonight. Right now . . ."

"A pillow is a poor substitute for you, but it'll have to do to fill the emptiness in my arms," Daryl said dramatically. It worked the magic he'd intended. Cydney laughed softly.

"Good night, Daryl."

"Good night, Cydney. See you tomorrow."

"With bells on," she yawned into the phone.

* * *

Cydney picked up the receiver of her telephone, then set the phone in its cradle again. She picked it up, started to dial a number, then slammed the phone down again.

"You must be out of your mind," she admonished herself. "You can't call him with something as trivial as this . . ."

She'd gone into her office with every intention of calling Daryl and telling him she just wanted to hear his voice. Yet she couldn't bring herself to do it; not after she'd warned him not do anything at the office that would draw attention to them. If she didn't follow her own rules, how could she expect him to? She picked up the phone again. Maybe she should call him and say she had a question about the open house scheduled for this Friday?

"No!" She wasn't going to start their relationship off with a silly game like that. But she did want to talk to him. She just wanted to see him. She closed her eyes, swallowing convulsively.

"Go on admit it, Cydney," she muttered. "You want him. Period."

On impulse, Cydney picked up a folder. She reached into her purse, and dropped two items into the folder. Squaring her shoulders, she then strode toward his office.

Dorothy Pinzer sat at her usual spot.

"Ms. Pinzer?" Cydney interrupted. "Is Mr. Burke-Carter in his office?"

"Yes," Dorothy said politely, but shortly.

"Well, would you buzz him, please, and see if he's available to see me?"

Dorothy paused, and glanced at the folder in her hand.

"If you're just here to get his signature on some papers, leave them in the in box. I'll buzz you when he's had a chance to read them." She extended her hand to take them from her.

"Sorry, no," Cydney said, holding the folder out of Dorothy's reach. "This requires more than just a signature. So, if you don't mind . . ."

Dorothy reached for the intercom button on the telephone. "Mr. Burke-Carter, Ms. Kelley is here to see you."

"Send her in, Dorothy," Daryl said, and prided himself on keeping his voice neutral, though he thought his heart was pounding loud enough to make his throat quiver.

Dorothy nodded her head in the direction of the door. "He'll see you now."

"Thank you, Ms. Pinzer," Cydney said, gave a jaunty wave, then strode through the door. She closed it, reached behind her to softly turn the lock, then waited by the door. Daryl stood up, regarding her carefully.

"Ms. Kelley," he said, with a cool nod.

"Mr. Burke-Carter," she returned. "I brought something I thought you needed to have." She waved the folder in front of him.

"Oh?" he said, focusing not on the folder, but on the subtle sway of Cydney's hips as she walked up to his desk and tossed the folder on top—scattering loose papers over the floor. She placed her palms flat on the desk and leaned close to him. He mimicked her stance, leaning across the desk so that his lips were only inches away from hers.

"And just what is it you think I need, Ms. Kelley?"

"A little T-C-L," she said, then smiled mischievously.

"You mean T-L-C," he corrected.

"No, sir. I said exactly what I meant."

"What's T-C-L?"

"Total carnal lust," Cydney said slowly, and deliberately pressed her lips against his throat to nip at the sensitive skin along his jaw. Daryl responded immediately, wrapping his arms around her and hauling her over the desk. She grasped his forearms, massaging the corded muscles as he crushed her to his chest.

"Cydney," he said hoarsely. "God, woman, I want you so much . . ."

"The folder," she responded, trying to maneuver the folder she'd brought in from under her.

"To hell with the folder," he growled, impatiently reaching for the buttons on her blouse.

"Trust me, Mr. Burke-Carter. You'll need the contents of *this* folder," Cydney insisted. She held it up, and tapped him on top of the head with it. Daryl plucked it from her fingers and peered inside. His face then lit up with a boyish grin.

"Proficient as usual, Ms. Kelley."

"I aim to please, sir," Cydney said primly. She shrugged out of her jacket, and leaned seductively across the desk.

"No. The pleasure is all mine," Daryl responded as he tore open the foil packet Cydney had conveniently provided for him.

"I thought this was a partnership. Share and share alike," she said, starting to protest the one-sidedness of his comment.

"You're right," Daryl said quickly. He smoothed his palms along her stocking-clad thighs. "You tell me what pleasures you the most."

"Oooh! I think you're making pretty good progress," Cydney whispered, throwing back her head.

"I'm only just getting started." Daryl explored farther, lifting her skirt higher. He then gave a low whistle of appreciation. Underneath the standard, corporate, two-piece jacket and skirt and prim silk blouse, she wore striking red lace panties with matching hosiery clips to keep her stockings in place. With one hand, Daryl unsnapped one clip, then another, then another until every clip was undone. His other hand worked its way beneath the waist band of her underwear. Once there, he stroked until she writhed against his hand. Cydney clenched her jaw, and pressed her lips together to keep from moaning aloud.

"I tried," she whispered. "I tried to stay away. I didn't want things to get out of control."

"If you hadn't come to me, Cydney, I would have gone to you," Daryl told her. "I couldn't have gone all day without seeing you, without touching you—or having you touch me."

At his insistence, Cydney unbuttoned his shirt. She pulled it from his waistband, the pulled up his undershirt. Trailing warm, butterfly kisses lightly along his chest, Cydney brought a moan from him that made her look up in alarm.

"Sh!!!" she warned him. "Or Doberman Pinscher will be in here before you can say, 'we weren't doing anything!' "

Daryl smiled, but his eyes gleamed. He bent his head forward, and drew one perky nipple into his mouth. Cydney gasped out loud, panting as Daryl continue to lath her with an expert tongue. She tried to lean away from him, but he held her tightly to him. One arm curled around her back to cradle her, while he maneuvered to position himself between her quivering thighs. She moaned softly, feeling heat and hardness separating them by a hair's breadth. Cydney pulsed against him in sync with the pulsing of her own womanhood.

Daryl guided Cydney back, cradling her head as he helped her recline on the desk. He shifted slightly, then in one smooth motion, entered her. She arched toward him, helping him complete the union. She started to move under him, but he held her hips immobile.

"Wait, sweetheart," he said in chagrin.

"What's wrong?"

"Nothing. Nothing's wrong!" he insisted. "It's just that I guess I'm a little, too worked up. If I don't get some control back, I'll go off like a rocket."

Cydney grinned up at him, then pulled his hands from her hips. "Don't hold back on me, Daryl. It's not as if we have a lot of time."

"Haste makes waste, my dear," he said in his best corporate voice.

"Time waits for no man," she retorted.

"Enough said," Daryl agreed, then began to move his hips. He slid forward, then retreated. Cydney caught him in a kiss. Her tongue probed the inner recesses of his mouth. Without realizing what she was doing, she probed and retreated in perfect time to Daryl's continuous, rocking motion. Her actions stimulated him, making him increase the tempo.

Cydney experienced that wonderfully delicious feeling of soaring away again. She arched toward him, lifting her hips to draw him deeper and deeper inside of her. By the expression on her face, Daryl knew that at any moment, she would fly away from him. She clutched at him, biting her lip as she neared release.

"No . . . no, not yet!" she lamented.

"That's all right, sweetheart," Daryl whispered raggedly in her ear. "Let go. . . . I'm right with you!" As soon as the words left his mouth, he stiffened as pleasure, sweet and strong, pierced through him. Daryl buried his face in her shoulder to still the cry rising from his soul. Cydney also made a concerted effort to still her sighs as tremors overwhelmed her. She finally collapsed, with a sigh bubbling from her lips.

Daryl lay perfectly still, allowing Cydney to stroke his neck, and soothe him as she would a small child.

"Do you think Dorothy is wondering what's going on in here?" Cydney asked, suddenly concerned how her meeting with Daryl behind closed doors might be perceived.

"And what if she is?"

"Do you think she'll talk?"

"And what do you think she'll say?"

Cydney shrugged. "Maybe she heard us. She's so close to the door."

"Again I say, so what if she does?"

Cydney started to rise, pushing Daryl away from her.

"You're being very cavalier about this."

"What do you want me to do, Cydney? Get nervous? Upset? Give everyone more reasons to look at us?"

"I just don't want anyone to get the wrong idea."

"That you're sleeping with me."

"Yes."

"But you are!"

"I meant to get ahead!" Cydney insisted.

"You can't help what people think."

"Sometimes you can."

"I'm not going to let you get away with denying that you care about me, Cydney. Even if I have to chase you up and down the halls until you admit it."

"You're not playing fair!" she accused him, pounding on his back with her fists.

"All's fair in love and war," he teased her.

Cydney regarded him with wide, serious eyes. "This isn't war, Daryl," she said.

"Then it must be love," he responded immediately.

"Love?" she mouthed the word without making a sound. He grasped her face between his hands.

"Yes, Cydney," Daryl said, smiling affectionately. "Don't you know by now that I'm in love with you?"

She stood up and walked away from him. "Love? That's ... uh ... such a strong word."

"You don't feel the same?"

Shrugging her shoulders, she replied uneasily, "I care about you, Daryl. And it's obvious that I'm attracted to you. Before I met you, I couldn't imagine ever feeling anything for anyone. You've brought a spark back to my life."

"But you can't say you're in love with me?!" Daryl sounded incredulous.

When she turned to face him again, her eyes glittered with unshed tears.

"I'm afraid to," she choked out.

"Afraid of what?"

"I don't want to be hurt again."

"And you think I do?"

"No!" she blurted out. "Of course not."

He approached her, shrugging back into his clothes. "Maybe I should have told you this from the start, Cydney, but when I play, I play for keeps."

"Love isn't a game, Daryl, or a business venture!" Cydney said sharply.

"I know that. But if you think I take my business seriously, you should see how I act once I meet a woman I want. What am I talking about?! You *will* see. You're that woman, Cydney."

She backed away from him, shaking her head in denial.

"I just want to know one thing, Cydney," he demanded.

"What?" she mouthed.

"What did you think I was talking about all those nights when we stayed up all hours of the night talking on the telephone. When I told you about all my future plans, didn't you think I was including you?"

"How could I think that? All of it was still so new!" Cydney lied. Of course she knew he meant to include her. She'd gone along with the conversation because she wanted to feel a part of someone else's life. She needed to feel connected. But sleepy ramblings that comforted her at night scared her to death in the calm, light of day.

Daryl started to say something, then changed his mind. He took a deep breath, running his hand over his mouth and jaw as he carefully considered his next words.

"Cydney, if there's one thing I've learned, it's that life is too short and too cruel to waste a moment. When you find something you like, something you want, you go for it. You grab it, and hold onto it, and devil take the person who tries to take it away from you. When I first heard about MegnaTronics, I wanted it. I wanted it so bad, I couldn't sleep for weeks until I figured out the best way to go after it."

"And now the business is yours."

"That's right. It's mine. It was no different once I figured out I wanted you. I wasn't going to stop until I had you." He stopped abruptly, seeing warning signs flash in her eyes.

"So, I'm just a thing, like a trophy, that you wanted? Something to brag about? A conquest?"

"You know better than that, Cydney."

"No, I don't," she denied. "You said yourself that you were determined to get me. Well, now you've had me!" she said bitterly. "You've had me in your office and in my home. Where next, Daryl? The lobby of the Chamber of Commerce!"

"Will you calm down?!" Daryl tried to silence her. "You didn't let me finish."

"I think you've said enough!" She jerked away from him and started for the door.

"What is the matter with you, Cydney? Why're you acting like this?" He grasped her arms, but she pulled away.

"Please . . . please don't touch me again. I should have never started this in the first place!"

"Don't do this to me, Cydney," Daryl said, shaking his head sadly. "Don't run away from me. Don't shut me out."

She paused by the door, composing herself before grasping the doorknob.

"Don't follow me, Daryl. You've given me something to think about and I need to do it alone."

"Don't you think you've spent enough time alone?"

His question stabbed at her, bringing a fresh veil of tears to her eyes.

She didn't turn to face him, but he could hear the pain in her voice as she said, ''That may be so . . . But this time, it's my choice.''

Cydney thought that episode in Daryl's office would set the tone for the rest of the week. It didn't. If she'd left his office angry and confused, she didn't have time to dwell on it during the week. There was too much to do in preparation for the open house. Organizing displays and presentations, and coordinating schedules with the other departments, she barely had time to think of herself at all. That didn't mean, of course, that she didn't think about Daryl. He was constantly on her mind. If she wasn't in his office, he was in hers, though each time they met, they talked of nothing but business.

She was the company's quality assurance director. It was her job to make sure that everything that bore the company's name, from the briefest correspondence to a hundred-page proposal, was the best that it could be. Along with her assistants and the rest of the department heads, Cydney made certain that every flyer, every brochure, every trinket and giveaway for the open house was top-notch quality.

When a scheduling conflict occurred between marketing and product development, Cydney stepped in to resolve that, too. She did so with her usual diplomacy, efficiency, and a few well-intentioned threats. Yet, through the whole ordeal, she felt as if someone else was acting for her. She didn't feel like herself—only a grim, dim copy of her usual vibrant self. While everyone around her seemed to be literally thrumming with excitement for the open house, Cydney felt as if she were mired in quicksand.

It's your own fault, she told herself over and over. Daryl had freely offered to lavish on her all of the love and attention she could ever want. And what did she do? She ran like a scared rabbit. It wasn't bad enough that she had to run, but she

had to fling him a parting shot before she left. Why did she
have to do that? He didn't deserve being treated that way.

The anger and the barbs she'd hurled at him were her way of
getting back the control she thought she'd lost. She'd demanded
space, and that's exactly what he gave her. During the days,
he didn't try to talk to her about anything but what was necessary
for the continued success of the company. And at night, he
never called. Not once.

By Friday afternoon, Cydney thought she would snap from
the tension brought on by her estrangement from Daryl and
the excitement in the office. When she found herself kicking
the snack machine all for the want of a chocolate bar that had
somehow gotten caught, she knew she had to do something to
end this.

Without waiting to see if Dorothy would check his schedule,
Cydney strode right past the protesting Dorothy, and burst into
Daryl's office. He sat at his desk, a sandwich half-raised to his
lips. The final copies of the brochures that would be distributed
that evening were scattered on his desk.

"I have to talk to you. Right now. It can't wait," Cydney
said breathlessly as Dorothy grasped her arm. Cydney jerked
her arm away.

"I told her you were in the middle of lunch, Mr. Burke-
Carter, but she just barged in and . . ."

"It's all right, Dorothy," Daryl said quietly, as he set aside
his lunch. Dorothy stood beside Cydney, with her arms folded
resolutely across her chest.

"Dorothy, would you close the door on your way out,
please?" Daryl said, nodding toward the entrance.

"Yes, sir," Dorothy responded. She threw him a puzzled
look. Mr. Burke-Carter hated interruptions almost as much as
he hated repeating himself. The more she thought about it,
since coming to this company, he was doing a lot of things he
didn't used to do. Then Dorothy glanced at Cydney. The way
they were looking at each other suddenly put the odd changes
in his behavior into perspective.

Good grief! Why hadn't she see it before? Mr. Burke-Carter
was in love!

Dorothy surveyed them again. They both looked angry, guarded, with nerves stretched taunt enough to snap. If it was love, it wasn't going well.

She closed the door, and made sure she locked it from the inside so there would no more unscheduled interruptions.

"Sit down." Daryl indicated the chair across from his desk.

"No . . . no thank you. This won't take long."

"Sort of like us, huh?" He smiled, but his eyes were troubled.

"I . . . I'm sorry," Cydney said, "for the roller-coaster ride I've put you on."

"Is that what you came here to tell me? I already knew that you weren't happy with what's been going on between us."

"It's been one strange week, Daryl. I'm surprised we got anything accomplished at all."

"Above all, I guess we're both consummate professionals."

"I'm not feeling very professional right now. I'm feeling pretty sick to my stomach. I want to go home."

"You don't need my permission to leave, Cydney," Daryl said softly. "You're free to go any time you want. You always were."

"I'll be back," she promised.

"For the open house," he elaborated.

She nodded once.

"And after that?" Daryl wanted to know. With a little more time, would she think it over and decide that she really wanted to be with him?

"I'll go home," she said. She knew what he was tacitly asking. Cydney decided that she didn't want to think about "after." She was barely coping with what was going on now. She didn't want to expend the energy thinking about what might happen, or even what might have been.

"Then I'll see you tonight."

"Tonight," she echoed. She started for the door, then turned around.

"Daryl?"

"Yes, Cydney."

"I just wanted you to know that . . . that I . . . I . . . I'm in love with you, too."

He looked up sharply and rose from his chair with every intention of taking her in his arms. She held up her hand to stop him.

"Oh, no, Daryl. Don't!"

"Don't what?"

"Don't look at me like that!" she warned him. "Don't look at me like you've won me over. You haven't. At least, not completely. Please, let me finish."

"What else do you have to do? Drive the nails in my coffin? God, Cydney! You're driving me crazy with this she loves me, she loves me not routine."

"It hasn't been any easier for me, Daryl. I'm not punishing you half as much as I'm punishing myself! I was playing with fire, thinking that I could make love to you and not let my heart get involved. But I did. And as soon as I did, I realized that my heart was still too fragile. Too many wounds and not enough stitches. When you told me you were in love with me, I panicked. I simply panicked."

"I can understand that," Daryl said evenly. "And we can work through it, if you just give it a chance."

"Haven't you heard a word I've said! I'm afraid!" Cydney said shrilly. She looked over her shoulder toward the door. Daryl understood the look perfectly. He grasped her by the shoulders and said severely, "Stop worrying about what somebody might think! If I had my way, everyone would know! I'd waltz in here this evening, with you on my arm, and dare anyone to say anything about it."

"You're insane," she whispered.

"Just crazy about you."

"You know all the right things to say, don't you?"

"I don't know. It seems lately with you, my timing's been a little off."

"It's not you, Daryl. It's me."

"Famous last words. It ranks right up there with, let's just be friends."

"Why can't we just be friends?"

"It's too late for that, Cydney, and you know it."

"I'm not sure I know anything anymore," Cydney sighed.

"Go home, sweetheart. Get some rest, okay? If things don't look better to you after tonight, then I'll raise the white flag. I'll let it alone. I'll let it go."

"Just like that?" Cydney teased. He squeezed her shoulders, then bent down for a kiss. When Cydney flinched, he gave her a soft, chaste, peck on the forehead.

"Tonight."

"Tonight," she echoed.

That night, as Cydney put the finishing touches on her hair and makeup, her son Cameron lay sprawled across her bed. His attention was divided between watching her and reading a sports magazine.

"Your Aunt Courtney will be through around seven to check on you, so you'd better make sure that you're in here by the time she comes by."

"I wasn't goin' anywhere."

"And make sure all of your friends are out of the house by then, too."

He looked up, giving her a sheepish and obviously guilty grin. "You don't have to worry about that, Mom."

"I was thinking about ordering a pizza for dinner . . ." Cydney began.

"Pizza! Man, what's the occasion?!"

"No reason. I just thought you and your friends deserved something special. You've been cool about me working so many late hours."

"Mom, stick to words from your own generation."

"How do you know cool isn't from my generation?" Cydney demanded, turning from the mirror to face him.

"Oh, yeah, I forget. You relics from the Ice Age would know about what's cool and what's not."

"You've got a real, funny mouth, you know that, Cam?"

Cameron laughed softly and buried his head back in his magazine.

"Mom?" he called, without looking up.

"Hmmm?"

"You look really nice tonight."

"Thank you," Cydney said, surprised by his compliment. She waited for the sweet talk to start. What did he want? To invite more friends? To stay up later than usual? When he didn't go on, Cydney's eyes grew even wider.

"Mom?" he ventured it again.

Uh-oh, she thought. Here it comes. Just when she'd complimented him on being such a good kid, he had to come right behind her and threaten that perception.

"What is it, Cam?"

"I'm glad you and Mr. Burke-Carter made up."

"Made up? Who says we were fighting?"

"You didn't call him this week and he didn't call you. If you ain't talkin', you ain't lovin' ...."

"Cameron Jason Kelley!"

"Well, it's the truth!" He sat up. "For a week now, you've been walking around here, muttering to yourself, snappin' at me, and lookin' like you're about to bust out with the tears if anybody even looked at you the wrong way."

"And now you think something's changed?"

He shrugged. "You're all dressed up; you're smiling ... That's gotta' mean something."

"I'm not going out on a date, Cameron. This is a business function. No cozy dinner, no romantic getaway."

"But he'll be there."

"Yes."

"And you'll be there."

"Yes."

"That's all you need, Mom."

"Cameron ...." Cydney began, then bit her lip to still her question. He was still a little boy. She had no business laying such heavy and personal problems on him.

"Yeah?"

She looked sharply at him.

"I mean, yes ma'am."

"Never mind."

"Mom, if you've got something on your mind, spit it out.

I'm the man of the house, remember? I'm supposed to help you.''

"You can't help me with this, Cameron."

"Can I ask you something?"

"You know you can ask me anything."

"If you don't want to be with him, why'd you let him stay the night?"

Anything but that! she screamed silently.

"I do want to be with him, Cameron."

"Then what's the problem?!" Cameron responded with what seemed to her a trifle more impertinence than she should let him get away with.

"He's my boss."

"Then quit."

"I need the job."

"And you need him, too," he said as a matter of fact.

"I don't need him exactly."

"I think you do. What you need is something that either Dad took away when he left or he never gave you. If Mr. Burke-Carter can give it back to you, what are you waiting for?"

"Then you don't mind if I see him?"

"*Duh!*" Cameron said, making the face and sound of what his friends used when they'd finally gotten their point across to the slower members of the group.

"If you don't mind, and he doesn't mind, what in the hell does it matter if anybody else cares!" Cydney declared, leaping to her feet.

"I say go for it, Mom!"

"Go for it!" she repeated. "Yeah! I'm going for it!"

"And while you're goin' for it, you can drop a quarter in the swear jar on your way out," Cameron said, turning back to his magazine. "On second thought, Mom, maybe you better save that quarter."

"For what?"

"To call home."

"I'll call from the office to check up on you, Cam," Cydney said, checking herself in the mirror again.

"Maybe you will; maybe you won't." Cameron shrugged.

Cydney paused at the tone of his voice. She sat on the edge of the bed. "Something on your mind, Cameron?"

"I just want to know, what about after this open house?"

"What do you mean after?"

"If you're gonna' go for it, maybe you might not want to come home. Maybe, you want to go somewhere else instead . . . like to Mr. Burke-Carter's place."

Cydney cleared her throat nervously. She and Cameron had talked candidly enough about sex; but it had often been in relation to him. She'd done her best to shield Cameron from expressing what her own needs were. After all, he was just a boy. He was her baby! Yet, the way he was looking at her with those eyes, so wise and old, she wondered how she thought she could conceal her own sexuality from him for so long.

"I'll be home tonight, Cameron."

"Alone?"

"Yes."

"You don't have to. I know you don't want to. Don't do it because of me . . . I mean, you can do it despite me . . . I mean . . ."

"Cameron!" she laughed, grasping his face. "There's a time and a place for everything!"

"I just don't want to mess up your plans, Mom."

"You are my plans, Cameron. Don't you know that? Everything I think and do and want involves you. You're my son, the most important man in my life."

"Not that I'm complaining or anything. I like all the perks of being your main man," Cameron teased. "But it's time to change, Mom. I won't be with you forever."

"You're not thinking of moving out are you, Cam?" she teased. "You want your own place?"

"Maybe . . . maybe with you being here, you're cramping my style."

"You're only thirteen. You don't have a style, yet. You'd better not," she threatened.

"Mom?"

"Yes?"

"When Aunt Courtney comes to check on me, do you mind if I go home with her?"

"I said you don't have to do that, Cameron," Cydney said, her voice strained.

"I want to," he insisted. "Besides, she's got better video games than I do."

Cydney kissed him on the cheek before grabbing her jacket from the bed.

"I'll call you later, Cam. Just remember that whether I reach you here or at Aunt Courtney's, I'll love you just the same."

"Bet," Cameron said, swiping at the lipstick smear. But as he heard his mother singing as she skipped down the stairs, his face broke into a wide, satisfied grin.

Daryl didn't even try to hide his grin of pleasure as he watched Cydney edging through the crowd, introducing herself to the potential clients, and rekindling friendly relations with their current ones. He marveled at how smoothly she switched roles—from expert on highly technical questions to "big picture" marketing strategist. Was there anything this woman couldn't do?

Make up her mind, he then thought grimly. If only she would make up her mind! He didn't just want her to make a decision. If he had to be honest, he wanted her to choose him. He'd done everything he could think of to move the process along—from outright honesty to laying low. Nothing seemed to work. What else could he do?

Daryl found himself more than a little irritated with his current state of mind. This was one of the most important nights in the history of MegnaTronics. He had to get out there and *schmooze*—not sit around and sulk because the woman he wanted hadn't said two words to him so far tonight. He had to snap himself out of this funk and get out there to perform! He had to be dazzling! Be charming! Show her that he could keep business and pleasure separate.

"Quite a turnout, big brother."

Whalen Burke-Carter quietly appeared at his brother's elbow.

With a small glass of white wine in one hand, a plate loaded with hors d'oevres in the other, he'd watched Daryl for several minutes. He watched him literally follow a woman whom he could only describe as stunning. It wasn't very noticeable at first. A glance here, a quick check there. But by mid-evening, it seemed as though Daryl wasn't interested at all in his long-awaited open house. All he could do was watch that woman. After a few, careful inquiries Whalen found out who she was. She was the director of the company's quality assurance department. She, as much as anyone, was responsible for the continued reputation and business prospects for MegnaTronics. Piecing together that information with what his wife had told him about the incident at the charity bazaar, Whalen thought that it was no wonder his brother was struck.

The woman was not only beautiful, but had a head for business, too. His brother never had a chance. Whalen watched Cydney circle the room. A polite smile here, appreciative laughter there, a few handshakes mingled with some corporately acceptable hugs—the woman worked the room like a politician. For a moment, she was obscured as the press of bodies surged around her, but when he caught sight of her again, it was in profile. Whalen quickly amended his assessment.

"Not a politician," he said aloud. "Like royalty."

"Excuse me?" Daryl asked, finally noticing his brother.

"That woman over there, the one in the blue, two-piece," Whalen said, nodding at Cydney.

"Cydney Kelley. She's the quality assurance director," Daryl said, keeping his voice neutral and matter of fact.

"She's like royalty; like some Nubian queen come down from on high to greet her subjects."

"No more wine for you tonight, Whalen," Daryl said, giving a short, nervous laugh. "I'm calling you a cab."

Whalen shook his head and wagged his finger at Daryl. "Come on, big brother, don't tell me you haven't noticed it, too."

"I don't know what you're talking about."

"I've been watching you, Daryl. And you haven't taken your eyes off that woman all evening. You want her."

Daryl lowered his voice. "So, what if I do?"

"Is the feeling mutual?"

"No."

"Are you sure?"

"She turned me down."

"Maybe she's playing hard to get," Whalen suggested.

"That's not her style, Whalen."

"So what are you going to do?"

"What can I do? Nothing but wait."

"That's not your style, either."

"Maybe I've changed."

"Because of her?"

"For her," Daryl corrected. "There's a difference."

"Shhh! She's coming this way." Whalen elbowed his brother, then plastered a wide smile on his face.

Cydney glanced from brother to brother—picking up on the resemblance immediately. For a moment, her expression was wary. Could Daryl have called in back-up to plead his case for him? He didn't have to do that. Didn't he know that she'd already made up her mind to take him into her arms and love him for the rest of their lives?

"Good evening," she said pleasantly, though her eyes still reflected suspicion.

"I was wondering when you'd get around to honoring me with a visit, Madam Director," Whalen said. He set aside his wine and plate and stuck out his hand.

"If I'd known you were waiting with a bated breath, I would have come around much sooner," Cydney responded.

Whalen introduced himself. "Whalen Burke-Carter, Daryl's younger brother."

"A pleasure to meet you," Cydney said, grasping his hand and shaking firmly. When Whalen raised her hand to his lips and held onto her just a fraction too long, she glanced quickly at Daryl. He did not look amused.

She pulled her hand away.

"So, what do you think of our company?" Cydney asked, quickly turning the subject to business.

"You've got a solid product and fine, fine people working

here," Whalen said, deliberately running his eyes along Cydney's curves. Cydney's eyes flashed.

"Yes, indeed," Whalen went on. "Fine, fine people. I don't see why you shouldn't be blue chip within five years."

"You're a professional basketball player, aren't you? Do you have time to dabble in commodities?" Cydney asked.

"Some," Whalen said with a shrug. "Maybe we can go off somewhere and discuss a little business."

"Just what did you have in mind, sir?"

"Oh, something appropriate for the evening—like corporate mergers and such?"

Cydney felt another knot build in the pit of her stomach. Just what was this man trying to prove? Why was he putting the moves on her with his brother standing right there? Then again, there was no way for Whalen to know the feelings she and Daryl shared unless Daryl had told him. And if Daryl had said something about them, and Whalen chose to ignore him, then Cydney could only come to two conclusions. Either the men of the Burke-Carter family didn't think twice about extramarital affairs, or Whalen was trying to goad Daryl. The question still remained—why? Could Daryl have put him up to it to test her? Or, was he trying to prove that he really was giving her the space she'd requested.

"Speaking of commodities," Cydney continued. "Know anything about gold, Whalen?"

"Gold?" Whalen threw Daryl a puzzled look.

"Yes," Cydney continued blandly, "like the gold band around your finger. That's a wedding ring, isn't it?"

Daryl burst out laughing when Whalen cleared his throat nervously.

"Yes, it is."

"You met Whalen's wife at the charity bazaar, Cydney," Daryl told her.

"What a lovely woman. I hope she shares your enthusiasm for business."

Without giving Whalen a chance to respond, Cydney excused herself and merged back into the crowd. Whalen gulped down his drink, then turned back to his brother.

"You're either a liar or you're blind as a bat, big brother," Whalen said.

"What are you talking about?"

"I just put my smoothest, mack daddy moves on that woman and she looked at me like I was something she could scrape off the bottom of her shoe." Then Whalen grinned. "Not that I wouldn't mind her using those gorgeous legs to walk over me . . ."

"See, Whalen, that's why you bombed out with her. She could smell hound all over you."

"Maybe she knew she was talking to the wrong Burke-Carter. I don't know what she told you, Darry, but that's the woman for you. If I were you, I wouldn't let another minute go by without letting everyone in this room know that Cydney Kelley is your woman. If that means sticking by her side and getting in her face every chance you get, you'd better get to it."

"She told me to back off, Whalen. I'm not going to crowd her."

"Look, big brother, I'm not saying she's playing hard to get. She's a smart, sexy woman who knows exactly what she wants. I don't think she has to play that game. But, I also think she needs to know that you think she's worth it."

"I told her how I felt and she shot me down."

Whalen shook his head. "You're pitiful. Since when do Burke-Carters give up with the first failure, or the second, or even the hundredth? Answer me this, Darry, why did you stand there and let me hang all over her?"

"She can take care of herself."

"I know that, and you know that, and she knows that. But don't you think that every now and then she needs a little taking care of? How do you know that she didn't want you to show a little feeling, some jealousy?"

Daryl opened his mouth to deny that Cydney would want that from him, then quickly shut it. The truth was, he didn't know. That was, he wasn't sure. Several times he'd had the opportunity to show that he wanted her exclusively for himself, and he'd let it go. Why did he do that? Because the first time he had shown a little jealousy, it had turned her off. He grimaced. That fiasco with Mike, the promotion, and the hug had almost destroyed them. Then again, his jealousy had been unfounded, out of place. It was a question of trusting her, and he had come back with the wrong answer.

Again, in the conference room, when Vernon Castle had obviously meant to belittle her by making overt, sexual references, he hadn't budged. He'd passed around a safe, uninvolved memo that might have shown his distaste for Vernon's tactics, but didn't tell Cydney how he'd taken the incident as personally as she had.

And when Whalen had challenged his right and his privilege, to call Cydney his own, he again did nothing.

"No wonder she can't make up her mind," Daryl murmured aloud. "I'm the one who's wavering."

"I take it I've gotten my point across," Whalen said, when Daryl seemed to shake himself out of a mental fog.

"Yeah, little brother, you've gotten your point across."

"So what are you standing here talking to me for. Go after her."

Daryl nodded and moved through the crowd. He tried not to make eye contact with any of the guests or employees as he searched the room for Cydney. He didn't want anyone to try to draw him into a conversation. No distractions.

"You're Daryl Burke-Carter, aren't you?"

A woman stepped directly into his path.

Barely hiding his irritation, Daryl answered, "Yes."

"I'm Debra Colton, Mr. Burke-Carter. It's nice to finally get a hold of you."

He quickly searched his memory. The name sounded vaguely familiar, if the face wasn't. Was she one of the clients? Daryl then held out his hand. "Thank you for coming to the open house, Ms. Colton."

"Thank *you*. You're a hard man to reach. Don't you return phone calls, Mr. Burke-Carter?"

Again he wracked his memory. When did he receive a call from her?

"I've been trying to reach you all week. When I called this

morning, I asked your assistant to put my message into your hand. I guess she doesn't take instructions very well.''

"I got your message, Ms. Colton," Daryl said, suddenly remembering the stack of messages he'd retrieved from Dorothy today. He also remembered seeing them scatter when he and Cydney exploded into passion in his office early this week. Daryl quickly squashed that memory. He was also starting to remember where else he'd heard Debra Colton's name.

"I got your message, Debra J. Colton," he reiterated. "Were you just calling to RSVP for tonight's function?"

"Hardly," Debra said, suddenly sounding very cool toward him.

"Then this is hardly the time and the place to talk about why you need to talk to me. Make an appointment with my assistant. I promise I'll get the message.''

"No, I don't think so. I don't think you're getting it all," Debra said, grasping his elbow. "You could be in a world of trouble, Mr. Burke-Carter. I'd think you'd be more concerned with what I have to say than the few, lukewarm promises to return phone calls or grant contracts you'll likely get at this function tonight.''

Politely, but firmly Daryl pulled away. "Her name is Dorothy Pinzer. She'll set up an appointment for you," Daryl said. "Now, if you'll excuse me. I have a business to run."

He moved away from her, his face stern and immobile.

"Maybe not for long if the SEC has anything to say about it,'' he heard her call after him.

That's all he needed tonight. How did that woman get through the door? In his haste to get away, he nearly plowed into Marty.

"Hey, Mr. BC," Marty said. "Boy, did we get a turnout."

"Yeah, sure," Daryl responded, blowing out his frustration. "Listen, Marty, have you seen Ms. Kelley?"

"She's in the small conference room with Vernon. He said something about needing help with his slide presentation.''

"Thanks," Daryl said. On further reflection he said, "Thanks for coming out tonight, Marty. Keep up the good work."

"Sure, Mr. BC. No sweat."

Daryl wove his way through the crowd again, heading for

the conference room. Whalen's encouragement, mingled with D.J. Colton's implied threat, and his own frustration with Cydney had him so worked up, that he thought his brain would burst. When he slipped into the back of the small conference room, used mostly for impromptu meetings, he had to pause to allow his eyes to adjust to the lack of light. There were about twelve people crammed into a room that normally held six, eight at the most.

Cydney sat at the front of the room, next to Vernon Castle. He handled the bulk of the presentation while Cydney offered additional information as questions came up that he could not answer. Daryl had come in on the tail end of the presentation. He had barely squeezed into the room when Vernon asked for someone to turn up the lights.

Daryl obliged. As soon as the lights came up, several attendees began to move toward the door. Daryl had to draw himself up to avoid being swept back outside. He tried to wave to get Cydney's attention, but she was occupied with setting up the slide projector for the next presentation. From his vantage point, Daryl saw Vernon slide into the seat next to Cydney. He said something to her—something to make her put on the face of polite, but definite disinterest. Vernon persisted, moving closer. Daryl's eyes narrowed when he saw Vernon's hand move subtly under the table. Cydney responded with a quick, definite movement of her own that forced Vernon to draw his hand back. A second later, he moved toward her again. This time, Cydney's movement was more noticeable.

Daryl was no lip reader, but he understand the one word that came from Cydney's lips. It was plain, simple, and to the point. With as much vehemence as she could muster with some of the attendees straggling in the room, she'd said, "No." It was enough for Daryl. No more standing by.

Almost to the point of rudeness, Daryl forced himself into the room. Cydney felt, rather than saw him coming. She looked up as Daryl edged around the table until he was standing directly behind Vernon.

"Hey, Mr. Burke-Carter," Vernon said. "Did you catch my . . ."

He was cut off in mid-schmooze as Daryl clasped him tightly on the shoulder and said, "Come with me."

He said it so quietly, so blandly, that if Cydney didn't know better, she'd swear that he was inviting Vernon out to discuss the weather.

"S-sure," Vernon said, not liking the look on Daryl's face, or the implication of the hand crushing his shoulder.

Cydney started to say something, then glanced around her at the attendees who'd stayed in the room to review reading materials that had been left out for them. Daryl read question in her eyes.

"You're prepared to give the next presentation, Ms. Kelley?"

"Yes," she said dubiously. She then asked, "Will it really be necessary?" Without having to ask him, she knew what had made Daryl so upset. He must have seen what Vernon tried to do.

"That'll be completely up to Mr. Castle," Daryl said, then turned to Vernon. "Let's go."

Daryl hustled Vernon through the corridors, away from the main crowd, to an area that had been darkened and roped off to prevent the guests from straying into sensitive areas of the company.

"So, what's going on, Mr. Burke-Carter?" Vernon asked, trying to make conversation. Daryl didn't say a word, nor did he let go until he'd forced Vernon into the archive room. He shoved Vernon against a stack of boxes.

"You tell me, Vernon," he said coldly.

"I don't know what you're talking about."

"Let me make it plain and simple so that even a weasel-faced idiot like you can understand. Stay away from Cydney Kelley. Don't talk to her. Don't touch her. Don't even breathe the air she breathes unless you have direct permission from her or from me. Is that clear enough for you?"

Vernon's eyes grew wide. "You think that I . . . Mr. Burke-Carter, I would never . . ."

When Vernon saw Daryl's fist convulse, he quickly changed tactics.

"Look, I didn't mean anything by it. It's just a little game that Cydney . . . I mean, Ms. Kelley and I play. It doesn't mean anything!"

Daryl grasped Vernon by the lapels and pulled him close so that his face was only inches away. "From now on, I'm calling the game, Vernon. And the name of the game is keep away."

"I . . . didn't know . . . That is, I thought . . ."

"No, you weren't thinking!" Cydney called from the door. Afraid of what she thought Daryl might do to Vernon, Cydney had canceled the next presentation, and had gone looking for them. "But that doesn't mean you should get your face pounded into hamburger because of it, Vernon."

"Stay out of this, Cydney," Daryl said. "This is between me and Vernon."

"You want to tell me who gave you permission to make something personal out of something that involved *my* person?" she asked, trying to diffuse Daryl's anger against Vernon by turning it on herself.

Daryl released Vernon to face her. "Are you trying to tell me that you didn't object to his touching you?"

"You know better than that," she said softly.

"So what's the problem?" he asked, straining not to raise his voice with the anger that was boiling near flash point.

"The problem is that this isn't the best time and place to deal with this. You've got an office full of clients and potential clients waiting for your attention, Daryl. Don't let something, and someone petty, take away your moment to shine."

"Cydney," Daryl sighed. He took a step toward her, ready to embrace her.

"I don't believe this," Vernon muttered. "I bust my ass trying to do my job and I find out that the VP promotion still winds up going to another employee."

"You say something?" Daryl half-turned, his tone menacing.

"Yeah, I said something!" Vernon said, feeling confident that Cydney would continue to intervene in order to avoid a scene. Cydney tried to wave him into silence, making slashing motions behind Daryl's back.

"Do you know how hard I worked to pull this sorry marketing

department together just so you can get all of the glory? How did you do it, Cydney? How did you get to be QA director? By doing the boss? And now you're going to be a VP. Let me congratulate you for stepping up. Or should I say sleeping up?''

Just like the day at the bazaar, Daryl moved so fast, that Cydney simply couldn't react fast enough to help, or hinder, what he was about to do. One minute Vernon was standing there, insulting her, the next he was lying flat on his back. Blood gushed from his mouth and nose and dribbled onto his starched, white shirt. Daryl stood above him, rubbing his fist.

''One more word, Vernon, and so help me . . .''

Vernon opened his mouth to protest, and Daryl's fist drew back again. This time, Cydney acted.

''Daryl, no!'' she screamed, grabbing his arm. Tightly coiled, and solid as the proverbial rock, the same arms which held her so tenderly, erupted quickly into violence. ''Please, don't! He isn't worth it!''

''I'm not going to let him talk to you that way, Cydney.''

''He doesn't matter!'' she insisted, tugging harder and pulling him away from Vernon. Daryl allowed himself to be pulled back.

''Get out now,'' he said, grinding each word. ''Don't bother to pick up your things Monday. I'll have them shipped to you. If you set foot on MegnaTronics property again without prior permission from me, I'll break your neck.''

''You're firing me?''

''You don't hear too well, do you?''

''You can't fire me! I'll sue you. I'll sue you for assault and battery.''

''How does a countersuit of sexual harassment sound, Vernon?'' Cydney retorted. ''It won't take much to get corroborating evidence against you from some of the other women who work here.''

''I don't believe this.''

''Believe it,'' Daryl said. ''Now get up and get out. If I see you hanging around in ten minutes, I'm calling the police.''

Swiping at his still streaming nose, Vernon scrambled to pick himself off of the floor.

"You'd better go after him," Cydney noted. "In his mood, I don't think you want him running into any clients."

"Are you all right?" Daryl asked.

She nodded solemnly.

"Wait here for me. I'll be right back."

Cydney started to tell him to be careful, then almost laughed at herself. She was reminded of all of those movies where the damsel in distress was left behind while the hero rode off to vanquish the enemy. She started after him. She wasn't the kind to sit back and wait for someone to fight her battles for her. Besides, there were guests out there. They were probably wondering why three key members of the company had suddenly disappeared.

"You do what you have to do, Daryl," she said. "I'm going to do what I have to."

"Meet me back here when you can get away," he said. "There's something I want to talk to you about."

She nodded, then split away from him. Daryl escorted Vernon out a side door while she returned to the guests.

Though she was on the lookout for any opportunity to get away, with the demands on her time, she wasn't able to slip away until more than an hour after the incident in the archive room. She caught Daryl's eye as she broke away from a group and headed again for the archive room.

Daryl met her and said by way of greeting, "I walked him to his car."

"You didn't have do that, Daryl," she said shaking her head.

"Yes, I did. I wanted to make sure that he was gone."

"Do you think he'll come back? Do you think he'll try to cause trouble?"

"Security won't let him back. I made sure of that."

Cydney sighed, "You did this to him because he tried to . . ."

"I couldn't stand by any more, Cydney," Daryl cut her off. "The man is filth, and I don't want him anywhere near you."

Making certain that they really were alone, Cydney wrapped her arms around his waist and drew herself to him.

"What am I going to do with you, Daryl Burke-Carter?" she said.

"That brings me back to what I wanted to talk to you about," he replied.

"What is it?"

Daryl kissed the top of her head, then said, "Marry me."

Every part of Cydney froze, from her breath to her heart. She lifted her head and stared incredulously at him. "What . . . what did you say?" she stammered.

"Why am I always repeating myself with you, Cydney Kelley?" He laughed at her. "You heard me."

"You . . . you asked me to m-marry you?" she somehow got out.

"Yes. And that's what I want *you* to say." He grasped her chin when she didn't respond. She didn't even blink. "You do love me, don't you?"

She dipped her head in a slight nod. Daryl helped her along by lifting her chin up and down. "That's a yes," he said. "And you know I love you, don't you? If I didn't, I wouldn't get so crazy at the thought of another man touching you."

Again, her head dipped once, so he helped her nod vigorously.

"That's two yeses. Let's try one more time. Cydney Kelley," Daryl began slowly. "I'm asking you again; will you marry me?"

Cydney paused, her eyes filling with tears. But, after what seemed a lifetime to Daryl, she nodded once, then again, and again, and again, faster and faster until he had to grasp her chin to still it.

She started to laugh, and to cry, and to speak all at the same time. So many questions, and still so many doubts. But there was one thing she was sure of—she was certain that she couldn't imagine her life without Daryl. She didn't want to think about it.

"Hold on a minute! Hold on!" Daryl laughed, trying to still the flood of questions that Cydney bombarded him with.

Cydney drew several deep breaths.

"Okay, Cydney, get a grip on yourself," she said. "You still have to go out there and face those clients."

"I want to face them together, Cydney."

"We will," she said. "But not yet, Daryl. Just hold off a little while longer. Will you do that for me?"

Daryl was reluctant. He wanted the whole world to know that Cydney was his. But, he understood her reluctance and had to respect her decision. That didn't stop him from silently grumbling the rest of the evening.

How Cydney got through the rest of the evening, she didn't know. Somehow, she must have. She remembered shaking hands and seeing the last of the open house attendees out the door. When the last guest had left, she turned and surveyed the room. To put it bluntly, it looked as if a hurricane had blown through the room. Tables and chairs were in disarray. Plates of half-eaten appetizers and glasses in various stages of being filled with wine or soda littered the tables. Forgotten fliers or brochures lay scattered on the floor. She gave a fatalistic shrug. Oh well, she'd helped to clean Cameron's room in worse states than this. With a little help, she thought they might be able to get the office back into order.

"By the year two thousand," she thought then in derision.

Only a handful of employees still remained. They were in various stages of cathartic collapse—without the energy to move or even speak. Cydney started to drag herself across the room, picking up trash as she moved.

"Don't worry about that. I've hired a cleaning crew. They'll be in tomorrow," Daryl said, bringing an appreciative, if not hearty, round of cheers from the remaining employees.

From across the room, Cydney caught Daryl's eye. Her eyes shone with pride. It was the first time she'd dared to look at him since he'd proposed to her in the archive room. She was afraid that if she looked at him while she was busy trying to convince a potential client to sign on with MegnaTronics, she would burst into tears of joy. She didn't have to wonder how her tears would be perceived. She could see headlines in the business journals now—quality assurance manager blubbers through business negotiations. Though the image would deliver a crushing blow to her carefully developed career, she started to snicker—the laughter of nervous tension bubbling to the surface.

She placed her hand over her mouth to still it; but something must have struck someone else as funny, too. Another chuckle from one of the employees, then another joined in. Within seconds, the room suddenly erupted into laughter and congratulations on a job well done. Cydney was surprised that everyone was so upbeat. She knew that at least one of the remaining employees must have seen Vernon leave in such a hurry. In a company this size, all it would take was one stray word, and within moments, everyone would know what had happened.

Though Daryl had done his best to hustle Vernon Castle out of the office without drawing too much attention to them, he was concerned that Vernon might try to wreck the open house with loud threats or accusations. He stuck by Vernon's side every step of the way. He ushered him through the corridor, out of a side door, and onto an elevator. He even alerted security so that Vernon could not sneak back into the office. Despite those measures, that didn't stop Daryl from expecting at any moment for Vernon to create vengeful havoc wherever and however he could.

He'd spent the remainder of the evening in various stages of mood swings. He went from being taut to the point of snapping with the stress of playing business host to furious at the idea of Vernon's accusations against Cydney. Each time he thought of her, his emotions swung to the opposite end of the spectrum. The thought of her made him giddy with elation. She'd said yes! He'd taken a chance and gambled that she would need him and want him as much as he wanted her.

"I can't believe we pulled it off!" Cydney said, throwing up her hands and collapsing into a chair.

"Without a hitch," Marty said, winking at her.

Daryl cleared his throat as if he'd make an announcement. Cydney stared at him, simultaneously pleading and daring him not to say anything that would make her want to crawl into a hole and hide.

"I have an announcement I want to make," Daryl said, deliberately using words that make Cydney think he was about to tell everyone of her proposal acceptance. He picked a glass of wine from one of the serving trays and indicated that the employees should join in on the toast. He cleared his throat again, "I just wanted to say how proud I am of all of you. You all pulled a full load at work this week and still gave hundred and one percent of your effort and attention tonight. I got a lot of good feedback from the attendees. A reporter from one of the local business circulars assured me that we'll get a positive write-up in next week's issue. I've scheduled meetings for the next six weeks solid for potential contracts and nearly all of our current clients gave verbal agreements to renew. In other words, we're on a roll. And it's all because of you, MegnaTronics. Give yourself a well-deserved hand."

"Here, here!" the employees cheered and raised their glasses in salute to each other.

"To Mike," Cydney said, "for the foundations of this dream."

"To Mike," echoed the room.

"To Mr. BC, for making us work to our full potential," Marty offered.

Cydney raised her glass to him; and just before taking a sip, she mouthed to him, "I love you." Whether anyone saw, she didn't know. But at the moment, she didn't care.

"All right, people, let's head on home," Daryl said briskly, motivated to clear the building to be alone with Cydney. "Is everyone okay to drive? Does anyone need a cab?"

"We're all cool," Marty said, echoing the sentiments of the remaining employees. Daryl had been very explicit in his directions about limited alcohol intake during the evening. Those who'd pushed the limit had already been driven home either by other employees or cabs.

Daryl moved to stand beside Cydney. "What about you?" he asked softly.

"What about me?" she returned.

"Do I need to see you home tonight?"

"You don't need to," she said. "I've only had one glass tonight. The question is, do you want to?"

"I want to," he said, straining to keep his tone low and his expression bland. "What about Cameron?"

"He's at my sister's tonight."

Daryl and Cydney waited until every employee had said their good nights. Only when the last car had pulled out of the drive, did Daryl feel free to hold Cydney as he'd wanted to all evening. Walking her to her car, he draped his arms around her shoulder. They walked in comfortable, companionable silence. Once they'd reached her car, Daryl said, "Let me drive you home, Cydney. I don't want to leave you, not even for a minute."

"What about . . ." she began.

"We can pick up your car in the morning," he said, kissing her lightly.

XII

The morning light streamed into Cydney's bedroom, bathing her in warmth. She stretched languorously, as supple as a cat. Her arm reached out to assure herself that she wasn't dreaming—that the blissful night of peace and passion she had spent with Daryl had actually happened. When her hand encountered empty space, she sat up with a start.

"Daryl?"

"Over here, sweetheart," Daryl soothed her. He'd been standing by the window, his attention focused on the rising sun. To be more honest, his attention was focused beyond the horizon. He was trying to see into the future. He knew that Cydney would be there. She would always be there. But would he? Now that he'd had more time to reflect, the conversation he'd had with that SEC investigator, Debra J. Colton, had him concerned—not worried, just concerned. He knew that he'd done nothing to generate an investigation. What bothered him was what made the SEC think that he had done something wrong? What did they have that pointed to questionable business practices? He'd worked so hard to get MegnaTronics. Would it, in the end, get him? Would it be the end of his illustrious career?

No! It couldn't be! He wouldn't let it. He glanced over at Cydney. He knew why she'd fought so hard to resist him. Her business reputation was hard won. She wasn't going to let a careless decision ruin it. He could say no less.

"What are you doing over there?" She patted the bed next to her. Daryl slid next to her, kissing her tenderly.

Cydney smoothed her hands over the worry lines in his face. "What's the matter, Daryl?"

He shook his head, starting to deny that anything was wrong.

"Don't give me that," she said. "You look like you've got the weight of the world on your shoulders."

"Nothing as heavy as that."

"Then what is it?"

He shook his head again. "Today is Saturday," he declared. "I'm not going to ruin this beautiful, summer day with business."

"MegnaTronics? Everything went well last night, except from a little noise from Vernon. What's bothering you about the company?"

He kissed her deeply, stilling her protests—and continued to kiss her until she was ready to relinquish her curiosity. Cydney filed her concerns away in the back of her mind, but reminded herself to bring it up again when they were both in the mood to talk.

She pulled the covers back, and invited him to slide in next to her. With her head resting in the crook of his arm, she snuggled close and tried to get back the drowsy comfort of half-sleep.

Daryl's palm rested against her hip where he caressed her in slow, absent, circular motions. Cydney sighed and snuggled even closer. Listening to the sound of his heart, the strong rhythm of his breathing, she convinced herself that if there was trouble at MegnaTronics, they would face it, and eventually solve it. She didn't know how long she lay there, listening and loving him. She felt the sun move across her bed to mark the passage of time. She heard the neighborhood slowly come to life with the usual, Saturday morning sounds—the thrum of lawnmowers, a blaring radio, the splash of water against a sidewalk as sprinklers came to life, the grind of engines as shadetree mechanics dragged out jalopies that, during the week, stayed hidden in the garage.

She wondered about the noises of Daryl's neighborhood as they would sound from his own bed. The thought of making love to him in the renowned Burke-Carter home prodded her from her drowsiness and pulled her toward desire.

She brushed her lips against his chest, feeling his heart pound against her mouth. Daryl grasped her head, pressing it closer. Cydney's tongue darted forward, tasting the unique saltiness of his skin. When he sighed softly, she kissed him again, moving back and forth over his chest. She slid her hands over him, marveling at the muscle definition that appeared in response to his increased breathing and her tender caresses. Her hands slid slower and lower, her kisses following in their wake.

Daryl clasped her head in his hands, trying to bring her up to kiss him. Cydney resisted, exploring farther beneath the covers. She found him and nestled closer to stroke the wondrous fusion of silk and steel. Daryl moved his hips slowly, drawing himself in and out of her searching fingers. Gaining confidence and control, Cydney carefully tightened, increasing the pressure and pleasure he experienced at her touch. She heard him emit a low moan. With an impish grin, she peaked out from the covers.

"Is that a cry of surrender? Do you want me to stop?"

He could only look at her, his eyes blazing. He tried to speak, and wound up biting his lip instead. His head fell back against the pillow. Cydney laughed out loud and ducked back under the covers. Last night, she was the one who had been speechless. He had touched her in ways and in places that she never knew could withstand so much pleasure. Before she'd drifted off to sleep, she'd promised that someday, she would return the favor. It seemed that this was her chance. He'd relinquished himself completely to her touch. She took full advantage of the fact that he was willing to let her explore without inhibitions. She moved lower so that even with his arms fully outstretched, he could barely grasp her shoulders.

In an act of total commitment to his pleasure, Cydney knelt

before him and took him into her mouth. She had done so with doubts and questions about how he would respond to her gift to him. Maybe he would be offended by her presumption. Maybe this was too intimate, too intrusive of his personal space. Maybe this act went against everything a refined Burke-Carter would consider proper in a future wife. A mistress or a casual affair, maybe. But the Burke-Carters were supposed to be beyond reproach. Maybe now he would consider her too daring, too promiscuous. She felt him quiver, then clench, then hold perfectly still. His hand rested on the top of her head. After a moment, she felt him subtly apply pressure. No words were necessary. A single touch erased all of the doubts.

She resumed her caresses; her lips smoothed over his entire taunt, throbbing, expanse of skin—from his waist, to his quivering, inner thighs.

"Cydney!" Daryl cried out, entwining his fingers through the dark, tangled mass of her hair. He was torn between allowing her to continue the sweet, torture of her probing tongue or ending it all with a brief, but explosive union. She ignored him, increasing the depth and tempo. Daryl submitted helplessly, hopelessly, caught in a spiral of everwidening intensity. Finally, unable to withstand her teasing, Daryl swore, then cried out, "Enough!"

In silent desperation, he threw his leg over her, then rolled Cydney over onto her back. She pressed her hands against his shoulders, pushing back against the intention she saw reflected in his dark eyes. Somewhere in the back of her mind, she wondered why she would resist now. She had welcomed, even goaded him to this ferocity.

"No! No you don't," Daryl denied her the opportunity to stop him now. Pinning her to the bed, he planted his hands on her hips then drove himself deeply into her. Cydney gasped aloud, wanting, yet not expecting the intensity of feeling from his forceful entrance.

"Daryl, wait! We didn't . . ." she began, vaguely remembering the condoms they'd left by the side of the bed.

He didn't pull away, but instead plunged deeper. He withdrew, then came to her again. Cydney arched toward him, whether trying to dislodge him or encourage him . . . she wasn't sure which. She only knew heat, and motion, and release—primal and overpowering. She met him again and again, with equal ferocity.

"Cydney!" Daryl suddenly whispered hoarsely into her ear. "Sweetheart, I can't hold back. I won't . . . I want to be in you. Please, let me. Let me stay!"

"And what if we make a baby?"

"Then we make a miracle," he said, pausing briefly to search her face for permission and ultimate acceptance.

Cydney touched her hand to his cheek. "Give me your miracle, Daryl."

Cydney yawned and stretched, feeling calm and relaxed. She glanced over at Daryl and found him staring at her, and smiling.

"What is it?" she asked, feeling slightly self-conscious.

"You know you snore when you sleep?"

"I do not!" she exclaimed.

"Yes, you do. But it's cute."

"What's so cute about sounding like pig?"

"Not like a pig," he said, kissing her on the nose. "Like a cat. You snore with a soft, little, mewling kind of a noise."

"Good grief. Now I am embarrassed!"

"Why?"

"I'm afraid to ask what else I do in my sleep."

"When you're dreaming, you reach out and touch me," Daryl told her.

"I touch you?" she repeated.

"In all the best places," he said, raising his eyebrows at her à la Groucho Marx. "It lets me know what you're thinking just before you go to sleep," he said.

"And it doesn't bother you?"

"As long as it's me that's making you dream those dreams," he said, kissing her passionately and possessively.

When he pulled away, Cydney said seriously, "I just don't want us to . . ."

"To what?"

"Burn too fast," she finished. "I need a slow, steady flame—one that I can count on."

"I'll be here for you, Cydney," Daryl said, taking her hand in his. "I'll always be here . . ."

"What's he doing here?" Cydney said, as soon as she and Daryl pulled into the MegnaTronics parking lot to retrieve her car.

"Who?"

"Mike," Cydney responded, pointing to his car. "Why on earth would he be here on a Saturday morning?"

"Afternoon," Daryl corrected, then leaned over to plant a kiss on her cheek. "We spent most of the morning—"

"I know how we spent the morning," Cydney interrupted him. "The same way we spent last night."

"The same way we'd spend the rest of the day if I had my say."

"Ummm. As tempting as the idea sounds, sooner or later I've got to get the day started."

"I know, I know," Daryl heaved a mock sigh. "And that means picking up your car."

"It's right over there," Cydney pointed out for him. "You don't think he's here to clean out his office, do you?"

"I don't know why he should. He agreed he'd stay on for six months."

"Do you think we ought to go up and see him . . . just to see if he's okay?"

"Maybe he wants privacy."

"Or maybe he's wallowing in a little self-pity. I wouldn't feel right not checking on him. Besides, if he saw my car parked here like I saw his, he'll probably wonder why I haven't come by to see him."

"Come on then," Daryl said, smiling despite the prick of jealousy that he felt. What made her want to share precious time with Mike instead of rushing back to her house where they could spend a few more moments together in privacy and passion? He took her hand and pulled her toward the office building.

Almost as if she'd read his thoughts, Cydney turned to Daryl and said, "I promise, we won't be long."

He flashed her a guilty smile. "Mike is your friend. Take all of the time you need. I'm sure there's something I could be catching up on in my office. Just swing by when you're ready to go."

She kissed him once more before entering the building, and withdrew her hand from his. Even though it was a Saturday, and even though she was dressed casually in jeans and a T-shirt, she still felt a strange sense of obligation to maintain office decorum. She cared for Daryl deeply, but as much as she hated to admit it, she cared more for what her employees thought of her. They could infer anything they wanted to; but she wasn't going to give them the ammunition to take potshots at her.

The guard stationed at the after hours security desk glanced up briefly. Recognizing them as occupants of the building, he pulled out a book to allow them to sign in under their company name.

"Busy day for MegnaTronics," he said simply, then turned back to his surveillance monitors.

The moment they stepped into the elevator, Daryl quickly wrapped his arms around her and drew her toward him.

"Will you cut that out! They probably have security cameras in here, too!" Cydney struggled to pull away, but only half-heartedly so.

"And you don't think there are cameras all over this building? Including my office?" He nibbled on her ear.

"Oh no! Don't tell me that!" Cydney groaned, twisting around to face him.

"They probably have every single thing we've said and done on tape!"

"Daryl!" Cydney squawked.

He raised his eyebrows wickedly at her. "What a show, huh?"

"This isn't funny," she chastised him. Cydney stepped away as the doors opened.

"Maybe next time we ought to charge admission," he suggested.

"Has anybody ever told you that you've got a sadistic streak?"

"A mile wide," he said promptly.

"Then I'll be sure to stay at least two miles away from it," Cydney retorted.

The front office was dark and locked. Daryl fished in his pocket for his keys just as the side door opened and Mike rushed out. He stopped short when he caught sight of the two of them.

"Daryl! Cydney, what are you doing here?" He glanced behind him, and shut the door before they approached him.

"We came to see what you were up to," Cydney said, with forced lightness.

"Up to? What do mean up to?"

"I don't mean anything. We saw your car in the parking lot and . . . that is, we . . . and . . . Mike, are you all right?" Cydney finally ended, reaching a hand out to him.

"I'm fine. Fine. Why wouldn't I be all right?" Mike said, Daryl and Cydney exchanged glances.

"She thought you might be trying to clean out your desk, Mike," Daryl said softly. "She didn't want you to do it alone."

"Why?" Mike demanded. His belligerent tone took Cydney by surprise. She moved closer to him. "No matter what else I might have been to you through the years, Mike, I've always been your friend. I'm your friend, Mike. I know how much MegnaTronics meant to you. I know how hard you worked to build it. Just because you're ready to go off and do something else doesn't mean you stop caring about the company. Maybe you needed a little private time to say goodbye. But I'm not going to let you say goodbye all alone. You stood by me, and now I'm standing by you."

"You're right, Cyd. I'm sorry if I came off sounding like a jerk." He cleared his throat. "I did come up to . . . to take care of a few, last minute things. But I couldn't do it. I just couldn't make myself say this was the end. So, now I'm cutting out of here. What are you guys doing here?''

"I came to pick up my car. I left it overnight after the open house.''

Mike raised his eyebrows, but he didn't comment on why Daryl would be the one escorting her to her car. Cydney was grateful for his obvious display of discretion.

"I've got a few things to take care of, too, Cydney,'' Daryl said. "If you and Mike want to go somewhere, have some lunch or something, I'll call you later.''

"How about it, Mike? Feel like grabbing a bite to eat?''

"When have you ever known me to turn down a free meal?''

"Who said anything about free?'' Cydney teased. She gestured toward the elevator. "Come on then.''

"The downstairs deli?''

"I'm treating. You sure you don't want something more exotic? You can get deli any time.''

"Not after next week.''

"Next week? I thought you were staying for at least six months.''

"Well, I've changed my mind.''

"Mike, what is going on?'' Cydney demanded. As she stepped into the elevator and stabbed the button indicating the lobby level, she said, "It's bad enough you sold the company. Now you're not even going to hang around to see if Megna-Tronics stays afloat.''

"That doesn't sound like you have too much confidence in your new boyfriend's abilities, Cydney.''

Cydney blushed. "That's not what I meant. Anyway, we're not talking about Daryl. We'll talking about you. Why are you in such a hurry to leave?''

"You tell me, Cyd. What's the point of hanging around? What good am I doing here?''

"This is your company!''

"Not any more,'' Mike countered tightly. "It's Daryl Burke-Carter's, for all it's worth. He wanted it, and now he's got it.''

"Because you gave it to him. You didn't fight to keep it.''

Mike shrugged helplessly.

"And now you've got regrets?" Cydney pressed.

"There's nothing I can do about it now. Every 'i' is dotted. Every 't' is crossed. Signed, sealed, and delivered."

"I don't understand you, Mike."

"I'm not asking you to . . . not yet," Mike said mysteriously. When Cydney turned a confused gaze to him, Mike simply grinned at her. The elevator doors opened, and he gestured grandly. "Come on. I'm feeling pretty chipper now. I'll even treat."

"Who are you, and what have you done with my old boss?" Cydney murmured as the elevator doors closed behind her.

Daryl closed the office door behind him and settled into the supple comfort of his leather chair. He propped his feet on his desk, and picked up a stack of labeled folders. He was reorganizing them in order of priority when he came to an unlabeled folder.

"What's this?" he muttered aloud. Then he laughed out loud, remembering the folder that Cydney had brought to him as an excuse to get to into his office. She certainly had gotten to him! Within seconds, she had turned him from business mogul to beggar—shamelessly pleading for her touch. In that same afternoon, she'd reduced him to total bewilderment when she had calmly walked out of his life.

Absently, Daryl rubbed the edges of the folder. He'd tried to calmly accept the fact that she didn't want him. But he couldn't. The facts just didn't ring true. How could she say she didn't want him when everything—from her eyes to her touch told him otherwise.

Daryl dragged himself away from that train of thought with a terse shake of his head. He didn't have to dwell on that now. That dark moment in his life was all over. Cydney had agreed to marry him. They could spend the rest of their lives together. He tapped the folder against the desk and grinned. Next time, he would bring the folder and . . .

A piece of paper fluttered from the open end of the folder and onto the floor, abruptly ending the thoughts that, he knew, would just distract him from work anyway. Curiosity gripped him again. The unmarked folder Cydney had brought to him hadn't held any paper like this. He picked it up, running his fingers down the list as he scanned the contents.

"What the—?" Daryl muttered. At first glance, Daryl thought he might have stumbled across one of Dorothy Pinzer's inventory lists. The items on the paper read like the kinds of items that MegnaTronics would normally keep in stock— software and memory upgrades, office equipment, subscriptions to trade magazines. Beside each item was the serial number and the cost of each item. Daryl started to search for the file where the lists belonged. He paused, scanning the list again.

"No!" he suddenly shook his head. "No way. This can't be right!"

He read the list again, carefully, checking each item. "Three hundred dollars for a file cabinet?"

No wonder the company was going broke before he took over. How could the company afford such extravagance? MegnaTronics might have been able to pass some of the expense on to their clients. With a little "padding" of some of the expenses agreed upon by company and client, MegnaTronics might have been able to recoup some of the costs of operating; but not nearly enough to justify the purchase of a three hundred dollar file cabinet.

He snorted in disbelief. "Hell, for three hundred dollars, I'll build a cabinet and keep the money in our own pockets."

Daryl read on. "Five hundred dollars worth of magazine subscriptions. Two thousand in memory upgrades. You could buy a brand new unit for that price. What is going on here?!"

He would have never approved a ridiculously inflated price like that. Did Mike? He checked the supposed dates of the purchases. They fell within the time frame he would have signed off on the purchases to approve them.

He wracked his memory. Could he have been so wrapped up in Cydney that he wasn't paying attention to what he was signing. No! He couldn't accept that. He wouldn't. If these purchases were approved, it wasn't by him. If he didn't do it, then who did? He'd have to find the original files. The purchase orders would be there. Someone had to sign them. Someone had to take responsibility for those deliveries, because he certainly wasn't.

"Mr. Burke-Carter?"

A voice hailed him from the hallway.

"In here," Daryl called out, sliding the paper back into the manila folder.

The building security guard opened the door, followed by a uniformed officer.

"Is there a problem?" Daryl asked, not liking the look on the officer's face.

"Would you step away from the desk, please, sir. Hands above your head."

"What's going on here?"

"Step away from the desk, sir," the officer repeated, and briefly passed his hand over his holstered gun to emphasize his point.

"Don't let him touch anything," Daryl heard someone call from the hall. A moment later, Debra Colton stepped through. She flashed her identification to the security guard and the police officer.

"What are you doing here?" Daryl demanded.

"We got a call that someone had broken into the Megna-Tronics office," the police officer informed him.

"This is my office," Daryl said tightly. "I have a key."

"I'll need that key to take into evidence." The officer held out his hand.

"This is my key, my office. I have a right to be here. You said there was a break in? We have a security system. Did the alarms go off?"

"No, sir," the security guard said. "Everything was quiet."

"So what makes you think there was a break in?"

"I told you; we had an anonymous call."

"An anonymous call?" Daryl echoed. He turned to Debra. "And what about you? Were you called, too?"

"Someone called and said that I'd find the match to this . . ." She held up a piece of paper. From what Daryl could tell, it looked similar to the one he had just been reading.

"And what is that?"

"A requisition list."

"And?" he prompted. "What's so illegal about that?"

"Nothing in itself," she replied calmly. "But if the revenue you made from passing on costs to your clients doesn't match what you've reported to the government, then we've got a problem."

Daryl felt a tight knot of apprehension squeeze his guts.

"If you wanted to see my records, all you had to do was ask. You don't have to go through this elaborate . . ."

"I tried to talk to you, Mr. Burke-Carter," Debra Colton cut him off. "You've made a bad habit of ducking me. Now we'll talk . . . my way, on my sweet time."

"Why the police? Did you have to get them involved?"

"I didn't call them."

"Who called you?"

"I told you, I don't know," Debra said impatiently. "If you've finished grilling me, I want some answers now."

"Ask away."

"Not from you, from your files."

"You're not touching my files."

"I've got a search warrant," she said, pulling out another piece of paper.

"Convenient," he said snidely, glancing at the security guard and police officer. He reached for his own manila folder and passed it to her.

"Here, Ms. Colton, I'll save you the trouble of tearing up my office. I think you'll need this."

"What is this?"

"The match to that," he said, indicating the requisition list she held in her hands.

She took it from him, read just a few lines, then nodded at the police officer.

"Take him."

"What?! You can't arrest me? On what charges?" Daryl exploded.

"Tax fraud and/or evasion for starters, Mr. Burke-Carter."

"Aren't you out of your league, Ms. Colton? I thought that was for the IRS to determine."

"Don't worry, Mr. Burke-Carter. There'll be plenty of time to get my friends at the Internal Revenue Service in when you're formerly charged."

"So, you're not charging me with anything?"

"Not yet. We're just taking you down to answer a few questions. If you answer them to my satisfaction, then you're free to go. If not, then, as I said before, we've got a problem."

"This is absolutely ridiculous! I haven't done anything wrong!" Daryl started to back away. "Don't you see, Ms. Colton? It's all too neat, too orchestrated. There's evidence here for your trumped up charges because someone put it here for you to find."

"Have you ever heard of where there's smoke there's fire?" Debra Colton asked.

"Have you ever heard of stupid is as stupid does?" Daryl retorted.

"A fool and his money are soon parted," Debra shot back. "Make sure you read him his rights, Officer. I don't want any slip ups. If he's guilty, I want him in jail to stay!"

"You're making a mistake," Daryl protested. He was still protesting as the officer read him his rights and escorted him out of the building.

Through the glass doors of the lobby deli, Cydney watched as Daryl was ushered into the back of the squad car.

"Daryl?" she whispered uncertainly. The man she saw being lead out looked like Daryl from behind. He had the same clothes. But this man was handcuffed. Her Daryl wouldn't have reason to be arrested. Not her Daryl!

"Daryl!" she called out then, standing abruptly, though she knew he couldn't hear her. Her half-eaten lunch scattered on the floor.

"Mike, look!" Cydney barely had the words out of her mouth before she pushed through the doors and dashed outside. Mike was directly behind her.

"Was that Burke-Carter?" Mike asked as the squad car pulled out of the parking lot.

"Yes! Yes, it was. What are they doing to him? Where are they taking him? Why are they taking him away like he was some kind of criminal?"

"I couldn't say," Mike answered.

"Come on then. Let's follow them."

"Cydney, you can't follow a squad car!" Mike protested.

"Why not?!" she demanded.

"You just can't." Mike shrugged.

"Don't tell me about can't. I'll tell *you* about can't. They can't take him away like that."

"If he's guilty, they can."

"Guilty? Guilty of what? Mike, do you know what's going on?"

"Cydney, why don't you go back home? He'll call you when he can."

"I won't leave him like this, Mike."

"I don't think you have a choice."

"Mike . . ."

"Go home, Cydney," Mike insisted. "If he can, he'll call you. I know he will. And then everything will be straightened out. You'll see. Everything will work out just fine."

Cydney shook her head. The beginnings of frustrated, confused tears stung her eyes.

"I don't understand," she whispered.

"Go home," Mike said again, turned, and walked away from her.

Cydney watched him walk away in stunned silence. She felt disoriented, confused, and as the seconds ticked by—angry. The more she thought about it, the more Mike's friendly advice sounded like a dismissal. How could he stand there and blindly mouth platitudes to her when the police had just taken Daryl away? Forget all of the personal reasons why she was upset. Why wasn't Mike more concerned? After all, didn't he just sell his business to Daryl? The man he'd entrusted with the livelihoods of his friends and coworkers was taken away like a common criminal. Why? What had he done? What had been his crime?

"Nothing!" Cydney said aloud. "He couldn't have! Michael Megna, you get your buns back here!" She shouted out his name, not caring who heard her or what they thought about her outburst.

Mike spun around.

"I mean it," Cydney said, her voice threatening bodily harm. "Get over here right now."

Mike walked back to her.

"I'm not going to run back and wait for someone to throw me some tidbits of information. You know that isn't my style. And it didn't use to be yours, Mike. If you care anything at all about MegnaTronics or Daryl, then you'll get in this car with me or you'll follow me to the police station."

"Cydney, you don't even know where they're taking him."

"Do you?" she demanded.

Mike hesitated, then replied, "No."

"Why don't I believe you, Mike?" Cydney frowned. Call it intuition, or familiarity with Mike's expressions and modes of dissembling, but he took a fraction too long to answer her. "What aren't you telling me?"

"Since when did you get a suspicious mind, Cyd?"

"I've always had one. You know that."

"Oh, yeah. I almost forgot."

"Are you going to tell me where they're taking him or not?"

"I can't be certain, Cydney."

"Just tell me what you know!" she said in exasperation.

"Cydney, Daryl's under investigation by the SEC."

"The SEC? The Securities and Exchange Commission? Why? What do they think he's done?"

"I'm not certain."

"Then how do you know . . ."

"An investigator was at the open house. Her name is D.J. Colton. She's been nosing around, asking questions, trying to get me to point to anything that said that Daryl got Megna-Tronics through unfair means."

"And what did you tell her?"

"What could I tell her? I had to tell her the truth."

"And that was?" Cydney prompted impatiently.

"As far as I know, Daryl Burke-Carter was nothing but open, honest, and fair in his dealings with me."

"Then why is the SEC after him?"

"I can't say."

"Can't say or won't say, Mike?"

"There you go with that suspicious mind again, Cydney. It's just an expression. Am I going to have to start watching everything I say around you now?" He pantomimed the motion of locking his lips and throwing away the key.

"This isn't funny, Mike. You tell me what you know, or so help me—" Cydney took a menacing step toward Mike and grabbed his shirt with both hands. She pulled him within inches of her face.

"I know . . . I know . . . You're worried about Daryl. I understand that."

"Don't patronize, Mike!"

"I'm not trying to. I'm just trying get through this unscathed."

"Oh, Mike . . ." Cydney let her hands drop, feeling completely deflated. "What are we going to do?"

"We can't do anything until we hear from Daryl. Would it make you feel any better if I came home with you? Do you want me to sit by the phone with you?"

"No. I don't need a baby sitter."

"You sure you don't want the company?"

"I'm sure." She gave a wan smile. "Thanks for offering, anyway. I'd better be getting home." Cydney wanted to make it back before Cameron made it back from Courtney's. She wanted time to compose herself. She didn't want her son to see her like this—wild and almost completely unstrung by the fact that Daryl had been falsely and unjustly accused. It was unjust, wasn't it?

XIII

"It wasn't fair! It just wasn't fair! I had him. I had him and I let him sleaze his way out of it!"

Cameron threw himself on the couch and looked to Cydney for sympathy. She sat in her favorite armchair, with her legs drawn up under her. She stared at the telephone intently, as if expecting at any moment that it would jump up and do tricks for her.

"Oscar promised he would let me have that new video game cartridge and when I tried to take it away from him, he went screaming to Aunt Courtney that I was trying to take his stuff. And then Aunt Courtney starts ragging on me about respecting other people's property. I should have just taken the cartridge and not said anything to anyone about it."

"Uh-huh."

"Mom?" Cameron looked up at Cydney in surprise. Since when would she approve of him taking things without permission? "Yo! Earth to Mom!" He waved his hands in front of her. "Mom, are you listening to me?"

"Uh-huh," she responded automatically again. Cameron snorted in disbelief and said to goad her, "I just wanted to let you know that I was quitting school and moving out. I'm going to move in with my new girlfriend.''

"Okay.''

"She's twenty-two, and dances nude at a bar.''

"That's fine.''

"She has a tattoo on her bottom that says 'Dancers do it in the dark.' She wants me to pierce my navel and my tongue.''

"Umm-hmm.'' Cydney didn't take her eyes off of the phone.

"What is it with you and that phone?!'' Cameron said loudly.

"What?'' Cydney looked up, blinking at her son. "What did you say?''

"What's the matter, Mom?''

"Nothing, Cam. I'm just waiting for a phone call.''

"From Mr. Burke-Carter?''

"Yeah.''

"It must be something totally heavy,'' Cameron mused.

"What makes you say that?'' Cydney looked up at him, marveling at how perceptive her son could be. Then Cameron burst out laughing, wondering how his mom could sometimes be so clueless.

"What's so funny?''

"Nothing, Mom. I'm going up to my room to let you have some privacy for when that phone call does come.''

"You don't have to run off, Cam.''

"You're just going to send me away when the call does come. I might as well start enjoying something now.''

Cydney held her arms out to her son. "Come here, boy.''

"Aw, man!'' Cameron could feel a hug coming on. "You're not going to smother me with kisses again, are you?''

"You'd better believe it!'' She laughed, drawing him close for a bear hug. Cameron groaned and made faces behind his mother's back; but on the inside, he felt warm—almost mushy.

"See you later, Mom.''

"Keep the music down,'' she responded. "Oh, and Cameron?''

"Yeah?''

She raised that scolding eyebrow at him.

"I mean, yes ma'am . . .''

"If you ever take anything without permission, I'll have to skin you alive. You know that, don't you?"

Cameron nodded and grinned. His mom may have seemed inattentive, but there was that inner "mom" that never missed a thing.

Cydney didn't want to get up from the chair. She didn't want to miss Daryl's phone call. But she couldn't just sit there. This was Sunday afternoon. Before she knew it, it would be Monday. Another work week would start. There was laundry to wash and put away, meetings to prepare for, school work to check. As many items as she could think of she had to do, she could think of just as many reasons why she shouldn't do them— why she shouldn't move.

"Where are you?" she whispered, and experienced a brief moment of déjà vu. It was only because she'd murmured that same phrase at least a hundred times an hour since she went home to wait for Daryl's call.

By six o'clock that evening, when he still hadn't called her, Cydney pulled her anxious, and somewhat stiff frame from the chair and ambled toward the kitchen. Cameron would expect dinner soon. Though he hadn't said so, she knew that he was hungry. She looked around her at the open wrappers left on the counters and in the trash. Maybe she could sit by the telephone a little while longer. By the look of the remains in the kitchen, he couldn't be too hungry. He'd left her alone for most of the afternoon—content to munch on chips, cookies, and anything else that wasn't bolted down in the refrigerator.

No . . . no more waiting. Her son needed her. If Daryl had needed her, he would have called her by now. The little voice inside of her that hinted that Daryl didn't need her really bothered her. To squash her anguish, she made herself focus on Cameron's needs. She pulled out fresh green vegetables, some frozen meat patties that she'd cooked earlier in the week, several potatoes, and a tin of biscuits.

By six forty-five, the vegetables were steaming, the meat patties were sizzling softly in their own juices, and the potatoes were whipped up into huge, fluffy mounds. The biscuits were high and golden brown and brushed lightly with a coating of real butter. She felt guilty for having neglected Cameron for so long. She didn't have the heart to cheat him with the no-salt, no-fat, low-cholesterol (and no taste) bargain margarine.

"Cameron!" she stuck her head out of the kitchen door and shouted. "Wash up, and come down to supper."

She pulled plates from the cupboard. When the door bell rang, she nearly dropped them from sheer nervousness.

"I've got it!" she called up to Cameron, trying to hurry to the door without looking like she was hurrying.

Cameron poked his head over the railing from upstairs and muttered, "I'd be safer getting in front of a speeding eighteen wheeler with no brakes than getting in front of you and that door."

Cydney flung the door open, knowing in her heart who it was without having to peer through the viewer.

Standing in her doorway, managing to look pleased, exhausted, and furious at the same time was Daryl.

"Daryl!" Cydney threw her arms around his neck.

He didn't speak. He just held her, and allowed the strength of his embrace to communicate all of the emotions he could not voice.

"Are you all right?" she whispered.

He nodded and started hesitantly. "I know you've got a million questions."

Cydney laid her finger gently across his lips. "They can wait," she said, and smiled a little to herself. She'd waited all afternoon. She could wait a little while longer. The look he gave her in response was full of gratitude.

"Something smells good." Daryl sniffed appreciatively. "Invite me to dinner."

"You know you have a standing invitation. It's not fancy, but . . ."

"You'll get no complaints here."

Cameron trudged down the stairs, nodding wordlessly in greeting to Daryl.

"Finish setting the table for me, will you, Cam?" Cydney indicated the dishes and silverware she'd left in the kitchen.

"Yes'm," he mumbled.

"Need a hand, Cameron?" Daryl offered.

Cameron's eyebrows nearly raised through the roof.

"You don't have to do that, Daryl," Cydney said. Then in a low voice. "You look exhausted."

"Let the man lend a hand if he wants to, Mom." Cameron grabbed Daryl by the elbow.

"It's all right," Daryl assured her. "I need to do something normal . . . to get the taste of this afternoon's fiasco out of my mouth."

Cydney opened her mouth to ask him about it, then shut it with an audible click. She promised she wouldn't grill him. Not now. Not in front of Cameron.

"You sit down." Daryl grasped her shoulders and steered her back toward the couch. "We'll handle things from here."

"She's been sitting down all afternoon—waiting by the phone," Cameron said, then cringed when he saw the heated look Cydney flashed him.

"Worried about little ol' me," Daryl teased.

"Just what makes you think I was waiting for you to call?" She tried to sound indignant. "What do you think I am? A silly, lovesick teenager?"

"Oh, *puh-lease!*" Cameron groaned aloud as he pushed the door open to the kitchen.

Cydney glared daggers as Daryl's laughter filtered back from the kitchen. He took the plates and silverware from Cameron.

"You know she doesn't really mean that, don'tcha, Mr. Burke-Carter. You know she really likes you, don't cha?" Cameron insisted.

"I know," Daryl said, without a hint of boasting. "I like her, too."

"Yeah, I know. Say, Mr. Burke-Carter."

"Yeah?"

"I gotta' baseball game this Wednesday afternoon. Are you gonna' let Mom off early so she can come to see me play? It's a pretty important game. If we beat this team, we're on our way to being division champs.''

"I'll let her go on one condition.''

"That you can come, too,'' Cameron added promptly.

"How did you know I was going to say that?''

"Oh, *puh-lease!*'' Cameron repeated. He set out serving dishes and tall glasses for the iced tea. On his way to the dining room, Cameron called out, "Hey, Mom! Mr. Burke-Carter said you can come to my game on Wednesday. He's coming, too.''

"That was generous of him,'' Cydney responded. "Are you *sure* you'll be able to make it, Daryl?'' Cydney offered without asking about what had happened to him that afternoon.

"We'll be there,'' Daryl said.

Cameron transferred the entrees to individual serving dishes, then called out. "Come get it while the gettin's good.''

Daryl held the chair out for Cydney as she moved toward the table. Cydney blushed, both liking the attention and wondering what Cameron was making of all of this. If he noticed, he didn't give any indication of it. Cydney supposed her son's stomach was doing all of his thinking for him. When he reached for a slice of bread, she tapped his hands.

"Put that back! You know better than that. Blessing first.''

"I'll say grace. You take too long, Mom, and I'm starving!'' Cameron volunteered.

Cydney felt Daryl's warm, strong hand close around hers. He reached out to Cameron, who after a moment's hesitation, took it. With a slight shrug and a grin, Cameron told Daryl that he would accept this new man in his mother's life—into their tight, exclusive circle of family. If the way Daryl was looking at his mom was any indication of his desire to stay, Cameron knew that Daryl wouldn't leave him alone until he'd become a permanent fixture at their family table.

Cameron quickly blessed the food, then looked up at Cydney for approval. She was glowering at him for his cursory prayer, but signaled acceptance of it by murmuring softly, "Amen.''

* * *

After supper, Cydney indicated to Daryl to take a seat on the couch while she made sure that Cameron made preparations for bed.

"Upstairs, young man." She pointed. "Hit the shower."

"I took a bath last night," Cameron complained.

"And you're taking another one tonight. Make sure you use soap this time," she added.

"Aw, man!" Cameron groaned—not so much for being caught cheating on his baths, but for having his mom call it to the attention of Mr. Burke-Carter.

"I'll be up in a few minutes to kiss you good night," she said.

"You don't have to," Cameron said quickly. If she offered to tuck him in, too, as she sometimes did, he would die of embarrassment. Cydney saw her son throw an embarrassed glance at Daryl.

"All right then," she agreed, feeling a pang of bittersweet nostalgia. Her baby boy wasn't a baby anymore. She had to stop thinking of him as her "little Cam."

Cameron darted upstairs, relieved that his mom knew enough not to suggest, even in fun, that she should lay out his pajamas and read him a bed time story. She watched him go, then turned to Daryl with a soft smile.

"What's the matter, Cydney? Is your baby growing up too fast for you?"

"Is it that obvious?"

"Screaming," Daryl said, his dark eyes twinkling at her. "You know what the cure for that is, don't you?"

"No, tell me," Cydney responded, though she could tell by the look on his face where this conversation was going.

He held his hand out to her, drawing her down next to him on the couch.

"We'll just have to have at least three more babies," he said, nuzzling her neck.

"Three!" Cydney shifted uncomfortably. She glanced in the direction Cameron had gone.

Daryl understood the look perfectly. He moved to put more space between them. Cydney then felt a pang of guilt. He'd been through too much today to have to wrestle for her attention. She took one last look toward the stairs, then leaned over to rest her head on Daryl's shoulder. After a moment, he closed his arm around her. Cydney sighed, snuggling closer to him.

For a long time, neither spoke. Finally, the curiosity that she had squashed came bubbling back to the surface.

"Daryl," she began, then hesitated. What could she say to him? Was there any easy way of asking someone why they were hauled away in a squad car?

"MegnaTronics," Daryl responded, know what Cydney was struggling to ask.

"What about it?"

"There are rumors that I took the company away from Mike."

"What do you mean took? As in stole? As in forced him to sell against his will?"

"Something like that," Daryl sighed. "And that's not all. They think I've been misrepresenting the companies assets and liabilities."

"I don't understand."

"Cydney, what do you know about the company's acquisition procedures?"

"A little," she said with a shrug. "I know when we sign a new contract with a new client, we project resource needs and have them agree to pay for a portion of it."

"When you and Mike were downstairs eating lunch, I found an inventory list—software, office furniture, standard stuff like that."

"And?"

"Cydney, the projected cost of what we supposedly paid for that stuff was nowhere near standard. Hundreds of dollars for a file cabinet."

"Are you serious?"

"As a heart attack," Daryl snorted. "There was no way I could justify passing that kind of cost on to our clients—not if I wanted to stay in business for very long."

"There has to be some kind of mistake. You'd never approve payment for overpriced office furniture. Besides, the accounting department would scream bloody murder if a bill like that came across their desks. The whole office would know if there was some price gouging going on. And no one has said anything to me, not even in gossip."

"Debra Colton doesn't agree."

"Who's Debra Colton?"

"An SEC investigator."

"SEC?! How did they get involved?"

"I don't know. Somebody's been making phone calls, pointing the finger at me. No sooner had I found that bogus list than they came bursting into the office like storm troopers, demanding to go through all of my files. She had a copy of a 'so-called' legitimate requisition list. When she compared it against the list that I had, she had them arrest me."

"Daryl, no!" Cydney breathed. "Oh, no . . . How did you get them to let you go?"

"They had nothing concrete. Since they had nothing to charge me with, they had to let me go. But that's not the end of it, Cydney. Sweetheart, someone out there is planting false evidence against me. When Debra and her goons find it, they're going to come back. And next time, they're not going to be so quick to let me go. I suppose the little episode this afternoon was supposed to serve as a warning."

"Or an opportunity," Cydney corrected. "She's going to do some digging. Well, so can we. You say that requisition list was planted in your office?"

"It had to be. It was in that folder you brought to me when . . ." he let his voice trail off, grinning foolishly.

Cydney blushed and said, "There couldn't have been too many people in your office from Friday morning to Saturday morning. It shouldn't be too hard to figure out who."

"Just three, Cydney," Daryl said soberly. "You, me and . . ."

"And Mike," she finished for him.

Daryl's jaw tightened.

"You're not thinking that he could have . . ." Cydney began.

"What else am I supposed to think? That you would plant that requisition? You know I'd never suspect you. And I didn't do it. There wasn't time for anyone else to slip into my office and put it there.''

"Daryl, no. Not Mike. He couldn't! Why would he?''

"I don't know. To get the company back, maybe.''

"But he doesn't want it! He sold it to you, Daryl,'' Cydney sputtered.

"You know and I know that we aren't overcharging our clients for nonexistent expenses. But somebody has indicated that we were. Finding that requisition was too coincidental. And then Debra Colton comes in with a similar list of materials. What are the chances of her having the exact same list on the day that I find mine? She told me somebody called her with an anonymous tip.''

"I suppose we could find out if there were any calls made from our office to hers,'' Cydney began.

"That's a start,'' Daryl agreed.

"Were those requisition lists on company letterhead?'' Cydney asked, getting the same "I'm working on a mystery'' look she got the night she helped find the virus on one of their client's computer systems.

"I believe so.''

"Everybody has access to that stock paper,'' she mused. "But maybe that's another way find out if that requisition was done in the office.''

"The lawyer that I've hired has a good team of investigators working for him,'' Daryl said. "They'll find out who swiped that paper to print up that bogus list.''

"They're going to be nosing around the office, asking unpleasant questions.''

"You'll have to forgive me if I upset the normal office routine.'' The stress Daryl felt manifested itself in sarcasm. Cydney didn't take it personally, but she was bothered by the fact that since she and Daryl had decided to pursue their relationship, the company had been plagued with mishaps. Daryl mistook Cydney's frown for injured feelings.

"I'm sorry, sweetheart,'' he said, drawing her closer again. "I guess I'm a little unnerved by all of this.''

"With good reason,'' Cydney responded.

"Cydney . . ." Daryl ventured.

"Umm-hmmm?"

"Can I . . . can I stay tonight?"

Cydney looked up at him as Daryl went on quickly. "I'm not suggesting anything that would embarrass you or make Cameron upset. I'll sleep on the couch by myself, if it makes you feel better. I just want to know I can wake up to you and with you tomorrow."

"Stay with me tonight, Daryl. With us," she amended. "I've accepted your marriage proposal. Cameron has to get used to the sight of you around the house."

"If I keep offering to help him with his chores, I don't think there'll be any problems." Daryl chuckled softly.

"If you do the dishes for him, you'll make a friend for life." She sighed. Both she and Daryl looked up when she heard Cameron move from the bathroom to his room.

"Good night, Mom. Good night, Mr. Burke-Carter!" he called down without pausing.

"Good night, Cam. Sweet dreams, son." Cydney started to rise, but Daryl pulled her back. They heard the door to Cameron's room close. Cydney almost smiled. It seemed that he closed it a little too forcefully to let her know that the coast was clear. He was in his room, and there he would stay until she indicated that it was okay for him to come out.

Slowly, deliberately, Daryl lay down. Cydney hesitated for a moment, then lay down next to him—her back to his chest. He snaked his arms around her waist and pulled her as close as he possibly could.

"I promise I'll behave," he whispered into her ear. "I just want to hold you like this for a while."

She nodded wordlessly, feeling cocooned in his arms. Within a few moments, she felt the deep rise and fall of his chest as he drifted off to sleep. Cydney didn't know how long she lay there, drifting in and out drowsiness and wakefulness, listening to the oddly soothing sounds of his breathing. When she thought she could move without waking Daryl, she slid off of the couch. She padded quickly upstairs to grab a blanket, then detoured to peek in on Cameron. She could hear his radio playing, but there was no light shining from under the door. She opened the door.

"Cam?" she called softly, so she wouldn't wake him if he were asleep. He was in bed, lying on top of the covers. She came in and grasped him by the shoulders. "Wake up, son," she continued in low tones. Cameron mumbled something in his sleep, but didn't fully wake.

"Get under the covers, Cam," Cydney directed. She knew that he wouldn't actually remember her late night visit. But he would wake up the next morning and *know* that she'd been there—had looked in on him. With just a simple gesture, he would know that she would continue to think of him, even when someone else competed for her time and her affection.

"I love you, Cameron," she murmured, kissed him, and hoped that love would work its way into his dreams. She turned the music down even more, checked the windows, then closed the door behind her. Grabbing the blanket she'd meant for Daryl, she moved downstairs to spread it over him. Just as Cameron had stirred, Daryl sighed softly in his sleep, and clutched the blanket in acknowledgment.

Cydney leaned over Daryl and kissed him lightly on the cheek.

"I love you, Daryl Burke-Carter," she whispered. She started to back away, then on impulse slid under the covers next to him. She fully intended to stay with him all night—even though she was too wound up to sleep. Whatever was going on at MegnaTronics was threatening her love and her career. She'd yearned for both for too long. And now someone, without caring, without feeling, was trying to destroy it all? She wouldn't let it happen. She couldn't. A fierce, overwhelming feeling of protectiveness surged through her. She hugged Daryl tightly, silently vowing that nothing would blemish their happiness. Nothing!

Though he was still deep in sleep, Daryl wrapped his arms around her and drew her to him. She felt his arousal press against her stomach. For a moment, Cydney's protective feeling faded as jealousy moved in. He was still asleep! He couldn't possibly know who he was holding—though his intention was clear enough. Even in sleep, his hands found their way to all of the sensitive areas of her body that aroused her desire even as he aroused her anger. How many other women, she wondered, had he sought out blindly in the middle of the night? Was he so practiced in these late night excursions that he didn't even have to open his eyes to look into the face of the woman he was about to make love to? Cydney started to squirm, trying to maneuver away from him. But as she moved against him, she felt her own desire growing. She pushed aside pride and anger, and clasped her arms around him.

Daryl whispered to her, with one word calming all of her doubts and fears. Softly, on a sigh, "Cydney!"

He knew! Cydney's heart soared. His feelings for her, rooted so firmly in his soul, burst forward to calm her—to claim her. When he came to her, he was still shrouded in sleep. Yet, Cydney could only smile as the love she felt for him wove its way into the fabric of his dreams.

Monday morning Daryl's time was eaten by meeting after meeting. Though he was edgy and distracted, he forced himself to go through the motions of running MegnaTronics. This was his business, damn it! His! And he wouldn't let some government pencil pusher take it away from him without a fight. During one meeting, he almost smiled at his mental bravado.

It was Cydney who had convinced to him to go on, business as usual, when all he wanted to do was spend the week at her home, wrapped in her arms.

"We're not backing away from this, Daryl," she warned him.

"What do you mean 'we'?" he teased her. "It's me they're after."

"Anybody who messes with my man will have to go through me first," she said toughly. Daryl knew she meant every word of it. In the meantime, she would do what she could to gather some facts for the investigator who was scheduled to come later that afternoon. If Daryl could just hold it together, keep his composure until the investigator found something concrete that would clear his reputation.

At one point, on his way to another meeting, he passed Cydney in the corridor. The smile, and the mischievous wink, she gave him did more to soothe his soul than all of the assurances of a hundred investigators or a thousand high-priced lawyers.

"Daryl, do you still have a copy of that bogus invoice?" Cydney asked him in low tones.

Daryl shrugged. "I don't. But I think the investigator who's coming this afternoon will. Why?"

"Just something I want to check," Cydney replied, tapping her cheek with her index finger.

"You have an idea?" Daryl asked hopefully. Cydney had that look—that I'm-not-going-to-let-this-get-the-best-of-me look.

"Nothing concrete. Sorry. I just want to follow up on an idea I've been kicking around in my head."

"I hope your idea pans out. If we don't come up with something soon, the stress from all of this will kick my butt," Daryl said, giving a rueful grin before moving off for his next meeting.

Cydney looked around to see if anyone was watching, then blew him an encouraging kiss before heading for Mike's office. She'd debated all Sunday going to see him. If he was the one trying to hurt Daryl, then she didn't want to tip him off. On the other hand, if he was innocent, her past history with him made her feel she owed him a chance to clear himself, too.

She poked her head in the door. "You got a minute, Mike?"

"For the soon to be new VP? You bet I do. Come on in."

Cydney closed the door firmly behind her. "I want to talk to you about what happened Saturday."

"You mean Daryl's arrest."

She nodded. "They let him go without charging him."

"Well, that's good," Mike sighed and smiled wanly.

"Mike, someone is trying to set him up." Cydney stepped out on a limb.

"How do you know?"

"Too many pieces are fitting together way too neatly. Somebody is setting him up."

"So, uh . . . why are you coming to me, Cyd? What do you expect me to do about it?"

"I want you to help me catch who's doing it."

"I'm no supersleuth, Cyd. And neither are you. If someone is trying to get him, you ought to leave it to the professionals to find out who."

"I can't sit by and let someone hurt him or this company. Can you?"

"If there's nothing I can do, then there's nothing I can do."

"I don't believe in being helpless, Mike," Cydney said tightly.

"So, what are you going to do?"

"Whatever I can."

"You've got a plan?"

"No."

"Have you got any leads?"

"No."

"What have you got?"

"I've got faith," Cydney replied.

"You really love him, don't you?" Mike asked, with a tinge of sadness that made alarm bells of warning ring inside of Cydney.

"Yes, I do."

"Funny, Cyd, I would have never guessed in a million years that that's the kind of man you would fall for. He's nothing like Jason."

"They're more alike than you think," Cydney said with a wry smile. "Believe me. I've made the comparison."

"I suppose you couldn't help yourself," Mike continued. "He is a sexy son of a gun. Rich, powerful, and smart. What's there not to fall for?"

"He's a good man, Mike," Cydney insisted. "He doesn't deserve to be treated like a criminal."

"Are you sure you're not just letting your emotions get in the way?"

"You mean hormones," she corrected. "I'm thinking with a clear head about this, Mike. I've got to help him."

"I still think you should leave this to the professionals, Cydney. Whoever's trying to get him seems like they're playing for keeps. They've called in the government watch dogs. Maybe you should keep out of it before someone starts to look at you too closely."

"Me? I haven't done anything."

"Guilt by association, my dear. It's been known to happen."

"I'm not backing off. Anything I can do to help him, I will."

"Think about this, Cydney. People could get hurt. Namely you."

"Mike, are you trying to tell me something? Was that a threat? Do you know something that you're not telling me? What do you know? Do you know enough to clear Daryl's name? If you know something, you've got to tell me. You can't sit on this!"

"I only know enough to have dumped MegnaTronics and get away as unscathed as I can," Mike said ominously. "Why don't you use that beautiful, brainy head of yours and do the same?"

His tone frightened Cydney more than she cared to admit. But more than frightened, she was furious. She stood up, almost seeming to tower over the seated Mike as she swelled with righteous indignation.

"We're not going to let this happen to MegnaTronics and to us without fighting back, Mike. I just wanted to let you know that. There will be investigators combing every inch of this company. Sooner or later, they're going to find that Daryl's innocent. So help me, Mike, if I find out that you knew something that could have ended this nightmare sooner and you didn't, I'll have your head on a platter!"

"Don't you threaten me, Cydney," Mike warned her.

"No threats," she countered. "A promise."

"I'm your friend, Cydney. I'm the man who gave you this job. Are you taking Daryl's side over mine?"

"I don't want to chose sides, Mike. I just want to get to the bottom of this," she said, pacing the room. She strode to the window to stare out, resting her elbow on the file cabinet next to it.

Mike jumped up from his desk. "Cydney!" he called out sharply.

"What is it?" she spun around, clutching at her pounding heart.

"What are you doing over there?" he demanded.

"What are you talking about? I'm not doing anything." She turned to face him. She could see a muscle working in Mike's cheek, twitching spasmodically.

"What's gotten into you lately, Mike? You've been just plain weird. You're making me wonder if you're not starting to crack up."

"It's the stress, Cyd. Too much stress."

"We're all under a lot of pressure. But you, of all people, have got to hold it together for MegnaTronics. Until this mess is cleared up with Daryl, everyone is going to be looking to you for strength, for guidance."

"Why can't they just leave me alone?!" Mike complained. "I don't want this anymore. That's why I quit. That's why I sold out."

"Like it or not, oh, fearless leader, you're all we've got now," Cydney said, a glimmer of her former teasing showing through.

"I don't like it," Mike grumbled. "I don't like it at all."

"Cydney, I'd like you to meet Albert Lister," Daryl made introductions to the investigator sent by his lawyer's office. "Albert, this is my quality assurance director, Cydney Kelley."

"A pleasure," Albert said, shaking her hand. Cydney took a seat in Daryl's office.

"What have you found out so far?" she asked, wasting no time in getting to the point.

"As you probably already know, the requisition list found in your office, Mr. Burke-Carter, was a forgery."

Cydney glanced at Daryl. For the money his lawyer was

demanding to help clear Daryl, this investigator had better come up with something better than this.

"And since you were able to narrow down the time when that list could have been planted, we're well on our way to discovering how it got here and who planted it."

"How?" Daryl wanted to know.

"Surveillance cameras. This office building is loaded with 'em. They're all hooked into some sort of sophisticated recording device. All we have to do is get a court order to surrender tapes from the past few days, and we've got your man."

Cydney closed her eyes, trying to fight down the sick feeling that had instantly risen to her stomach at the idea of Daryl's office being monitored.

"How often are those tapes reviewed?" Daryl glanced over at her and couldn't help grinning at the look on Cydney's face.

Albert Lister's head swiveled to follow Daryl's gaze. He mistook Cydney's expression for an admission of guilt.

"Maybe we don't have to look so far to find whoever's responsible for planting that paper," he suggested. "What about it, Ms. Kelley? Something you want to say?"

"What are you saying? You think I put those papers in Daryl's office?" Cydney was outraged.

"You can eliminate Cydney from your list of suspects, Mr. Lister," Daryl assured him, choking back laughter. "I think I can provide a perfect alibi for Ms. Kelley's whereabouts over the past few days."

"Then why don't you want those tapes . . ." Albert began trying to read both Daryl's face and Cydney's. He then let out an understanding, "Ohhh . . ."

"I told you the office was probably monitored, Cydney." Daryl shrugged fatalistically.

"Yeah, after the fact," she retorted, crossing her arms across her chest and settling back into her chair. Just when she thought she could walk into Daryl's office without becoming inflamed by the remembrance of the passion they'd shared . . . Now, it seemed as though perfect strangers would be privy to that memory.

"My investigative agency is very discrete, Ms. Kelley," Mr. Lister tried to assure her. "I promise you, we'll use only the parts of the tape that we need to clear Mr. Burke-Carter."

"How soon do you think we can get access to them?" Daryl asked.

"It depends on the judge who signed the search and seizure warrant. There are a lot of other, delicate, right-to-privacy issues the judge will have to consider. But, given the prominence of your family in the community, I don't think it'll take too long to get what we need."

Cydney snapped her fingers as if something had just occurred to her. "Speaking of which, Mr. Lister, you have something I need."

"And what is that, Ms. Kelley?"

"A copy of that requisition list, the fake one. Something about it is nagging me."

"What is it, Cydney?" Daryl asked.

"Something about it seems familiar. If I see it, it may jog my memory."

Albert Lister opened his portfolio and handed her a copy of the list. Daryl waited expectantly while Cydney scanned it.

"Anything?" he asked. Again, the hope in his voice stabbed directly at her heart.

"Not yet. But it'll come to me. Until then, I just hope the surveillance tape will be the answer to our prayers," Cydney sighed.

"Say your prayers, big brother, you don't stand a chance!" Whalen took careful aim, then let the basketball fly from his fingertips to start their regular, Monday night basketball game.

Daryl leaped into the air, knocking the ball away from the rim. He hit it so hard, it flew halfway across the basketball court. Whalen spun around to chase after it, but Daryl had already beat him to it and was taking aim for a shot of his own.

"Man! I see you came to play!" Whalen let out a frustrated breath as the ball sank through the hoop with an audible *swoosh!*

"Three-point line! In your face!" Daryl grinned as the spectators who'd stopped their own game to watch the infamous Burke-Carter brothers let out an appreciative shout.

"Keep shooting like that, and you'll put me out of a job," Whalen complained, dribbling the ball. "I'm supposed to be the basketball star. Remember?" He bounced the ball once, then twice between his legs to show off his fancy footwork— and to gain the attention and respect of the spectators. "You don't see me sitting in your high-rise office, showing you up by making multi-million dollar deals, do you?"

Daryl raised his hands. "I'll try to take it easy on you tonight."

"Don't mind me, big brother. If you've got the juice and need to show me up a little, go on ahead. Blow off some steam. Get it off your chest. Run up and down the court. Pound those boards until even the ball begs for a time out."

Daryl nodded. His brother knew the trouble he was having at MegnaTronics. He'd even tried to give him early warning that it was coming.

"Come on, little brother. Are you going to talk or are you going to shoot some hoops?"

Right now, Daryl didn't want to think about MegnaTronics. He didn't want to be the boss. He didn't want to think about the SEC or padded invoices or taxes. He wanted to be just plain Daryl, out to play and play hard.

Whalen brought the ball inbounds and started to drive toward the goal. Daryl shifted to block him, but in a move almost too fast to follow, Whalen pivoted and spun around him. He leaped into the air, smoothly, gracefully, and let the ball roll from his fingers into the hoop.

"Lucky shot," Daryl snorted. "If you weren't almost seven feet tall, little brother, you'd never be able to shake past me."

"Yack. Yack. Yack! That's the trouble with you baby moguls, all fluff and no stuff."

"I'll show you stuff," Daryl returned as Whalen tossed him the ball. He bounced the ball experimentally, building up momentum. Daryl stared his brother straight in the eye, determination clearly written on his face. Whalen crouched low. "Oh, you think I'm gonna' let you jam the ball on me? You think you're gonna' stuff the ball into the hoop with me standing here? You just try it. You'll get yourself hurt."

"Over or through you, son. Over or through you!" Daryl said, as he started toward Whalen.

On and on the game went. Sometimes Daryl was ahead, sometimes Whalen. Eventually, they stopped keeping score. The point of the game was not to gain the most points, but peace of mind. The fast-paced, competitive game drove out the demons they'd brought to those Monday games. With Daryl, it was the trouble with MegnaTronics. With Whalen, maybe it was a bad practice session. By the time the two brothers fell, exhausted and perspiring on the bleachers, they could almost believe that this day had been the best one in their lives.

"Ready to hit the showers?" Whalen asked, mopping his brow.

"Calling it quits?"

"Not that I'm tired or anything. I just don't want to keep Shana waiting. Don't you want to get back to Cydney?"

Daryl felt a pang of conscience. He hadn't thought of her in well over an hour. Though she hadn't said so to him, that session with the private investigator really shook her. The fact that someone might be looking at those tapes of her and Daryl making love in his office really bothered her. He shouldn't have teased her about that. He shouldn't have laughed at her. The first thing, right out of the showers, he'd head for a florist, buy her the biggest, most obnoxious bouquet of flowers, take them over to her and apologize.

"You've got that goofy look on your face," Whalen teased. "You're thinking about her now, aren't you?"

"I'm going to marry her, Whalen," Daryl said softly.

"Tell me something I don't know. Have you told Dad yet? Have you set a date?"

"Nope. But the sooner the better. As soon as all of this is over . . ."

"How's she taking it?"

"She's a rock," Daryl said incredulously. "I don't know how one woman can be so strong. Sometimes, when all I want to do is say, to hell with it . . . sell the company and move on, she makes me hang in there.''

"I knew she was the one for you the first time I saw her.''

"No you didn't, you dog! You tried to put the moves on her! Try that again after we're married, and I'll have to give you a worse butt-stomping than I gave you tonight out on the basketball court.''

"Man, you've got to be out of your mind. I creamed you out there tonight!''

"In your dreams,'' Daryl countered. They pulled themselves up from the bleachers. "Just one way to settle this.''

"We play to twenty.'' Whalen followed his brother back onto the court.

Three games later, the Burke-Carter brothers agreed to call it quits.

"Shower!'' Whalen gasped, sucking for air.

"Sauna,'' Daryl countered.

"See you next Monday?''

"Count on it.''

Daryl clapped his brother on the back; then in an uncharacteristic display of affection, hugged him.

"It's gonna be all right, Darry,'' Whalen promised him. "Go on, hit the sauna. Then call your woman.''

"Say hello to Shana for me.'' Daryl waved then headed for the sauna room. He stripped down, wrapped a towel around his waist, and settled against the stone bench to relax. Because of the lateness of the hour, he was alone in the steam room. He sighed in pleasure. He didn't feel like making small talk anyway. Part of him wished he'd brought his cellular phone into the sauna with him. He did feel like talking to Cydney. He wanted to hear her voice. He wanted to hear her say how much she loved him, needed him, and believed in him.

This deal with MegnaTronics had shaken his confidence. He was starting to doubt whether he still had the edge, the skills to take a company, on the verge of collapse as this one had been, and make it pay off for everyone. Whoever had planted that evidence against him had also planted the seeds of self-doubt that were slowly eroding his sense of what was best for he company. What if evidence continued to stack up against ~~him~~? What if this thing went all the way to trial? What if he were found guilty? His knew his family was on his side, but that was almost obligatory. They had nothing to lose by sticking by him. Cydney, had everything to lose. If the business failed, if he failed, how could he expect her to still want him?

He put his head in his hands, suddenly overwhelmed with fear and self-doubt. If he lost her, would he want to start over again? Not just with another business, but with another woman. He'd revealed so much to her, exposed so much of himself. If she wanted to, she could really hurt him. He could always buy another business. But there was no amount of money in the world that would buy back his willingness to trust, to love.

Daryl lifted his head as the door to sauna room opened. An elderly man entered the room and sat across the sauna from Daryl. Daryl ignored him, wanting to get back to his own thoughts. Yet, he felt the man staring intently at him with an unwavering gaze.

"Burke-Carter." The voice coming from the frail-looking man was surprisingly strong.

Daryl looked up without saying a word.

"Seems to me like you would know when it was time to get out of the heat, son."

Something in the man's inflection, in the soft mocking laughter that came after the statement, made Daryl think that he wasn't just talking about the sauna. His jaw tightened. He'd come here tonight wanting to purge the trouble of Megna-Tronics from his system.

"What do you want from me?" Daryl demanded.

"I came with a bit of advice."

"I don't need it," Daryl said, standing as if to leave.

"Maybe you do!" the man said sharply. "Sit down."

For a moment, Daryl considered ignoring him. What could this old man do to him? Still, his intense gaze pinned him, held him immobile.

"My advice, son, is stop trying so hard. Let things take their natural course."

Daryl shook his head. "I'm not going to sit back and let

some fool take my company from me. You can take that back to whoever sent you.''

"I'm no errand boy, son."

"Stop calling me son. I'm not your son!" Daryl snapped then clamped his mouth shut when he realized how childish he must have sounded.

"No, you're not. But you are a babe in the woods, trying to play big, bad business tycoon. You thought you could beat out the big boys and not suffer the consequences. Trouble is, young man, you're letting your hormones do your thinking for you. Can't say I blame you, if I had a woman like that doin' me . . .'' The man grinned, his thoughts obvious in the dry chuckle that followed.

Cydney! Daryl's heart froze.

"Did Dalton Keller send you?" Daryl hissed. "Is he trying to scare me out MegnaTronics? You tell Keller to stay away from me, my company, and my woman! Is that clear? You stay away from us!"

"Shut up," the man snapped. "You don't know what the hell you're talking about. I'm telling you this for your own good. Stop digging into affairs that don't concern you. Just lay low; in a few days, all of this will blow over. If you don't . . .well, let's not even consider that as a possibility . . .''

The man stood up and left the sauna. Daryl fell back against the stone bench. It felt cold to him now. He leaped up again.

Cydney! Had he been to her, too? Had he threatened her? He flew into his clothes and drove to her house in record time.

Cydney opened the door to his frantic pounding, barely clutching her robe around her.

"Daryl, what are—'' she couldn't get the words out for his crushing kiss.

"Are you all right?" he asked, pulling her back into the house.

"Of course, I'm all right. What is it? What's wrong?!" His look frightened her. He started to deny that anything was wrong.

"I . . . I just wanted to see you," he said lamely.

"Daryl," she said, putting her hands on her hips and staring at him, unconvinced.

"Hold me, Cydney," he said, desperate for her again. "Just hold me."

Without a word, she went to him. He stroked her back, her hair. "You mean more to me . . ." His voice trailed off as he looked into her dark, concerned eyes. "More than money, more than MegnaTronics. If you asked me to, I'd give it all up. I'd walk away."

"I wouldn't ask you to do that, Daryl, anymore than you could let me give up my career."

"If . . . if I did give it up, if I lost it all, would you still have me?"

"What kind of question is that? I don't care about any of that, Daryl. It's you I want. I love *you!*"

He relaxed, blowing out a deep sigh. "I know you do, Cydney. I just wanted to hear you say it to me."

She took his hands in hers. "I'll say it as many times as you need to hear it, Daryl. I love you. I love you!"

He squeezed her tightly to his chest, then held her away from him.

"I didn't mean to scare you tonight, sweetheart. I guess I started to think about what's going on at MegnaTronics and I started to panic."

"Then let me soothe your heart tonight, Daryl," she said, taking his hand in hers and leading him up to her room.

"Batter up!"

The shout went up that called Cameron to the plate. It was the fourth inning of the crucial, Wednesday night game that he'd goaded Daryl into letting his mom attend. She'd promised she would, each time responding with the same patience as he badgered her. "You're gonna' be there, Mom? You sure you're gonna' be there? You're not gonna' get stuck in a meeting are you, Mom?"

"I'll be there, Cameron. I promise I'll be there."

Now that night had come. All of the nervous energy he'd worked up during the week was manifesting itself in not-so-subtle ways. His first two innings were a complete disaster.

He'd struck out his first time up to bat. The second time, he attempted a bunt and was thrown out at first base.

Now that he was "on deck" again, he threw down the other two bats that he'd held to loosen up his swing, and clung to his favorite one. As he stepped up to the plate, he scanned the crowd for his mom.

Cydney whistled shrilly, drawing Cameron's attention.

"Knock it out of the park, Cam!" she shouted. "Nail that sucker!"

Cameron grinned, partially out of embarrassment and partially out of pride. Nobody could whoop it up like his mom. He'd seen her outshout his coach and several of the veteran referees. He gave a half wave and nodded at Daryl, waving and whistling just as loudly. Cameron swung once, then twice, experimentally before stepping into the box. He tapped the bat against his cleats to knock off the dust, then tapped home plate for luck.

The pitcher, a burly eighth-grader who could almost pass for a fully grown man, shouted something at him. Cameron ignored him. Nothing could rattle him now. His mom was here. She would make it all right. She always did.

The pitcher blazed one by him.

"Strike one!" The umpire shouted, holding up a single finger. The crowd booed, remembering Cameron's first two times at bat. Cameron ignored them, accepting the strike in stride. He almost never swung at the first pitch. The first two times he did had resulted in his outs. Comfortable in the fact that his mom would always be proud of him, no matter how he fared, he could take the luxury of being more selective about his pitches.

"That's all right, baby! Take your time!" Cydney encouraged.

"You can do it, Cameron!" Daryl shouted, and whistled shrilly through his fingers.

The pitcher wound up, then released again. Cameron waited and waited, for what seemed like ages. But as the ball approached him, he sensed, rather than felt the bat connect soundly. He reacted immediately, sprinting for first base.

Cydney rose up, shouting. Coupled with Daryl's cheers and the rest of the parents and friends who'd come to cheer Cameron's team on, the air around Cameron seemed to crackle with excitement. He pumped his arms, driving himself on. He considered waving triumphantly to his mom, but decided that he would be better off if he concentrated on making it to the base first, and gloating later.

The first base coach was urging him on, indicating that he'd hit the ball far enough to make another base.

"He's gonna' make it! He's got a double!" Cydney shouted.

"Slide, Little C!" one of Cameron's teammates urged him. The second base coach agreed. He shouted, then signaled for a slide. Cameron saw the second baseman of the opposing team crouch low, his entire body covering the plate. The ball had dropped far into left field. By the time the outfielder chased the ball down and hurled it to the relay man, Cameron was a just a few feet away from the plate. He increased his efforts, then stretched his body out. He hit the ground with a thud. For a moment, the wind was knocked from his lungs as a cloud of dust plowed into his mouth and nose. His helmet tipped forward to cover his eyes, then rolled away into the dust. The second baseman was shouting for the ball. In seconds, Cameron's fingers would reach the plate.

The relay man spun and flung the ball at second base. The ball was coming in fast, but high. The second baseman would have to leap to catch it. Cameron squinted through teary eyes as the baseman leaped into the air. He even thought he heard the ball drop into the baseman's glove with a dull *fwoomp!* But it was too late. Cameron's outstretched hand flailed and landed on the base as the umpire shouted, "Safe!"

Cameron started to grin, wanted to shout. He'd made it. As he looked up to acknowledge the umpire, his grin quickly faded. In that split second, the sun was blotted out by the sight of a pair of size nine cleats. Those feet were coming down and coming down hard. No force on this earth could stop it.

"Uh-oh!" was all he had time to say before the second baseman landed on top of him.

"Cameron!" Cydney's hands flew to her mouth. "Did you

see that? That big bully stomped on my baby on purpose! Foul
Unsportsmanlike conduct!'' She grasped the fence separating
the spectators from the playing field and rattled it.

The homeplate referee glanced over his shoulder, but didn'
make a comment. When the second base coach called for a
time out, and shouted for the team sports trainer, Cydney went
from furious to afraid.

''He's hurt!'' she said over her shoulder at Daryl as she
climbed down from the bleachers.

''Ma'am! Ma'am, you can't go out there!'' The referee tried
to stop her.

''That's my son!'' Cydney protested. ''He's hurt.''

''Yes, ma'am. But the trainer is out there. It's just a precaution to make certain he's all right.''

''But . . .''

''As soon we know something, we'll let you know, ma'am.
Please . . .''

Cydney ground her teeth. When she saw the trainer turn
Cameron over to examine him and noticed how limply her son
reacted, Cydney panicked.

''You let me out there to see my baby, or so help me, *I'll*
stomp every coach or referee, that tries to get in my way!''
she threatened. She wasn't shouting now. Her voice was low
and tight. Daryl recognized that look and that sound immediately. When the referee turned to him as if to ask Daryl to
control Cydney, Daryl shook his head. No way. He wasn't
getting in the way of Cydney and her son.

The trainer said something to the head coach, who also
had gone out to the middle of the field. They were shouting
something. What were they saying? Cydney strained to hear.
They were calling for a stretcher. Cameron was unconscious!

''Come on,'' Daryl said, grasping her by the hand and moving
around the referee. He and Cydney ran across the diamond,
meeting the team trainer, the head coach, the referee, and a
few others Cydney didn't know as they carefully lifted Cameron
onto the stretcher. She fought down another wave of panic
when Cameron's head, covered in blood, lolled near the edge
of the stretcher.

"No! Oh, my God, no! Cameron, baby, speak to Mom!"

She grasped his hand and jogged alongside them as they headed for the parking lot.

"There'll be an ambulance here within five minutes, Mrs. Kelley," the coach assured her.

"How . . . how bad is he?"

"He took a pretty nasty clip on the back of the head. But, the good thing about scalp wounds is that they usually bleed worse than the damage seems at first."

"But he's unconscious!" Cydney screeched, then bit her lip to keep her anger in check. She didn't need to lose control now. She had to be strong for Cameron. She had to be there, confident and composed, when Cameron came to.

The ambulance pulled into the parking lot, lights flashing. "I'm riding in the ambulance with him," Cydney announced, and silently dared anyone to keep her from trying it.

Daryl squeezed her shoulder. "I'll follow behind. I'll be right there. Don't worry, Cydney, he's going to be fine. Cameron's a tough young man."

"He's my baby," she contradicted in a whisper, but smiled at his encouragement.

"Where are you taking him?" Daryl asked. The paramedic told them the name and location of the nearest hospital.

"Good . . . good," Daryl nodded in satisfaction. He turned back to Cydney. "That's a teaching hospital, Cydney."

"Nobody's going to experiment on my son!" Cydney threatened. "You take him somewhere where the doctors will know what they're doing."

"That hospital is one of the best in the country, Cydney," Daryl assured her. "They'll take good care of Cameron. Don't you worry, now. I'll be right there," Daryl promised again, as he backed away and headed for his car.

Cydney could only stand by while the paramedics performed their own examination of her son. After relaying Cameron's condition to the hospital, they loaded him onto a gurney, and pushed him into the back of ambulance. Cydney climbed up immediately after, scrambling as if she expected someone to grab her legs and pull her out again.

"This is a nightmare," she groaned. "I can't believe that this is happening!"

The flashing lights, the sirens, the sight of her son's gray, pinched face frightened her so that she could barely breathe. Her lungs fought for every breath. She glanced around her, trying to follow the paramedics as they tossed back and forth medical terms that meant absolutely nothing to her. Nothing in their speech indicated to her that her son would be all right.

Though it seemed much longer to Cydney, in less than ten minutes, they were storming through the doors of the emergency room. A second medical team swarmed around the gurney and took over where the first paramedic team had left off. Before Cydney knew it, they were wheeling Cameron away. Someone else has grasped her arm, leading her away from her son.

"No! I want to be with him." Cydney struggled.

"Yes, ma'am, but the doctors are going to have to examine him first."

"I need to be there for him."

"Yes, ma'am. As soon as we knew more . . ."

"I know, I know. You'll let me know," Cydney said irritably.

"Yes, ma'am. If I can just get you to come this way, we need to get your son admitted." The medical assistant thrust a clipboard into her hands.

Paperwork? How could she even think about filling out forms when her son was lying there hurt, possibly bleeding to death, or in a coma!

She felt a warm, strong hand grasp her shoulder. She spun around, then flew straight at Daryl.

"They took him away. They won't let me see him!" Cydney sobbed into his shoulder.

"They will," Daryl soothed, smoothing her hair. "They're going to take very good care of him first. Then you can see him, Cydney. Come on over here." He guided her to the waiting room chairs.

She sat down weakly, the clipboard sitting untouched in her lap. She stared down at it, without seeing it. Words and lines blurred before her as her eyes filled with tears. Daryl took the board away from her and pulled out a pen.

"Patient's name," he said crisply, forcing Cydney to clear her mind.

"Cameron Jason Kelley," she responded automatically.

"Date of birth," Daryl went on quickly, not giving her a chance to think, only respond.

Within ten minutes, he'd gone through every question. When he got to the line for her to sign consent for treatment, he placed the clipboard back into her lap. Cydney penned her name with careful, deliberate strokes. Daryl smiled further encouragement at her as he took the papers to the nurses' station.

When he got back, he asked, "Is there anyone you want me to call?"

"My sister Courtney," Cydney said, and rattled off the number. "She'll get in touch with my parents and let them know what's happened."

When he returned from making the call, Cydney reached for his hand again.

"He has to be all right, Daryl," she whispered. "He's all that I have."

Daryl nodded in sympathy, then pressed his lips together. He'd wanted so badly to say, *You have me.* But he knew that nothing could fill the void if she lost her son, not even if he devoted his entire life to her.

Cydney leaned her head on his shoulder. "Thank you for coming."

"Did you think I wouldn't? I told you I'd be there for you, Cydney. That means every part of you. And Cameron, if anything, is the best part of you."

She closed her eyes, allowing her tears to flow down her cheeks.

"You don't know the half of it," she said. "He wasn't an easy delivery."

Half smiling at the memory, she went on. "He was almost a breach baby, you know, turned feet first at the time of delivery. But, like a miracle, at the last minute as they were planning a cesarean section, he turned around. When most babies are born into this world, they come out mad, howling for all they're worth. Not Cameron. He faced the world—grinning the most precious, toothless grin. He's my special, little man. If I lose him . . .''

"You won't," Daryl insisted. "You won't : . ."

Cydney shuddered, allowing the negative thoughts to wash over as she pushed them aside.

When, after thirty minutes, she still had not received word about Cameron's condition, she began to prowl the waiting room.

"What's taking them so long?!" she asked over and over.

"Why don't I see if I can find out anything," Daryl offered.

She nodded gratefully, squeezing her arms against her mid-section to still the queasy, unsettled feeling that had risen inside.

Daryl disappeared around the corridor. Cydney turned away. She didn't know how long she stood there, staring at a blank wall, and trying to will herself not to cry.

"Cydney!"

She turned as her sister Courtney rushed to her and wrapped her in a tight hug. "Are you all right?"

"I'm fine. It's Cameron I'm worried about."

"I met your boss in the hall. He said that Cameron was hurt at a baseball game."

Cydney nodded curtly. "One of those big bullies deliberately stomped him for sliding into second base."

"Don't you worry, little sister. Cameron will be fine. He's got a head as hard as a rock."

Cydney smiled despite herself.

"Sort of like his dad," Courtney went on. "Uh, Cydney, I have something I think I should tell you."

"What is it?"

"I . . . uh, I . . ."

"What is it, Courtney? Spit it out."

"When Daryl called me and told me that Cameron was hurt, I called Mom and Dad immediately."

'And?"

"Then, Mom used the three-way connection on her phone and called Jason."

Cydney swallowed convulsively. "He *is* Cameron's father.

He has a right to know what's going on with his son." She squared her shoulders.

"I'm glad you feel this way. Because he said he was on his way to the hospital."

Cydney's eyes widened, but she didn't respond.

"Did you hear what I said, Cydney? Jason is coming here."

"I heard you."

"Are you going to be all right with that?"

"It doesn't look like I have a choice. He's coming and there's nothing I can do to stop it."

"You're not going to get into a fight, are you?"

"I think I have enough on my mind without getting into some mess like that, Courtney. For Pete's sake, give me some credit for being able to be adult."

Courtney wrapped her arm around Cydney and led her back to the waiting room.

"I know you're an adult, Cydney. It's him that I'm worried about. As soon as I saw Daryl here . . ."

"Daryl will be fine, too," Cydney said stoutly.

"If everybody's going to be so okey-dokey fine, why do I feel like I'm about to witness a train wreck in the making?" Courtney grumbled.

Daryl knew the hospital staff would do its best to treat Cameron, but trying to get answers was like to trying to find out one of the hospital's deepest, darkest secrets. He didn't think they were being deliberately callous, but for someone to actually stop what they were doing and answer the questions of a nonrelative was almost too much to ask. Daryl decided that if the staff was stonewalling him, he'd just have to find a way around them. What he needed was a little clout—someone on the inside who could get his answers for him and wouldn't mind coming right back—as so many that he'd questioned promised they would.

He picked up a hospital courtesy phone and dialed an extension.

"Burke-Carter, here . . ." came the reply after several rings.

"Dad? I'm glad I caught you here today. It's me—Daryl."

"Darry? What are you doing here?"

"The son of one of my employees was injured in a baseball game, Dad. They brought him in about half an hour ago, but we don't know anything about his condition. We don't know who the attending physician is or anything . . ."

"We? This wouldn't be that Kelley woman, would it?"

"Yes, Dad. It's that Kelley woman. Her name is Cydney, and right now she's worried out of her mind. Is there anything you can do?"

"I haven't been called to pediatrics in a while, son. Anything I can get will be purely a professional courtesy."

"After a half-hour of professional, but polite snubbing, we'll take anything."

"All right, then. I'll see what I can do."

"Thanks. I appreciate it."

"Meet you down in the waiting room in about ten minutes."

"See you then."

"Daryl, before you go, I have to know . . . you wouldn't be involved in this because of personal reasons, would you?"

"What do you mean?"

"I mean, are you sleeping with this woman? Is this boy your son?"

"No, Cameron is not my son," Daryl said stiffly. He didn't answer his father's other question. He didn't think it was any of his business. All he needed to know, he would know soon enough when Daryl announced his engagement.

"You're in love with her, aren't you?"

"What has this got to do with Cameron's condition, Dad?"

"If I'm going to throw my weight around here, Darry, I've got to know that it's for a good cause."

"It is," Daryl said softly. "I care about Cydney very much, Dad. I can't stand it knowing she's in so much pain. The only thing I know to do to ease some of that pain is to find out for her how Cameron's doing."

"That's good enough for me. I'll find out what you need to know or turn this hospital on its ear trying."

"Thanks, Dad."

Harlan heard the grin in his son's voice.

Daryl returned to the sisters. When Cydney looked hopefully up at him, it nearly broke his heart.

"I wasn't able to find out anything," Daryl said quietly. "But I contacted someone who can."

"Who?"

"My father. I told you this was a teaching hospital. In addition to his private practice, my father also instructs the residents. He'll find out something. He said he'll be here in ten minutes."

"Ten minutes, ten hours . . ." Cydney murmured, "It's all the same. It seems as though all I've done is wait!"

Courtney looked up at Daryl and shook her head. "Don't think we're not grateful, Mr. Burke-Carter," Courtney began and pinched her sister to remind her that Daryl was going above and beyond the call of duty in seeing to her.

"Call me Daryl," he indicated with an outstretched hand.

Courtney smiled and took it without hesitation. "And I'm Courtney."

"I'm sorry, Daryl. I didn't mean to sound ugly," Cydney said. "I'm just so worried."

"I know . . . but it's going to be all right."

"What happens if he's in a coma? Or paralyzed! I can't afford any extended hospital stay . . . even with insurance," Cydney wailed, suddenly tired of hearing the same assurances. "I just can't afford it!"

"Cydney," Daryl said, grasping her chin and forcing her to look at him. "*I'm* telling you, you don't have to worry about that. Let the cost of Cameron's care be the least of your worries."

Courtney and Cydney exchanged glances. It didn't take a genius to figure out that, without going into details, Daryl was offering to help her pay for the expenses. When she opened her mouth as if to protest or reject Daryl's generous offer, Courtney pinched her sister again.

"Will you chill out!" Courtney admonished. "Stop borrowing trouble. The man said everything will be all right."

"You didn't seem him, Courtney," Cydney flared. "He was lying there, all limp and cold and . . . for all I know, he could be dead, and they're just not telling me!'' She stood up quickly. "That's it, I'm going in there. Just let them try to stop me!"

"Cydney, stop it," Daryl said. "Let them do their job. If you go in there now, you could be making it worse for Cameron."

"How could it be much worse, Daryl? How?" she demanded to know. Daryl held his hand out to her and took her into his arms. He stood, rocking her, and soothing her. "He's going to be all right, sweetheart. You have to have faith."

"I'm so scared," she murmured into his shoulder. "I feel so helpless. I should be there with him so he knows he isn't alone."

"He knows," Courtney stood also, and patted Cydney. "Cam knows you'd never leave him." She looked over Daryl's shoulder and suddenly grimaced. "Uh-oh."

Cydney didn't hear her but Daryl did. He looked at her and raised an eyebrow in question. Courtney indicated with a slight tilt of her head what had caused her sudden dismay. Daryl recognized the man approaching them immediately. He'd stared often enough at the image of Cydney's former husband—Jason Kelley. It was not good timing. Not good timing, at all. He squeezed her shoulders, as much to brace himself as her.

Courtney moved away, trying to intercept Jason before he made it to the waiting room.

"Hello, Jason," Courtney said quietly, placing one hand lightly against his chest and raising a finger of the other hand to her lips to indicate not to announce himself just yet. He stared down at her, his brow furrowing.

"Courtney," Jason said in sharp, clipped tones that she knew so well. It was as if common courtesy was too painful for him to grant. He pointed with his chin at the still embracing Daryl and Cydney. "What the hell is this? What's he doing groping my wife?"

"Ex-wife," Courtney corrected. "You'd better remember that."

"How could I forget? You and that high-priced lawyer you got for her pounded it into me at every opportunity. Now, who is he?"

"That's Daryl Burke-Carter, Jason," Courtney said. "Don't

you go ticking him off, either. He just offered to pay for Cameron's medical bills.''

"I don't need help taking care of my son," Jason snapped and moved around her.

"Cyd—" he called out to her.

Cydney jumped visibly and pulled away from Daryl.

"Jason, what are you doing here?" she said, then realized how silly that must have sounded to him. Once he knew Cameron was hurt, did she really expect him to stay away?

"How's my son?" Jason ignored the question rather than state the obvious. But by referring to Cameron as his son, he had begun the age-old tug of war that ended bitterly with the court awarding custody to Cydney.

"I don't know. No one's come out to tell us yet . . . but we expect some news at any minute." She turned to Daryl and said, "You said your father would be here in a few minutes with some news?"

Daryl nodded once.

"Uh-huh," Jason snorted. He eyed Daryl from head to foot. "So, this is the man you've been—" He ended with a crude suggestion that sent the heat of embarrassment and resentment to her cheeks. She felt Daryl tense beside her. She squeezed his hand, both in assurance and admonition. This wasn't the time or the place.

Jason saw the warnings flash in her eyes, and for a moment was taken aback. A year ago, a comment like that would have reduced Cydney to tears. She moved within inches of him, face-to-face and said in a carefully modulated voice, "If you want to wait in here for news about Cameron, you can. You're welcome to stay. But if you try to screw with my head again, I'll just have to send you to a room where you can wait by yourself. How does a nice, private room in the intensive care unit sound to you, Jason?"

"Hey, baby, chill. I'm not here to start anything. I just want to see my son."

Jason backed away and moved to a seat on the couch. He threw himself down, as if unconcerned about Cydney's uncharacteristic assertiveness. But he glared at Daryl through hooded eyes.

"Cameron Jason Kelley. I'm looking for Cameron's parents." A physician entered the waiting room, followed closely by Harlan Burke-Carter. When Cydney, Courtney, Jason, and Daryl all converged on the doctor, the doctor raised his eyebrows in question. "I take it this is his extended family."

"The only thing that's extended is my patience," Cydney snapped. "Cameron is my son. I want to know how he's doing. And I want to know right now. Tell me in plain English, please, not hidden behind all of this medical gibberish and jargon."

"All right, Mrs. Kelley. I'm Doctor Angelo. I'll be handling your son's case, at the insistence of Dr. Burke-Carter, here."

Cydney glanced over her shoulder at Daryl's father. He winked back at her—his broad face so much like Daryl's that she instantly knew what Daryl would look like in twenty or so years.

"How is he, Doctor? I'm Cameron's father," Jason pressed.

"Cameron suffered a blow to the back of the head. He required several stitches and he has a slight concussion. But, as far as the X-rays can determine, there is no damage to the brain or the spine. That means no coma, no paralysis."

"Oh, thank God!" Cydney gasped, feeling so weak in the knees, she had to sit on one of the couches for support.

"We can see him?" Daryl asked.

"He's sleeping now. We gave him something for the pain. When he wakes up, we'll perform a series of tests to double-check the X-rays. I'm afraid I can only authorize immediate family to see him, and only for a few minutes. He really needs to rest."

"Where is he?" Cydney pressed.

"He's in the intensive care wing, just overnight so we can monitor his progress very carefully. Tomorrow, we'll move him to a private room."

"A private room," Cydney echoed. Daryl knew exactly what she was thinking. She was thinking of the cost again. He squeezed her shoulder and said, "Why don't you go see him, Cydney? We'll be here when you get back."

She smiled up at him.

"ICU is on the third floor," Doctor Angelo told her.

"I'm coming, too. I may not be able to go in, but I can peek in to make sure he's all right," Courtney said. Jason followed behind them both, but not without a slightly triumphant grin for the small, petty victory he had over the man who now shared his woman's bed.

"Thanks, Mark," Harlan said, shaking Dr. Angelo's hand.

"Not a problem. Glad I could help. See you around." Dr. Angelo shook hands briefly with Harlan. Then, after nodding to Daryl, he returned to his rounds.

"Thank you, Dad, for stepping in," Daryl said.

"Don't mention it. Mark owed me a couple of favors anyway."

"Did you get a chance to see the boy?"

"I did. He looked fine—nice and healthy."

"He's a good kid, Dad."

"Come over here, Darry," Harlan said, grasping his son's elbow and leading him away from the remainder of the waiting room occupants. "I want to ask you something."

"Dad, I know what you're going to say . . ." Daryl began.

"Do you? Then you know a lot more than I do at this point," Harlan said with a wry smile. "I'm not sure quite how to put this. I just want to ask, are you sure?"

"About?"

"You know what about. Are you sure about your involvement with that Kelley woman?"

"Her name isn't that Kelley woman. Her name is Cydney, and I've never been more sure about anything in my life."

"You think her husband is going to let you come in and take over his responsibility."

"I don't think he'll have too many complaints about me paying the hospital bill. He's not that big of a fool."

"So you are paying for her. What about her husband?"

"She didn't ask me to pay, if that's what you mean. And

she's not married to him any more. She's divorced and hasn[t] had anything to do with him in years.''

''I didn't think she would. She seems like a proud, capab[le] woman. But it's more than just hospital bills, son. Raising [a] family is hard enough in itself; but to take someone else[s] family when that someone isn't out of the picture . . . Darr[yl] you're asking for a world of trouble.''

''She's worth it, Dad. I can handle it.''

''Well, all I can say is, it's obvious she's made a differen[ce] in your life. I don't think I've ever seen you so committed [to] anything, or anyone. If she's the one for you, then I wish yo[u] all the happiness in the world. You just watch out for that e[x] husband. He may not want her anymore, but that doesn't mea[n] he wants anyone else to have her either. And as for his so[n,] he's not going to give him up without a fight, either.''

''I won't let him use Cameron in some kind of macho tu[g] of war. I won't play that game, Dad.''

''Good boy.'' Harlan clapped Daryl on the back. ''I've g[ot] to run, son. I've got a class in about ten minutes. Will you b[e] around long? Maybe you, me, and that Kelley woman . . . [I] mean, Ms. Kelley . . . can have dinner together. You know, ge[t] to know each other.''

''Maybe some other time, Dad. I don't think she'll feel muc[h] like socializing. She won't want to leave Cameron's side.''

''Some other time, then.''

''Thanks, again, Dad.''

''Don't mention it.''

''Did I mention that Dr. Angelo is one of the foremo[st] pediatricians in the city?'' Courtney was saying as they waite[d] for the elevator that would take them to the intensive care uni[t.]

''Only about a hundred times,'' Jason muttered under hi[s] breath.

''Nothing but the best for our little Cameron,'' Courtne[y] continued. ''I can't believe that Mr. Burke-Carter is going t[o] pick up Cameron's medical bill.''

''Burke-Carter,'' Jason echoed. ''Of *the* Burke-Carters?''

"Do you know of any other Burke-Carters with that kind of clout?" Courtney retorted. Jason turned to the still silent Cydney. She'd allowed Courtney to engage Jason in conversation because she didn't think that she had the energy or the desire to think about anything but Cameron. All she wanted to do was get to her son's room and hold him.

"Well, I'll be damned," Jason went on. "You didn't do too bad for yourself, now did you, Cyd? No wonder you didn't want to hang with me. What could I offer you that could compare with Burke-Carter's money?"

Cydney turned blazing eyes to him. "I would have stayed with you until my last, dying breath, Jason Kelley! But you were too busy reminding me why I wasn't worth your time! Don't you dare try to drag me down because I've finally, after all this time, found someone who values me."

"And you always told me that money didn't matter—that some things, like our so-called love, couldn't be bought anywhere. I guess I was wrong."

"About a lot of things," Courtney interjected.

"Stay out of this, Courtney," Cydney snapped. She glanced around her as her outburst drew attention from the hospital staff and visitors. She whispered tightly to Jason, "You have a problem with my relationship with Daryl?"

"Yeah, I have a problem with it. I don't appreciate him coming in here, throwing his money around, and thinking he can just take my son away from me."

"He isn't trying to take him away. Why should you care anyway? You gave up your right to call him your son when you left us."

"I didn't give it up. You, that lawyer, and that judge took him away from me."

"You left us, Jason. You did that. No one forced you to leave."

"I had to leave, Cydney. Nothing I ever did was good enough for you. You didn't like the way that I dressed. You didn't like the way that I talked. You didn't like the work I chose. What else was I supposed to do? Change?"

"I loved you, Jason," Cydney said, shaking her head. She

blinked rapidly, trying to hold back the tears that stung he eyes. "You didn't have to change. But you could have talke to me, told me what you were feeling. You could have sai 'What you're doing to me is making me want to leave you But you didn't. Instead, you just said goodbye.''

"And you think this Burke-Carter is going to stick around What happens when you get tired of him, too? What happen when you start harping on him?"

"That won't happen.''

"Yeah, I suppose money makes a man really interesting.'

"That's not what I want from him, Jason.''

"But you're not turning it down, either," Jason accused her

"She's not stupid," Courtney stepped in.

"Do you mind?!" Cydney said tightly. "Will you let m handle this?''

"Well, handle it, then. Don't let him talk to you that way If Daryl Burke-Carter wants to take care of you, then let him.''

"I'm taking care of me!" Cydney said loudly. She clampe her mouth shut and was relieved when the elevator finally arrived. There were only the three of them waiting to go up. They could finish this conversation in relative privacy. She wanted to end the conversation and end it quickly. She didn't need Jason's suspicions to poison her mind and her spirit. When she went to Cameron, she wanted to focus all of her love and attention on him, without being distracted by Jason's accusations.

"Yes, Daryl's family is well off. Yes, he has money. But I also admire his work ethic. He works for his pay, Jason. He works hard for everything he has—including me. Nobody bought me. He earned my trust, my respect, and my love.''

"I'm relieved to know that you weren't as easy for him as you were for me. If I'd thought back then that you'd whore yourself out to the first man to flash you a little green, I could have had the judge hand Cameron to me in a heartbeat.''

Cydney's hands clenched into tight, balls of fury. She stepped toward Jason as the elevator doors slid open.

"Let it go, Cydney." Courtney grasped Cydney's sleeve and tugged her toward the open door. "Don't give him the atisfaction.'' She glanced over at Jason and gave him a wide, icked smile. "Save that for Daryl."

Cydney smiled a little in return. By releasing some of that nsion, she could now focus on her son. She stopped the first oor nurse she saw and asked about Cameron.

'I'll take you to him.'' She smiled that professional, sympa-etic smile that was starting to annoy Cydney in an irrational ind of way. She knew the woman was only doing her job. ut how could she suggest, even by way of a smile, that she nderstood her pain and her concern? She probably didn't even now Cameron. How could she know about the funny, vibrant, evoted spark that was her son?

"How is he?" Cydney asked.

"He's doing just fine. But I'm afraid I can't let you stay too ong. As soon as he's moved to a private room, you can spend aore time with him."

"And when will that be?" Courtney asked.

"The doctor said tomorrow, Courtney. Weren't you lis-ening?" Jason interrupted.

Cydney threw him another warning glance. Not here. Not ow. If he ruined any chance of her getting to see Cameron, he really would put him in the hospital.

"That's right,'' the nurse confirmed. "By tomorrow, we hould know if he's well past the critical point. He's a fine, trong young man with every reason and chance in the world o recover fully."

"Thank you,'' Cydney breathed. When the nurse smiled at er again and patted her shoulder, Cydney relaxed. The concern n the woman's face was genuine. Maybe she didn't know Cameron, but the look in her eyes told Cydney that Cameron vas more than just a name and number on a chart to her, too.

When the nurse indicated Cameron's room, both Courtney nd Jason hung back. The look Cydney flashed told them if hey tried to get ahead of her to see Cameron, they'd regret it.

"Just remember,'' the nurse offered, "that all of those moni-ors are just a precaution. Don't let that equipment in there care you. We're just making sure he's all right.''

Cydney nodded, then pushed aside the door. Despite the

nurse's effort to prepare her, her first reaction on seeing t^
beeping, flashing, whirring equipment in the room made h^
cry out softly in dismay.

"My baby!" She moved quickly to Cameron's bedside an^
took his slender hand carefully in her own. She didn't want t^
jostle him too much. She didn't want to disturb the intravenou^
drip going into the back of his hand.

"It's all right, Cameron," she whispered, smoothing hi^
forehead with a trembling hand. "It's all right. Mom's her^
and I'm not leaving you. Do you hear me? I'll be right he^
for you."

She leaned over him, kissed his cheek. She was startled whe^
she felt something warm and wet touch her lips. For a second^
she thought he might have stirred and kissed her back. Whe^
she pulled away to check for signs of motion, she realized tha^
the wetness was from her own tears which had finally broke^
to the surface.

She started to reach up to wipe them away, and felt anothe^
hand reaching behind her to wipe them away for her. She crane^
her neck around.

"My turn," Jason said softly. All of the animosity was^
stripped from his voice and his expression.

Without a word, Cydney nodded and stepped aside to allow^
Jason his moment.

"Thanks for giving me the time off to be with Cameron."

Cydney lay on the couch, her head resting in Daryl's lap.
As he stroked her hair absently, he read through the business
section of the newspaper.

"Cameron really appreciated it," she continued.

"A man would have to be crazy—trying to come between
you and your son," Daryl remarked, and tweaked her nose
affectionately. Cydney immediately grimaced. Not because she
didn't appreciate Daryl's tender touches, but because of the
fact that she had allowed a man to come between her and
Cameron. The only reason she wasn't at the hospital now was

ecause she and Jason agreed to take turns staying overnight
ith Cameron.

Daryl's father arranged for a special cot to be brought in so
at she and Jason could remain with Cameron during the length
f his hospital visit. The only equitable way for them to decide
ho would watch over him first was to flip a coin. When the
oin came up heads, in Jason's favor, Cydney immediately
emanded a rematch.

"We can stand here all night and argue over who gets him
ke we did in that court room, or we can take a lesson from
ere," Jason snapped.

Not willing to be "out-adulted" by Jason, Cydney took a
eep breath and agreed.

"All right. You stay with him tonight. I'm sure it will do
im a world of good to see you when he wakes up."

"See you tomorrow."

Before she left, Cydney leaned over Cameron and kissed
im softly on the forehead.

"Sweet dreams, Cam. I promise, I'll be right here, by your
ide, first thing tomorrow morning."

On her way out, Jason blocked the door. "What? No kiss
or me, for old times' sake?"

"You can kiss my . . ."

"Ah-ah-ah, Cydney," Jason said, wagging his finger in front
f her. "No swearing in front of the baby."

"Take a good look, Jason. He's not a baby anymore. You've
ost a few years."

When Jason's expression softened, Cydney almost felt a tiny,
limmer of sentimental feeling for him.

"I know . . . Just look at my little man. My main man,
Cameron. Before you know it, he'll be off finding a wife of
is own and trying to raise his own little crumb snatcher."

Cydney laughed softly at the term, remembering how Jason
eferred to Cameron the first day he was able to hold his
ewborn son.

"I didn't think you had any more smiles left for me, Cyd-
ey," Jason mused.

"Jason, we don't have to be enemies—or even strangers.

We had a life together, and now we have a teenage son. That a bond that no divorce papers could break.''

''So what are you trying to say, that you want to take m back? That you want to try again?''

''No, Jason, that's not what I'm saying at all,'' Cydney sai trying to keep the horror she felt at the thought out of h voice. At the same time, she didn't want to destroy the fragi beginnings of healing she felt with Jason now. ''We're differe people now. We can't go back. I'm saying, let's go forwar from this point. We can make a real effort to . . .''

''To what? Be pals? Do you think your rich new boyfrie will go for that? Is he into the group thing?'' Jason was immed ately bitter.

''Don't talk about Daryl that way! You don't see me tryir to drag down the woman in your life. And don't try to tell m that there isn't one, Jason. I know you haven't spent all of th time alone. It isn't in you. If you've made a life with her, want to say that I'm happy for you. Why can't you be happ for me?''

''It's not easy, Cydney, watching you with him. You kno that, don't you? Knowing that he's touched you in the place that I used to, knowing that you're saying the kinds of thing to him that you used to say to me. . . How do you expect m to live with that? It was easy when I didn't know, when I hadn seen him. I could pretend that there would never be anothe person after me.''

''You wanted me to spend the rest of my life alone?''

''You have Cameron.''

''It's not the same and you know it. Jason, as much hurt a we've given each other, I'd never wish that on you. I woul never want you to be miserable.''

''You say that now. What about back then?''

''Yes, I wanted to hurt you. But that was because I wa hurting so much. All of that has changed, Jason. I've change I'm happy now and I want you to be happy, too. I don't wa to fight you. The time and energy we've spent fighting, w could have spent more productively.''

''We could have spent the time being more reproductive

It's a shame Cameron never had a little brother or sister to watch out for. Though it wasn't for the lack of trying!''

Cydney blushed despite herself. ''So, do we call a truce or do we tear the hospital down trying to rip each other apart?''

''Truce,'' Jason agreed, holding out his hand to her. Cydney took it and squeezed. Without warning, Jason suddenly yanked Cydney toward him and brought his lips swiftly over hers. Cydney squawked in indignation, but didn't immediately pull away. For the briefest of moments, she allowed herself to remember.

She felt her memories and her emotions dragging her back to the time when she hungered for a kiss like this from him. She thought about the sulky, silent nights when they lay side by side, when she wished he would have broken through the barrier of silence and healed all of the hurt with a kiss just like this.

With her reluctance and her resistance weakening, she felt her lips becoming pliant and mobile under Jason's emotional onslaught. Her arms crept around his neck, her body molded into his with almost painful familiarity. Jason responded immediately. His hips jutted forward, moving against hers.

''Jason,'' she sobbed, then placed her hands against his chest. She wanted to push him away, but she let her hands linger against him a little too long. ''Why are you doing this to me?''

''I wanted to make sure,'' he said, his voice unsteady.

''Of what? That you could still get to me? I could have told you that!''

''I wanted to know for myself. I wanted to know if there was anything left for me.''

''I love Daryl now, Jason,'' Cydney said, swiping at her face as if she could wipe away the memory of Jason's touch.

''I know,'' Jason said, stepping away from her. ''Kissing you . . . as good as it was, I knew . . . I could feel you slipping away from me. Go back to your new love, Cydney,'' Jason dismissed her. ''I don't know if I can handle trying to be friends with you, but I think we can muddle through a cordial reunion or two—for Cameron's sake. I want him back in my life.''

"He will be. I'm make sure of that," Cydney whispered, and kissed him on the cheek before leaving the room.

"You sure you have enough room?" Daryl asked, as Cydney seemed to squirm uncomfortably on the couch. The memory of Jason's kiss pricked her conscience.

"I'm fine," she said, but sat up anyway.

"Are you sure you're all right, Cydney? You seem a little restless." Daryl searched her face. He knew she'd had a confrontation with Jason. He didn't have to be a mind reader to know that the man probably wouldn't let her go without trying to get in a few parting shots. But she hadn't come back from the hospital angry, or even fuming about her ex-husband. Daryl experienced another bout of jealousy. He wondered if the man had tried to get her back, to use Cameron's injury as an excuse to worm his way back into her life. He didn't say so to her, though several times he was on the verge of asking her. He resolved to respect her privacy and hoped that what they'd built together could now withstand a brush with her past.

"I guess I'm anxious about Cameron. I'll be all right. I just need to settle my nerves. I'm going to the kitchen to fix myself something to drink. Can I get you anything?" she offered. She saw the worry in his face and intuitively knew that it wasn't worry about her alone that put that look there.

"Whatever you're having is fine. Why don't you sit back and relax, Cydney. I'll get it for you."

"Don't get up," she waved him back to the couch. On impulse, she leaned over and kissed him on the top of the head. "Thanks for offering, boss man."

She'd made it halfway to the kitchen when the doorbell rang.

"I can at least get that for you," Daryl said. He tried to keep his expression light. Inwardly, he thought that if that was Jason Kelley at the door, he'd stop him before he could weasel another foot into Cydney's life. "Do you feel like visitors or should I run interference for you?"

The news of Cameron's accident had spread quickly. The phone was constantly ringing from well wishers—from her coworkers to his friends at school. Unable to get any rest, Cydney finally recorded a message, briefly giving the details of Cameron's accident and his condition. She then turned the ringer off on the phone. She grumbled that it was too bad that she couldn't turn the ringer off on the doorbell. She was glad that Daryl was there to take messages, accept gifts, and to turn aside anyone who wasn't family.

"I'm all right," she said, nodding at the door. As she poured two, small glasses of wine, she heard Daryl open the door and then a familiar voice was calling out to her.

"Mike?" she poked her head out. "Mike, what are you doing here?"

"I came to see about Cameron. When you didn't come in to work today, I asked Daryl what was up. He told me about Cameron. Cyd, I'm so sorry." He held out a small, sympathy plant and get well card to her. "I tried to deliver these in person to Cam. But since I wasn't family, they wouldn't let me see him. I thought I'd drop them by here instead."

"Thank you, Mike. That was very sweet of you to come out all this way. But he's going to be fine. He's got a mild concussion. And he has some stitches that'll leave a nice little scar to impress all the girls with."

Mike then glanced over at Daryl. "I didn't know you'd be here. I should have known, you being who you are and she being what she is to you. I suppose it's best that you are."

Daryl frowned, puzzled by Mike's disjointed, almost incoherent conversation. "I didn't want to leave Cydney alone, not with her being so worried about Cameron."

"I'm so sorry, so, so sorry," Mike muttered then, looking down at the carpet in an effort to avoid Cydney's gaze.

"I said he's going to be fine. He's resting comfortably at the hospital." Cydney watched Mike's throat bob, as if he were fighting down the urge to cry. "Mike?" she reached out to touch his arm. "Mike, it's going to be all right. Cameron's fine."

"Don't!" Mike said sharply, pulling away from her. "Don't touch me!"

"Mike, what the hell's the matter with you?" Daryl demanded in defense of the hurt look on Cydney's face.

"I don't want her sympathy. I don't want her to be kind to me—not after what I've done."

"What have you done?" Daryl and Cydney asked in unison. Mike shook his head, pacing the room in obvious agitation.

"I didn't think it would go this far," he muttered aloud. "It's not working out like I thought. I didn't count on you two falling for each other. I didn't count on anyone getting hurt . . . If you could have just stayed enemies, it would have been so perfect, so much easier."

"Mike, if you don't start making sense, I'm going to have to knock some sense into you," Cydney threatened.

"Cydney, why couldn't you have just stayed out of it?!" Mike suddenly shouted. "What did you have to go and get involved for?"

"You can't choose the people you fall in love with, Mike. It just happens," she said, shrugging helplessly. She looked to Daryl. He shrugged, not understanding any of Mike's ramblings.

"You should have just stayed out of it!" Mike ranted on. "Now, because of you, everything's ruined . . . all of that planning . . . for nothing!" He took a step toward her, frightening her with the naked anger written on his face. She gasped, and involuntarily reached for Daryl.

"Cameron, poor Cameron. He didn't deserve that . . . I never thought they . . . that is . . . I . . ."

"What about Cameron?!" Cydney quickly got over her fear. She grabbed Mike and shook him. "What are you trying to tell me? Tell me! Did you do something to my son?"

"Not me. It wasn't me. If something happened to him, don't blame me. It wasn't all my fault. I told you to leave it alone, not to get involved. I warned you that people could get hurt."

"What are you talking about?" said an angry, frustrated Daryl. "Did you have something to do with Cameron's accident?"

"It wasn't me!" Mike insisted. "It was them. The only

reason I'm here tonight is to warn you, so that you can try to stop it!''

"What are you talking about?" Daryl grabbed Mike by the elbow. "Stop what, Mike?"

Mike turned pleading eyes to Cydney. "Cyd, you've got to believe me. I never meant anything to happen to Cameron. If I'd thought in a million years that—''

Cydney's heart hardened. "You tell me what you know. Tell me everything. Tell me now, Mike! Now!"

"They were going to kill me if I didn't agree to it . . . if I didn't give them their money."

"Who? What money?" Cydney was thoroughly confused now.

"Keller!" Mike finally got out on a moan. "Dalton Keller."

"Who's Dalton Keller?" Cydney asked when she saw Daryl release Mike out of pure astonishment.

"Dalton Keller? Mike, what are you doing dealing with Dalton Keller?"

"Will somebody please tell me what's going on?" Cydney pleaded.

Mike slumped into a chair and nodded to Daryl to give an explanation.

"Dalton Keller, among other things, is rumored to be one of the richest, most powerful men in the southwest, Cydney. Oil, real estate, utilities—you name it, he's got a piece of it. He's another venture capitalist with a knack for recognizing potential. He and I both made a play for MegnaTronics."

"And you got it."

"Not without pulling in every favor I had owed," Daryl said, shaking his head.

"But gobbling up small companies is just one of his legitimate businesses, Cydney," Mike elaborated. "Because he pumps so much money into the economy, no one pays attention to his side business, his so-called hobbies . . . But I paid attention."

"And that was?" she prompted.

Mike shook his head, unwilling or unable to answer her. Again, he looked to Daryl for back up.

"He's talking about drugs, Cydney," Daryl said in disgust. "It's also rumored that Keller turns a nice little bit of pocket change by supplying drugs to people like Mike."

"Not just people like me," Mike said with a hint of snobbery. "He does his bargain basement stuff, too. I wouldn't be surprised if that guy you caught at the bazaar wasn't on Keller's client list."

"Oh, Mike," Cydney moaned, shaking her head. She sat down weakly, staring at him.

"Don't look at me like that, Cydney. I told you that I didn't want your pity. What I'm going through, I did to myself. I've got to face it alone."

"But you're not alone," Cydney said, reaching out to touch his hand.

"No. Of course he's not alone. He sure as hell dragged a lot of innocent people through the garbage with him!" Daryl snapped. He didn't want Cydney to waste her sympathy on Mike.

"Mike, you weren't selling to the employees, were you?" Cydney could barely bring herself to ask the question.

"No, Cydney! God, no! I couldn't do that!" Mike exclaimed in horror. "How could you think that?"

"I don't know what to think anymore, Mike."

"Besides," Mike went on with a grin that chilled Cydney, "with your salaries, you couldn't afford the designer merchandise that Keller was passing on to me."

"Evidently, you couldn't either. Is that why you started embezzling?" Daryl accused him.

"Embezzling?" Cydney echoed.

"What else could explain the missing funds? What else could account for the bills that couldn't be paid on time? And what about the padded invoices? You were trying to make up the difference for what you took." Daryl went on. "I should have known. I thought it was just mismanagement. But when I took over the company and saw how efficiently everyone worked, I knew there had to be more to it than just financial negligence."

Mike rubbed his jaw and muttered, "I didn't know what else to do. Though the company was falling apart around me, I knew I could afford to lose it. I could always start fresh. But those people at MegnaTronics depended on me. I had to figure a way out.''

"Then I walked in," Daryl said.

"Mike, I thought you said that you approached Daryl," Cydney interjected, "that you initiated the buy out."

"I did lead him to MegnaTronics," Mike gloated. "I knew what kind of man Daryl was and knew he couldn't resist a challenge, especially if he had a chance to beat out Keller. With your reputation for go-for-the-jugular business tactics, I knew you wouldn't stop until you had MegnaTronics. So, I put the word out about the company's weakened position, knowing that I would either get you or someone just like you."

"But you knew the SEC would be looking over that deal," Daryl accused. "You knew that I was being watched like a hawk because of my last investment venture."

"I thought if you could just pull things back together, help the company turn a profit, I could bail out, sell my stock, and get Keller's money back to him. All I needed was a little time."

"You were stalling," Cydney whispered.

"Everything would have worked out; I just needed more time. But Keller knew what I was doing. He demanded his money in full. I told him I didn't have it. He called me a liar and threatened to kill me, to hurt my family. I got desperate. I had to make him believe that I was really broke. The only way to do that was to make him believe that the company was in real trouble." Mike swallowed hard and looked up at Daryl.

Daryl shook his head, naked fury blazing in his eyes. "You set me up," he ground out. "You son of a gun! You set me up. You planted that evidence against me."

Daryl crossed the room in three, long strides, and wrapped his hands around Mike's throat.

"Daryl, let him go! You're killing him!" Cydney jumped up and tugged against Daryl's arm.

"Worthless piece of filth!" Daryl shook even harder.

"I thought they'd question you, maybe watch you for a while!" Mike gasped, clutching at Daryl's squeezing hands. "Keller knows the SEC. He'd know the routine. He'd see that you were under investigation and then he'd back off. Once the SEC proved that you were on the level, they'd let you go. The business would start thriving again. You know, free publicity! Keller would get his money; you'd be clear."

"But it didn't turn out that way. What went wrong?" Cydney asked, managing to pry Daryl away.

"I'll tell you what went wrong!" Daryl snarled, giving Mike a vicious shove away from him. "Keller isn't a patient man. He isn't stupid either. If he thinks he's being treated like a fool, he gets mad."

Mike massaged his throat. "When you two called that investigator, Cydney tipped him off about where she'd seen that requisition list before. All he had to do was ask a few questions. Everyone knows that the last file you and I both worked on was the Janski file. It was stupid of me to use that file. I should have used a more obscure one, but I was desperate. It was the one I knew the best. I guess I made it too easy to see where the padded numbers had come from and who'd padded them. If Keller had someone working for him on the inside of the SEC, he'd know it, too. I really wish you hadn't gotten involved."

"Cameron!" she said, understanding dawning on her. "Because of you, they went after him. I'll kill you!" She launched herself at Mike with fists flailing. She connected solidly with his temple, sending him sprawling over the side of the chair.

"I thought they'd leave you alone. I thought they'd want Daryl's name cleared so that he could start making money. Cydney, I don't have proof that Cameron's accident wasn't what it seemed. I'm just afraid. I had a gut feeling. Once that SEC investigator Colton found out who was embezzling and why, I knew the investigation would lead her straight back to Keller. I've had enough meetings with him, Cyd. There are enough witnesses to tie us together. If he did try for Cameron, I guess he just wanted to shut you up. He'd rather lose the money I owed him than lose everything."

"So why are you coming to us with this now?" Daryl demanded.

"I told you, I came to tell you so that we can stop him."

"Seems like the damage is already done," Cydney said bitterly.

"You don't understand!" Mike said impatiently. "Keller wants his money. One way or another, he's going to get it."

"How? There's nothing to give?" she said, throwing her hands up in despair.

"There will be after . . . after . . . after the fire . . . after we collect on the insurance."

"Fire!" Cydney squawked. "Where?"

"At MegnaTronics," Mike said. "It was the only way."

"You're going to torch MegnaTronics. Have you lost your mind?!" she started for him again. Mike ducked behind the chair. "Suppose someone is in there! Someone could get hurt! Killed! How could you be so stupid? So callous?!"

"Who's going to start it? How?" Daryl demanded. "No, you should be telling this to the police. I don't want to know."

"It's too late, you're both already involved."

"Don't you dare try to implicate us in this, Michael!" Cydney yelled at him.

"I can't believe you're going to destroy my company," Daryl said, racing for his car keys.

"My company," Mike objected.

"No!" Daryl snarled. "It's mine. And I'm not going to let you flush it down the toilet. If you want to wallow in your own filth, then you go right ahead, Mr. Megna. All I ask is that you stay out of my way."

"Daryl!" Cydney called out to him. "If it's a matter of you or the company, let it go. Don't take any chances. You hear me? You'd better come back to me."

Daryl smiled briefly. In that one moment, she erased all of the doubts and insecurities he had about her and Jason. He kissed her deeply, quickly. "Call the police," he said then.

Cydney snatched the phone to her ear and dialed 9-1-1 emergency. As she relayed what little information she knew, she glared at Mike. When he stood as if to leave, she snarled. "Sit down! You're not going anywhere!"

"You can't stop me, Cyd; I've got to go."

While she still had 9-1-1 on the line, she demanded that squad car be sent to her house immediately.

"You took from the company. You put my son's life i danger. If I have to knock you down and sit on you mysel I'm not letting you out of here, Mike."

"Cydney," Mike started to plead. "You have to understand I had a sickness. I couldn't help myself."

"Don't!" she held up her hand to stop him. "I don't war to hear it. I might accept that excuse if weren't for that fac that nobody forced you to even start that garbage, Mike. I know drug addiction is a sickness. Heaven knows we've all been sensitized to that. But you . . . you must have known what you were doing at some point. You must have been able to contro your thoughts, your actions. The devious, complicated, calcu lated ways you came up with to hide what you were doing. I you spent half as much energy looking for help instead of trying to get yourself in deeper, you might have been on your way to recovery. I'm sorry. I have no sympathy for you."

"Don't preach to me, Cydney. You don't know the hell I've been through."

"Don't I? I just spent the last twenty-four hours in a hospital praying for my son. And now you tell me you might have been responsible for his being there? Don't you dare tell me that that I don't know suffering."

"I'm sorry . . . I'm so sorry," Mike repeated.

"Save it," she snapped, then turned to the door. She peeked through the viewer. "The police are here, Mike. Now's your chance. You can turn this around."

"I'm scared, Cyd. I confessed to you because I care about you. I care about Cameron. I confessed to you before I told my own wife. I can't tell the police. If I tell them what I know, there'll be nothing on this planet to keep Keller from coming after me."

"If you testify against him, and put him away, they can protect you."

"Yeah, right," Mike snorted. "I thought you were a realist, Cydney. Don't try to sugarcoat things for me."

"I'm going to open the door now, Mike. You can either be

man and stand up for what you know is right or you can go
being afraid. You can go on hurting innocent people to save
ur own sorry hide."

"Ouch, that hurts, Cydney. You don't have to be so cruel.
ut I guess that's why I wanted you to be VP. You always
uld make the tough decisions. Go on, open the door. Ready
not, here they come."

Cydney nodded, took a deep breath, then ushered the officers

Flanked by building security guards, an arson investigator,
e police, and the insurance adjuster, Daryl moved slowly
rough the waterlogged offices that used to be MegnaTronics.
rue to Mike's word, he had rigged a computer to "spontane-
usly" combust. But the robust security and sprinkler system
uickly snuffed out the fire before any heat damage could be
one. The damage by the sprinklers themselves, however,
ould probably put MegnaTronics in the red and keep the
ompany there until who knew how many years.

"Cure worse than the disease," Daryl muttered, shaking his
ead.

"Come here, Mr. Burke-Carter," the arson investigator
aved him over. "It looks like a small blaze broke out in here
nd caught two other units before the sprinklers kicked in."

"This is our server room, Ms. Ochoa," Daryl said. "We
eep the computers running twenty-four hours a day, seven
ays a week."

"I imagine if a fire would start naturally, it would most
gically start here," she commented.

"I have it on good authority that this fire was neither natural
or logical," Daryl said bitterly. He slammed his hand against
ne of the computers in anger, knocking it to the floor and
ending off a shower of sparks."

"Hey, Mr. Burke-Carter, do you mind?!" one of the police
fficers called out. "It's not as if our shoes are rubber lined."

"Sorry," Daryl responded woodenly.

"So you're admitting this fire was deliberately set?" t‖ insurance adjuster made notes in a small, wirebound noteboo

"I already gave my statement to the police," Daryl sai‖ trying to maintain his composure in the midst of seeing h‖ dream company literally go down the drain. "Unless I'm mi‖ taken, the person responsible has already been taken into cu‖ tody."

"With a full confession," Cydney said, stepping into t‖ server room.

"Excuse me, ma'am, this is a restricted area." One of t‖ officers tried to restrain Cydney.

"It's all right, let her in. She's the company's VP," Dar‖ said, smiling ruefully. "What's left of it, that is."

"Oh, Daryl," Cydney breathed. "I'm so sorry. What are w‖ going to do?"

"What can we do? Salvage what we can, give the employee‖ their severance ... and wish them good luck finding ne‖ work."

The insurance agent stepped up to Daryl, referring to h‖ notebook.

"You don't have be so drastic, Mr. Burke-Carter. Send you‖ employees on an extended sabbatical. With your insuranc‖ policy, you should be able to maintain their full salaries unt‖ your office is restored."

"I don't get it," Daryl said, shaking his head. "You mea‖ the insurance company will honor the policy even though th‖ fire was deliberately set?"

"I was under the impression that Mr. Megna was no longe‖ an employee of MegnaTronics," the agent said, and referre‖ to his notebook again.

"That's right," Cydney spoke up excitedly. "Mike resigne‖ several weeks ago, effective two days ago as a matter of fact.‖

"Then, as far as our company is concerned, the damag‖ won't be perceived as a deliberate attempt on your part t‖ defraud the company. The policy and the company are in you‖ name, Mr. Burke-Carter. The events that transpired here wer‖ obviously beyond your control. Call it an act of maliciou‖ mischief, if you like. It's covered under your policy as long a‖

ou can prove to our satisfaction that you were in no way
nvolved, either directly or indirectly.''

"The person responsible is, at this moment, giving his statement to the police," Cydney said, squeezing her hands together
to keep her from hugging Daryl in light of what the insurance
gent was telling them.

"Then you've done everything the policy requires. Adequate
ecurity measures, sprinkler system . . . you should have your
rst check within the week.''

Cydney let out a whoop, unable to contain her joy. She
eaped up, wrapping her arms around Daryl's neck and planting
 huge kiss firmly on his lips. Daryl held her close, responding
oftly to her with assurances that, moments before, would have
ounded hollow and insincere to him.

"What did you say you were VP of? That wouldn't be
orporate relations, would it?" the insurance agent teased
Cydney.

"I'm sorry," Cydney said, pulling herself away, and tugging
t her clothes to regain her composure.

"Don't be," the agent said, then held out his hand to Daryl
nd Cydney. "Good luck, Mr. Burke-Carter." He glanced over
t Cydney, then added, "In all your endeavors. With such
bviously dedicated employees, you should be back on your
eet in no time.''

Epilogue

Cydney didn't have to watch Cameron's feet as he kept perfect time to the music which helped them move across the polished floor of the church reception hall. She wished she could say the same for some of the relatives she'd danced with that day. She couldn't count how many times she had to dust footprints from her white, satin shoes.

"My little Cam," Cydney said in pleasant surprise. "I didn't know you had such smooth moves."

"Why do you think all the girls are ringing my phone all of the time?" he teased.

"What all?" Cydney teased in return. Then she squeezed her son, and kissed him on the forehead.

"Aw, man . . . look what you did. I'll bet I got a big, bright lipstick stain right in the middle of my forehead. How do you expect me to make moves on some of these girls in here when I'm a marked man?"

"You'd better be careful, Casanova. Half the young girls in here are your relatives."

"Then I guess I'll have to talk to each and every one of them until I find one who ain't related."

Cydney cleared her throat with subtle correction.

"Isn't related." Cameron got the hint. "Come on, Mom
Let me get you back to Daryl before you give me anothe
homework lesson—and on your wedding day, too," he sai
in mock dejection. Then Cameron guided his mom, in a swi
of white satin and lace, with a train that seemed a mile lon
over to the new bridegroom.

"Here you go, Daryl," Cameron said grandly. "She's a
yours. Take good care of her."

"Rest easy, Little C," Daryl adopted Cameron's nicknam
"I've made taking care of your mother my lifelong ambition."

"Even above MegnaTronics?" Cameron wanted to know.

"Not MegnaTronics anymore," Cydney corrected, smilin
so wide her face was beginning to hurt. "DBC & Associates."

"With you being an associate," Cameron grinned in return
"My mom—a vice president. You'd better watch out, Dary
Pretty soon, she'll be aiming for your job."

"She wouldn't be the woman I married if she didn't," Dary
said. "But I get to keep the comfy chair!"

Without missing a beat, he swept Cydney into his arms an
maneuvered her back onto the dance floor.

"Happy?" he asked, though he knew the answer by th
shining in her eyes.

"Miserable," she replied laughing. "Absolutely miserable."

"Then I can't wait to see downright dejection," he whis
pered, his lips pressed to her cheek. The warmth of his breath
against her skin never failed to make her shiver with suppresse
excitement. As he spun her around, she caught sight of a familia
face on the edge of the crowd.

"Daryl," Cydney murmured. For a second, her expressio
clouded.

"I see him," Daryl returned. "Who invited him? I didn't
Did you?"

"No," Cydney said. "But maybe I should have."

"After everything he's done?" Daryl glared daggers a
Michael Megna as he indicated half-heartedly that he wante
to see them.

"He did bring us together," Cydney said, trying to look on
the positive side.

Daryl laughed and nodded his head in acquiescence. "You're right. Come on. Let's go see what he wants." As they left the spotlight and moved toward the exit where Mike stood, Cydney whispered. "Who are those two guys with him?"

They were dressed conservatively in dark suits; but it was obvious to Cydney and Daryl that they weren't part of the wedding party, relations, or invited guests. Daryl's eyes flew open, recognizing one as the man who'd warned him in the sauna.

"Sooo—" Mike hailed them as they approached, "you two finally did it. You finally tied that old knot. Congratulations, Burke-Carter. Cydney, I've never seen you look more radiant."

"Thank you," she said simply.

"Sooo," Mike said again, awkwardly. "I just came by to say congratulations, and goodbye. I don't expect I'll be seeing you again—not that you'd want to see me after everything that I've done to you."

"It's over and done with, Mike," Cydney said. She smiled warmly and said, "You can put it behind you now. I'm really proud of the way you testified against Keller."

Mike cleared his throat gruffly, "Well, you know, I had to . . . civic duty and all that." He looked over at Daryl. "You're not buying it, are you?"

"Not a word," Daryl said, folding his arms across his chest.

"I guess the last thing you bought from me was almost a total wash out . . . no pun intended," Mike elbowed Daryl. "Funny how that insurance policy just happened to cover you, huh? Even though the fire was set by an ex-employee?"

"Yeah, funny how that worked out," Daryl said, his eyes narrowing.

"You knew!" Cydney exclaimed. "You knew he would be covered. That's why you moved up your quitting date!"

"Smart lady," Mike replied. "It was the only way to completely reel Keller in. I was never after you, Daryl. I just had to make it look like I was to get to Keller. I really am sorry."

"Mike, I just have to know," Cydney stepped closer, "were you really taking Keller's drugs?"

"Taking them, but not *taking* them," Mike said gravely.

"We met several times, and I gave him the money, but everything I got from him I gave straight to the police, Cyd."

"Good grief, Mike, you changed your story so many times, I don't know whether to kiss or kill you!" Cydney exclaimed.

"This time I'm on the level, Cydney. You've got to believe me."

"I do," she whispered, then held her hands out to him.

"Second time you've said that today, huh, Cyd?" he joked to cover the sudden, emotional constriction of his throat as he took his friend and former employee into his arms.

"So what happens now?" Daryl asked.

"I'm going away," Mike said. "They're relocating me and my family. This really is the last time I'll see you."

Daryl extended his hand in wary friendship. "Good luck, Mike. Despite everything, I think I can honestly say that I'm going to miss you around here."

"Oh, I think you'll find something and someone else to occupy your time," Mike assured them. He took Daryl's hand, then joined it with Cydney's.

"All the happiness in the world, you two. You deserve it." Then Mike looked over his shoulder as the two strangers who had accompanied him indicated that it was time to go.

"Take care, Mike," Cydney said.

"I will. I promise. And who knows, Daryl, in a new place, under a new name, I just may be giving DBC & Associates a run for its money."

As Mike was being escorted out, Daryl muttered under his breath, "Don't count on it."

Daryl twirled Cydney back onto the dance floor.

"So, do you believe that version of his story?" Cydney wanted to know.

"To be honest, Cydney, I don't know what to believe about Mike anymore."

"Some of it had to be true. He went to trial, didn't he? He testified against Dalton Keller."

"I suppose," Daryl said dubiously. "I still won't ever trust him again. Don't ask me to."

"He put a lot on the line to put that man away," Cydney said.

"After putting the company, Cameron, and you in danger, I can't believe that you're ready to forgive him," Daryl said incredulously.

"I wouldn't go that far!" Cydney exclaimed. "Not completely, anyway. After everything that he did, he still managed to take care of his employees—and his friends. I guess I have to admire his commitment."

"You want to admire a commitment?" Daryl's voice dropped as he pressed his lips to Cydney's ear. "I'll give you a commitment to admire, Mrs. Burke-Carter."

Mrs. Burke-Carter, Cydney echoed in her mind. She liked the sound of that. She leaned her head against his shoulder and sighed. She didn't have to say anything. Daryl knew exactly what she was thinking, how she was feeling. Whatever she was feeling, he was certain that he was feeling the same, only tenfold. If he could, he would stay just like that, wrapped in her arms, with the warmth of her love flowing around them as free and as voluminous as the folds of her dress and train.

Looking over her head, Daryl saw Jason Kelley lift a champagne glass to him in silent salute. Daryl almost frowned. Another person he would have considered barring from the door if he could have. With a barely perceptible nod, he acknowledged Jason's salute. If he had to think of a positive reason for Jason's presence, he could almost thank Jason for bringing Cydney into his life. One man's trash, another man's treasure. One bond broken, another bond forged.

Daryl suddenly squeezed Cydney tightly, making her ribs squeak in protest. He wouldn't be fool enough to let her go. Not ever! When he repeated the sacred vow to seal himself to her, he meant now and forever. And Heaven help the one to try to come between them!

"Cutting in." Whalen suddenly appeared by Daryl's side, tapping him on the shoulder. He laughed when he saw the expression on Daryl's face. "Don't worry, big brother. I'll bring her back," Whalen promised.

"You'd better," Daryl mock threatened.

He watched Cydney swirl away, his expression serious, but not grim. He had nothing to fear. She was his, and he was hers—with enough love between them to withstand a tiny bit of separation. Daryl waited for as long as he could—almost two minutes—before cutting back in on his brother.

"Man, you've got it bad!" Whalen said, shaking his head. "Can't you two stand to be apart for more than five minutes?"

"Nope!" Cydney said definitively. "And I wouldn't have it any other way."

Whalen watched as Daryl swept Cydney into his arms and maneuvered her back onto the dance floor. A moment later, Shana joined him.

"I knew it would come to this," she said. "The first time I saw them together."

"I knew it before you did," Whalen boasted. "I'm the one who told him to find a good woman."

"Do you think he can handle it all, Whalen? A new wife, a new son, a new company?"

"Are you kidding! That's a Burke-Carter out there. We Burke-Carters can handle anything!" When Whalen saw the SEC investigator D.J. Colton raise her glass in salute to the newly married couple, he laughed out loud. "Well . . . almost anything."

The music played on. Family and friends swirled around her. But Cydney didn't notice. She only had eyes for Daryl—the man to whom she had given the ultimate commitment—her life, her love, her all.

ABOUT THE AUTHOR

Geri Guillaume is the pseudonym for an author who lives in Houston, Texas, with her family. A technical writer, she is also the mother of two children and raises horses.

COMING IN NOVEMBER ...

THE ESSENCE OF LOVE   (0-7860-0567-X, $4.99/$6.50)
by Candice Poarch
Once falsely accused of fraud, Cleopatra Sharp managed to flourish in her new aromatherapy shop outside of Washington, D.C. But suspicion falls on her again. Postal inspector Taylor Bradford goes undercover as a repairman at her shop, determined to keep dangerous drugs and fraudulent miracle cures out of his community. When he realizes Cleopatra is nothing but a tender, giving woman, he must choose between his head and his heart.

LOVE'S PROMISE   (0-7860-0568-8, $4.99/$6.50)
by Adrienne Ellis Reeves
Beth Jordan refused a marriage proposal from her long-time boyfriend, only to find that he was quickly engaged to another. Determined to show everyone in Jamison, South Carolina that she wasn't too flighty to accomplish anything, she took part in a community service contest. Cy Brewster, her contest partner, tested her good intentions, for now she was in it for love. And a secret from Cy's past tests whether theirs is a love that promises forever.

EDEN'S DREAM   (0-7860-0572-6, $4.99/$6.50)
by Marcia King-Gamble
Eden Sommers fled to Mercer Island, in the Pacific Northwest, after a tragic plane crash claimed her husband and left her devastated. As she searches for answers, the mysterious man who moves in next door and bears a striking resemblance to her husband, manages to distract her. Is it mere coincidence that has brought Noel Robinson to Mercer Island? Eden will discover his secrets before she submits to the love welling up between them.

ISLAND PROMISE   (0-7860-0574-2, $4.99/$6.50)
by Angela Winters
Dallas schoolteacher Morgan Breck's reckless spirit led her to make an impulsive purchase at an estate sale, that plunged her into the arms of sexy investor Jake Turner. Jake is only interested in finding his missing sister, and when Morgan stumbles onto a clue that might locate his sister, he is thrilled to be with her. But when they are on the island where his sister may be, intense passion will force Jake to surrender to love.

Available wherever paperbacks are sold, or order direct from the Publisher. Send cover price plus 50¢ per copy for mailing and handling to Kensington Publishing Corp., Consumer Orders, or call (toll free) 888-345-BOOK, to place your order using Mastercard or Visa. Residents of New York and Tennessee must include sales tax. DO NOT SEND CASH.